Dedication.

Saleah Micci, thank you for approaching me to join a writer's group that you felt led to start. Your wisdom and encouragement have been invaluable, as you have walked with me on the journey of seeing my unfinished manuscript be the finished product it is today.

Thanks also to Lilly Brown, another member of the writer's group, for your support, kind words and belief in me to go forward and fulfil my dream.

Table of Contents

Chapter One

*D*iving and manoeuvring through the crowds, Olivia and Carol finally arrived at 'Italia Bellini'. They were relieved that they did not have to wait too long for a table. Shortly after their arrival, a waiter showed them to a quiet corner. They both slumped down, exhausted, releasing the numerous bags they had accumulated whilst out on their shopping spree.

The restaurant was elegantly decorated throughout with white poppies and lilies, creating a homey Italian ambience. Italia Bellini paid great attention to detail, with the staff appropriately attired to fit in with the theme. The waitresses wore white linen blouses with puffed sleeves to the elbows and red frilled skirts, whilst the men wore white shirts, black trousers and red waistcoats with an embroidered pattern down the sides. The restaurant was a favourite of Olivia and Carol's, as the owners and staff always extended a warm and friendly welcome to their customers. The atmosphere and surroundings encapsulated the finest of Italy's culture and heritage.

In the evening, guests were treated to the tranquillity of serenading Italian music, which is why it was popular with the locals and difficult to get a booking at short notice.

When they had given their order to the waitress, they were able to relax and casually converse. "Well, in two weeks' time, you'll become Mrs Mills and will be jetting off into the sun for your honeymoon," said Olivia, smiling. Olivia was pleased that Carol had met Michael, whom she had been dating for the last three years. The outcome of that chance meeting was their upcoming marriage.

"I think on the day you'll have to pinch me, as I still can't believe it's really happening to me. A few years ago, I was moping around the house saying that all the good guys had been swooped up and now in a couple of weeks my life is going to change drastically. I'm really going to miss sharing a house with you though." Carol sighed, as she put her hand on top of Olivia's and squeezed it tight.

"Everything is going to be fine," Olivia reassured. "I will always be here, although playing a slightly different role in your life." Olivia playfully rolled her eyes at Carol. "And besides, Michael is a great guy. I have no worries that you won't be anything but extremely happy." Olivia smiled, as she gave Carol a comforting look. "You both love and trust each other and in my books, that's a great start and, most importantly, you both have God."

Olivia's comments reassured Carol. Not that Carol was having second thoughts or doubts, but she knew that marriage was sacred. Many a couple started off with good intentions and for various reasons, the marriages had ended in disaster. Carol's idea of marriage was that it was for keeps. Her strong Christian beliefs cemented that notion. At that point, the waitress arrived with their order. Carol ordered lasagne and a Diet Coke and Olivia, the spaghetti bolognese and a freshly squeezed orange juice.

As they ate, they carried on talking. "Anyway, if it can happen to me, at the age of 40, then it can also happen for you too." Carol tried to reassure Olivia that her time too would come, especially as they both had been waiting a long time.

"Oh well, I think I've given up looking. Once you've passed 40, it just seems that bit harder." That was Olivia's way of dealing with the subject any time it came up in conversation. Olivia was attractive, medium built and about 5ft. 8in, but always found it a problem meeting any decent guys to complement her height. The thought of ending up with a 'midget', as she put it, was her worst nightmare and she and Carol often laughed about her trepidation. As a teacher, Olivia was reasonably confident and was able to channel any frustration regarding the topic into her work. Olivia loved her work and had a special, God given talent when it came to working with children. Not only did she teach in her secular job, but she also taught the Sunday school class at her local church. Sometimes on weekends Carol would have to put up with screaming children running around the place, as Olivia would give their parents a break. She especially had a knack for reaching out to challenging or withdrawn children. Who, in Olivia's opinion, often only needed that extra love and one-on-one attention.

As they left the restaurant, Carol could see how exhausted Olivia looked and was appreciative that Olivia accompanied her whilst she did some last-minute shopping for her honeymoon. By way of a thank you, Carol took care of the cheque and on leaving the restaurant, hailed a taxi, which took them home.

Michael Mills was one of the doctors of a small practice in the suburbs of green and leafy Bricket Wood, a village in the county of Hertfordshire, England, 4.2 miles south of St Albans and 4.2 miles north-northeast of Watford. The practice was run by three doctors: Michael Mills, Joan Webb and a new doctor, Christopher Harris, who had just taken over. His predecessor haven taken up a new post abroad.

Michael first met Carol at their local church and whilst they had noticed each other at meetings from time-to-time, they only managed to exchange the politely rehearsed "hellos" and "goodbyes". It was only when Carol twisted her ankle on a toy left by one of Olivia's weekend visitors that brought them together. Carol often joked with Olivia that it was well worth the pain she endured if bagging Michael was the end result. Because of that incident, Carol would forever be indebted to Olivia.

Chris Harris moved to the suburbs for a quieter life from the hustle and bustle of city life. He had a 5-year-old son, Ben, and was a widower, having lost his wife to cancer when Ben was just three years old. Chris had found it hard to come to terms with bringing up his son as a single parent but always tried his best to give Ben a normal childhood. Not coming from a large family, Ben hadn't been exposed to the dynamics of experiencing a strong family unit and therefore at times struggled with his behaviour. With his father busy furthering his career, Ben had not always been afforded the attention he has craved. Chris recognised that he needed to slow things down, for the sake of his son, which is why he made a drastic change in his lifestyle and made the move to the suburbs for a better quality of life.

"Hi Janet, is Michael ready yet?" Carol inquired as she walked over to the reception desk in the surgery.

"No Carol, he's seeing a patient and he has one more

after that one."

"I don't mind wa_ting, I think I'm a bit early anyway," sighed Carol.

"Well, you just take a seat and I'll buzz him through to let him know that you're here."

"Thanks Janet."

"By the way, how are your wedding plans coming along?"

"Oh, not too bad. Everything seems to be coming together, but I'll be glad when it's all over. It can be a bit of a headache at times." Janet smiled, as she buzzed through to let Michael know that Carol was waiting.

"Okay, Janet, thanks for letting me know, I'll be with her as soon as I can."

The waiting room had five other patients who were waiting for Dr Webb and Dr Harris. Janet kept the waiting room spic and span, with the main centre of attention being a colourful aquarium. It was a pleasant distraction that patients could appreciate if they got bored with reading the posters on the wall or browsing through the variety of magazines on the coffee table. Carol could never sit down for too long when she occasionally came to the surgery to whisk Michael off for lunch. She would often go over and chat with Janet in between her seeing to patients, trying extremely hard not to disturb her and be a nuisance.

Carol looked up and saw that Janet had a quiet moment. She put the magazine back on the table and quickly rushed over to the reception area. "So, what's this Dr Harris like then? I haven't been introduced to him yet," Carol whispered as she leaned on the counter looking intently into Janet's face.

"He seems quite nice Carol. Quite tall. A reserved sort of person, I would say, but he's very good with the patients, considering he's only been with us for a short time. But deep down it seems that he's got a lot on his mind, as I often catch him wandering off deep in thought."

"Every time I've been here," voiced Carol, "he's either been at the hospital or dealing with a patient. I hope I get to meet him today."

Right on cue, the intercom rang. "Mrs Williams, Dr Mills will see you now, go straight through; third door on the left."

"Thank you, Janet," said Mrs Williams, a frail elderly lady, and went on through to see the doctor.

"Last one and he'll be with you. I don't think Mrs

Williams will be too long. I think she's only here for a repeat prescription, and then you can whisk that future hubby of yours off to lunch."

Carol smiled and went back to her seat trying to settle and flick through a magazine again. As she sat down, out of one of the surgery rooms emerged a tall, dark and strikingly handsome gentleman in a white coat with a stethoscope around his neck. Behind him followed a frail old lady aided by a walking stick. He walked towards Janet. "Janet, would you mind popping across the road and picking up Mrs Woods' prescription; her leg is giving her a bit of trouble today. I'll sit here and man the telephones until you get back." The doctor proceeded to walk around the counter, as he passed Janet the prescription.

"Not at all. Dr Harris," said Janet as they swapped places. "I won't be too long."

"Thanks Janet. Please take a seat, Mrs Woods. Janet will be back in a few minutes. Are you sure I can't call you a cab? You really need to rest that leg," he said as he helped Mrs Woods to a seat next to Carol.

"Oh no, doctor, I'll be fine. The bus-stop is just outside, and it drops me across the road from my bungalow. Besides, with the cost of living these days and my limited pension, I can't afford such luxuries." Mrs Woods smiled with him as he went back behind the counter.

Carol was trying hard to act as if she was reading the magazine, but her eyes were peering over it. She couldn't help but notice how kind and caring this man was treating his patient. Carol also observed how attractive he was and the only thought that kept running through her mind was *how perfect he would be for Olivia.* He was the right height, seemed to be the caring type. Definitely attractive and he was a doctor, just like her Michael. In Carol's opinion, what else did Olivia need? Almost as if she couldn't stop her thoughts from getting out of control, Carol started to visualise the dinner parties that they could all go to as devoted couples. She really was letting her imagination run wild, especially as she had only seen this man in action for all but 5 minutes, if that.

Still in a daze, Carol didn't even see Michael's patient leave or that he was now walking towards her, putting on his jacket ready to take her to lunch. "Hello, is anyone there?" he said tapping her forehead.

"Oh, sorry hon," she exclaimed, rather embarrassed, knowing what she had just been thinking.

He kissed her gently on the lips. "I hope I didn't keep you too long?"

"Oh no, that's okay, I got here early, plus I've been

catching up and chatting with Janet."

"By the way, where is Janet?" Michael asked as he looked over at the reception desk and saw Chris sitting there.

"Oh, she just popped across the road to the pharmacy for Mrs Wood's prescription. Here she is now," said Chris.

"Sorry I took so long, there was a bit of a queue." Janet sighed as she tried to catch her breath.

"Thanks very much Janet. Here you are, Mrs Woods. I'll see you in two weeks' time and try to keep that leg elevated in the meantime."

By this time Carol had been nudging Michael in the ribs and muttering under her breath that he introduce her to the new doctor.

"Oh, haven't you met him yet? Chris, before you go back in, I'd like to introduce you to my fiancée, Carol."

"Pleased to meet you, Carol," he said, as he extended his hand to greet her. Carol found herself lost for words as she shook his soft, warm hand, whilst looking up into his deep brown eyes. "In the short time I've been here, I have heard a lot about you, from Michael of course." He smiled.

10

"All good I hope," replied Carol as she tried to pull her thoughts together and take back her hand, which seemed to have got stuck in her trance.

"But of course," Chris said, and everyone chuckled.

And he has a sense of humour too, he's perfect for Olivia. As Carol and Michael left the surgery, Carol squeezed Michael's hand and had a cheeky grin on her face. "Uh oh, when you have that look on your face, I know you're up to something."

"Oh, never you mind, I just think Chris is charming, that's all."

"Eh, steady on, you're a soon-to-be married woman. Keep your eyes off."

"Don't be silly," Carol said as she playfully tapped Michael on his shoulder. "I can look, but not for me. I just think that he would be perfect for Olivia." Carol smiled as she drew close to Michael squeezing his arm.

"Give the man a break, Caz. He's new in town, has a young son to contend with and plus he only lost his wife a few years ago. I think he has come here for a fresh start and perhaps to get away from the reminders of his past. If you're asking me if he's ready to start dating again, I'm afraid I couldn't help you there, as the subject hasn't really come up."

"And Olivia is just the fresh start that he might be looking for, don't you think?" Carol quickly interrupted.

"Don't go there, Caz. I know Olivia is your best friend and you want the best for her but keep out of any kind of matchmaking for the time being and let nature take its course. If God wants it to happen then nothing can stop it. Just give the man time to settle and find his feet."

"Okay, okay," Carol said, poking him in the ribs. "But you'll see I'm right. I can just feel it in my bones. Now come on and take me to lunch, I'm starving."

———————◄O►———————

Chapter Two

"**O**livia, can I have a quick word before you go back to your class?" Mrs Barratt shouted as she saw Olivia walk pass her office.

"Yes of course." Mrs Barratt was the Head Teacher at Newmont Primary School where Olivia had taught for the past five years. She was highly thought of by her colleagues and had also developed a good rapport with the children. Olivia especially had a gifting for dealing with children who needed specialised attention due to behavioural issues, issues at home, or children who had been emotionally scarred.

"Take a seat Olivia, I won't keep you long." Olivia took a seat in Mrs Barratt's large and spacious office, which was decorated in a child friendly way. Children were encouraged to draw pictures in their art class and the best pictures would be hung in Mrs Barratt's office as picture of the month. This made the office quite colourful which encapsulated a friendly atmosphere for the children, especially if they were naughty and had to be sent to her office to be reprimanded.

"I've asked you in because I wanted to discuss a little boy by the name of Ben Harris. He's been with us for about two months now and he's in Barbara's class, but she just can't seem to make any real progress with him. I can't pinpoint what exactly the problem is, but I do know that he lost his mother when he was just three years old, and I wonder if he has been slightly traumatised by this. I know you have a special gift in reaching out to your students and I wondered if you wouldn't mind taking him into your class until the end of term?"

Mrs Barratt had Ben's personal folder opened and flicked through it as she tried to find some more information for Olivia that she thought might be helpful. "His father had a busy career as a doctor in the city and thought the move to the country would help Ben to be exposed to a quieter and tranquil lifestyle."

"I don't see any problem with that, Mrs Barratt," Olivia complied.

Mrs Barratt was quick to add, "I have nothing against Barbara's teaching methods, but some of us in the teaching profession have a different approach and style with certain children. That's why I feel Ben would benefit greatly from being in your class. I think you would be able to bring out the qualities we know he has buried deep inside and give him that extra push he needs to improve his grades," Mrs Barratt continued.

"He's still young and if we can help him now, it will be beneficial to his future development."

"Well, you know me," said Olivia, smiling as she got up and started to walk towards the door, "I'll do my best. I can't promise any overnight miracles, but I shall certainly do everything within my abilities to help Ben with his development, after all that's what I'm here for."

"Thanks Olivia, I knew I could count on you. I'll go and get him and bring him along to your class in a few minutes. I've already run the idea by Barbara, and she doesn't have any problem with the change, so there should be no need for any awkwardness on the matter. Our main objective is that our children receive all the help and encouragement they need, and this school will always be there to provide that." Just then, the bell rang to indicate that the break was over, and Olivia left Mrs Barratt's office and walked down to the corridor back to her own class, 1D.

"Okay everyone, as you go quietly to get your milk. I just want to let you know that a new pupil will be joining our class called Ben Harris. Mrs Barratt will be bringing him in shortly, so I expect you all to be on your best behaviour when they arrive." The children rushed back to their desks with their milk bottles clutched tightly and Olivia gave them all a chocolate digestive biscuit.

At that point Mrs Barratt knocked the door and brought Ben in. All the children rose to their feet as Mrs Barratt walked in. "Good afternoon, Mrs Barratt," hollered the children in unison, with some chatting amongst themselves. Olivia looked over at them, rolling her eyes and indicating that they needed to be quiet.

"Good afternoon 1D, please be seated. I'd like you all to say hello to Ben who will be joining your class until the end of term, and I hope that you will all be kind to him and show him how things are done in your class."

"Hello Ben," chanted the children. Ben shyly dropped his head and fidgeted with his pockets, slightly kicking Olivia's table leg.

"Okay Olivia, he's all yours," whispered Mrs Barratt as she pushed Ben closer to Olivia. "Good luck," she said as she left the room.

Olivia smiled and pondered within herself, *I don't believe in luck, but I do believe in God and if anything is going to happen, then it is going to happen because God is in control of the situation.* "Come on, Ben," Olivia said

16

as she placed her hands on his shoulders and directed him to his seat. "Have a seat next to John and I'll go and get you a bottle of milk and a biscuit."

As he sat on his seat, Ben looked up at Olivia and smiled as if to imply that he was comfortable and belonged in her class. Somehow, he could feel a warmth radiating in her eyes and even at the young age of 5 sensed that she actually cared.

"After our milk, we will have a story chosen from our book corner. Now let me see who is going to be my special helper today and choose our book?" The children started to fix their desks and sit up straight, raising their hands so that Olivia would choose them. Firstly, Olivia got the children to take their empty bottles back to the milk crate and then walk quietly back to their desks. As the children went back to their seats, some almost fell off their seats in an attempt to be the helper for the task.

"Please Miss Dupont, can I pick the book today?" they cried, extending their hands high in the air. That was the only real time Olivia got all the children's undivided attention because it gave them a chance to pick their favourite book and look at the colourful pictures.

"Oh, I don't know who to choose," said Olivia teasingly, "Everyone is behaving so well, but Ben is sitting very quietly and as it is his first day in Class 1D, we will let Ben go to the library corner and pick a book."

Ben looked surprised that Olivia would choose him. However, he got up and walked to the back of the room towards the left-hand side. Olivia had arranged a library corner for the children, who had a story read to them every day before they went home, which they eagerly looked forward to. As Ben loved animals, he picked the book called 'Dirty Harry', about a canine dog who was always getting into trouble. As Olivia read the story you could hear a pin drop as the children listened intently, laughing loudly in all the right places and thoroughly enjoying their story-time.

The afternoon bell sounded, and the children were aroused as they waited for Olivia to give the signal to get their coats, hats and scarves and wait for their parents to collect them. All the parents came and collected their children, with Ben being the last one to be collected. There was a knock on the door which was already half opened. "Hello, my name is Dr... I mean Mr Harris and I've come to collect my son, Ben, who I understand is here."

"Oh yes," said Olivia as she rose to her feet and extended her hand to shake his hand with a warm smile on her face. "I'm Miss Dupont, Ben's new form teacher."

"What happened to Miss Rogers?" he exclaimed with a puzzled look on his face.

"The Head... I mean Mrs Barratt thought it was necessary for Ben's progress that he changed classes until the end of the term."

"And when was I going to be informed of this move?" Chris retorted as he helped Ben put on his brown duffle coat and wrapped his multicoloured scarf around his neck.

"Oh, well I'm very sorry if you feel you were not informed of this change, Mr Harris," Olivia said as she collated her books and carried on tidying her desk. "But the person you need to bring this up with, if you are not happy with things, is Mrs Barratt. I can take you to her office on your way out if you like?"

"No," he said abruptly as he held Ben's hand and led him out of the class, "I haven't got the time right now."

"Maybe I can get Mrs Barratt to give you a call tomorrow during the day," Olivia said as she followed them out, turning off the lights and locking the door.

"I'm quite busy during the day at the surgery. Maybe I'll get an explanation at a later date. However, in the meantime, perhaps you could pass on my sentiments to Mrs Barratt and let her know that I would like a full explanation." And on that snappish note, he and Ben left the school grounds.

"Hi there." Carol heard the rattle of keys as Olivia came through the front door, returning from work.

"Hey girl," Olivia replied in a sullen tone.

"What's up? Didn't you have a good day? Did those kids send you round the bend again?" said Carol laughingly, sensing that something might be up.

Olivia started walking up the stairs of the semi-detached house they jointly owned. "I was actually having a good day, up until the end of the day that is."

"Why? What happened at the end of the day?" replied Carol, voicing her concern.

"Oh, I suppose it wasn't as bad as I am making it out to be. I just had a run in with one of the parents," she shouted back as she had reached the top of the stairs. "I'll tell you all about it a bit later, but right now I just need to soak in a hot bubble bath and unwind."

"Okay, but don't soak for too long, dinner is nearly ready." It was a mutual agreement between the two friends that whoever got home first would start the dinner. The lot fell on Carol that night who was preparing chicken, which was simmering nicely in the slow cooker. It gave off a strong, but pleasant, spicy aroma, and with just the rice left to cook, the meal would be finished in a matter of 15 minutes. Carol appeared reasonably happy with her accomplishments, since Olivia was the better cook out of the two of them and retreated to the living room with a glass of wine to relax before dinner was ready.

Their semi-detached was a three-bed house with a large garden, which, as a keen gardener, Carol tried to keep tidy. However, her efforts were to no avail, especially when Olivia's 'little helpers' came over to stay or visit and ran all over her much-loved flower beds. The décor of the house was attractive with neutral colours and pine wood IKEA furniture. Again, Carol was more of the domestic type in comparison to Olivia's rather laid-back approach. Not that Olivia was messy; it was just that the lot fell on Carol being the one to always put her foot down if things were not up to scratch. Carol was very precise and made sure the house was kept clean and tidy, while Olivia was more of the maternal type and loved a house to look as though it was lived in rather than a show piece. Even though they both had their own strong individual character, they complemented each other well, which was the cement to their friendship since meeting at university in their early twenties.

"That's better," Olivia said as she entered the living

room, casually dressed in a long white T-shirt and black leggings, barefoot and with her thick black hair flowing behind her. "Something smells good. You'll make someone a good wife one of these days. Have you been practising?" she teased.

As Carol brought the food to the table, she couldn't wait to tell Olivia all about her day and the new person she had met. "I'll say grace, shall I? For what we are about to receive, may the Lord make us truly thankful."

"Amen," Olivia said loudly in a sarcastic voice. As Olivia began to dish out her meal, she glanced over at Carol who was staring at her with a big grin on her face. "Uh oh, you're up to something. I know that look and it always means that you're about to get into somebody's business. So, whose business is it this time, eh?"

"Whaaaat! I don't know what you mean." Carol smirked, trying to deny she was up to anything. "Pass the hot sauce please," Carol said as she reached her hand across the table to where Olivia was sitting.

"The food is hot already; you don't need any more pepper."

"I like my food hot and spicy."

"Like your man eh!" replied Olivia to which they

both fell into a fit of laughter.

"Anyway," Carol continued as she tried to have a half decent conversation with Olivia. "Aren't you going to ask me what sort of day I've had?"

Olivia rolled her eyes as Carol poured the sauce over her chicken. "Well, seeing you had the day off, I'm sure it was a lazy one."

"Yes, it was lazy actually. After I got up at 10.00 am I might add."

"How the other half live, eh," interrupted Olivia.

"I had a bath and then cleaned the house from top to bottom. I hope you noticed that I tidied your things from under the stairs."

"I had." Olivia nodded whilst taking a mouthful of rice.

"And then I went and had lunch with my fiancé."

"I thought Michael's name would come up in the conversation sooner or later." Ever since Carol and Michael had started dating, they had been inseparable with Carol being completely besotted by him to the point that he was always the topic of conversation. Not that Olivia minded though, as she was happy to know that at least one of them found an eligible suitor, which seemed to be getting harder and harder the older they got within the Christian community. They both felt strongly that it had to be a Christian man that they wanted to eventually settle down with.

"Well anyway," continued Carol, "whilst I was waiting for Michael to finish with his appointments, I finally met the new doctor. His name is …."

Before Carol could finish her sentence, Olivia interrupted her flow. "Dr Harris" she said sarcastically in a high-pitched voice.

"How do you know?" Carol replied inquisitively and slightly perturbed that Olivia had rained on her parade.

"Dah!! It's a small town and when a man comes to your school to collect his son and introduces himself as Dr Harris, it doesn't take rocket science to realise that he may be Michael's new partner. Anyway, I thought he was quite rude."

"He's not," Carol said defensively. "Well, what I mean is that when I met him this afternoon, he seemed quite charming." Again, there was that cheeky grin on her face.

"Well, he wasn't very charming when I met him. In

fact, he was rather abrupt with me." At that point, the telephone rang, and Olivia rushed to answer it, using the opportunity to excuse herself from the conversation. Although her first impression of Chris Harris did not start off on the right foot, she could not dismiss the fact that he was strikingly attractive, with a physique to die for.

"Hi Michael, how are you? Yes, Carol is here. I'll just call her; take care of yourself. Carol, the phone is for you, and I'll give you three guesses who it is?" Olivia said as she held the phone up in the air, causing Carol to jump to reach the phone.

"Is it Dr Harris?" whispered Carol as she took the phone from Olivia.

"You really don't give up, do you?" Olivia cleared the table, whilst in the background the voice of Carol reverberated as she exchanged romantic undertones with Michael. It got a bit too much for Olivia and to give Carol some privacy, Olivia shut the door to the living room, leaving Carol on the other side, sitting on the stairs in the hallway to finish off her conversation.

As Carol had done her share of duties throughout the day, Olivia felt obliged to tidy the dinner dishes. She looked for a gospel CD to keep her company and selected 'The Call' by one of her favourite gospel groups,

Anointed, and turned up the volume to drown out Carol's tone and to be respectful of her call. As Olivia leaned over the sink and washed the dishes, she mused to herself. *Why is it that I am in on a Friday night with no where to go? When is that hunk going to come and sweep me off my feet? Oh Lord, where is he?*

At that moment, Chris Harris' face flashed across her mind. *Oh, don't be silly Olivia, you hardly know the man.* But in another breath, she thought, *He is fine though!* Again, Olivia dismissed the thoughts that were invading her 'me time' with the Lord and tried to convince herself that Chris Harris was arrogant and that she was not remotely interested in a man she only just met and knew nothing about. Nevertheless, yet her intrigue of him was compelling, which she struggled to grasp.

"You don't have anything special on tonight, do you, Olivia?" Carol had finished her call and came into the kitchen where Olivia had just finished the dishes and was about to sweep the kitchen floor.

Staring at the ceiling, pretending to think about if she had anything to do, Olivia replied, "Well I don't think I have, but let me consult my diary in case I have an important appointment I forgot about."

"Okay, Miss Busy Bee. Anyway, one of our badminton

partners can't make it tonight and Michael was wondering if you could fill in."

Olivia swept the floor swerving around Carol. "Might be able to and then again I might not. I was looking forward to a relaxing night in."

"Oh, come on Olivia, we all used to have a great time on a Friday night at the leisure centre until you dropped out." Olivia had taken an evening course in creative writing as a side-line, which interrupted badminton with a small group of friends that met on a Friday evening. Carol and Michael still went ahead playing and found a replacement for Olivia amongst the Mature Adults Group at their local church. Whilst Carol and Michael were quite serious and skilled players, Olivia didn't take it that serious. It was just a bit of fun to her, which she used as a means of keeping fit. The course Olivia was taking had finished a few weeks earlier and she found herself at a loose end on a Friday evening. After realising that it would be a laugh to get out and enjoy herself, Olivia agreed and shortly thereafter they left for the leisure centre.

————◄◉►————

Chapter Three

" They will be here soon," screamed Carol as she flew down the stairs. It was the night of her hen party, and everyone had agreed to meet at their house. After which they were going out to dinner at their local Chinese restaurant, The Golden Palace. Carol was getting quite excited, with the reality that in three days' time she would be getting married. Olivia had been a great support to her these past couple of weeks and they both knew that things would be different after Carol and Michael were married.

Carol and Michael had bought a three-bedroom house not too far from Olivia. The house was run down and in desperate need of repair and a lot of 'TLC'. A task that did not seem to bother the pair, as they wanted to take on a project that they could refurbish together and at their own pace. This gave them the opportunity of putting their individual stamp on it. It was also an added bonus that Carol was an interior designer and was able to produce several suggestions on how to add value to the property.

Olivia had bought out Carol's share in their property and had decided that she would advertise for a suitable lodger, to help with the mortgage, which she was now paying on her own.

The first guest arrived and, not long after that, one by one the other guests started to stroll in. There were about 12 of them in total, mainly consisting of friends from church, Carol's work friends and a few family members. The house was filled with laughter and joviality as the ladies chatted, joked and introduced themselves to each other.

"Right ladies." Olivia got up from their large soft sofa and shook her skirt, releasing the crumbs that had accumulated from stuffing themselves with nachos and nuts that Carol had prepared earlier. "We better be leaving now. The table's booked for 8 pm and we don't want to be late."

At that prompt, everyone started to get themselves ready. "I'll take my car and four others can come with me," said Carol as she started to get everyone organised and led the massive exodus.

"You're supposed to be taking things easy Carol, and here you are, as usual, organising everything. Well, I'm doing the planning tonight," exclaimed Olivia and carried on getting the cars organised. "I've got room for four. Janice, would you mind driving?" Janice was a mutual friend of them both who attended their church.

"No, I don't mind driving."

"And Jenny, are you okay to drive too?"

"Yeah sure," added Jenny.

"Right, that's settled. Now let's get going and give this girl a night to remember."

"Olivia, you better not have anything dodgy up your sleeves," Carol said in a slightly nervous tone.

"Like what?" Olivia chanted back. "The stripper-gram said he would be there about......oops, now I've let 'the cat out the bag', oh dear." Everyone started to laugh as they walked to the cars, but Carol wasn't laughing and thought to herself, *Lord they better be joking.*

It took the hens about 20 minutes to get to the restaurant. Having found suitable parking spaces, the party arrived at the restaurant and were shown to a banqueting room that was prepared specially for the festivity. To save time with ordering, everyone had already pre-selected their main dish beforehand. This gave the restaurant the opportunity to have the selected dishes partly ready, whilst everyone enjoyed their starters. The waiters brought to the table prawn toasts, hors d'oeuvre rolls, served with sweet and sour sauce, long soup and stuffed mushrooms. The evening was enjoyed by all, as well as the food being excellent.

Carol was having a great time, trying not to look too worried, but still wondering if Olivia was really going to pull a stunt on her. Olivia was always the joker between them and over the years pulled many pranks on Carol, sometimes to her detriment. But Carol had got used to Olivia larking about and had grown, albeit reluctantly, to accept her warped sense of humour.

"Are you having a good time, Carol?" Jenny asked, as she put her arm around Carol and gave her a big hug.

"Yeah, I'm having a great time; thanks for coming all this way." Jenny was Carol's older sister and had been married to Tony for 10 years, having been blessed with three children. Carol and Jenny didn't get to see each other as often as they would have liked due to their distance in location. However, they talked often on the telephone which gave them the opportunity to keep up to date with each other's lives.

After the main meal, Olivia stood up with a glass in her hand. And with a spoon in the other, tinkled the glass as it made a reverberating sound. "May I have everyone's

31

attention, please? Will you all raise your glasses and join me as I propose a toast to the happy couple; to Carol and Michael."

"To Carol and Michael," everyone echoed.

Olivia added, "May God bless their lives and may they have a long and happy marriage."

"And may they have lots of babies," shouted Janice and everyone cheered "amen" in unison and clapped as they congratulated Carol.

As everyone started to get themselves ready to leave, Carol whispered to Olivia, "Thanks for not playing any pranks tonight, Liv."

Olivia grinned. "I wouldn't have done anything, not tonight anyway. I'm giving you a prank free zone until you get back from your honeymoon." They both smiled and gave each other a hug.

The other hens hugged Carol and each other as they said their goodbyes. They wished Carol all the best for Friday, reassuring her that she should remain calm, relaxed and just enjoy the day since everything she had put in place for her big day would go according to plan. Having the wedding on a weekday rather than a Saturday meant that the couple saved a great deal on costs, using the extra monies to put into their renovation project.

It was a warmish Saturday afternoon in March. Olivia was pottering around the house tidying up the things that Carol had left behind in her hurried state when she came back to the house after the wedding to get changed for her honeymoon. They had flown out at 8 am that morning, departing from Gatwick Airport's South Terminal. Michael's best man, Steve, who was also single and often tried to get a date with Olivia, drove them to the airport. Olivia's mind could not help but go over the events of the previous day. She too was exhausted.

As Carol's maid of honour, Olivia was busy running around ensuring everything ran smoothly and that Carol remained as calm as possible for her big day. That picture would be etched in her mind forever when she first saw Carol in her wedding dress, which fitted her neat trim figure beautifully, with her train flowing elegantly behind her. Carol was not an elaborate dresser and the only thing that made a daring statement was her beautiful head piece which made her look like a Nubian princess. Michael also looked his usual cool dapper self in his black pinstriped suit and white shirt. They looked the perfect couple and surprisingly the day went well, without any obvious disasters.

Well, nothing that Olivia was prepared to tell the

33

couple about. Maybe she would share those stories with them when they got back from their honeymoon on the exotic island of Barbados. One such story being that whilst they were waiting for Carol to arrive at the church, one of her flower girls, Jenny's daughter, who was only four years old, somehow locked herself in the toilet. It was only with Olivia's gentle coaxing and soft talking that made her stop crying and somehow reach the lock and let herself out. Olivia was sure Carol would see the funny side of that story.

As Olivia was deep in thought the telephone rang. She closed the wardrobe door in Carol's room and ran to the telephone situated downstairs in the stairway. "Hello."

"Hi Olivia, it's me."

"Oh, hi Steve; how are you?" Olivia said as she sat on the bottom stair. Steve was quite a talkative guy and as she thought the call would be lengthy, she decided to rest her legs.

"Are you still trying to recover then? That was some wedding huh! I wonder if you are as exhausted as I feel," Steve asked.

"I am actually. Just sorting a few things out, and then I'm off to the surgery."

"Oh," he exclaimed, becoming a little concerned. Steve was an incredible guy, who said all the right things any woman would want to hear, and Olivia knew that someday Steve would make someone a great husband, but she didn't feel the same way about him.

Even though, he would qualify on the height criteria, he just wasn't her 'Boaz'. And for Olivia it was important that she found her 'Boaz' and not just settle for a substitute all because she could not find her Boaz. Steve was aware that Olivia wasn't interested in him romantically, and only saw him as a good friend. However, he still could not help the way he felt about her.

"I hope it's nothing serious," he said.

"Oh, nothing to be concerned with," Olivia replied. She propped the phone up on one side of her ear and shoulder whilst using the finger on her right hand to finish chipping off the nail varnish on her nails that was starting to look shabby.

"Anyway, I called to see if you would like to come to the cinema tonight. One of Tyler Perry's movies is showing at the Odeon, and I thought it would be fun for us to see," Steve said, finding it quite amusing.

Olivia thought to herself, *It's Saturday and even though I'm tired, what am I really going to do tonight?*

Absolutely nothing. Steve is a nice enough person, and his heart is in the right place. After all, there's no harm in going to the cinema with a friend; why not? Olivia got up from sitting on the stairs with a sigh as her bottom had literally gone numb from sitting there too long. "Okay Steve, I'd like that."

"Good, I'll pick you up at 7 pm. Maybe we can get a pizza before the film. I'll book us seats for the 9.30 pm show."

"Okay Steve, I'll see you at 7 pm."

It was a pleasant afternoon and since the traffic was not too heavy, with drivers taking advantage of the weather and leaving their cars at home, Olivia pulled up at the surgery with minutes to spare. The practice opened their doors on a Saturday once a month, which benefitted individuals who worked in the week and could not attend appointments on a weekday.

As Olivia entered the surgery, Janet was sitting at the reception with her usual warm and welcoming smile. She really was an asset to the practice and well respected in the community. "Hello Olivia, you're just in time. You're the last one for the day. I shall be glad to get out of here and put my feet up."

"You work too hard Janet; you're a Saint. I hope they

know how fortunate they are to have you."

Janet smiled; everyone was always telling her that throughout her twenty-year history at the practice. Olivia took a seat as Janet took her file into the doctor's office. As usual, the surgery looked spic and span; you could not fault it. The fish appeared content, swerving around in their spacious tank, inter-weaving amongst the coral and greenery. "Dr Harris will see you in five minutes." Janet smiled.

"Dr Harris!" Olivia squeaked in a high-pitched voice rather puzzlingly. "I'm here to see Dr Webb."

"Oh, I'm sorry, Olivia. With Michael away on his honeymoon, Joan had to take the emergency calls today and all her appointments have been transferred to Dr Harris. I hope it isn't too much of an inconvenience."

"Oh, err...., no, I suppose it will be alright." Olivia put the magazine she had started to read back on the table as Dr Harris came out of his office.

"Ah, Miss DuPont, sorry to keep you waiting; please come in." Chris held the door open as Olivia walked in and he followed her through. "Please have a seat." His office was the smallest of the three doctors' offices, but very comfortable.

Olivia glanced at the table and noticed a frame with two pictures. She recognised Ben, although slightly younger, with a big grin on his face and in the other picture was a very beautiful petite lady, who Olivia guessed was probably Chris' late wife. Remembering his mannerism the last time they met a few weeks prior, Olivia did not want to pry by asking who the lady in the photograph was.

On the walls, she noticed some of the pictures that Ben had drawn in her class. Whenever Olivia had asked Ben who his pictures were for, he would say they were for his daddy, who would put them up in his office. Olivia started to sense a warmer side to Chris, like the one that Carol had bragged about. Chris clasped his hands and looked at Olivia rather embarrassingly.

"Firstly, I would like to apologise for the way I came across when I first met you. It was totally out of character. I was having problems that day trying to find a housekeeper and I'm sorry I took it out on you."

Olivia felt embarrassed too as she wasn't expecting him to apologise or even bring the matter up. "Oh, don't worry about it. I know parents often have a lot on their minds. Consider the matter closed, so let's start again," Olivia said with a smile on her face as she looked into his dark but striking eyes.

"I had planned to apologise to you at the wedding, but you seemed quite preoccupied in your maid of honour role. And then I tried to pinpoint you to ask for a dance, but another man seemed quite occupied with you all night, almost taking every dance." *Wow, he noticed me!* "Was that your boyfriend?"

Olivia thought, *This Dr Harris is getting a bit too friendly for my liking and* didn't want to be discussing her personal life with Chris as in many ways he was still a stranger to her. "No," Olivia said rather confused. "Actually, I really wanted to see Dr Webb," Olivia exclaimed, quickly changing the subject.

"Joan is taking the emergency calls today." Chris had Olivia's file in his hands and flicked through her notes, periodically looking up at her.

"Yes, I know; Janet told me."

"Anyway, I've been reading your file. So, what can I help you with today? How have your fibroids been behaving? No major problems I hope," Chris articulated, as he preoccupied himself looking at one of the charts in Olivia's file. "I see that you are due another scan to see if they have grown in size."

"I've been experiencing extreme discomfort on my bladder," Olivia exclaimed, feeling more embarrassed by the minute that she was actually having this kind of conversation with him. *Firstly, He was too good looking to be a doctor,* Olivia thought. *And secondly, he's my pupil's father for goodness sake. How would I feel on Parents' Day when he came to talk about Ben's progress and future knowing what he knew about my gynaecological history?* Olivia's mind started to race ahead of her. *There's no way I can let this man examine me; I'll just die of embarrassment. He may have done this procedure hundreds of times and seen various uteruses in all different shapes and sizes, but he hasn't seen mine and nor will he.*

Olivia came back to the land of living to the sound of Chris' dulcet tone. "Let me just examine you to feel if the fibroids have dropped any further which could be the reason why they would feel as though they are pressing on your bladder. You can get undressed behind the screen."

He must be mad Olivia thought and picked up her bag with the idea of leaving. "Dr Harris, you may think this a bit old-fashioned, but I would prefer to be examined by a female doctor. So, I think I better make a new appointment with Janet to see Dr Webb next week."

"I hope you're not embarrassed by me, Miss DuPont?" Chris tried to reassure Olivia that this was strictly a professional assessment.

"Oh no," Olivia said hurriedly trying to exit Chris' office. "It's just that Dr Webb has been my doctor for many years now and I've kind of got used to dealing with her. Thanks all the same. Goodbye." Olivia could not get out of his office and the surgery fast enough, flying past Janet and waving her hand in a gesture to say she was leaving. By the time Chris was able to run after Olivia, he got the tail end of her car as it zoomed speedily out of the car park.

That night Olivia was extremely quiet which was unusual for her. Steve wondered if he had said something to offend her, but Olivia reassured him that the events of the previous day had finally caught up with her and she was feeling a little tired. Olivia apologised to Steve after they left the Pizza Hut and explained that she would have to give the cinema a miss. In Steve's usual, kind-hearted way, he understood and drove her home.

Chapter Four

Sunday service was, as usual, a special time for Olivia to spend the time to reflect and exhale. After the last two eventful days, Olivia was grateful that she wasn't on the rota that morning to teach and really enjoyed the worship, followed by an inspiring message by Pastor Frank Turner. 'PT', as he was fondly referred to, was a vibrant young minister of this friendly community church and would often take the opportunity to challenge his congregation to seek the higher places and deeper depths in God to enhance their Christian walk. Olivia had been a Christian for as long as she could remember, having been brought up in a Christian family and it was her faith that brought her through when she faced various challenges in her life, especially in the area of her singleness.

New Dawn was a family-oriented church, predominately made up of married couples and young families. Therefore, whether Olivia wanted to address the issue of her singleness or not, she was thrust into being surrounded by couples, thus having to deal with it. For her part, Olivia aspired to have a family of her own someday. However, with Carol away on honeymoon, Olivia knew she would be going home to an empty house, which was something she now had to get used to.

Olivia made the decision to go for the easy option and eat out, rather than going home to start cooking from scratch, and for one at that. As a confident, mature woman, Olivia was comfortable with her own company and eating on her own was not something she saw as a problem, which she had done many times before to give Carol and Michael personal space at their house for them to spend quality time together. As Olivia left the car park adjacent to the back of the church, she hesitated on which way to go. *If I go left it will be Chiquitas. Now do I want Mexican or Portuguese?* In her spirit, she felt a strong inkling to go Mexican and turned left en-route to Chiquitas.

On arriving at Chiquitas, the waiter found Olivia a lovely spot in the corner by the window, which delighted her to no end, as she enjoyed peering through it, observing the various people that went by. Wondering who they were, what they were up to and where they were going was a game Olivia often played in her mind. She loved to let her imagination run wild at times as she conjured up elaborate stories about them.

After ordering her meal, the waiter brought Olivia a virgin colada, a coconut and pineapple drink topped with crushed ice, and a bowl of nachos with a spicy salsa dip, whilst waiting for her main meal to arrive. Again, back to her pastime of gazing through the window and being a nosey old thing, Olivia didn't quite notice a couple of individuals who had entered the restaurant, since she was rummaging through her bag trying to locate her mobile phone which was ringing.

"Hi Steve; yes, I'm fine. Sorry I left so quickly last night; I'd like to refund the price of those tickets." Steve reassured Olivia that it wasn't necessary and that he was in a hurry. He just wanted to check up on her to see if she was okay. "Well... okay Steve, you take care of yourself and enjoy your Sunday afternoon." As Olivia hung up the phone, she glanced in the corner of her eye that the waiter was showing another party to a table adjacent to hers.

Olivia heard the sound of fast, running feet and an out of breath little boy stopping at her table. "Hello, Miss DuPont." Olivia looked up as she recognised the voice as Ben from her class who had run off from his father and made a dive in her direction. Ever since Ben had changed classes to Olivia's class, he had made a remarkable turnaround and appeared a more confident and bubblier little boy, compared to the withdrawn boy she had first been introduced to.

Losing his mother had had a profound effect on his life and had drawn him into a world of silence where no-one was allowed in, not even his father. However, Olivia had a special gift of bringing out the inner hidden qualities in a child and whatever methods she was using seemed to be doing the trick.

"Hi Ben. Who are you with?" Olivia looked around to see if there was an adult with him as she couldn't see Chris lurking behind one of the columns that obscured her view.

"He's with me." Chris emerged from behind the column, also slightly out of breath. "Ben, you are not to run off like that." Chris placed his hands on Ben's shoulders, trying to guide him towards the table the waiter was showing them to.

"Hi, Dr Harris, how are you?" Olivia tried to avoid eye contact with Chris.

"I'm fine. Thanks to you, I had an extra half an hour on my hands yesterday and got to leave the surgery early, so that can't be a bad thing." Chris used a touch of humour to put Olivia at ease following her speedy departure the previous day, imagining how awkward it must have been for her.

"Yes, I'm sorry about running out yesterday, but I thought it was better to wait until Dr Webb was available to see me than to go through everything again with you, especially since you aren't fully familiar with my history." Olivia felt herself falling deeper into the pit that she was creating and was saved by the waiter's dulcet tone.

"Sir, can I show you to your table, or will you be joining your friend? I can bring another chair; that won't be a problem." The waiter's eyes glanced at another chair on the next table.

"Oh no, we don't want to intrude on this lady's space; we'll take our table, thanks."

"Oh Dad, pleaseeeeee, can't we stay with Miss DuPont? Pleaseeeeee, Dad?" Ben looked into his dad's face and then into Olivia's, like a helpless puppy looking for a new home.

"Oh, go on then, who couldn't resist that angelic face?" Olivia smiled. "I'm eating alone anyway, and the company would be nice."

"Well, if you're sure we won't be a problem; thanks very much."

"No, you won't," laughed Olivia, especially since

Ben had already taken his cue and sat down, smiling confidently in her face as if he had just achieved a huge victory.

The waiter brought over another chair and Chris sat down also. The waiter turned towards Chris, who was adjusting his seating, trying to get comfortable. "Can I get you something to drink sir?"

"Yes, can I have an apple juice for my son, and I'll have one of those please." Chris pointed to Olivia's long slender glass, complete with a slice of pineapple and an umbrella on the side.

"That's a virgin colada," voiced the waiter.

"Sounds good to me," Chris responded.

"I'll get your drinks and give you a little time to look over the menu."

Lunch was enjoyable and relaxing, with no uncomfortable moments, which considering the previous day's events, Olivia was thankful for. Whilst Ben was busy scribbling away with the colouring set the waiter had given to him, Chris took the opportunity to attempt to get to know Olivia a little bit better.

"So, Miss DuPont!"

"Please, call me Olivia; you make me feel as if I'm back in the classroom," Olivia interrupted.

"Yes, I see what you mean. Well Olivia, you can call me Chris and then I won't feel like I'm back in the surgery either."

"Deal," Olivia responded and they both chuckled. Chris noticed how stunningly attractive Olivia was with her dark velvet features, long black hair and dark eyes, and a smile that brightened up any dark room. Being in her presence generated a warmness that made him feel at ease whilst conversing with her.

"So, Olivia, what is a nice lady like you doing having lunch on her own on a Sunday afternoon?"

"One word; laziness," Olivia said casually. "I just didn't feel like cooking for myself today and with Carol not around now, I felt like treating myself. I left church and said to myself whichever way I turn out of the car park that is the restaurant I will go to and here I am." Olivia raised her hands as if to indicate that the decision was divinely taken out of her hands.

"You go to church? So, you're a Christian then?"

"Guilty as charged," Olivia said flippantly. "What about you? What's your opinion on faith and God?"

48

"Well….." Chris fidgeted with his hands trying to think of a way he was going to explain how his own faith in God had been shattered somewhat, following the death of his wife two years ago. He finally got his thoughts together. "I'm at a low place right now in terms of my faith, so I don't really know how I feel."

"But you haven't given up on God altogether, have you?" Olivia enquired inquisitively.

"No, not at all; I just need some time to process my thoughts and move forward. We prayed fervently and believed that Jill…. that was my wife's name, would be healed when she first got sick; but she died anyway and it was something I hadn't quite anticipated, because I felt strongly that she would pull through."

Olivia could see the strain on Chris' face and didn't want to probe him any further, if talking about his late wife was too difficult for him. "I'm really sorry for your loss." Olivia put her hand on his hand to offer sympathy. "But please don't feel you need to talk about it any further if it is too difficult to do so."

Chris composed himself as he gently pulled his hand away. "Actually, it isn't difficult talking about it, although for the first time, in a very long time, I feel a weight has been lifted from off my shoulders without feeling overwhelmed by the whole experience. I guess time really is a healer."

At that moment, Ben jumped in and interrupted their conversation. "Daddy, look at my picture." He showed Chris the picture he was painstakingly working on.

"That's nice, son," Chris reassured and patted Ben on the shoulder.

"I think we are going to have to put that one up in our classroom, Ben," Olivia said as she smiled at him. Ben smiled back, feeling extremely proud of himself and his artwork, which prompted Chris' next move.

"Right Ben, I think it's time we better be making tracks." Chris beckoned to the waiter for the bill. "Since we crashed your party, I think it is only fair that lunch is on us, if you don't mind, that is."

"Well, it was a nice enough intrusion all the same and thank you very much." Olivia was thankful for Chris' gesture, as she reached for her bag and started to put on her jacket.

"Oh, let me." Chris rushed over to help Olivia with her jacket.

"Why thank you, kind sir." Olivia smiled, and in that moment, they both gazed into each other's eyes and then quickly looked away.

As they exited the restaurant, Chris held the door open for Olivia. "Here, let me get that."

"Twice in one day, eh?" Olivia said playfully as if her Prince Charming had come to her rescue.

"I would have offered to give you a lift home, but since you already told me that you drove here, I guess this is goodbye for now then."

"Yeah, we sistas are too independent for our own good sometimes huh," Olivia giggled.

"Bye, Miss DuPont," Ben said as he waved to Olivia with one hand, the other hand holding tightly his masterpiece.

"Bye Ben, see you tomorrow and don't forget to bring your picture with you. Bye Chris, I really enjoyed myself and thanks again for paying."

"Yeah, I enjoyed myself too, perhaps we can do it again some time."

"That would be nice." They all left the restaurant and headed in opposite directions. As Olivia parted company from Chris and Ben, Olivia wanted to look back to see if Chris was looking at her as she walked to her car but did not want to get caught and therefore kept her face straight ahead. However, what she did not see was that Chris did turn around, taking a quick glance at Olivia, whilst reflecting intently on the lunch and the time they had spent for those few hours, which brought a pleasant smile to his face.

Chapter Five

*A*fter a hectic week with OFSTED visiting the school, Olivia was looking forward to spending quality time and a girlie evening with Carol. Carol and Mike had returned from their honeymoon two weeks prior, however, the two friends had not yet had the opportunity of catching up since the wedding and they had planned Friday would be the day to remedy that.

Olivia had agreed to cook and decided to make Carol's favourite: Thai green chicken curry with jasmine rice and a selection of roasted vegetables, followed by honeycomb and caramel cheesecake. The spices and aroma in the curry were infusing nicely, permeating throughout the kitchen, and Olivia took the opportunity to run upstairs and change whilst the jasmine rice simmered in the rice cooker. Olivia came back downstairs in a pair of jeggings and a Betty Boop T-shirt and set the table in anticipation of Carol's arrival within the next 10 minutes.

Ever since they had known each other, Carol was always the punctual one and sure enough, at 8 pm and right on cue, Carol was knocking the front door. "Hey girl, look at you, with your tanned self." Olivia embraced Carol with a warm hug on the front porch.

"I'm doing good. I've been looking forward to this evening for the last couple of weeks, so let me in girl, and let me see what you've done with the place," Carol asserted, as she jokingly pushed her way past Olivia. Her gaze checking out the place, whilst scrutinizing methodically the changes Olivia had made.

The changes were not that significant, but Olivia did attempt to put her own personal stamp on the place, since she didn't have Carol, the resident interior designer, breathing down her neck anymore to ensure everything was spic and span, looking like one of her 'show homes', as Olivia would always tease.

"Umm," Carol hummed, smiling as she followed the tantalizing aroma and headed towards the kitchen, being familiar with the layout of the house. "Wow, you're making my favourite, Thai green chicken curry."

"Yep, thought I'd make the effort." Both girls started to laugh. "Right, the food should be ready in about 10 minutes, but let's go into the lounge and then you can give me the low down on life as 'Mrs Mills' and tell me about those amazing beaches in sunny Barbados. Can I get you something to drink?" Olivia asked as she walked towards the kitchen.

"I'll have an Apple and Raspberry J20 – thanks," which Carol knew would be in the fridge.

"One J20 coming up; make yourself comfortable. I mean, it's not like you don't know where everything is, and I'll bring them in."

Olivia brought the drinks in and sat down, joining Carol on the sofa. It was the first opportunity that the friends got to talk about the wedding. "Carol, the wedding was amazing, and you looked so beautiful."

"Thanks, we had a great day, and everything seemed to go according to plan," Carol exclaimed as she sipped her drink.

"Well, I won't tell you about the horror stories then," Olivia giggled.

"What horror stories? I don't think I want to hear them now, as it will only mar my perfect image of the day." Carol smiled.

"Well, to be fair there weren't that many, and Steve and I managed our best to keep them from you both, like the fact that little Lucy locked herself in the bathroom."

"Wow, a whole lot of drama eh!" Carol said inquisitively, holding her hands over her ears as if not to listen.

"Saved by the bell," Olivia yelled as she got up to turn off the cooker's timer. "Right the food's ready," she hollered to Carol, "So take a seat at the table and I'll bring the food through."

"I think I like this being waited on; it makes a change from me doing all the serving now, but I'm not complaining, I love being the dutiful wife," Carol said, smiling.

"I know you are still in the honeymoon period, so I'll give you another month, then come back to me and tell me that he isn't getting on your last nerve." They both fell about laughing, after which Olivia blessed the food.

"So, what was Barbados like, girl? I've always wanted to go there."

"It was just like the pictures you see in the brochures. White sand and the bluest, greeny coloured sea, yet so clear, the clearest that I have ever seen. We had a private villa, with our own personal maid and private chef. Michael really did push the boat out to make it a special and memorable time."

"And was it?"

"Girl, indeed, it was." The girls did a high five in the air, with a cheeky smirk on their faces.

"So enough about me," Carol said, as they tucked into their food, and she took a sip of her J20. "What's been going on in your world; how's work?"

"Work's okay, although we had an OFSTED inspection this week and you know what it's like when we have an OFSTED inspection. Everyone was running around like a headless chicken." Olivia sighed whilst nodding her head. "But I'm confident we will do well. When the inspectors visited my class, whilst they don't give away much from their facial expressions, I could sense that they were quite pleased with the lesson plan they observed of mine." Olivia was smiling, indicating a real sense of pride and achievement.

"Well done, Livy," Carol congratulated. "And now to your personal life; what's new on that front then?" Carol said rather curiously.

"You said that like you've had some top secret inside information; care to share?" Olivia said, rolling her eyes and looking over at Carol, who she knew loved a good ole story and loved to be the first to share it.

"Well Michael may have let slip that Chris said the two of you had a date."

"A date!!" Olivia screeched rather sharply. "I would hardly call it that. He saw me in Chiquitas the Sunday following the wedding and happened to crash my party of one." Olivia smirked. "Plus, he had Ben with him, so I don't know how you could interpret that as a date…" Olivia quickly got up from the table with the intention to clear the table but didn't quite manage it somehow. "So… are you ready for dessert?"

Olivia was trying to change the subject, but Carol quickly picked up on that. "Hey, stop trying to change the subject. What's wrong with Chris anyway?"

"Nothing's wrong with him, I just don't know the man that well. His background etc; I mean, he could be anyone." Olivia went to the kitchen and came back carrying dessert plates with two well-crafted honeycomb and caramel cheesecakes. "Now I haven't put any single cream on them, as I'm watching my figure, but now that you've found your man, do you want some on yours?" Olivia chuckled as she sat back at the table.

"Listen girl, just because one is married, it doesn't mean that one should let themselves go, you know, and yes please, I would like some cream with mine." They both fell about laughing. They could always find something to laugh about and continued to enjoy themselves throughout the evening, catching up on things that they had missed in each other's lives.

"So," Olivia communed, "how is the project coming along?" Olivia was referring to the house in much need of repair that Carol and Michael had bought.

"Well, we didn't realise how much of a project it was going to be, having now moved in, but it's all good. You know me; I like an empty shell with the opportunity of being able to put my stamp on it and turning it into a masterpiece. And the best thing about this particular project is that I am going to enjoy doing it with the man I love, the man who makes me happy." Carol tilted her head to the side, as she munched on her cheesecake, which was her favourite dessert of all time. "Is there another piece going?" Carol enquired, looking towards the kitchen.

"There sure is," Olivia said, rolling her eyes, as if it were a given that Carol would want seconds. "I'll go and cut you another piece." As Olivia brought another slice of cheesecake and gave it to Carol, they both found a comfortable position on the sofa to continue the conversation they had started. "I envy you Carol; it must be quite satisfying knowing that you have finally found the man of your dreams."

Carol agreed, nodding her head and taking a bite of her dessert. "Yes, it is, Livy," Carol proudly responded with a mouthful of cake. "But you'll find your Boaz too and I'm sure it will be sooner than you think."

"There you go again," Olivia butted in. "I know where you're going with this; you're such a matchmaker."

"But I only want you to be happy; just like me and Michael are."

"I know you do Caz, but sometimes the wait is just so hard, and I keep asking God, when will it happen. I'm nearly 40 for goodness sake and I bet all my eggs have shrivelled up by now too."

"Don't be silly Liv. Many women in their forties have produced children in their older years and don't forget Sarah in the Bible; she had her first child at the age of 99 years old."

"Now you're tripping, Caz," Olivia smiled sheepishly. "What about you and Michael, are you guys going to try soon, seeing that you're in the same age group as I am?" Olivia enquired.

"I guess we will at some point, however, the house is our main priority at the moment. Once we've got it how we want it, then I'm sure we'll have a sprog or two."

Carol smiled.

"Caz, you do want kids, don't you?" Olivia asked puzzlingly, as she had always noticed when they shared a house together and children were around on the weekends that Carol wasn't really a natural around kids, but she just put that down to Carol not wanting them to disturb her beautifully prepared, picture perfect, home. "But Michael wants kids, right?"

"Oh yeah, he's keen, but as I said, right now, the house is our priority and who knows how long that could take." Olivia sensed that there was something off with her friend about having children but could not quite put her finger on what she was feeling uncomfortable about, so she decided not to pry any further and let the subject die a death.

"Oh well," said Carol rising to her feet. "It was a lovely evening, but I need to get back to my hubby, he'll be wondering where I am as it's getting late."

"I know," said Olivia. "Us singles don't really have a man to answer to, but for you, things are different now and you have another person's feelings to consider. My, my how things have changed eh." Olivia rose to her feet.

"Oh nooooo, look at the table!" Carol shrieked looking over at the table where the plates and glasses remained from their meal. "I should at least stay to help you tidy up."

"Don't be silly, girl," Olivia exclaimed, waving her hand across her face. "That's what dishwashers were invented for. I'll load the dishwasher when you've gone, and they'll be done before you get home. You get going, as Michael will be waiting up for you," Olivia said as she embraced Carol. "And yes it was a lovely evening and long overdue at that. When you next have a free moment and can squeeze me in, maybe we'll go out next time; save me from cooking eh." Olivia chuckled.

"Or better still...." Carol jumped in. "You can come to ours; that way you can see how things have progressed from when you last saw the house in its original state and then you can let me have your honest thoughts. Not that it's going to make a blind bit of difference, 'cause after all, I'm the professional..... right!" Carol laughed at her sassy comment, picked up her things and walked to the door.

"Drive safely hon and text me when you get in."

"Will do, night hon."

Olivia waved Carol goodbye until the car went out of her gaze before locking the door and drawing the curtains for the evening. Olivia didn't want to leave a dirty dining room until the next day and cleared the table and loaded the dishwasher before she retired for the night. As she recalled how the evening transpired, Olivia was thankful that she didn't take on any unnecessary commitments and had a relaxed weekend to look forward to.

Chapter Six

*M*onday mornings always seemed to come around quickly. However, Olivia was grateful for the relaxing weekend she had enjoyed, after the hectic OFSTED inspection the previous week. And equally grateful that she had the day off, which was booked as she had a doctor's appointment, following which she had to go to the hospital for another scan. Olivia wasn't looking forward to the scan since one of the requirements was to have a full bladder prior to the scan. In the past, this was always a difficult feat for her when trying to retain water, for any given length of time, due to her weak bladder.

It was quite a bleak day and Olivia would have preferred to stay in bed and pull the duvet covers over her, but she knew the inevitable could not be avoided. Olivia got herself ready and drove the few miles to the surgery for her 11.00 am appointment. She got to the surgery in good time and was surprised that the surgery was not that busy for a Monday morning. Olivia was grateful that Dr Webb was back to her normal schedule and that she would be able to be seen by her.

"Olivia, go straight in, you're Dr Webb's first appointment today, so she doesn't have anyone in with her now." Janet gave Olivia her notes and proceeded to call Dr Webb on the intercom to let her know that Olivia had arrived and was on her way down. Olivia walked the length of the corridor towards Dr Webb's office, which was the last door at the end, having to pass both Michael and Chris's offices.

I wonder if Chris is working today, or if he is at the hospital this morning? Olivia pondered, *and if so, I wonder if we'll bump into each other?* Since their initial meeting at Chiquitas a few weeks ago, neither of them had seen each other and despite Chris's assurances that he would keep in touch, he had not done so. *Oh well, it's his loss.* Olivia arrived at Dr Webb's office and knocked the door.

"Come in Olivia." Olivia entered Dr Webb's spacious office, complete with all the latest mod cons.

"Looks like you have a completely new office since I've last been here," Olivia exclaimed as she sat down on the seat opposite Dr Webb.

"Yes, Olivia, it was about time we updated things. We have recently received some extra funding and we have

65

been able to stretch our resources a bit further to bring things into the 21st Century." Joan smiled. "Now, what's all this about you not completing your last visit with Dr Harris?" Joan sighed, as if talking to a naughty child who would not eat the vegetables that had been put on their plate.

As Olivia recalled that last visit in her mind, it reminded her of how embarrassed she felt. The thought of stripping from the waist down in front of Chris was not an option she was prepared to undertake, especially as she found him drop dead gorgeous and to die for. Olivia directed her thoughts back to the matter in hand.

"Oh, that was nothing," Olivia exclaimed. "I was in a hurry that day and since I didn't think Dr Harris was that familiar with my history. I felt it best to wait and see you when I could discuss things in more detail." *Olivia, oh what a big fat lie you just told, and you're supposed to be a Christian too.* If Olivia's skin were not a dark complexion, she was sure Joan would have seen her flushed face and was glad that she seemingly got away with her 'white lie'.

"Well, madam, that delay is what has prompted the hospital appointment you now have today. Your last scan showed some cause for concern, which should have been treated at that last visit." Olivia was ridden with guilt and felt rather silly now that she had put her own health in jeopardy over what was simply an element of pride on her behalf. "Anyway, when you see the consultant today at the hospital, they will be able to give you further options on the way to proceed. If you come back and see me in a couple of weeks, we can discuss your treatment plan and other things again then."

Olivia felt like one of her students who was being scolded for something they had done wrong. "Thank you, Dr Webb. I appreciate your time and I'll see you in a couple of weeks." As Olivia left Dr Webb's office and walked the corridor, both doctors' doors were still closed. Olivia thought she had missed her opportunity to bump into Chris, but on reflection was somewhat relieved since she wasn't sure how their meeting would fair. Or whether there would be any awkwardness, which she was glad to have averted.

Olivia had a couple of hours to spare before her hospital appointment and decided to pop into town and do a spot of shopping, her favourite pastime. Olivia had her eyes on a particular pair of red wedged heel shoes that she had wanted since they first came out but could not justify paying the £89.50 they had cost. However, now that the sales were on, she prayed that they had gone down. Olivia popped into John Lewis to see if the Roland

Cartier shoes had been reduced and, to her delight, they had gone down to £44, which she thought was a bargain and quickly snapped them up. Carol always teased her, accusing her of being frugal when it came to shopping, but Olivia disagreed and believed there was always a sale, further down in the year, to take advantage of and it was only a matter of time. Her motto was 'good things come to those that wait' and with that mantra, saved herself several pounds over the years and had a healthy bank account balance to show for it too.

Olivia's appointment was at 2.30 pm and she got to the hospital at 2.15 pm, allowing sufficient time to park the car and check in at the receptionist's desk. Following the scan, Olivia was pleased with herself that she had managed to retain her water, enabling the medical professionals to take the necessary ultrasound.

Olivia's next stop was at the clinic, where she made herself comfortable and took out her kindle. As from past experiences, hospital clinics never ran to time and always ran over. With her kindle in her bag, she could always catch up on any reading she was behind on or listen to music on Amazon Music or iTunes.

As she glanced up from behind her screen and looked up at the wipe-board with the information of the various doctors' names and the rooms they would be using, she read the names out in her mind. *Dr Khan, Dr Mann, Dr Leith and Dr Harris.* Olivia's mind retracted the names she had just reverberated. *'DR HARRIS; you have got to be joking. Please God, don't say that this is the 'Dr Harris' I know. But it's a small community and he wasn't at the practice this morning, so it must be him. Oh nooooooo.* Olivia grew anxious and suddenly the kindle book she was reading did not seem to hold her attention. Olivia pondered further. *Well, there are four doctors' name on that board, what are the odds that I get him, 4 to 1 right! God are you having a laugh? This just can't be happening, I'll just die if I get him, as I won't be able to back out this time.*

Whilst Olivia was deep in thought, she did not hear the receptionist call her name twice. "Miss Dupont!" That loud third call snapped her out of her trance.

"Oh yes, sorry that's me," Olivia shrieked as she quickly gathered her things, having dropped her keys and glasses on the floor from sheer nerves, and proceeded to the reception desk. "Please go to room one." As Olivia walked to room one, her thoughts raced ahead as to whom she was going to find behind door one. She knocked the door.

"Come in." As Olivia walked in, to her horror, Chris was sitting there with two other individuals; a man and a woman, who were quite young and looked like trainee doctors. "Hi Olivia…. Sorry I mean, hello Miss Dupont," Chris said as he cleared his throat and changed his voice to that of a more professional tone. "Please take a seat, Miss Dupont." Chris motioned to the seat that was opposite him and tapped the keyboard on his computer, pulling up Olivia's records on the screen. As Olivia sat down, she realised that her fate was sealed, and that this time she was unable to run, and once and for all, would have to deal with her fears head on.

"You don't mind the student doctors being in the room whilst I examine you, do you?" Chris was obligated to ask permission before assuming that his patients would be comfortable with such an option.

Olivia thought long and hard. *Well at least there is a woman in the room, so I should be grateful for small mercies eh.* "No, that's okay," Olivia affirmed.

"That's great. Well, if you could go behind the curtains and get undressed and put on one of the gowns, then pop yourself on the bed, we'll see what's been going on, shall we?" Chris smiled, attempting to reassure Olivia that this interaction between them was strictly professional.

I don't know what he's smiling at. I don't find anything about this whole situation to smile about. I just want to die.

Olivia emerged from behind the curtains, robed in an emerald-green gown, with its unflattering gape at the back. Olivia wondered to herself what moron designed such a contraption designed to bring embarrassment somewhat to its users, rather than make them feel good about themselves. She grudgingly plopped herself on the bed. Chris explained to her that he was going to examine her pelvis to check the size of her fibroids and to see whether they had increased in size. His hands were firm, yet soft and Olivia felt vulnerable and slightly embarrassed, given her professional relationship with Chris as the parent of one of her students.

This just isn't right.... God helpppp. However, there wasn't much Olivia could do about it, apart from pray that it would be over as quickly as possible. After allowing his students to also have a probe of her pelvis, Chris asked Olivia if she would get dressed and come back to his desk when she was ready.

Olivia sat back at the desk after she had got dressed and put the gown in the bin provided. "The prognosis isn't good I'm afraid. Your fibroids have grown quite significantly; therefore, the only option now is surgery."

"Ohh," sighed Olivia.

However, Chris interjected with hope quickly, "But the good news is that we can save your uterus and there is no need for a hysterectomy. Whilst the fibroids have increased in size, they are manageable and therefore a simple myomectomy procedure will be performed instead, with the view of saving your uterus. I know it's a lot to take in right now, but what are your thoughts about the information I have just shared with you, and do you have any questions you'd like to ask me?"

Olivia pondered for a moment. "Yes, it is a lot to take in, however, I'm very grateful that the procedure will keep my uterus intact. It's my desire to have children one day and to take that opportunity away from me would have been quite overwhelming." *I can't believe I just said that to Chris out loud, argh.* "What are the next steps?" Olivia asked, slightly relieved by the news she had just heard.

"Well, we will schedule you in for surgery within the next month or so, as there is a waiting list, but I don't see any problem with me reaching those fibroids and getting them all out."

"What! You'll be doing the surgery?" shrieked Olivia. *Unbelievable. Is this man going to haunt me for the rest of my life? God, this isn't really what I had in mind when I said that I'd like to get to know him better; it wasn't this direct.* Olivia smiled to herself. God truly had a sense of humour, but in her mind, this really was beyond a joke now.

Chapter Seven

"You really are competitive, aren't you?" Chris sighed, as he grabbed his towel and wiped the sweat from his face. Michael laughed as he gathered up his squash racket and bag.

"No pain, no gain." Michael chuckled as he slapped Chris on the back. "Plus, if you keep your form up, you'll be thanking me when you see the difference in your core abs."

"Let's hope so, because this kind of pain just isn't right." They both laughed as they walked to the changing rooms to take a shower.

Having refreshed themselves, they grabbed a burger in their local leisure centre's bar. "Is this a good idea?" Chris eyeballed Michael puzzlingly, especially as it looked like they were going to undo the hard work they had just achieved.

"Protein is important." Michael laughed. "And we need to retain our stamina."

"So how are you finding married life?" Chris poised the question to Michael as he settled down to enjoy his burger, feeling a little less guilty. "What has it been, about three months now?"

"Yes, three glorious months. It makes me wonder why I didn't do it sooner. But I guess us guys are always weighing things up before we eventually get around to doing anything concrete."

"Are you saying that you had concerns then?" Chris probed.

"Not concerns as such. I just wanted to be sure that Caz was the woman God had for me, because I only plan on getting married once," Michael reassured Chris as he didn't want to give him the wrong impression of his love for Carol.

"Do you think God is interested in those kinds of issues concerning our lives?" Chris enquired.

"Of course, Chris. God is interested in every area of our lives. His Word encourages us to cast all our cares upon Him, because He is concerned about every area of our lives and I'm a firm believer in standing on the Word of God. Man, this burger really is good." Michael gulped, washing it down with a bottle of mineral water. "Sorry, I didn't mean to stop your flow and talk about carnal things." He smirked.

"No, that's okay; I still have a lot of questions that I need to ask God about. I guess in time I'll get them answered."

"Why don't you come along to an Alpha Course we've been running at our Church?" Michael suggested. "I know you're not new to faith, but it generates a lot of honest questions and answers about God from non-believers and you might find it helpful to address any underlying issues you're facing."

"Thanks, I might just do that," Chris confirmed. "I know I can't keep running from God, and at some point, I will have to address my fears. I just want the empty and hollowness I feel in my life at present to be filled."

"Chris, you know that everything you'll ever need can only be found in developing a relationship with Jesus Christ."

Chris nodded. "I know you're right, Mike, and it's up to me to make the first move. Thanks for the invitation, I think I will come along and see what it's all about. Anything right now would be a big improvement on how I've been feeling." Chris rolled his eyes as he contemplated the internal torment that was churning on the inside of his soul.

"Chris, I just want to shake your hand brother, and to congratulate you on re-dedicating your heart to the Lord." Michael extended his hand to Chris as he grabbed him and gave him a hearty embrace.

"Yes, well done, Chris," Carol reiterated as she leant over and gave Chris a peck on his cheek.

Chris was overwhelmed. He had taken up Michael's offer to attend one of their Alpha classes and felt an amazing presence of God's Holy Spirit, prompting him to repent and re-dedicate his life to the Lord.

"I must admit," exclaimed Chris, "I feel a lot lighter, as if a weight has been lifted from off my shoulders. I had allowed the grief of my late wife's death to take me deeper and deeper into a valley of despair, but tonight I felt that weight just drop off instantly; I really am free!"

"You'll have to share your good news with Olivia when you next see her!" Carol was quick to drop that remark in, as she knew they had not had much contact with each other since Olivia's surgery.

"Oh yes; I will." Chris smiled as he nodded, with a noticeable glint in his eye. "I will have to check in on Olivia anyway, as part of her post-op care. Do you know if she is at home, or whether she went to her parents' house?" Chris pried, trying to ascertain where Olivia chose to recuperate following her major surgery, since it was a hospital requirement that, upon discharge, Olivia was not allowed to recuperate at her own house by herself.

"Actually," Carol smiled, as if she were happy to offer the information, "Olivia's recuperating at our home. It just made sense since my hubby is a doctor after all."

"That's the best care a patient could want for; I'm pleased," Chris said. "If it's alright with you both, I'd like to check in on her."

"Oh, I think I might open the door for you if you came knocking," teased Carol.

Michael wrapped his arms around Carol and said, "You're not right, woman! Chris, take no notice of this little wife of mine, you are welcome anytime and I'm sure Olivia would be grateful for some decent company aside from us two loved up birds in her face every waking moment."

Chris smiled. "It's a date then!"

Let's hope so, Carol mused to herself. *God only knows what those two knuckleheads can't seem to see what's blatantly obvious and staring them right in front their faces.*

"Well thanks for a great evening. Carol, you take care

of yourself and Mike, I'll see you at work tomorrow." Michael and Carol returned the sentiment as they all walked to the car park and departed.

Olivia had spent a couple of weeks at Michael and Carol's home recuperating after her surgery but was now starting to feel like a spare wheel, especially as they were still fairly newlyweds. She was a firm believer that married couples should have quality time to enjoy together, without interference from a third party. This scenario wasn't her idea to begin with. Olivia was all set to recuperate at her parents' house, but Carol was insistent that it made sense for her to stay with them, and when Carol had an idea in her head, woe betide anyone who tried to change her mind.

Olivia was grateful for the kindness of her friend, since the thought of going back to live with her parents, after having left the parental home for so long, was a daunting prospect, which somehow, she would have got through, with the help of the Lord. Whilst Olivia loved her parents dearly, there was something to be said for having your own independence and doing things 'your own way', so to speak. Olivia knew her parents wouldn't have been able to help themselves; reverting back to treating her as a teenager once again, especially since her room was practically the same as how she left it. Give or take a few posters on the walls of upcoming Christian bands she used to idolise.

Carol was quite flexible with her job and was able to spend several days working from home, which was another reason she convinced Michael and Olivia that her recovering at their home was the better option. Neither of them would dare talk Carol out of her 'master plan'. Working from home also had its added benefits too, as it gave Carol the opportunity to work a bit on the house. Her and Michael had made great strides in the renovation, and it was starting to take shape and look like a real forever home with its period features and quirky character.

Carol really did have a flare for design and had started to put her and Michael's stamp on it, moving it away from the 'badly in need of repair' shell that they had bought, which they got at a reduced-price due to its dilapidated condition.

Carol was in the kitchen area cooking up a storm as Michael was due home shortly and she loved the fact that she was in a position where she could have a meal prepared for him after a busy day at the surgery. Olivia was relaxing on the sofa, listening to a local Christian radio station.

"Carol," Olivia shouted. "I think I'll go home at the

weekend."

Carol rushed into the room in hysteria with a pair of oven gloves in her hands. "That was quite random."

"No…. I have been giving it some thought and it's time I started to get myself prepared for going home, going back to work, etc, before I become a permanent feature." Olivia smiled.

"I know the District Nurse has visited you a couple of times, but you'd think Chris would have popped in to see you, especially when he said he would," Carol disappointedly voiced her opinion.

"Oh, it's no problem," Olivia remarked in Chris' defence. "I am sure he's been very busy, and I think I'd avoid me too if I was him."

"Why do you say that Olivia?"

"Well, the whole thing has been quite embarrassing for the both of us. I can't really look him in the face, and I guess he has seen more of 'me' than he bargained, if you get my drift." Carol walked over and gave Olivia a hug, reassuring her that her fears was not necessarily the case.

"There could be another reason, you know." Carol smiled. "I did forget to share with you that Chris re-committed his life to the Lord you know; so, I guess he's taking the time to make up for lost time."

"Oh, I didn't know that," Olivia said with a positive glow on her face. "That's great news; he'll feel more at peace with himself now, as he seemed to be carrying the world on his shoulders. I'm so pleased for him."

"Yes, it is great news," Carol agreed. "I must have got distracted with something else that I forgot to mention it, which really isn't like me at all, is it?" They both chuckled, because it really wasn't like Carol to miss being the first to share important news like that. Carol wasn't a gossiper according to her summarisation of herself. She just prided herself in being the bearer of 'good news', which was the way she saw it, and in her opinion, that was that.

Whilst they were having a moment, there was a rattle at the front door, followed by the sound of voices. Michael came through the door with another figure accompanying him. He hung his coat up on the banister and left his bag in the cupboard under the stairs.

"Hi hon." He entered the lounge and walked over to Carol and gave her a warm embrace and gently kissed her on the lips. "Look who I've got with me," Michael said sheepishly, referring to Chris who followed closely behind him. "I'm sorry that I didn't ring ahead to let you know and hope you don't mind."

Carol smiled, still embraced in Michael's arms. "Of course, I don't mind; I always make extra, as you well know, because you usually have second and thirds." They both grinned. "This man can't get enough of my cooking," Carol said, digging Michael in his stomach.

"Hello Olivia," Chris uttered as he walked over to her. He felt a bit awkward and didn't know whether to shake her hand or hug her, but because Olivia was sitting on the sofa, he leant over and gave her a peck on the cheek, which took Olivia by surprise. However, she smiled, and to put him out of his discomfort, returned his greeting.

Michael went on to explain the reason for Chris' random appearance. "Chris said that he wanted to pop in to see Olivia before he went home, and I convinced him to stay for a bite to eat."

Chris mentioned that he wasn't able to stay too long since his housekeeper, Mrs Jenkins, was looking after Ben and he wanted to read a story to Ben and tuck him in before he went to bed.

"Now let me see what my lovely wife has cooked me for dinner; it smells great." Michael and Carol discreetly made their exit from the dining room, allowing Chris and Olivia some privacy.

"So how have you been?" Chris enquired, as he gazed

at Olivia, who was trying hard to straighten up as she had been slouched on the sofa, not expecting any other person than Michael to show up.

"Yeah, I'm bearing up; thanks. Although I can't wait to go home." There was a slight hint of exhaustion in Olivia's tone. She quickly glimpsed an outlandish expression on Chris' face. "Don't get me wrong, whilst my hosts have been a great blessing and a real God-send, there's really no place like home, being surrounded by your own creature comforts!" Olivia got up slowly and walked over to the window, where she glanced out.

"Yes, I know the feeling," Chris sympathised. Olivia's striking physique held Chris' gaze. They both seemed a little awkward in each other's company and small talk was proving a bit strained, almost as if they did not have much in common with each other. The teacher in Olivia alluded to this fact and therefore she tried quickly to say something to rouse the silence.

"I hear congratulations are in order." Chris looked a little puzzled as his eyes followed Olivia as she slowly moved around the room attempting to stretch her limbs as if she was about to warm up for one of her exercise classes. When Olivia saw the confusion on Chris' face, she continued to finish her statement, "Carol mentioned that you had re-committed your life to Christ; I'm really pleased for you." Olivia walked back to the sofa positioned directly opposite Chris.

He rolled his eyes as if the penny had just dropped. "Ahh yes; I'm back in the fold, so to speak, and it feels like I'm back home," Chris said with a confident smile. That foresight on the part of Olivia paid off; after their initial hiccup, the conversation that followed flowed and their banter and laughter was evident to those in the other room.

"I wonder what those two are laughing at," Carol said, as she put her ear close to the wall, trying to hear what was going on in the adjoining room.

"Carol, stop it; you're so nosey. You just can't help yourself, can you?" Michael rolled his eyes as he attempted to pull Carol away from the wall or from being anywhere near the door. "When are you going to learn to stop prying in other people's affairs, Caz? I've told you before that if you let things take their natural course; you'd be surprised to know that the world doesn't revolve around you. You know, the Gospel according to Carol and all that."

"Ha! Ha! Very funny, Mr Mills." Carol walked to the other side of the kitchen and back to what she was doing. Carol hated when Michael told her off, in that manner, because he was always the voice of reason and usually made a lot of sense. However, from a young teenage growing up, she had always been fixated on romance, her happy ending and all that goes with it, and would often have her nose buried in books plotting out the future she one day dreamt she would have.

"Anyway, whilst we're on the subject, when are we going to start trying for a family?" Michael said as he crept up behind Carol and held her petite waist, intimately giving her a kiss behind her right ear.

"Did I miss something?" Carol said, feeling slightly perturbed by Michael's revelation. "How was that on the subject?"

"Well, every time I attempt to bring it up, you always have some sort of excuse, so I thought I would take my chances and give it another go." Michael was an only child, therefore, having a large family was quite important to him, and he wanted a house full of kids.

"We're still working on the renovations. I thought we agreed to get that out of the way first, and then see how things go," Carol quickly retaliated. "Plus, I plan to go back to work shortly as I have two large projects I'll be working on which is going to be quite time consuming." Carol seemed to find all sorts of excuses to justify why she was not ready to start a family any time soon.

"Caz, you do want children, don't you? I thought we had talked about this and had both agreed that this is what we wanted for our future." Michael's voice sounded emotional as he turned and looked intently into Carol's eyes.

Yet Carol's response did not do much to settle his concerns. "Yes, we did talk about this, but I didn't think it was something we were looking at immediately. Certainly not in the first few years of our marriage. My business has finally broken even, and I feel it's now making inroads. I thought we agreed that you'd give me time to establish my clientele. Plus, you also have had a few changes with the practice. Can we really add a baby and the enormity of what that would entail to our busy equation?"

"Caz, neither of us are getting any younger," Michael said frustratedly.

"Oh, thanks a lot." Carol showed her annoyance and treated the cutlery and dinnerware more harshly than was normal. It sounded like World War 3 was about to break out.

"Sorry Caz, that came out wrong. Rather what I meant was that at least if we started trying for a family now, if either of us had any unforeseen issues in that department, then those issues could be ironed out now as opposed to finding out later down the line that there could be potential problems." Michael tried further to reassure Carol. "I have had patients over the years who put things off for the sake of their careers or other various reasons, only to find out later that they wish they had started a family when they were in the prime of their lives."

Carol walked towards the door, carrying the dishes she had prepared the food in and said rather abruptly, "Excuse me, whilst me and my decrepit eggs get out of this place, because I am done with this conversation." Carol walked out of the room leaving Michael in mid-discussion.

Michael tutted and rolled his eyes. *This attitude is becoming too frequent; I don't know what has changed since we got married, but I intend to get to the bottom of this.* Michael knew he could easily have reacted to the situation but decided not to make a scene or embarrass Carol and, instead, made use of the situation and brought out the rest of the dishes Carol had left behind. He rejoined his guests with a cheery greeting, hoping that they did not overhear the ruckus that was happening in the kitchen area a few minutes earlier.

Chapter Eight

*O*livia was glad to be back home and back to normal. The place seemed hollow from the emptiness of chatter and the laughter of her friends, but that didn't matter to Olivia, as she could once again do exactly what she wanted to the way she wanted. There was something to be said for living a single lifestyle, depending on how that was viewed by others. To some it could be interpreted as living selfishly. Just concentrating on number one. And to another, more about making the most of the cards life deals you. Just appreciating one day at a time, regardless of what a person's preferences are. Olivia was always strong in her opinions and lived by the motto "Enjoying where you are at, on the way to where you are going," which was a phrase she borrowed from listening to Joyce Meyer's ministry, and that truth kept her content and structured.

Olivia only had the weekend to get herself sorted out as she was returning to work on the Monday. She was really looking forward to seeing all her pupils as in her mind she had spent far too much time away from them and did not want them to forget her. From as far back as Olivia could remember, she always wanted to be a teacher. Her own experience as a child growing up brought back happy memories, especially of the teachers that had poured into her life and made her education a positive experience. This planted seeds in her heart to reciprocate back to others what she had been privileged to receive in those formative years.

As Olivia glanced around her surroundings, a thought she previously contemplated came back to her mind. *This place is too big for me, and I do need help paying the mortgage. I'm going to advertise on Christian Flat-share for a house mate.* It wasn't that Olivia couldn't live on her own. And whilst she certainly valued periodic moments on her own to focus and enjoy the solitude, Olivia felt that perhaps it wasn't where she should be at this juncture in her life. Since this was a thought that popped out of the blue again. Olivia knew that when random thoughts came to her like that, she needed to commit it to prayer and get God's perspective on the matter before she made any rash decisions.

The buzzing sound of her mobile phone interrupted her thoughts. "Yes, Carol, I am fine, thanks, and no, I don't miss you and that hubby of yours," Olivia said sarcastically, just to wind Carol up. Olivia wondered how long it would take Carol to call, since Carol was the mother hen of the two of them.

"Well, you take it easy, Olivia, and don't do anything too strenuous. Even though you've been given the all-clear to go back to work, you still have to be sensible." Olivia smiled as she continued walking around the house with the phone nestled tightly under her chin, finishing off what she was doing.

"Sometimes it's hard to tell who's the doctor, you or that hubby of yours."

"I know, but it's only because I love yah hon; you know that right?"

"Yes hon, and I love you too. What honestly would I do if you weren't in my life? I tell you, the world would be one dull place, that's for sure."

"Ahh bless you, Livy. Likewise, too hon. Now you take care of yourself and if there's anything you need, don't hesitate to ask."

"I won't; bye hon."

It was a tough week making the transition back into work mode. But Olivia did what she did best and just put her heart and soul into her students and got through it. Likewise, the children were also glad to have her back.

Whilst Olivia was convalescing, the school brought in a substitute teacher. However, Olivia's stamp and imprint on her students' lives was something quite special and really could not be replicated, not even by a substitute. The children missed the way Olivia made them all feel very special as if they were the only 'little person' in her class. Which Olivia's Head Teacher praised her for as being quite a rare quality that was only possessed by those truly gifted and called to teach.

It was Thursday afternoon and school would soon be over, but Olivia was a bit puzzled by a telephone call she got earlier from Michael asking to meet up with her after work but requesting that she was not to discuss it with Carol since it was a private matter he wanted to run by her. Ever since the call, Olivia had been slightly distracted as she tried to wrack her brain as to what Michael could possibly want to discuss with her, without Carol's knowledge, since he knew they were tight and literally spoke on the phone every day. It was not her birthday; that was later in the year. Nor was it his. Perhaps it was something to do with the house and Michael wanted to surprise Carol with something special and he needed Olivia to help him.

It could be anything, Olivia thought. There were just the last few students to be collected by their parents and then Olivia would head to the coffee shop that Michael had suggested. And even that was a bit off the beaten track, which was another thing that was making Olivia slightly nervous and suspicious. Olivia wasn't in the habit of meeting up with married men in coffee shops, in areas she was not that familiar with, but she did not consider Michael a 'married man as such'. Olivia always just saw him as 'Carol's Michael' and really hoped that Carol would not call her on her way out, because Carol was like that and would always want to know how she was doing.

Now that she had just gone back to work, Carol had literally called her every day that week as she was going home to see if she was okay and not too tired running around all day after a room full of active children. On cue, just like on the movie set with a scene being played out, Olivia's mobile rang. She had to negotiate the books she was carrying whilst trying to find the phone in her bag and when she found it and looked at it; Carol's name appeared on the screen.

What should I do? Do I answer it or not? If I don't, she'll start to worry and then continue to ring me until I answer it. And then if she rings when I am with Michael, I won't be able to hold my nerve and she'll wonder why I'm talking strangely and then will start to ask more questions that I won't be able to answer. I'm just going to answer it; tell her I'm on my way home but am stopping off to meet a friend for coffee; hopefully, she'll think it's with Steve and that will be the end of that. Even though Steve had cooled off pursing Olivia, they still met up on the odd occasion to touch base. Olivia appreciated the fact that Steve was easy to talk to and get along with. Their meetups were always fun times and Olivia often wondered who Steve would eventually end up marrying as he was such a good catch.

"Oh, hi Carol. Yeah, I've just finished for the day and I'm in a bit of a hurry; can I catch up with you later?" Olivia's eyes rolled up to the ceiling in the hope that her quick thinking did the trick.

"Oh okay," said Carol in a subdued tone. Before Olivia could end the call, Carol was not giving up so easily and tried to elongate the conversation. "So, what are your plans for the evening? Doing anything nice?"

OMG Olivia thought, still hurrying along having finally reached her car. "Carol, I've just got to my car now; catch you later hon." Olivia terminated the call swiftly and got into the driving seat and exhaled with a sigh of relief as she tossed the books she was carrying on the passenger's seat. Olivia knew Carol would quiz her later as to what the hurry was all about, but at that moment in time, Carol was the least of her worries. Olivia was now running a good 10 minutes late and hated arriving anywhere late, which she found quite a rude trait and prided herself on not being one of 'those individuals'.

With the help of her satnav, Olivia found the coffee shop and thankfully, someone was pulling out just when she was driving up, and she cleverly manoeuvred into the space and thanked God for His favour.

Michael was already inside. Olivia went into the coffee shop and was about to approach a staff member but saw Michael waving his hand and beckoning her over to the table that he had already secured. It was a quaint little coffee shop, quite popular with a constant flow of individuals in office attire that probably stopped off for a coffee and chat before going home. Michael stood up as Olivia got to the table and they exchanged greetings with a gentle hug. Michael was always quite the chivalrous gentleman and Olivia loved it when men acted like men and treated those of the opposite sex with dignity and respect, like holding doors and giving up their seats on transportation and those other little touches that women, who enjoyed that type of behaviour, appreciated.

"So, what's this all about, Dr Mills?" Olivia made herself comfortable by taking off her scarf and allowing her flowing hair to nestle on her shoulders, resting her coat and bag on the spare seat next to her. Olivia always referred to Michael by his professional title when she was intrigued by something he said or did.

He looked and shifted nervously in his seat. "What would you like to drink?" Michael drew Olivia's attention to the menu that was on the table.

After pondering over it for a couple of minutes, Olivia made her choice. "I'll have the honeycomb latte with soya milk please." Olivia was not about to risk anything that had lactose in it, especially as she was in an unfamiliar area and did not want to be caught short in an embarrassing moment were she to have an adverse reaction from drinking the wrong type of milk in her coffee.

"Anything to eat?" Michael added as he got up to go over to the counter.

"How long are we planning on being here Dr Mills?" Olivia teased. "Oh, go on then, I am feeling quite peckish, so I'll spoil myself and have one of their oatmeal and raisin cookies too." Michael was gone for a few minutes and came back with Olivia's latte and cookie on a tray and got himself a mocha coffee and a ham sandwich. "You definitely got that made with soya milk, right?" Olivia quickly interjected, looking quite concerned.

"Yep, don't worry Olivia; I know all about you and your delicate ways." Michael tutted with his eyes raised and they both chuckled. When it came to all things related to Olivia, Michael was very much clued up since Carol would tell him chapter and verse on most things concerning Olivia's life, except for those very private conversations which had to be protected by the 'girl code', which meant you took that secret to the grave than dare break a confidence.

Michael sat down and positioned himself comfortably. "I know you must be wondering what you are doing here and why I was a bit sheepish about asking you not to mention it to Caz. Even choosing somewhere off the beaten track. But I just didn't want us to be seen by anyone who knows either of us and then somehow it getting back to Caz, because that would only make it more complicated to explain ourselves."

"Yesssss," Olivia sighed. "And we know how Carol would interpret that too." Carol was known to be quick tempered and often blurted things out first before processing the situation and ascertaining if there was another alternative to the situation. Olivia was only too aware of that, but Carol was her girl and she loved her to bits. Even her quirky ways that she did not always understand, she just figured that you had to accept your friend's strengths, as well as their weaknesses since the world is made up of all types of personalities which was necessary to embrace if friendships were to work and stand the test.

They sat drinking their coffees and consuming their food and Michael attempted to explain the real reason he wanted to speak with Olivia in private. "I've just been a bit concerned of late." Michael's face sank, and his tone sounded serious, very different to the playful Michael Olivia was used to interacting with. "Have you noticed anything odd about Caz's behaviour of late?" Olivia looked at Michael puzzled, and he continued, "I just wondered if she has ever spoken to you about having children, since you guys talk just about everything? Lately, we can't seem to talk about the subject without ending up in an argument."

Olivia could see the seriousness in Michael's face and felt a great empathy for him. Olivia was mindful that Carol wasn't particularly crazy about children. Purely because of how she responded to them when they shared a house, and Olivia had various children over for weekends. Olivia was going to have to be very careful how she painted her best friend to her very concerned husband, because at the same time she didn't want to betray her friend's confidence. Olivia had to think quick on her feet and homed in on her teaching skills to convey a creative explanation that might be plausible to Michael.

"Carol was always more career driven, as you indeed know. But I don't think she has ruled out kids. I just think perhaps that it's something she feels she wants to do in her own time." Olivia hoped that explanation might soothe things somewhat, but the nervousness in her voice might have given her away.

"But we spoke about this prior to getting married and Caz knew how important children and having a family was to me. Having grown up as an only child and being adopted at that, having a family of my own is a big thing to me." It was important to Michael that he marry the right person. Someone who shared a similar outlook on life to him and wanted the same things, like a family and at least two or three kids. Michael would be the first to admit that he dated quite a few women before he met Carol, but that was purely because he was gathering 'information', which is how he described it. Trying his best to ascertain what the women wanted out of life and if they shared the same values that synced with his; the deciding factor being whether they wanted to start a family immediately or not.

Michael wiped the sweat from his forehead as he started to feel slightly warm and undid the top button of his shirt and loosened his tie as he continued on, "And we aren't getting any younger either and should really start to try for a baby now. Olivia, I see this in my practice all the time, women preferring to pursue their careers and so they put off motherhood for a later stage and then at that later stage, they run into complications and their chances of having a child have diminished somewhat. I don't want that for us, but I just feel there is more to the matter that Carol isn't divulging, which is why I wondered if she had said anything to you. I'm not asking you to betray a confidence, if there is an issue, but I'm just getting nowhere whenever I broach the subject."

Olivia wanted to reassure Michael and she rested her hand tightly on his hand, almost squeezing it. "Michael, I think you are probably worrying about nothing; you know what Carol's like. When she gets her head into a project, she gets quite focused on that particular task. I'm always teasing her that I can't believe that she's an interior designer and yet can't multi-task."

Michael smiled. "You're probably right, Olivia. Perhaps it's just me trying to interpret things with my medical hat on and maybe I should give her some more time. After all, we're still technically newlyweds. Maybe I should just cool off and let nature take its course, eh?"

"Too much information, Dr Mills, too much information," Olivia screamed as she playfully put her hands over her ears.

Michael sniggered. "Okay, okay. Well thanks for meeting with me, Olivia. Now enough about me and my marital woes, more importantly, how have you been feeling and how are things?" Michael was referring to Olivia's health and the surgery she had undergone a couple of months prior.

"Oh, I'm fine. I've slowly transitioned back into the swing of things at school and the children certainly missed me, so that was nice to hear."

Michael butted in. "Olivia, you know those kids absolutely adore you. Look at young Ben and the strides you have made with him. Chris can't stop singing your praises at work."

Oh yeah, Olivia thought, *yet he can't even pick the phone up and say 'hi'....* Olivia really didn't know what to make of Chris; was he interested or not? Olivia felt Chris started off well by making the right noises at the beginning of their friendship, which looked like it could be promising. However, post her operation, Olivia noticed that Chris had backed off somewhat, with Olivia not being able to read between the lines. And she had no intentions of chasing any man that could not be 'a man' and go after what he really wanted. Olivia had strong principles on this point and wasn't about to change it at this juncture in her life.

"Oh really?" Olivia said sarcastically.

"Now what's that supposed to mean?"

"Nothing really. It's just that I don't get that kind of feedback from him, that's all. A little compliment here and there goes a long way for a woman's ego you know." Olivia tried to laugh it off, rather than let Michael see her vulnerability.

"I know I'm always telling Caz off, but I have to agree with her, I don't know why the two of you can't get your act together. You're single; he's single and the both of you would make a great couple, but for some reason, it looks as though it's a non-starter."

Olivia rolled her eyes. *Pahleeeeze.* "Michael, you know I'm old-fashioned in that respect and believe that the man should make the first move and I guess the reality is that he just isn't moving; well not fast enough for my liking." Olivia shrugged her shoulders in a defiant 'what really is the point' manner.

"Let me have a gentle discreet word with him."

Olivia grabbed Michael's hand. "No don't Michael; I wouldn't want him to think that I've been pressuring you to say something. I'm a firm believer that if God's in something, then it will happen."

"Olivia, I also am a firm believer in that, but God does expect us to do our part you know and not just sit around on our 'blessed assurance' and do nothing. Look I said it would be discreet and he wouldn't even know what I am doing; us guys are dumb like that you know." He smirked.

"Tell me about it." Olivia winced back.

"I can't believe that I am turning into my match-making wife. And she would throttle me for having a go at her when she tries to put her two cents in."

Olivia rose to her feet and started to gather her things, putting her scarf around her neck and slipping on her coat. "Well Michael, I'm going to have to love you and leave you now. I have a few things to do this evening at home. But I'll have a word with Carol 'discreetly', as you put it, and see what she says and what her feelings are at this moment in time. That's the best I can do without my line of questioning sounding like the Spanish inquisition."

"Thanks Olivia. I would really appreciate that and as you say, it is probably something and nothing."

They both got up, exchanged a hug and left.

Chapter Nine

*O*livia was glad to finally be home. She had an early start that morning and what with meeting Michael straight after work, it turned out to be a long day. As Olivia soaked in her bubble bath, she enjoyed the warmth of the water against her body, absorbing the pleasant pomegranate scent of candles that she had lit, which were positioned on a corner shelf for the aroma and their calming effect. Olivia's mind couldn't help but wonder what really was behind Michael's concerns. He seemed genuinely worried, and she sensed that it wasn't just 'baby-gate', but perhaps something a lot deeper. Olivia also knew it was a conversation she was going to have at some point with Carol in a roundabout way, so as not to draw suspicions that she was in cohorts with Michael and that they were ganging up on her. It was a conversation that Olivia certainly wasn't looking forward to.

"You were home later than usual this evening," Carol quizzed Michael as they prepared for bed. Michael was busy brushing his teeth in their en-suite, which was a section of the house that was completed to a high standard and Carol could tick off her to-do-list. Carol was moisturising her face and removing the residual makeup with cotton wool. She had met a client earlier in the day for an important meeting and whilst she didn't need make-up when she worked from home, Carol always wanted to look her best and come across professional when she met potential clients. And if that helped clinched the deal, then make-up had to be slapped on, even though she wasn't too comfortable with all that kind of stuff. Olivia was the more creative one in that department out of the two of them and would occasionally give her friend a makeover or give her some beauty tips, which certainly helped her bag Michael in their earlier courting days, so that was a lesson worth having in Carol's opinion.

Michael couldn't respond as he had a mouthful of toothpaste and Carol could hear the water in the bathroom still running. When Michael was able to talk, he came into the bedroom with a towel in his hand as he wiped his mouth. "Oh yeah; sorry, I forgot to text you to let you know that I'd be running late tonight." Michael hoped his brief response would suffice, but he knew it didn't really answer the question and knowing Carol, he knew the questions would not stop there.

"So, did you have some consultancy meetings at the hospital then, as when I called the surgery, I got the 'out of office' message, which gave the impression that everyone had gone for the day?"

"Ahh yes, I had to meet up with an old friend. We had coffee and a good chat. We must have got carried away not looking at our watches." *Technically, I'm not lying; Olivia is an old friend, right LORD?* Michael wanted the questions to stop and quickly tried to change the subject. "And how did your day go, my lovely? You were meeting with a new client today, weren't you?"

"Yes, I was" Carol said excitedly and was proud to announce that she got the business and then proceeded to tell Michael all about the finer details of her meeting, so much so that she was completely thrown off the trail of unearthing who Michael had met up with. Michael appreciated he had just dodged a bullet and released a sigh of gratitude that he had got away without having to tell a blatant lie to his wife, even if he had concealed important facts about whom he had spent the evening with.

As they climbed into bed, Michael embraced Carol. "I'm so proud of you, Mrs Mills, for securing that new project. I know how hard you worked on your proposal." Michael gently kissed Carol on the lips.

"Why thank you, Mr Mills." Carol smiled as she gingerly accepted her husband's gesture of affection. Michael attempted to go further by taking baby steps, being wary of recent rejections he had experienced over the past couple of months, which he tried to reason might be down to Carol working too hard on the renovation of the house, as well as running her own business.

Carol pulled herself away from Michael's embrace, stretching her arms in the air and exhaling a loud waning yawn. "Gosh it's been such a long day; I'm so tired – we both could do with a good night's rest." Carol turned to her side of the bed, switched off her side lamp and pulled the duvet over her shoulder.

A disappointed and deflated Michael understood what Carol's demeanour meant, since this seemed to be the norm lately. He turned off his side lamp and turned the other way also with his back to Carol, and went to sleep.

A couple of weeks had passed since Olivia had met up with Michael for coffee. She knew that she couldn't put off having the conversation with Carol any longer. However, with being busy at work and Carol working on her new project, their diaries could never sync to find a suitable time for each other. Olivia took it upon herself and made the bold move of insisting that they meet up after a women's breakfast meeting that the church had scheduled.

Olivia was now used to having her Saturdays to herself to rest after a hectic week at work, but as she had to get up early for the breakfast meeting, she felt it was as good of an opportunity to kill two birds with one stone, so to speak. As a teacher, Olivia was a great planner and very resourceful with time, especially when it was her time. And whilst Olivia would not have been the first to admit it, but she did notice of late that Carol had not been calling her as often as she used to. It was almost as if she was trying to avoid her, but Olivia quickly put that thought to the back of her mind. After all, they were the best of friends and thick as thieves, which is how most people described them, almost like the Thelma and Louise of their day.

"I loved the theme of this morning's meeting; 'Resting in His Presence'," Olivia verbalized as she and Carol met up afterwards in Costa Coffee for a girlie chat.

"Yes, I thought so too; I think it has come at just the right time. Of late, I'm finding it hard juggling all the things I have to deal with, such as the reno at home, work and spending time with Michael." Carol seemed exhausted. If the truth be told, Carol did not seem her bubbly and inquisitive self and her appearance looked quite shabby in contrast to her casual, yet understated, usual self. Carol's eyes looked swollen, like she had constantly been crying and her manner seemed sedate.

"Well, you certainly don't seem yourself hon, that's for sure."

"Well, I've also had a lot on my mind that has been weighing me down." Carol looked directly into Olivia's eyes with a deep and piercing look that Olivia had not seen from Carol before. After getting past the pleasantries, having not spoken to each other for a couple of weeks, which was quite unusual for the two of them, Carol's voice changed somewhat into a more sarcastic tone. "So, is there anything you need to tell me, that you haven't told me, Olivia?" Carol's words were pronounced and a higher pitch in volume as she emphasized the word 'Olivia'.

Olivia looked slightly confused and shifted nervously in her chair. "I don't think so." Olivia took a sip of her coffee. "Why?" Olivia tried to interpret Carol's train of thought. *She must think that I've been out with Chris and not told her. Typical Carol; always wanting to be the first to get the latest gossip, never one to hear it second hand.*

"Okay, perhaps I can help jog your memory, seeing that it seems you're suffering from a slight bout of amnesia." Olivia started to feel uncomfortable with the way the conversation was going and rolled her eyes wondering where the dialogue was leading to. This really wasn't the way they spoke to each other and even in jest, it was never disrespectful. They always had each other's back whatever the situation was.

Carol resorted to tapping her fingers rhythmically on the table quite loudly, like she was about to explode similar to a pressure cooker when its ready to let off steam. "Okay, let me put it in plain English that you can understand." And then just like a pressure cooker, the steam gushed out. "Are you having an affair with my husband?" Carol raised her voice a decibel higher than her original tone.

Olivia looked shocked and stunned and could not believe what she was hearing, yet was quick to respond. "Absolutely not, Carol, and why would you come out with a ridiculous accusation like that?" Olivia didn't know where to put her face and felt slightly embarrassed, since customers at the tables either side of them turned around to see what the noise was, which apparently disturbed the peaceful environment, caused by Carol's agitated state.

Olivia didn't know if the looks of disgust were aimed at her, being the alleged 'adulterer' or at Carol being the downtrodden 'victim', but if the floor could open up at that moment in time, she would happily have crawled into it for solace.

Olivia quickly defended herself. "Again, I don't know where this line of questioning is going, but it's crazy. Me and Michael? As if! No disrespect to Michael, but he's your husband and I would never ever come between you and him, or any other woman's husband for that matter. And how you can sit there and accuse me of something like this shows me where your head is at this particular juncture in your life."

Olivia was seething and Carol knew that perhaps she had pushed her too far; after all they did have a long history of being friends and had helped each other out through some tough times in their lives, but it did not stop her from continuing in the sarcastic tone that she had adopted. It was almost as if Carol was having an out of body experience and was sitting there watching herself, but yet could not stop what was gushing out of her mouth.

"So, you never met Michael a couple of weeks ago in a secluded area at a quaint little coffee shop? I guess that wasn't you then; perhaps it was your twin?" And then the penny dropped. Olivia looked stunned and knew that she wasn't going to be able to worm herself out of this one and because of the way Carol had reacted to the information she had received from God knows who, Olivia knew she had to confess to everything, even if it showed Michael in a bad light. She couldn't risk losing her friendship over a simple misunderstanding, especially since it wasn't something she had instigated in the first instance.

"Aha," Carol said, pointing her finger towards Olivia's face. "I see your memory is starting to come back, so now you can tell me why a client of mine went to great lengths to rub in my face that she saw my husband having coffee with another woman and they were holding hands? And boy did she just love getting one over on me, seeing she wasn't happy that I recently had to increase a quote by £2,000 that I had originally quoted her."

OMG Olivia thought, *this just gets worse by the minute.*

"I only knew it was you," Carol continued in a distressed manner, "because she described your long flowing black hair and physique to a tee." A tear fell from Carol's eye, and she frantically rummaged through her bag looking for a tissue.

Olivia felt a prompt from the Holy Spirit not to go in all guns blazing with her response, but rather to be sensitive to what she now knew was a delicate matter. In a lowered and calming voice, Olivia responded, "I'm sorry, Carol. I know how it must look, but I can assure you, it wasn't how your client described it and there is a perfectly plausible explanation as to why I was with Michael that evening." Olivia looked Carol straight in the eye.

"Michael had asked to meet me there as he was concerned someone might see us having coffee in our vicinity and thus put two and two together, but it seems that all his best efforts still did not take into consideration that there would always be eyes that see you from anywhere." Olivia tried to reach for Carol's hand, but Carol pulled it away.

"And why would he want to meet up with you in some secluded area; what has he got to hide?" sobbed Carol.

Still in a calm voice, Olivia continued, "Carol, he's really worried about you and the fact that you won't discuss starting a family soon. He said every time he tries to bring the topic up, you always argue with him about the matter. And since we are so close, he wanted to ask me if I knew of any reasons why you won't have a serious conversation about starting a family."

"That's a private matter, between the two of us," snapped Carol. "And why would he bring a third party into our personal situation? He had no right talking to you about this."

"I'm sorry Carol, but I really didn't know what he wanted to talk about, but he seemed so insistent that I didn't want to say no. I naively thought that perhaps he

113

was organising something special for you and wanted some ideas, which is why he chose the location he did. I too was taken aback by the content of the conversation and felt uncomfortable by betraying your confidence in any way and I told him that I did not think he had anything to worry about and to give you some time."

Carol's sniffles died down as she responded to Olivia's calming tone, dabbing the tears from her eyes and blowing her nose. Olivia was glad she followed the Holy Spirit's lead and was reminded of the scripture in Proverbs, 'A soft answer turns away wrath'. Olivia certainly felt Carol's wrath that morning. Now that she had calmly explained the real reason for meeting up with Michael, she hoped that Carol would believe her side of the story. Not the version of some disgruntled client who took great pleasure in looking for a way to get even with Carol, no matter how that information could be damaging or hurtful to her marriage.

Olivia reached again for Carol's hand, but this time she did not pull it away and allowed Olivia to gently stroke it. "I'm sorry," Carol said in a more repentant manner. "I didn't really think you were having an affair with Michael. I just saw red when that awful woman delighted to tell me what she saw. And it has been playing on my mind for the past few weeks. Michael seemed distant also, so I just put two and two together and got a rather inconceivable figure."

Both women looked into each other's eyes, and smiled, and just like that, their friendship was back on track. "So where do we go from here?" Olivia asked, because she wanted to know that this morning's outburst was not going to have a damaging effect on them moving forward and that this incident would not always be there hanging over their heads until another outburst.

Carol dropped her head, just like one of Olivia's students who was being remanded by her. "I've got some things that I need to deal with, which I haven't been totally honest about and perhaps that's my first step to finding the wholeness I think I have lost over these past few months."

Olivia seemed confused and wondered if it had anything to do with their friendship, but something told her that it was not their friendship she was talking about, but at the same time, knew not to pry as Carol was still slightly fragile and she didn't want to undo the significant progress they had just made. Her friend had a husband now and perhaps this was the right time to slowly let go of the reins on their friendship in order that Carol could instead rely more on Michael which might draw them closer to each other. Olivia knew that was the kind of relationship she would want with her future husband, one of intimacy and trust. She had dreamt and imagined it for so long and certainly would not want him having to set up secret rendezvous with his wife's best friend to ascertain what was wrong with her.

Chapter Ten

*A*fter the morning she had, Olivia knew she needed to have some normal conversation with an element of fun to lighten the atmosphere and the only person she could think of who would fit that bill, and whose company she wanted to be in, was Steve's. After finishing her shopping at the local Sainsbury's and packing the groceries away, Olivia poured herself a glass of apple juice, which she rested on the side table and plopped herself on her soft leather armchair, initiating the button at the side to extend the foot rest, which elongated her into a comfortable position.

She slid her mobile phone out of the side pocket of her skinny jeans and opened the contacts tab and found Steve's number. *I hope he's in; I really could do with cheering up. I've not seen much of him lately, only the odd glance at church.* As Olivia dialled the number, she took another sip of her juice.

The phone only rang two times before Steve answered the phone. "Hi Liv, how are you?" Steve's voice conveyed his usual calm tone.

"Hey Steve, how are you doing? I didn't think I'd get you," Olivia spluttered, not realising that Steve would answer the phone so quickly, and started to wipe the spillage from the sides of her mouth with a tissue.

"You okay, girl? Sounds like you're choking there," Steve said teasingly.

"I know, but you could have let the phone ring a bit longer; I was just taking a sip of my drink."

"Well, I can always put the phone down and let it ring a bit longer if you like." Olivia chuckled. Steve already made her feel comfortable and in a jovial mood and that was exactly what she needed after the unpleasant morning she had, having been spoilt by Carol's allegations.

"So, this is a bit of an 'on the spur moment', and you can say no if you want to, but I was wondering whether you fancied doing something this afternoon? I've had a difficult morning and I need cheering up and I thought who can cheer me up and the Holy Spirit dropped your name in my spirit." Olivia waited for Steve's response, wondering what he would think.

"So, this was the Holy Spirit's idea was it?" Steve responded inquisitively. He had known Olivia for a while now and could read her like a book. "And what have you done with your best friend, for me to have this honour?"

"Err, ummm, well, that's a long story, which we could talk about on another occasion if you like. But I really need a complete change of scenery and some fun company." Olivia tried to change the subject and hoped Steve would not press her further on her relationship with Carol.

"But I thought Michael had mentioned in passing that you and that new Dr Chris were an item now; why didn't the Holy Spirit bring him to your mind instead?"

Olivia jumped in before he could continue. "Who told you that we were an item? Because we're not."

Steve pressed a bit more. "Well, the way I saw him looking at you at the wedding, it looked that way to me."

"Steve, you're not still hung up on that are you? The wedding seems like it was a lifetime ago, and a lot has happened since then. Anyway, if you don't want to hang out with me, I did say that you didn't have to." Olivia was annoyed by Steve's comments, plus she felt like 'Billy-no-mates'. Her friendship with Carol was strained and she didn't have a romantic relationship in her life and felt like life sucked. Yes, she had her relationship with God, but those two things were at two opposite ends of the spectrum and there was no comparison.

Steve could hear that he was losing Olivia in the

119

conversation. "Okay, I am going out this evening, but I guess I can spare a few hours to cheer a friend up; you fancy going ice-skating?"

Olivia paused and smiled on the other side of the phone. "You know I love ice-skating." Olivia sounded like an excited schoolgirl about to be given an ice-cream cone by a parent.

"Well get your skates on, girl, 'cause I'm coming to pick you up in an hour."

"I'll be ready. Oh, and Steve… thank you." Olivia pushed herself back in the upright position of her chair and ran upstairs to get changed. *Thank you, Jesus; that's really nice of him. And no, I'm not using him; he's a friend after all and that's what friends are for.* Olivia was responding to the conversation going on in her head since she felt that her 'conscious' was not being fair to her by questioning her motives like that and she convinced herself that her intentions were purely honourable.

True to his word, Steve was there within the hour. That was one of the many qualities Olivia liked about him. His punctuality and his reliability. You could set your clock by him. If he said he would pick you up at a certain time, he would be there without fail. It was a quality Olivia hoped her 'Boaz' would have too. If the truth be told, Steve had quite a lot of great qualities that were on Olivia's 'checklist' of 'must-haves' in a future spouse, but there was always something that held her back from seeing him as anything other than a good friend.

The horn tooted, and Olivia knew that was the cue that her ride was outside. She quickly took a scrunchie from off her dresser and tied her hair back in a bun. Olivia knew that when gliding around the ice, she did not want to have to deal with her wavy hair getting in the way and potentially causing her to fall. Although it did not take much to do that since Olivia was not the best of skaters, but then again, neither was she the worse. Plus, Steve liked taking her ice skating as he got the opportunity to show off his skills, since he was quite an accomplished skater, which also meant he could sneakily try and get closer to Olivia and assist her around the rink when he saw she was waning.

After an hour or so of skating around, Steve suggested they take a break, and they found a table in the eating area of the ice rink. They ordered two iced teas and a bowl of cheese and jalapeno nachos to share.

"So where are you off to this evening then?" Olivia enquired as she loosened her jacket and slid comfortably into a corner booth. Her curious nature got the better of her, since she knew that there weren't any evening activities at the church that she knew of.

"Why are you all up in my business?" Steve teased, as he knew Olivia's personality inside out and could bet money on the fact that she would have asked the question at some point throughout their afternoon. He was just surprised it took her so long to raise the subject.

Olivia felt slightly embarrassed because she knew Steve had outed her. "No, I'm not. I just don't remember anything being announced this weekend at church." Their fingers kept touching each other's every time they reached in the bowl for a nacho and for the first time, Olivia almost allowed herself to enjoy the moment of that light touch of Steve's hand near to hers. However, as usual she would suppress whatever was happening between them, since he was not her 'Boaz'.

Reluctantly, Steve sighed. "Oh well I guess you might find out at some point. I'm going on a date."

"A date!" Olivia shrieked yet did not realise that her voice had elevated or that she had a look on her face which told a telling story. "Who are you taking on a date then?" Steve's revelation provoked Olivia's curiosity even more as to the extent of Steve's evening activities.

"I'm not sure if you know her. She's that young lady who recently joined our church a couple of months ago.

She's in my cell group and we seem to have hit it off. She's really easy to talk with and I like the way she interprets the Bible and what she shares and brings to the group." Steve reached for a napkin to wipe his sticky fingers and then took a sip of his iced tea.

"You mean, Jen Walton?"

"Oh, you know her?" Steve seemed surprised.

"Yeah, I've met her." Olivia continued, "Well, you know I've been looking for a flat mate; PK introduced me to her and said she might be looking for somewhere to live, and I met up with her a few weeks ago. I didn't know she was in your cell group."

"So, are you going to give her the room then?"

"I've got a couple more ladies to see before I make my decision. Plus, I need to pray about it also. Carol is going to be a tough act to follow."

"Of course, she would be, you were best friends.... Dahh!" Steve chuckled as he raised his hands in the air. "Goodness look at the time. I'm going to have to make treads and take you home, young lady, as I've got to go and get myself ready." Steve started to put his jacket on.

"Oh, yes of course; you did say you only had a small window and I really appreciate you spending time to cheer me up." Olivia looked at him and smiled warmly.

"Sorry, I never did ask you why you had a rough morning, but perhaps we can catch up again eh?"

"Ah yes, of course, that would be nice and it's fine, don't worry; you've no idea how you have helped me to erase the bulk of that memory." Olivia exhaled. They both picked up their belongings and left the ice rink. Steve drove back effortlessly, taking the shortcuts back to Olivia's home. He jumped out the car and ran around to her side and opened the door for her. Olivia smiled, they embraced, and he jumped back in his car and revved up the engine.

"Thanks again Steve.... Oh, and have a pleasant evening."

"Thank you; I will try to." Steve tooted his horn, waved his hand to Olivia and drove off. Olivia watched him drive away with the smoke from his exhaust filling the air. Olivia felt a tinge of jealousy rise on the inside of her and could not help from wondering what kind of date Steve and Jen would have and wished she knew where her relationship with Chris stood. Olivia also longed to be wined and dined and have some romance in her life. At times it made her sad and reflective as to how long she would have to wait until God opened the right door for her.

With the Wednesday morning staff meeting ending earlier than usual, Michael, Chris and Joan vacated the conference room in a jovial manner, ready for the busy day. Janet entered the room after them and started stacking the used coffee cups on top of each other and gathered the leftover croissants, side places and used napkins, and placed them on a tray, which she took to the kitchen, adjacent to the conference room.

"How is it that I ended up with the mums and toddlers group this month…. Again?" Michael said suspiciously. "I feel I've been set-up. Haven't I gone the last two months in a row now?" The practice gave back to the community by visiting a local mums and toddlers group down the road from the surgery. Offering support to young single mums and giving advice as to basic healthcare tips that they could carry out to ensure that their children remained healthy and up to date on any necessary jabs and services required.

Joan and Chris laughed to themselves as they walked down the corridor to their individual rooms, with Michael walking shortly behind them. "Well, I guess we thought you needed the practice; since out of the three of us you are the one most likely to be in the position of starting a family soon," Joan teased as she arrived at her office first and opened the door.

"Yeah, I'm in total agreement," Chris voiced. "So don't look at me, I'm the furthest from all that baby talk. That's why we made an executive decision that you were the right person, and, by the way, you're outnumbered two to one anyway." Chris was next to reach his office, and the hinges creaked as he opened his door.

"Well, this just sounds like a stitch up to me; that's all I'm saying." Michael peered over his glasses like a headmaster about to reprimand a couple of loitering kids who had not gone directly to their classroom after the school bell had rung. Michael wasn't quite finished talking when he got to Chris's office. "Chris, have you got a few minutes; I'd like to pick your brains about something?"

"Yeah sure." Chris motioned his hand inviting Michael inside and closed the door behind him. Neither of them had any imminent appointments, since the surgery opened 30 minutes later than its normal opening time on Wednesdays, which gave the practice time to incorporate staff meetings and discuss any pressing matters.

"What seems to be on your mind, my friend? I must admit, you haven't seemed your cheery self of late. I thought I'd give you some space to feel free to share whenever you were ready. Is everything okay at home?"

Michael sat down in the seat opposite Chris, in a reversal of roles, almost as if he was now the patient sitting in the doctor's office. "It's funny you should be so perceptive and yes, you're right, I haven't been myself, and a lot has been weighing in on my mind of late." Michael's countenance dropped, and his face appeared as though he was carrying the weight of the world on his shoulders.

Michael shared with Chris in detail some of the real struggles that he and Carol were going through in terms of communicating and even being on the same page with what they both wanted in life. Michael felt that the goalposts had changed somewhat, and they seemed to be at opposite ends of the spectrum in the type of lifestyle they both desired. Michael sensed that Carol's personality was changing daily, and he was struggling to recognise the person he fell in love with and wanted to spend the rest of his life with. Carol had got touchy and moody in recent months, and every conversation they had engaged in, especially around the topic of starting a family, just ended in heated arguments, with one or the other of them walking out of the room. Michael was at his wits end to determine how to amicably resolve the matter, which initially led to the meet up with Olivia to ascertain if she could offer some sort of explanation, especially with the pair being as close friends as they were.

127

Having listened to Michael really bare his soul, Chris felt his pain, having remembered his own personal struggles at one point in his marriage when it felt that he and his late wife were on the verge of a divorce. But it was the help of a good Christian counsellor that helped them to get back on track and got them to break down their issues, line by line, until they reached a satisfactory compromise. What clinched things was the counsellor asking them both to write down a list of all the qualities they liked about each other, no matter how simple it was and then getting them to swap lists. With each party looking at things through the lens of their partner's perspective of them, that brought a new-found respect from both parties, which eventually brought healing to their relationship. As Chris reminisced, he would give anything to be in Michael's shoes, even if it were just dealing with a silly argument which he knew, with a lot of work could easily be remedied if both parties were willing to do the work.

"Have you thought about going down the counselling route? I know it helped me and Jill when we had a low point in our marriage," Chris expressed, after allowing Michael to exhale and get everything out in the open. Men, by nature, don't really talk about their feelings with each other as such, which was a trait that came a lot easier for women, but Michael was slowly dying on the inside and knew that keeping his problems in any longer would not be helpful for anyone in the long run.

Michael scratched his chin. "I would be open to it, I guess. I just don't know if Caz would be. A few weeks ago, I tried picking Olivia's brains just to see if she could shed any light and Caz found out about our meeting and literally blew her top, accusing us of having an affair as such. I totally made a mess of the whole thing." Michael sighed in despair and slumped back in his chair.

Chris knew he really didn't have the expertise to deal with marital issues. Him sharing his story was one thing, but to solve the problems between Michael and Carol was on a whole different scale. Chris had a thought, almost as if the Holy Spirit dropped it into his thoughts. Tapping his pen on the table he said to Michael, "What about PT? Why don't you both make an appointment to see him? I'm sure he has spoken to many a couple on their marital woes and steered them in the right direction. I know that I probably don't know him as well as you do, but he seems easy going enough and I always enjoy his sermons. I feel he has a knack of interacting with his congregation and his stories are always relatable. I've often left the service uplifted and motivated."

"You could be right you know." It was as if Michael had a flash of inspiration and the light bulb had been turned on. The tone of his voice lifted. "We both get on great with PT and his wife and I think Caz may feel a bit more comfortable talking with him as opposed to a total stranger. I think I'm going to suggest it and see how she feels. What have we got to lose eh!" Michael stood up and extended his arms in a large stretch. "Well thanks for your listening ear, but I guess we both have work to do, and in just under an hour, I have to go over and visit the mums and do my clinic, offering them advice and assistance."

"You're very welcome, Michael. You have not only been a good work colleague, but you've also been a true friend to me since I first moved to the Wood and have helped me with many an issue that I needed ironed out. I just hope being a listening ear has helped you offload some of what you have been carrying around for a while." Chris got up from his seat and went around to the other side of the table and gave Michael a pat on his back. "I would offer to pray for you, but I'm not that comfortable praying openly like that yet, but will keep you in my prayers."

Michael smiled. "I totally understand; one step at a time eh?" They both chuckled as Michael left Chris's office.

Chapter Eleven

*M*ichael arrived home that evening and put his key in the front door. An aromatic flavour captivated his nostrils as he entered the house, which smelt like his favourite dish, slow cooked stew chicken, with basmati rice and vegetables. Michael hung his coat on the metal coat stand, nestled in a space in the corner of their hallway and placed his bag at the foot of the stairs and headed towards the scent.

Michael prayed the mood would be light and that Carol's attitude would be warm and welcoming. He had had quite a busy day with visiting the mums and toddlers' group, and conducting headlice checks on the toddlers was not exactly his morning of fun. That was followed by a stint at a specialist clinic at the hospital, finally returning to the surgery for his last appointments, that went on into the evening, which was the norm on Wednesdays to compensate for the late start.

Carol was busily singing away, melodically, to a worship song that was playing on her DAB radio, which was tuned to Premier Christian Radio, and did not hear when Michael entered the kitchen. Michael saw this distraction as an opportunity to affectionately greet Carol. "Hi hon," Michael whispered as he got close to Carol, not wanting to startle her, and gently hugged her waist from behind and kissed her on the side of her neck, pushing her hair out of the way.

Carol did not flinch or wriggle her way out of his embrace as had been the case over the past few weeks when Michael had tried to show her affection. She was positioned towards the hob in their newly refurbished kitchen which was finally finished. The kitchen project took slightly longer than anticipated, due to a change in the layout of the design by the ever so perfectionist Carol. Carol would be the first to admit that she was not exactly a domestic goddess in the kitchen. But that did not mean they couldn't have a swanky, super-sized kitchen in their home, with all the latest gadgets and mod cons. After all Carol was a designer; it was to be expected.

"Hi hon." Carol turned around and gave Michael a warm embrace as she kissed him on the lips. It took Michael back a bit, this sudden change in her demeanour, but at the same time, he was not about to complain about it. Having a bit of normality in their lives was a welcome change. Carol took her hands and squeezed his chin and lightly kissed his lips again.

Michael smiled. "I smelt a lovely aroma when I came in the door and if I'm not mistaken, it smelt like my favourite." Michael took the lid off from one of the burnt orange cast iron casserole dishes, which came as a set of three and was a wedding present. He tilted his head towards the dish to savour the moment.

"Yes, it is, there's no pulling the wool over your eyes, is there?" Carol chuckled. "Go and freshen up and I'll just finish things off and then we can sit down and eat; there's a few things we need to talk about."

Michael also knew he had some things he wanted to bring to the table, so he was all for clearing the air and getting things out in the open. "Okay," Michael said as he kissed Carol on the top of her head and went upstairs to freshen up.

Michael came downstairs, having showered and heavily sprayed himself with his favourite aftershave, Paco Rabanne Pour. He especially liked using that brand as it was a birthday present from Carol.

"Wowww." Carol frantically fanned the area with her hand as Michael walked past her. "Seems to me like somebody swallowed the whole bottle."

Michael laughed. "I just like to smell good." He pulled out one of the pinewood chairs, matching their elaborate pinewood table that Carol had set with various dishes and plates for them to sit down and enjoy their meal. It was something they had not done for a while, instead often just getting a tray and eating their dinner on their laps in front of the TV. That was when they did find the time to eat together.

Carol dished up. "Bon appetite," and they both started their meal that she had sweated long and hard over for the past couple of hours, having had a half day off from the current project she was working on. Carol wasn't the greatest cook, which everyone close to her was aware of, but her food was at least edible. However, Michael just appreciated the fact that Carol was a tryer, and he felt the love that she had exhibited when attempting to provide a meal for her husband. Michael poured them both a glass of Ariel Cabernet Sauvignon, a non-alcoholic red wine that they saved for special occasions.

He raised his glass to Carol's in a toast. "To good times," Michael said, as the glasses clinked.

"To good times," Carol repeated as she looked directly into his eyes.

As they ate, Michael complimented Carol on

preparing the meal and thanked her for her efforts. He was almost tempted to ask her what he had done to deserve such special treatment, with his wife preparing his favourite dish, especially since for a while things had been quite strained between them. He wondered if this was finally a peace offering on Carol's part, with them now having reached a turn of events. Michael wondered if Carol had been talking things over with Olivia, since the two friends had sorted things out between them. He was pleased to see them back where they were before the unexpected fall-out they had experienced. Perhaps he didn't even have to bring up the subject about making an appointment to see PT and decided he would gauge how the rest of the evening progressed.

"How was your day?" Michael said as he looked directly at Carol making the effort to show that he was genuinely interested in how her day went.

"It was productive. We are nearly through and I'm quite pleased with the way the project is progressing. I'm looking to finish things off in about three weeks' time. My clients have also referred me to one of their contacts who has a massive outfit, which I need to size up. But if I do take it, it's going to mean a lot more work, which I'm excited about because a contract like that could raise the profile of my business and would be good exposure for my website too in terms of referrals. To have acknowledgement from a company of this magnitude would take me places." Carol's face lit up as she talked about her business.

Wow, extra business, thought Michael; *seems to me that she's not going to have time to deal with anything remotely personal if she doesn't pull in the reins.* "Sounds great." Michael half-heartedly smiled, as he tried to show support to Carol.

"Well, I'm glad you're happy for me, because that's partly what I wanted to talk to you about." Carol's voice mimicked someone who wanted something but knew they shouldn't be asking for it.

Here it comes, Michael thought. *I knew there just had to be something behind this sudden change of behaviour and pleasantry towards me.* Michael felt a sharp cut to his stomach as if someone had given him a punch deep in his core. He genuinely thought Carol wanted to make amends for how things had been between them lately, but instead she was buttering him up for something that would be to her gain. *And she didn't even ask what kind of day I had either.* Michael felt disappointed but tried not to show any emotion of displeasure in his demeanour. He also wanted to hear fully what Carol had to say. Perhaps it wasn't something bad but was something that involved them both in the interim. "Oh yeah?" Michael voiced, trying not to sound as if he had sussed Carol out and had unravelled her cunning plan to bribe him with his favourite meal in the hope that she would get her own way, whatever that way was.

"Well, you know things have been a bit strained between us of late!" Carol continued. "I think we could do with some space, just so that we aren't on top of each other; giving us a chance to clear our heads. You know what they say, 'absence makes the heart grow fonder.'" Carol was trying to make light of the situation, after dropping such a large bombshell.

Michael looked at her, slightly puzzled. He didn't know where this train of conversation was leading to. "I don't quite understand what you are trying to say, Caz; are you suggesting that we should split up?"

"No, I'm not," Carol said nervously, trying to find a way of explaining herself. "That new business I just told you about that I am looking to secure is a new regeneration project. As I explained earlier, it would be huge for me, but the only snag is that the project is in Manchester."

There, she had done it. Carol had dropped the bombshell, which was a conversation she had been toying in her head ever since the proposition was put to her. In her heart of hearts, Carol knew that she should have first discussed the matter over with Michael, but her focus was blinkered, and she wasn't really thinking straight or rational. Carol quickly took up her glass and gulped her drink.

"Manchester!" Michael uttered, slightly alarmed. "Do you know how far Manchester is from us?"

Before Michael could finish his sentence, Carol jumped in. "It's about 145 miles."

"Sounds to me like someone's already done their homework," Michael said sarcastically.

"Well, I had to do so before I agreed to the job."

"Hold on a minute!" Michael jumped back in. "A minute ago, you were talking about going to size up the job. Now you're telling me that you've already agreed to the job. Without even discussing it with me, Caz what is going on? And what is happening to us?" Michael slammed his hand on the table in frustration. "And if this job is in Manchester, what are the terms of it? How long is it?"

Carol started to feel annoyed at Michael, that he wasn't as excited as she was and couldn't understand why he was feeling frustrated. Carol had always been able to wrap Michael around her little finger and he often gave in to many of her weird and strange ideas. Her reasoning behind her decision was that she thought he would have been glad for a bit of space between them to work on himself.

"We hadn't been on very good talking terms for a while, so it wasn't really something that I could bring up," Carol attempted to justify her decision to totally exclude Michael from such an important decision which would greatly affect both of their lives. "In answer to your question as to how long the contract is going to last, it's for approximately three months; but I am only going to commit to eight weeks."

"Eight weeks!" Michael shouted and shook his head in disbelief. "Caz, when married couples have an issue in their relationship, they usually talk about it or go to see a counsellor. Or do something to work on things, but they don't run away from each other and just hope that distance, oh and in our case, we're talking of 145 miles to be exact, will solve whatever is really going on between them. When I came home this evening, I was going to discuss with you and suggest that we make an appointment to see PT just to see if we could have a third party, like someone who we respect, who would be willing to help us. Note, I said I was going to discuss with you; not tell you," Michael said sarcastically.

"There you go again," Carol said angrily. "Always trying to muster up any third party you can find to bring into our business."

"Caz, whether you'll admit it or not, we need help. We've been married shy of seven months now and we both know it has been up and down at times. If truth be told, I feel we started off really great, but it just seems that our problems arose every time the topic of starting a family came up." Carol started to shift nervously in her seat whilst Michael continued, "I don't mean to embarrass you, but I don't know why this topic has created such hostility between us as this is something we talked about strongly before we got married. Children were a key feature in the mix. We were both on the same page about this."

Carol snapped back sharply and in defiance, "I don't really want to discuss this now; I've said yes to Manchester. I've given my word and I can't go back on it now. Our marriage will survive this. Lots of couples have time apart from each other for all sorts of reasons. All I'm asking is that you support my decision. You said you would support my career and business, so I'd appreciate you supporting me in this." Carol stood up from the table and started to clear the dishes giving the impression that she was finished discussing the matter and her mind was made up.

"Unbelievable," Michael said as he watched her totally dismiss finishing off the conversation in a mature manner. "So what timeframe are we looking at then?" Michael tried to ascertain the rationale behind Carol's decision.

"I'll be leaving at the end of the month."

"So, in three weeks' time at the end of January then. Well thanks for the notice." Michael walked out of the room in a rage, grabbed his jacket from the coat rack and slammed the door behind him. Carol scurried through the lounge, knocking the side of her hip on a sharp corner of the table, to reach the front window and twitched the blind, only to catch the tail end of Michael's silver Corsa as it drove away at speed in a cloud of smoke.

Chapter Twelve

A lot had happened within the last couple of months. Olivia had taken in a new lodger. Having interviewed a few ladies to be a potential housemate, Olivia did not have the time for drama in her life and wanted a peaceful and quiet life. Of all the prospects she interviewed, she found she had more in common with Jen Walton and was drawn to her cheerful personality. Olivia could see how Steve enjoyed her company.

Jen and Steve had had a couple more dates and Olivia felt relieved that things had fizzled out between them as she felt it would have been awkward if Steve had started coming around to see Jen and not particularly to see her. Even though Olivia would not allow herself to admit that things between her and Steve was anything other than a friendship, resembling something of a Christian brotherly/sisterly relationship, she knew something had changed in her heart towards him, especially when she had to sit and listen to Jen comment on '*what a nice guy he was.*' '*A true gentleman in fact*' were her words; and that '*he was just too good to be a single guy without already having been snapped up by some lucky woman.'* Steve hadn't discussed with Jen his past feelings for her new housemate, so Jen was none the wiser and felt quite comfortable in sharing girlie banter with Olivia about her hopeful love life, to Olivia's discomfort.

However, Olivia still wanted to pursue things with Chris to see if there was anything there worth developing, before calling time on the relationship. If that is what it could be called, as things had proceeded quite slow between them from the get-go. One minute Chris seemed keen, and the next minute he was distant, which Olivia had put down to him still processing matters in his mind over his loss. And whilst she did not want to seem as if she was not being sympathetic, Olivia just wondered how much time was expected to be seen as *'being considerate'*.

She also had feelings that needed to be met and didn't want to put her life on hold whilst waiting around for some man to get his act together. At least the solid relationship she had with Carol was back to normal. However, Olivia was surprised when Carol had called her, prior to leaving for Manchester, to say that she was going away for an extended period to work on a project.

Olivia didn't want to press Carol too much on her motives since she did not want to damage the progress they had made, but in all honesty, she questioned why Carol would want to put that kind of space between her and Michael's relationship. The Carol she knew would not have taken a contract that would have taken her away from Michael for a week, let alone for eight, and yet Olivia suspected there was more to this rationale than met the eye, but she just could not put her finger on what the mystery was.

At least she felt reassured that Carol would not be totally isolated and on her own in Manchester since, her sister Jenny lived in a 4-bed barn conversion in Cheshire, on the outskirts bordering Greater Manchester. Carol had admitted to Olivia in the past that she was in awe of the home Jenny had built with her husband and, if truth be told, was a bit envious of the lifestyle she enjoyed, having moved to the area following her marriage. Olivia revelled in the fact that Carol was also only a phone call or text message away, and they had already texted each other quite frequently.

Olivia and Jen sat next to each other during the morning service at New Dawn church. The church was packed, and the worship service was exciting and uplifting. The worship team did an excellent job in leading the congregation in a heartfelt expression of worship to God. Olivia glanced in front of her and saw that Michael was seated a few rows in front of them and next to him was Chris and Ben.

On the screen, the words were displayed of one of Olivia's favourite worship songs, The Reckless Love, by Bethel Music. The song expressing the love God has for mankind and the way He will recklessly go after the one who had lost their way, based around the scripture that describes the farmer going after the lost sheep. New Dawn was blessed with several talented musicians, worship directors and singers, and as well as Pastor Frank's uplifting sermons, the worship time was a highlight of the services.

After worship, the welcome and notices were given, the offering was collected, and the children were dismissed to their classes. Olivia watched as the children made an exuberant dash to their classes and chuckled when Ben ran back halfway to get his Bible from Chris. He was always forgetting something or the other and Olivia loved the fact that she got to teach him at school. However, she was even more grateful that she wasn't on duty that day to teach the Junior Church and was delighted when PT's sermon coincided with her favourite song of the morning.

Pastor Frank took to the platform and placed his iPad on the podium. Speaking from Matthew 18 in the New International Version, he reminded the congregation of one of Jesus's parables and read from verses 12-14. 'If a man owns a hundred sheep, and one of them wanders away, will he not leave the ninety-nine on the hills and go to look for the one that wandered off. And if he finds it, I tell you the truth, he is happier about that one sheep than about the ninety-nine that did not wander off. In the same way your Father in heaven is not willing that any of these little ones should be lost'. Pastor Frank elaborated on the verses, going to great lengths to encourage the congregation that God is a loving Father and no matter what mistakes they had made or how far they had strayed from God, He would ensure that He found them, just like how the farmer in the scripture pursued his lost sheep until it was back amongst his flock. Similarly, God's love is reckless and will go after us at the expense of all the others who are already safe within His fold and have no need to be rescued as such.

As the service ended and the congregation noisily dispersed; some went straight home, but others gathered in small groups, chatting with friends over tea, coffee and biscuits at the back of the church in a reserved area cornered off specifically for hospitality. New Dawn was a friendly church, and this was just one of their many ideas to ensure that individuals felt included and did not feel isolated on a Sunday, following the main service. Which some individuals voiced were some of the loneliest times of the day having spent the morning at church, only then to go home to an empty shell.

New Dawn prided itself on being a church for the entire family, incorporating the whole community. Olivia and Jen were standing by the table holding disposable cups enjoying a hot beverage and watched as Michael and Chris walked over and joined them.

"Hi ladies, do you mind if we joined you?" Michael whispered.

"Not at all." Olivia stepped aside to make room for Michael and Chris to join their space.

Ben's class had not yet been dismissed and it was only a matter of time when an excited little boy would come tearing his way through the crowds looking for his dad. Chris kept an eye on the door where the children's classrooms were located as he was a bit farther away from where he usually would be when Ben came out of his class, and he didn't want Ben to be running aimlessly around the church looking for him.

"Hi Olivia... Jen; how are you both?" Chris said slightly distracted somewhat, continually glancing towards the door.

"Well, I'm fine," Olivia said as she sipped on her

milky lactose free coffee.

"And me too," said Jen with a smile as she grabbed another jammie dodger from the table with refreshments.

"You better not let Ben see you eating his favourite biscuit; he'll think there's none left for him," Chris said smiling. He relaxed his gaze for a bit and gave his full attention to Jen.

"Oh okay, well I'll make sure I wipe the crumbs from my mouth when he comes." Jen chuckled. Jen really liked New Dawn church and felt welcomed as a newcomer. She found it easy to settle in and did not really experience that awkward transition period that can occur sometimes when you go to a new church and try your best to fit into already established cliques. Chris knew what it felt like to be the newbie on the block for a while, and he wanted to ensure Jen felt included.

As Chris and Jen continued to compare stories about their time being new to the area and the church, Olivia took the opportunity to pull Michael aside. He seemed a little lost without his other half who would normally have been by his side on a Sunday morning.

Olivia felt Chris was more comfortable talking to Jen and she wondered if he was trying to avoid her, and if he was, she really did not have time for his insecurities.

Olivia had just sat enthralled by an inspirational talk by her pastor which made her feel loved by God, and she wasn't going to let anything, or anyone for that matter, spoil the moment. Plus, she had her friend that needed her attention and that was where her priorities lay for the short period of time they would spend socialising.

"Have you heard from Carol recently?" Michael had just put his empty coffee cup on the table. He had downed his coffee very quickly as if he was drinking a shot. *Gosh he drank that coffee quick*, Olivia noted. *Perhaps he got a lukewarm cup*, Olivia rationalised.

"Yes, I spoke to her last night and she's coming home at the weekend." Michael seemed to perk up, and a smile lit up, what seemed to be a subdued face, on the prospect of seeing Carol at the weekend, as he hadn't seen her for about three weeks.

Carol had initially promised that she would come home on the weekends, but the initial start of the contract was taking up a lot more of her time than she had anticipated. Carol was a workaholic and perfectionist by nature and did not always know when to say 'no', to her detriment. "She seems chirpier," Michael added. "We've talked and prayed over Skype and have texted a lot too. I have also been meeting up with PT for counselling and he has been teaching me not to react in ways that would cause Caz to stress out and it seems to be working. But I haven't let her know that we've been meeting up as she probably wouldn't be happy about that prospect."

"That's great, Michael." Olivia lightly touched the top of his arm, expressing her happiness that they were making progress as a couple and dealing with whatever issues had intruded and tried to throw a spanner in the works of their marriage. The scripture of John 10:10 came to her mind '*The thief comes only to steal and kill and destroy; I have come that they may have life and have it to the full'*. There was no doubt in her mind that this was an attack of the enemy on the lives of her dear friends, and she too had taken to her knees in prayer and intercession that God would heal their marriage. Olivia was grateful to learn of their progress and answer to prayer.

Michael continued, "I think she's enjoying spending time with her sister and her nieces and nephew so it's good that she's getting time to spend it within an environment of children." Michael was still hopeful that the idea of children was still on the table, even though it seemed to be the source of their past arguments. However, PT had counselled him to go easy on that particular subject for the moment and rather just concentrate on rekindling some of the things that brought happiness throughout their courtship and the first part of their marriage. He felt for sure that with less pressure on the subject of starting a family, things would just take their natural course.

As they were rounding up their conversation and about to return to Chris and Jen, not wanting to appear as if they were being secretive or exclusive, an excited Ben ran at speed towards their group, waving in his hand the handouts that he had been colouring whilst at Junior Church. "Look Daddy, look what I did." Ben crashed into him, at which point his eye caught the jammie dodgers on the table.

"What have you got there buddy?" Chris looked down at Ben and took the handout from his hand to examine Ben's masterpiece.

"Daddy, can I get one of those biscuits please?" Ben was excited because they were his favourite biscuits. Chris always added them to the shopping list whenever they went to the supermarket, since Ben finished them off as quick as Chris could buy them.

"Course you can buddy." Jen reached for the table and took up a plate and placed it at Ben's level. "You've got good taste you know, Ben, because these are my favourite too."

Ben smiled as he took two biscuits and immediately put them to his mouth, licking the centre which was filled with sticky jam. "Mine too," Ben said, with crumbs and jam smudged at either side of his mouth. Jen placed the plate back on the table and thought she had better not take another one as she did not want Chris to get the wrong impression of her.

Jen had enjoyed their conversation and found that they had quite a lot in common. Not only on a personal level, but also in their professional jobs since Jen was a paramedic. That allowed them to interact and exchange medical jargon with each other, which if Olivia was still a part of the conversation, she might have felt lost for words and a spare wheel amongst the two of them.

Olivia wondered what everyone was doing for lunch. She and Jen had agreed to lunch out and she didn't like the thought of knowing Michael was going back to an empty house. Olivia took the opportunity on a whim to invite him to join them and extended the invitation to Chris and Ben also. To her surprise, they both agreed, and the party dispersed to exit the church to go to their various cars in the carpark, where most cars had already vacated. They agreed to go to Olivia's favourite Italian restaurant.

Olivia was grateful that she would get to continue her conversation with Michael. Chris was grateful also for the opportunity to get to know Jen a bit better. He had seen her in church over the last month or so, as she usually sat with Olivia and had been aware that she was her new housemate. He was struck by her simple, yet beautiful features, but ordinarily would not just go over to her and say hello without a good reason to do so. He was grateful that he got to talk to her in the safety of a group setting so that getting to know her followed a more natural flow. Chris was mindful that everyone was trying to push him and Olivia together but questioned whether that was only because the two of them just happened to be single or whether they really thought that they were well matched.

Chapter Thirteen

*C*arol was pleased with the way the project was developing. Even though the initial workload was more than she had projected in her timeline schedule, she had missed home and was looking forward to the weekend. Carol was especially looking forward to seeing and spending time with Michael. Their conversations over the past weeks had taken on a different tone and she was enjoying being rekindled with the warmer side of Michael's character. And the fact that there was no baby talk was even better. Since Jenny was near to where Carol was staying, they were able to meet up often which felt good for Carol to be able to touch base with her big sister and bond with her nieces and nephew.

Carol pulled into the drive of Jenny's barn conversion property and immediately felt a sense of warmth and comfort and was looking forward to spending time with her family a few days prior to going home for the weekend. Her nephew, Christian, opened the door and gave her a big hug. Carol embraced his hug.

"You're getting taller than me, Chrissy boy." Carol slid her hand on his head and ruffled his curly hair. Christian smiled and took Carol's jacket and put it in the cloak cupboard under the stairs.

"Is that you Carol?" a shallow shriek vibrated from the back of the house, the voice getting softer the more it reached the hallway.

"Yes, it's me. You did say 7.30 pm… right?" Carol wondered if she had got the time wrong from the surprised tone of Jenny's voice.

Jenny met Carol in the hallway and gave her a big hug. "Hey little sis; it's so good to see you again." Jenny held Carol's hand and led her towards the kitchen. "The children have already eaten and are upstairs playing on the computer and Tony is working late; so, it's just me and you kid. Spag-bol okay?"

"Yeah, that's great. I've been on take-out for the past couple of weeks, so a home cooked meal is like a treat." Carol gleamed at the prospect of something tasty and hot, and the fact that she didn't have to lift a finger in its execution was such a blessing.

Jenny went over to the ceramic hob and turned off the pasta that was al dente in texture, and dished up the spaghetti bolognaise, which released a spicy aroma of tomatoes, garlic and basil. She took the garlic bread out of the oven and placed it on the centre of the table. As they sat down, the conversation spanned several topics, with them laughing as they reminisced some of their childhood antics.

"Well, the reason why you can't cook that well is that you never stuck around to see what mum was doing. You'd always run off and play with your Lego and dolls house. No wonder you got into interior design."

Carol smiled as she bit on a slice of garlic bread and was quick to defend herself. "Well, I felt you and mum didn't want me there as you were always so close. I felt she thought you did a better job than I did anyway, and to be fair, you are her favourite child." Carol raised her eyebrows as she looked attentively at Jenny.

"No, I'm not." Carol's comment surprised Jenny. As the sisters were in a jovial and playful mood, Jenny thought it would be a good opportunity to quiz her on the recent issues that had been going on in her marriage.

When she first learnt that Carol was coming to Manchester for an extended period, she questioned in her mind why Carol would want to be away from Michael for so long and further questioned why this was the first time in three weeks that she was now going home at the weekend. What was going on? And why did Carol take on this project and did not sub-contract it out to someone else and then come in at the final stage of the project to oversee the work, like she had done on previous projects that were a long way from home? All these questions had been going around in her head and she knew she would have to tread carefully as Carol could be quite volatile when being pressed on a topic she did not want to talk about, which is why it wasn't something she had broached before.

"Michael must be missing you then," Jenny said as she dropped his name into their conversation. It caught Carol off guard, since she was trying to avoid having the conversation as she knew Jenny's personality would press her to talk about things she didn't want to discuss and coughed slightly as she gave her response.

"Yeahh, he is. We've been talking via Skype as well, so it's not like he hasn't been seeing my face." Carol tried to convince herself that all was well in her relationship with Michael.

"Yes, but is that enough? You haven't seen each other in the flesh for, what, is it three weeks now?"

"Have you been counting then?" Carol replied quite sharply.

"Not really. If I'm being honest, I just don't think it was a wise move on your part by taking this contract, potentially putting a distance between you and Michael and placing a strain on your marriage. I'm your big sister, so I can say this to you truthfully, but you're still what is considered a newlywed couple and you need to continue to put the work in to maintain a healthy marriage. I should know, having been married for over 10 years now."

Carol knew Jenny was right. As the older sister of five years, she was always the voice of reason in their relationship and knew she had to come clean on a conversation they had had many years ago, which she had tried to bury. Carol's voice lowered in tone. "He doesn't know!"

"Doesn't know what?" Jenny replied confusingly.

Carol continued, "I haven't told him yet."

"Haven't told him what?" Jenny's eyes suddenly widened as the penny dropped. "Carol, please tell me that you don't mean what I think you are referring to. Please tell me that Michael knows that you can't have children?"

Carol's head dropped, and she put her hands over her face. "Jenny; I just couldn't tell him. From the first time we met, I knew he was my soulmate. As we developed in our relationship, he talked more and more about his love to have children one day. I knew that if he had any inclination that I couldn't give him a child, he would have ended the relationship there and then."

"No, no, no, Carol." Jenny covered her hands across her face in absolute horror. "You should never have deceived him like that." Jenny was in utter disbelief and couldn't believe what she was hearing. Whilst Carol had shared with her that she and Michael had been arguing a lot of late, she hadn't divulged what it was over. Now everything was making sense and the penny had fully dropped. Even though Carol was her younger sister, she would normally have her back in most instances. However, Jenny felt on this occasion that it was hard to justify such a lifechanging situation that not only affected Carol's life, but that of her husband's too.

Carol felt a sense of relief. She exhaled and finally released the dreadful secret she had been keeping for years. Jenny only knew of the secret as it was something that Carol had shared with her at the time when she was walking through that dark season of her life. Carol was 18 years old when she got involved in a relationship with an older married man, which resulted in her getting pregnant. Carol wasn't a committed Christian at the time, but the married man did not want to have anything to do with Carol and a baby that would potentially jeopardise his relationship with his wife and young family.

His constant pressuring forced Carol to have an abortion; convincing her that he would set everything up and pay for the procedure. At her young age, Carol felt she did not have a choice and went ahead with the abortion. Sadly, it was not carried out by a licenced abortion clinic and, as a result, Carol experienced a considerable amount of excess bleeding and damage to her internal organs, which is when she shared her dilemma with Jenny who took her to A&E, unbeknown to their parents.

Carol was treated as an adult, which meant that the authorities did not need to contact her parents for parental consent. The prognosis revealed that unfortunately the abortion was badly botched. Carol's hope of having children in the future had faded away and would not be a possibility due to the damage done to her womb and fallopian tubes. Since the sisters were not living at home at the time, Carol's recovery period went undetected by anyone and thus the secret was safely buried between them…. until now.

The relief of finally releasing the lie that she had been living for these past years took its toll on Carol and she let out a loud screech and sobbed uncontrollably. Jenny did not like to see her baby sister in such a state and always came to Carol's aid whenever she ran into any kind of trouble. Jenny pulled Carol towards her and embraced her, trying to calm her down. Her sobbing was so loud that Jenny's children ran downstairs to see what the commotion was all about.

"Is auntie Carol okay mom?" Jenny's eldest looked very concerned as he had never seen Carol in such a state.

"You go back upstairs, Chrissy. Your auntie is just upset over a matter, but she will be okay. You all don't have to worry as everything is going to be fine." Their mum's reassurance was enough for all three children to believe there was nothing to worry about and they all trotted back upstairs, one behind each other, and went back to occupying themselves with what they were doing before.

Jenny got some tissues and a couple of tablets for Carol to take with a glass of water to calm her nerves and knew it was time to have the difficult conversation with Carol.

"Carol, I know you're upset right now, but you can't continue to live this lie; it's eating you up. You need to come clean with Michael and you need to do it sooner rather than later. If I were you, I'd tell him when you go home this weekend." Jenny didn't want to seem as if she were pressuring Carol to confront her issues, but knew the longer this lie went on, the worse things would be with her and Michael when he eventually found out.

"I'm not sure if I can do it this weekend Jenny." Carol sobbed as she continued to dab the tears from her swollen, darkened eyes. "He really is looking forward to seeing me this weekend and is convinced that we have been making progress. To tell him now would crush him. I can't do that to him. I will tell him, but I won't do it this weekend. I just won't."

Carol had a lot to ponder over on the long drive back to Bricket Wood and her conversation with Jenny a few days prior still weighed heavily on her mind. Listening to her Hillsong CD helped gather her thoughts as the music was uplifting and inspirational. It was in her CD collection in her car because it always gave her the boost she needed whenever she had issues to sort out in her head. Carol was looking forward to seeing Michael. They had been apart for too long, and she knew the real reason why that was. Carol deliberately took a contract that ordinarily she would have passed over to another company, so that she could escape and get away from the way her marriage was spiralling downward and out of control, right in front of her very eyes.

After a few weeks' space and spending time with God in prayer, Carol felt at peace not to bring up the situation until after this weekend had passed because it would not be fair to Michael to drop a devasting bombshell like that on him. Carol pondered to herself. *When was the right time to tell your husband that you couldn't give him the one thing he wanted most in the world, and you tricked him into marrying you under false pretences?* Carol wasn't quite sure, and if she could get away with living the lie continuously, she would have. But Carol knew that eventually she would be caught out because the Holy Spirit had been speaking to her conscious and yet she was doing a good job ignoring its prompts and the numerous opportunities God had given her over time.

As she continued to meditate, Olivia's face flashed across her mind. Olivia wasn't aware of her big secret either, and she wondered how she would react to it. Olivia was a stickler for honesty in a relationship, so she would not fathom or excuse what Carol had done. Yet Carol was getting a strong sense in her spirit that she should talk to Olivia about it before she spoke with Michael. At least if she gauged Olivia's reaction, then she would get a sense of how Michael might react. Well, that was the craziness that she was pondering over. *Should I tell Olivia this weekend whilst I am down, or should I do it another time?* Again, this was a big dilemma Carol needed to contemplate.

Carol pulled into her road and the familiar feelings

of warmth, and a sense of security flooded through her body, reminding her of why she and Michael had chosen to live in the area. Everything looked the same, apart from the trees. The leaves had turned an auburn colour, due to the change in season. Carol imagined Michael frantically clearing away the leaves from the drive, before she arrived, as he knew how much the mess of scattered leaves in front the house drove her crazy. That thought brought a smile to her face of how thoughtful a person he was and what a kind man she had married. He did not deserve to have dumped at his door the emotional junk that she had been carrying over the years, which was sure to hit him like a ton of bricks.

Carol approached the drive and, as she had suspected, the entrance was spotless, and Michael's car was in its usual spot on the drive, so she knew he was at home. *Why would he not be at home?* Carol pondered. It was Friday after all and, if he could, Michael liked to get away early so that he could maximise his time well and spend his weekends with Carol. Sometimes they would book a hotel and have a weekend away, just for a change of scenery. At other times they would go to a museum or visit an exhibition. Or go and catch a movie, followed by a meal. But their favourite pastime, by far, was spending time together at their home and just chilling and watching tv. It didn't matter what was on; whether it was documentaries,

Christian tv or even rubbish tv, the key part was the quality time they spent with each other. Carol felt strongly that this weekend was going to be one of those 'spending it at home times', since there was much to talk about, and they needed to spend quality time with each other for obvious reasons.

Carol let herself in the house and placed her small suitcase in the corner in the hallway and went in search for her hubby, who she had really missed. As she manoeuvred herself throughout the house, there was a fresh fragrance and she observed that everything looked nice and clean, and appreciated that Michael had gone to a lot of trouble for her benefit. She loved him for that since housework really was not his forte. He was more of a DIY maestro.

"Caz, is that you?" An excited Michael came rushing out from the back of the house and ran straight towards Carol. He picked her up and spun her around and they embraced each other and kissed passionately. It was a kiss like two lovebirds who were courting would engage in to show their deep affection for one another. Regardless of the distance that had separated them over the past weeks, that passion between them was still there and it was clear that they both wanted to make every effort to enjoy and make the most of their weekend together. Michael affectionately flicked Carol's hair behind her ear and then slipped his arm around her waist and walked her into the lounge.

"Ummm. Something smells good," Carol exclaimed as they sat cosily snuggled up to each other on the sofa, their feet intertwined.

"Ahh, yes," said Michael sheepishly.

"What's that look for?" Carol could read him like a book and always knew when he was up to something.

"Okay, okay; so, I cheated a bit." Michael had a cheeky grin on his face. "Since I knew you wouldn't have wanted me to slave over a hot cooker having worked all the hours God sent today, I thought I'd order in a takeaway. One of our favourites, Thai food. So, I got Pad Thai, Thai Chicken Meatballs and Thai Corn Fritters. Plus, I knew you would want me all to yourself too." Michael sniggered, as he tickled Carol on the side of her ribs.

"Oh, you did, did you?" Carol wriggled and tried to get out of his hold. Michael knew tickling Carol was a way he got the upper hand, as Carol was ticklish, and was just putty in his hand as her limbs loosed and she totally lost control until she got away from him. "Right, that does it; let me go and freshen up so that I can enjoy some of this scrumptious food."

Carol eventually got herself free and retrieved her case and started to go upstairs when Michael shouted, "No probs, I'll set the table and get the food reheated in the microwave. You go and enjoy yourself and I'll see you when you come back down. Don't be long now." Michael knew that once Carol got in that bathroom, she could be in there for ages. He could never understand what women did so long once they were in there, but he had learnt throughout their married life just to get used to it and ask no questions.

As Carol put things away in the drawers on her side of the bed, it was evident that it was a while since they had been in the same bed, let alone been intimate with each other. Carol got undressed and quickly jumped in the shower. As the water trickled over her face and down her body, thoughts went to the warm reception she got from Michael when she had arrived earlier and the intimate embrace they shared and the playful way they interacted. A shiver came over her body. The thought that she would have to come clean to Michael soon about the secret she had been keeping from him crippled her.

I've spoilt everything. I'll never earn his respect or get back what we have once he knows how I have deceived him......what am I going to do? I really need to talk to my best friend, Olivia, but she's going to be just as horrified as he will. What a mess. The change in the temperature of the hot water jilted her back to consciousness. "Ouch," Carol squealed as the water got unbearable and she adjusted the temperature. She quickly finished showering and reached for the towel she had thrown over the top of the shower. She dried herself and got dressed and slipped into the special kaftan that Michael had bought for her on their honeymoon, which always made her feel special and appreciated because of the sentiment.

As she came downstairs, she went straight into the dining room and Michael's gazed just held her. "Wowwww, you look gorgeous hon, and that outfit sure brings back memories of where we bought it from."

Carol's hair was moderately styled in a scrunchie on the top of her head and her trim shape and figure was lost in the oversized kaftan, which might have been deliberate on Carol's part. Nevertheless, Michael thought she looked stunning. He had only seen her via Skype over the last three weeks, so, to see her in the flesh and to hold her in his arms, felt like a treat to him and he pondered over the words and counselling he had received from PT. *I mustn't talk about babies or pressure her about starting a family. Instead, I'm to keep it neutral and just concentrate on us getting back to where we were.* Michael had laid the table for two. He put out a couple of wine glasses on the coasters and brought in the sizzling, aromatic food and a bottle of white grape and elderberry Shloer for them to enjoy with their meal.

Dinner was enjoyable, and the conversation flowed freely which reminded them of the good old days when this was something they did naturally. "So, what are our plans for the next couple of days?" Carol asked inquisitively. She knew Michael was a planner and would not miss the opportunity to impress her with his lavish plans.

"Well, I'm glad you asked," Michael said mysteriously. "It's a surprise, but Sunday does involve us going to church in the morning. I thought it would be nice for us to go together which would give you the chance to touch base with all your friends. That's if you don't mind," he said in a lowered voice.

Even though Carol had a quick turnaround before she had to leave for Manchester early on the Monday, she reasoned within herself that she could handle a few hours seeing everyone. It wouldn't be long until the project was finally finished, and she would be home for good, but also home to face the consequences of her grave decision, which was a chapter in her life she wished would magically go away.

Michael and Carol played a quick game of scrabble,

which always brought the competitive side out of them. And Carol was pleased to see that her winning streak was still intact. There was a lot of laughter. It was almost as if they were trying to drag the evening out without stating the obvious, that at some point they would have to go upstairs and share a bed together. And what were the rules when you had been separated for a while? Does one have sexual intimacy with their partner on the first night or would they wait until the following night? That was the dilemma.

Chapter Fourteen

*C*arol reached her hand over to Michael's side of the bed, only to find the space empty. *Where's that man gone now?* Carol was pleasantly surprised that given the distance they had had between them, how easily it was for them to enjoy a time of intimacy with each other. Neither of them felt awkward, which just made the decision that she had to deal with even harder. *If I told him now, would we still have intimate times like we had last night?* The thought of losing that oneness with Michael was unbearable.

Carol loved Michael deeply. Even more so than when she first laid eyes on him, which is why telling him in those earlier times was not an option. Carol rationalised that she wasn't going to lose the best relationship she had ever had with someone of the opposite sex. Yes, she dated other men, but there was always something missing. She didn't feel any of them were her real soulmate, until she met Michael and then she knew, that he was the one. She was confident that Michael felt the same way about her also.

Over the past few weeks, Carol pondered how things would have panned out between them had she come clean initially and was honest by confessing upfront with Michael that she could not have children. Would he still have married her anyway because his love for her could conquer anything that came their way? Or would not having the chance to be a father have been the deal breaker? Carol instead chose to make the decision she did as she felt she knew what his response would have been. She wasn't able to live with that. In hindsight, Carol now wished she had let Michael make that decision for himself. She should have trusted him, but more importantly, she should have trusted God.

Michael had got up early to prepare breakfast so that Carol could relax and enjoy it in bed. Carol was special to him, and he wanted to treat her like a princess would be accustomed to. The bacon was sizzling under the grill and the eggs were poaching. Michael buttered the toast and once the bacon and eggs were cooked, he arranged everything on tray, and gently placed a single stemmed red rose in a vase and put it in the middle of the tray.

Michael also reminisced over the previous night and felt thrilled with the way things had gone. He was glad that he had started the counselling sessions with PT. He felt they had helped him to separate his personal desires from what really was important and that was ensuring his wife's happiness was paramount. Michael had enjoyed feeling the silkiness of Carol's body next to his and embracing her in his arms when they enjoyed intimacy. He felt disappointed that the weekend would soon be over but knew it wouldn't be long until Carol's project was finished for good and then they could concentrate on getting back to where they were. Eventually, with time, they could then try to start that family they had talked about when they had first got married.

"Ahh what's this?" There was a hint of surprise in Carol's voice, as Michael tapped opened the door with his toe, gripping tightly the tray arrayed with a feast of delights fit for a princess. "I thought my nose buds weren't mistaken as I went to the toilet, when I whiffed that bacon coming up the stairs. This is lovely. Thank you, my kind husband." Carol gave him a peck on the lips. Michael positioned the tray on the bed in the middle of them and they just stayed in bed and enjoyed a hearty breakfast. "Umm, I could really get used to this." Carol smiled, biting on her toast and feeling totally spoiled by Michael.

"Well, when you're back for good there's no reason why we can't, eh?" Michael reassured her. "But this morning we need to get ourselves ready, because the first surprise is looming."

"Ohh okay. Well, I enjoyed this breakfast, Mr Mills, so I'm just going to jump in the shower and get myself ready." Carol casually strolled to the bathroom to take a shower, whilst Michael cleared away the breakfast things.

Michael had arranged to take Carol into London to see a matinee at the theatre. The musical, Fiddler on the Roof, was a favourite story of hers. They got a train into town and Michael enjoyed teasing Carol as to where they were going. The more she tried to guess every time they passed something she thought it might be, she would get it wrong. Michael enjoyed watching her squirm because Carol always had to know everything or be the first to know everything. This time, however, Michael was in the driving seat, and he was loving it.

They got off the train at Charing Cross, the heart of theatreland, where the area was buzzing with commuters and visitors. Michael took Carol's hand and glided her through the crowds until they got to the Playhouse Theatre. As they arrived outside the theatre and joined the queue that had formed, Carol saw the distinctive green and yellow sign 'Fiddler on the Roof'.

"Yeahh!" She clapped her hands with glee, jumping up

and down. "It's one of my all-time favourite storylines," said Carol as she cradled Michael's arm. "Thanks hon. This is really a treat…. love you." Michael smiled back at her because he knew he had done good in Carol's eyes anyway as that smile was priceless and a sign of her approval.

The musical was everything Carol had hoped it would be, full of emotion, humour, outstanding singing and a spectacular set and stage to appreciate. After the final scene, the cast came back onto the stage to take their bow and were given a standing ovation. The audience applauded vibrantly, whistling and jeering. Carol joined in, cheering loudly, whilst clutching her treasured program under her arm, so as not to drop it.

Michael had arranged for them to have dinner following the play at a four-star Michelin restaurant in the vicinity. As they ate and chatted, they reminisced over their favourite parts of the play. Whilst Carol loved the performance, it was the exquisite set and décor that captured her gaze. Being an interior designer by profession, she was mesmerised by the grand opulence and attention to detail that the designers worked with, and roughly sketched around the sides of her program some of the styles that she liked that she felt might be useful in her work.

After dinner, they enjoyed a stroll along the streets, looking in the shops and just enjoying the buzz of what being in the heart of London brings. It was soon time to head home. Carol felt truly spoilt. In her opinion, Michael really pulled out the stops, in fact she would go as far as to stay he excelled himself. It reminded her of their courtship days, which were happy days.

Dark thoughts soon turned to what things would have been like had she told Michael the night before, what her big secret was. They would never have had such a magical day and all Michael's plans would have been ruined and money wasted as he would have been speechless, angry, or even mortified. Those were just some of the words that she could imagine would have described the situation. *I will tell him soon,* Carol reasoned to herself, *but I know now, for certain, that this wasn't the right weekend to do that, so thank you Holy Spirit for guiding me on that front.*

Carol felt better within herself if she thought her delusional thoughts were a result of the Holy Spirit's promptings, because then she could hide under that notion and appease her guilty conscious in the process. There was still another five weeks to go and her contract in Manchester would be finished and then 'life' as she knew it would resume; or would it? That was the question. The guilt was crippling her and she felt a deep sense in her spirit that five more weeks to wait and spill the beans to Michael was just too long. There and then, she made up in her mind that she would only commit to two more weeks and then delegate the rest of the project to a trusted associate who could project manage the end of the contract. She could still oversee things from home, which was something she would normally have done, if she wasn't trying to run away from her problems.

The ride home was comfortable and even though it felt like a busy day, with a lot crammed into it, they both enjoyed the day and concurred that they were now beat and were glad to be heading home. The plan was a nightcap and then off to bed. They both had church in the morning and Sunday was going to be Carol's last full day before heading back to Manchester on Monday.

As they climbed into bed Carol thanked Michael for a lovely day. Michael assured her that it was his pleasure because she was worth it. Exhausted from the day's activities, they kissed each other goodnight and slept comfortably.

Carol was glad that she attended the Sunday service and equally glad she got to touch base with old friends and her extended church family. Carol felt slightly awkward and convicted, to say the least, by the morning's sermon. 'Putting Your Trust in Jehovah El-roi – The God Who

Sees', which was given by a guest speaker, as PT and his family were away on holiday. Carol felt the sermon was directed, like a dart, straight towards her heart. Her heart being the bullseye. The preacher shared that God sees everything and that when individuals tried to do things in their own strength, it often worked out disastrous, citing the story of Abram and Sarai. The couple were promised by God that they would have a son, but instead of waiting for that promise, they went ahead in their own strength and tried to orchestrate their interpretation of how that would look, especially since they were well advanced in age and in the natural way, it did not look possible.

Alright God, Carol sighed within herself, whilst sitting next to Michael who affectionately held her hand and seemed to be enjoying the sermon. *And I bet he is imagining that this sermon fits nicely with us trying for children, being slightly older.* Carol's mind was spiralling into overdrive. Had PT preached a sermon like that, she could happily have accused him of preaching at her. But for a visiting minister to be on point like that, Carol knew it was the Holy Spirit once again prompting her and this time she knew there was no way she could back out again. *I could tell him now and then he would have a couple of weeks whilst I am in Manchester to process things on his own, but I want to speak with Olivia about it first, so I think I'm going to leave it until when I finally come back home*. Carol and Olivia had a nice chat over coffee after the service and their friendship had really got back on track, so she felt comfortable about now being the right time. Carol had intimated to Olivia that she wanted to pick her brain over an issue when she got home, so Olivia was already clued up, so to speak, that there was a chat imminent. She just didn't know to what extent that chat would turn out to be and how costly.

Chapter Fifteen

*I*t had been obvious to Olivia over the past few months that nothing further would materialise between her and Chris' relationship. If you could even call it that, because other than the pleasantries at school and the odd occasional 'hello' at church, Chris was not pursing her like how a man, when he is interested in a woman, pursues her. And that was fine with Olivia, she just wished he had the decency to end things properly and yet knew in her mind that, as a man, he would argue that there was nothing to end, since technically, nothing had officially started.

Well, he shouldn't have flirted with me then or gave the impression that he might have been interested. That really annoyed Olivia when guys did that. Olivia also noticed that her housemate, Jen, had been getting a lot of phone calls of late, where she would excuse herself from the lounge area to take in private and yet Olivia knew, in her heart of hearts, that Chris was on the other side of those calls. *Well, she's welcome to him. I don't need a man like that. I deserve someone who is warm, genuine and is generally interested in me and who will treat me the way I ought to be treated.* Just as Olivia was putting the romantic world to right, her phone rang.

Olivia answered it and heard Steve's voice on the other end and almost gasped with shock. "Ohh. Hi Steve," her voice said, trembling.

"You okay girl? You sound like you're in the middle of something. Is this a bad time?" Olivia sat on the settee, shocked by the way she was just complaining to God about the type of guy she deserved to pursue her and yet such a very guy, who had been under her nose for the longest time, just happened to phone at that same time. *Holy Spirit: did you have anything to do with this call?*

"Err no," Olivia fumbled. "I was just deep in thought when you called, so your call jolted me out of those thoughts." Olivia hoped she had got away with that lame excuse.

"Well, I hope it was me you were thinking of," Steve joked.

"Oh pahleeze." Olivia smiled.

"Anyway, I called to see if you wanted to go to a jazz festival? Remember we both talked about going to one and I said I would do some research and keep you informed when I had information of any such festival. Well, I happened to be looking online recently and saw that the North Sea Jazz Festival was on. So, I bought two tickets in the hope that you were still interested, especially as you know how quickly these tickets sell out."

Olivia paused and gathered her thoughts. "No, that would be cool as I love jazz and really wanted to experience going to a festival. Thanks Steve. So, when is it?"

"It's next week, but there's a small catch." Steve's voice changed somewhat as if he knew that Olivia wasn't going to like what the catch was!

"Okayyy, go on then," Olivia said suspiciously. "You're starting to sound weird though. Am I even going to like what you have to say?" Olivia wondered what Steve was up to. She and Steve were good friends, so they knew the tone of each other's voice, especially if there was a change to it and something slightly out of the ordinary was about to transpire.

Steve continued, "Since I knew you really wanted to go to a jazz festival, as I did, I took the liberty of booking the tickets, however they are in Rotterdam." Steve waited for Olivia's response, which could have gone one of two ways in his opinion.

"Rotterdammmm. Really. And it's next weekend you say?" Olivia was a little taken aback, yet somehow, she wasn't surprised and laughed inwardly to herself. Steve really was a guy of surprises. He would plan things and then hope for the best. He did not allow limitations to put him off in life. If he wanted something, he usually went for it and with a lot of patience and trust in God, would end up just like the cat that got the cream. "Well okay then." Olivia was stunned and could not actually believe the words that were coming out of her own mouth. "And I guess you have things like travel, accommodation etc in place have you; or is that a silly question?" she chuckled.

"Well actually, I did put some provisional plans in place in the hope that you would want to go." Steve smiled as he too knew that Olivia loved to be swept off her feet and loved it when a man took the initiative on things in a way that was not forceful or manipulative, but instead respectful and thoughtful. "I do have a hotel provisionally booked. Separate rooms," he was quick to add.

"Well of course," Olivia followed. "I would expect nothing less."

"And the rooms aren't adjacent either. In fact, I asked for them to be on separate floors; just so I don't get accused of planning any funny business." Steve's voice was playful. "I hadn't booked the airline tickets yet, since they aren't something you can do provisionally with EasyJet and normally have to be bought there and then which is why I thought I'd call you as I can book the flights now, if you give me the green light to say all is well." Steve was hopeful that Olivia would agree to go.

Even though he had backed down on pursuing his love for her, when Chris came on the scene, he had observed that there wasn't anything genuine there threatening his pursuit of Olivia and he felt he needed to give it one more try since it couldn't do any harm and he had nothing to lose. Steve deduced that if he kept knocking on the door of her heart, that she would eventually open it and feel the same way about him like he felt for her.

"Yes Steve, I would be honoured to go, but do I need to take off the Friday or anything like that?" In her mind, Olivia had started to get excited and was rushing ahead, thinking about what type of clothes she would have to pack and any toiletries she would have to top up on for the weekend.

"No Livy, we can get a flight out on Friday evening as I know the school curriculum isn't in favour of you taking days off outside of the normal term time. Plus, most of the bands don't perform until the Saturday, finishing midday on Sunday. We can get a flight on Sunday around 5 pm, which should give you sufficient time to recoup and be ready for work on Monday."

Ever the considerate and thoughtful soul, Olivia reflected. *What am I scared of LORD that I won't allow myself to commit fully to this man?* Perhaps this was a question that God would answer over the course of the upcoming weekend. "Oh great," Olivia said hopefully. "Let's book it then before I have a chance to ponder this craziness over and change my mind. I can't believe we're doing this!"

"Great," Steve uttered. "Let me go now and book the flights. Trust me, it's going to be a memorable weekend. I'll let you know how I get on! Stay blessed." And with expediency, Steve hung up the phone in a hurry to see if the tickets he had looked at earlier for a reasonable price were still available.

Friday had finally arrived, and Olivia was looking forward to her weekend away with Steve. She hadn't really told anyone, as Carol was due back in a week's time, and she didn't want her to start putting two and two together and coming up with the wrong outcome and felt that it really wasn't anyone else's business at this juncture. Olivia had told Jen, out of courtesy, that she was going away for the weekend but did not say where she was going or with whom. Jen was such a trusting soul that she would not have asked either. The ladies had a great respect for each other's privacy which made their partnership work from the word go.

Olivia wanted to get away quite speedily and began to feel agitated that Ben's housekeeper, Mrs Jenkins, was late in picking him up. She was usually quite punctual, which Olivia was relying on, especially that evening, as she had a flight to catch. Ben was sitting patiently with his hat and scarf on, looking warm and cute, nervously tapping his fingers on the table.

"Oh, dear Benny, looks like Mrs Jenkins is running late today, isn't she?" Olivia patted Ben on the head and walked back to finish off tidying her desktop. All the other children's parents had already collected them, and Ben was the last one, which meant that Olivia could not dash out as she had planned. As Olivia got to her desk her mobile phone rang. She rushed quickly to answer it in case it was Steve with any last-minute changes to their plans. They had agreed that Steve would pick Olivia up and he would drive to Heathrow Airport and leave his car in the short stay car park.

The call, however, was not from Steve. The name that illuminated was 'Chris-doctor/parent'. That was how Olivia had stored Chris' name in her phone, reminding her of his dual roles in the capacity she had to deal with him. Olivia answered the call. "Hi Chris." *He better not make me late tonight. This is so typical and insensitive of him.*

"Hi Olivia; I'm glad I caught you." *Like I can really go anywhere whilst your son is still here*, Olivia grimaced. "There's been a bit of an accident. Unfortunately, Mrs Jenkins was in a car crash and has badly damaged her leg and had a few other bruises here and there, and I am here with her at the hospital." Olivia felt guilty for her earlier thoughts and was upset for Mrs Jenkins but wondered how things would now pan out with Ben.

"Oh gosh, I am so sorry to hear that Chris. Poor Mrs Jenkins; how is she coping?" Olivia was almost ready and had her laptop bag over her shoulder and her car keys dangling in her hand.

"She's a bit shaken up," Chris expressed, "but she's as tough as old boots that one." He smirked. "I don't mean to put you out and under normal circumstances, I wouldn't ask, but could you take Ben home with you until I am able to collect him later, once I have left the hospital?"

Olivia's mind spiralled into a frenzy, and she began to get flustered. "Well under normal circumstances Chris, I wouldn't have minded helping out, but unfortunately, I am going away this evening for the weekend and I am literally rushing home now to get my bag and then I'm out of the door again."

"Oh, I see," Chris uttered as he tried to think quick on his feet of an alternative plan. "I wonder if Jen is at home and could look after him instead then?"

"Well, I'm not sure what Jen's plans are like this evening. Anyway, whatever you decide Chris, you're going to have to be quick, because I really have to go. Couldn't I bring him to the hospital?" Olivia felt sorry for Ben, as once again, he was being passed around like some commodity that nobody wanted, Surely, he deserved more security than this.

Chris rang Olivia back. "I've just spoken to Jen and she's at home this evening and is happy to keep Ben until I am able to collect him." Chris felt relieved that Jen was in a position to help out. *I bet she is,* Olivia surmised.

"Well, it looks like that is sorted then; Ben and I are leaving now." Olivia hurriedly tried to rush Chris off the phone.

"Thanks Olivia and have a nice weekend. Are you going anywhere nice?" Chris wanted to end on a pleasantry. *Oh no,* Olivia gasped; *what do I say now?*

"Just catching up with an old friend; and you're welcome. Anyway, I must dash, or I'll be late." Olivia grabbed Ben by the hand and headed for the door. She didn't feel it was her place to tell him about Mrs Jenkins' incident, after all, that's what he had a father for, to break down the difficult conversations in life.

All Olivia explained to Ben was that Mrs Jenkins or his daddy were unable to collect him today, but that she was taking him back to her house to spend some time with Jen and then his dad would pick him up later. Olivia was aware that Ben and Jen were getting along quite well of late, so such a drastic change of circumstances, wouldn't have fazed him, especially if Jen had a packet of their favourite biscuits for them to consume together.

Olivia got home with time to spare and took Ben into the lounge where he was greeted by a smiling Jen who gave her the thumbs up. Olivia had already called Steve, on her way home, and asked him to meet her at the bottom of her road instead, so as not to draw any undue attention to themselves. She grabbed her bags, said her goodbyes to Jen and Ben, shut the door and walked to the end of her road, where Steve picked her up five minutes later and they headed off to Heathrow to get their flight.

Chapter Sixteen

Steve and Olivia got to Heathrow in good time to check in for their flight. They decided to have a quick beverage at Costa Coffee, prior to boarding. Olivia ordered a Chai Latte with soya milk and Steve had a peach flavoured iced tea. "I thought we were meant to be going on an EasyJet flight," Olivia smirked.

"Well, you know how quick those flights get booked up. When I got back to my screen, the flights had gone, so I had to get a couple of BA flights instead. But really there is no comparison, you know that they are a better class of travel…. right?" Steve released a cheeky grin.

"Oh yeah, I know," Olivia nodded. The conversation flowed steadily between the pair.

"So, Carol is back next week eh. I wonder how that's going to feel for them both."

Olivia raised her eyebrows as she sipped her drink and agreed with Steve. "Yeah, I know, but I have been talking with Carol via skype and she said things are really good between them right now. Albeit the small problem of them being in separate locations, of course."

"I don't think I could ever do that," Steve professed.

"Do what?" Olivia asked inquisitively.

"Have an extended period away from my wife."

"Well in reality, there will be days when you'll be apart for a variety of reasons," Olivia quickly defended.

"Yeah I know that," Steve affirmed, "but theirs was deliberate. Carol orchestrated the whole thing and pretty much left Michael high and dry. I should know, as I had to console the poor guy and try and pick up the pieces. It's almost as if she is running away from something. It really knocked the wind out of Michael; he just couldn't understand it. Did she confide in you about anything as to her rationale behind her sudden exodus?"

"Not really," Olivia said, shaking her head. "I too was a bit puzzled by the whole thing myself and, no she didn't confide in me about anything that was troubling her. So, I can't really comment on that front!"

Steve looked up at the departures board, which was visible from where they were sitting. "That's us showing. Gate 38 it is then. It states it's a 15-minute walk to the gate, so we better start walking now. You didn't want any duty free, did you?" Steve enquired, suddenly realising that they had not allowed any time to browse, since they were busily chatting away.

"No, I'm good; I'll have a flick through the inflight magazine on the plane to see if there are any bargains that catch my eye." They both finished off their drinks, gathered their hand luggage and headed for the departure gate.

Once at the departure gate, they did not have long to wait, and Olivia was surprised when Steve directed her towards the line for priority boarding. *Typical of Steve paying a bit extra so that we could board the aircraft first.* However, Olivia didn't envisage what would follow next.

As they boarded the plane, the flight attendant asked to see their boarding cards and directed them both to the first-class area and Olivia gasped with excitement. "Steve; what have you done? Olivia smiled as Steve helped her put her suitcase in the overhead compartment and she snuggled into the window seat, with Steve in the cubicle adjacent to hers.

"It was a surprise for you," Steve said as he peered over at her.

"Well, I am truly surprised, now buckle yourself in as we'll be taking off soon." Olivia's thoughts reflected on how thoughtful Steve had been in all that he had done for her. When she tried asking him what her share of the trip would cost, prior to the trip, he told her that he had this one and to see it as an early Christmas present. Again, Olivia reminded herself that he had all the qualities she was looking for in a husband and resigned herself to the fact that if he were ever to bring the subject up again about them being together that she would finally stop fighting the inevitable and succumb to his charisma. After all what did she have to lose? They were great friends, enjoyed each other's company and had similar interests; plus, he was fine, beyond fine, and she would be a fool to let him slip through her fingers for another time, or let anyone else have him for that matter.

The hour-long flight went smooth and was comfortable, with Steve and Olivia laughing and chatting about a range of topics for the duration of the flight; coming up for air when they were served a selection of drinks and snacks by the flight attendants.

Steve had arranged for a taxi to meet and greet them at the airport and take them straight to the Mercure Sheffield Parkway, a 4-star hotel, situated 4 miles from the city centre. As the taxi pulled into the hotel car park, they were both taken aback and wowed by the decor and plushness of the hotel. Once they had checked into their rooms, which were spacious and luxurious with free Wi-Fi, and had freshened up, Steve and Olivia took advantage of enjoying a late meal in the hotel's stylish restaurant, before retiring for the night. It had been a long evening and as they had already selected which artists they wanted to see, the plan for the next day was to get up early and see a bit of the city centre, before going to the Rotterdam Ahoy Arena for the jazz festival.

Steve walked Olivia to her room. He was true to his word and their rooms were indeed on different floors. As they approached Olivia's room Steve made way for Olivia to take the lead.

"Well Miss Dupont, this is where I say goodnight." Steve watched as Olivia fiddled in her bag for her key card, which she retrieved and unlocked her door.

"Thanks for a lovely evening, Steve," Olivia said as she smiled at him. They were always affectionate to each other as friends and Steve lent over and kissed Olivia on the cheek. To be on the same floor as Olivia, Steve knew the temptation was too great. Many couples had succumbed to that mistake under the guise of 'just having a night cap' and he had no intentions of being another statistic. Steve really cared for and respected Olivia and if she was to be his wife, as he hoped she would, then he would have to prove to her that he was a man of his word and indeed a Godly man, if that; one who could keep his flesh under control and show restraint.

"Sleep well and don't be late for breakfast." Steve turned around and started to walk towards the lift. Olivia smiled.

"I won't, and you sleep well too."

Steve got to his room and reflected on the evening. Dinner that night went well, and the conversation flowed between him and Olivia naturally. They were never short of conversation when they got together. But in the back of his mind, he really wanted to approach the subject of him and Olivia officially making a go of things and he hadn't yet found the right opportunity to do so. It was something that he had planned to do over the weekend, and felt he still had at least two more days to broach the subject. But the setting had to be right, and Steve hoped that he would discern when that time would be.

The two days flew by quickly with Steve and Olivia exploring the sites of Rotterdam as well as enjoying the various jazz artists at the festival. Sunday was their last day in the Netherlands and Steve had booked a plush, 4-star restaurant for them to have their final meal before leaving for the airport to catch their evening flight. At the restaurant they both ordered a traditional Sunday roast and over dessert, talk turned to the weekend.

"Steve, I can't believe it's over already. I've had such a good time and you have gone above and beyond to make sure we both have had a great weekend." Olivia put her hand over Steve's to thank him.

Steve blushed slightly and had an inward dialogue within himself. *Come on Steve, speak up now or you will miss the moment.* "Actually, it wasn't hard to plan as I did it all for you, because you are very special to me." Steve sensed that the timing was now or never and decided to go for it and then deal with whatever the outcome would be. "I know I have previously told you how I felt about you, but, at the time, you didn't feel the same way, and yet I have still pursued you. Well, the feelings haven't gone away. In fact, I think they have only grown deeper. And this weekend has only proven to me how much I'd like to have something more with you than just a great friendship." Steve sighed and came up for air. *Well, I have laid my heart bare for her to see; and the ball is now in her court.*

Olivia listened to everything Steve had to say, before commenting and then looked him straight in the eyes. "Steve, we've known each other for years. You're my dearest and most trusted male friend that I have…"

As Olivia paused in her speech, Steve felt his insides churn as he deliberated that it was the moment when he was going to get punched in the stomach with a line of rejection again, but instead he was pleasantly surprised with what transpired next.

"...I am not sure why I have resisted your advances to me for so long, when clearly you are the right man for me and have been under my nose this whole time. But I have and I'm not going to fight my feelings anymore. I'm going to be true to myself and say yes to whatever you are asking of me." Olivia exhaled a gasp of air and with their hands clasped tightly, they both smiled knowingly at each other, as this was a decision that was a long time in the making and long overdue.

The waiter interrupted Steve and Olivia at a crucial time when they were deep in conversation to take their order, which after placing their order, they found it natural to pick up right from where they left off. "Olivia, you don't know how happy you have made me; I'm the happiest man alive right now."

"Well, I feel ecstatic too you know." Olivia smiled.

Then Steve asked Olivia a direct question. "You know when you said you were ready to say yes to whatever I asked of you. Have you ever heard of the concept of

197

supernatural marriages? I've been seeing a few articles online and that's what I have been praying into."

"I think I have. A few of the girls were talking about it once at our women's fellowship; why?"

Steve stopped and wondered how Olivia was going to process his next comment. "Olivia, I am not asking you to be my girlfriend as such."

"Ohh, you're not?" Olivia said slightly puzzled but nevertheless was intrigued as to where the conversation was going. Olivia knew that Steve was quite a character and there was never a dull moment when she was in his company and knew that she could trust his judgement in whatever he was contemplating.

Steve continued with his train of thought. "What I am asking of you is to enter into a courtship with you, with the intentions leading to marriage."

Olivia looked at him nervously and said, "Steve Adams; you really don't do anything by halves do you? But I know this is God's plan, and I feel the same way too. You're right I did say that I would say yes to whatever you asked of me; so, I guess that is a yes."

Steve was over the moon and knew his life would not be the same. He was a strong believer in if you took matters to God and trusted wholeheartedly in His providence, that things would work out in your favour if He was in it. He had never felt surer about anything in his life and was confident that together, he and Olivia would be a powerhouse couple for the Kingdom of God, bringing great glory to the church.

Chapter Seventeen

*I*t had been a few weeks since Olivia and Steve's trip to Rotterdam and with the events that had transpired, they both decided to keep their relationship quiet until they had had the opportunity to process for themselves the enormity of such a big decision that would eventually change the trajectory of their lives. Olivia knew at some point that she would have to share the news with Carol. After all, Carol was one of her dearest friends and she wouldn't take too lightly being left out on such meaty news for any great length of time. Plus, she needed to catch up with Carol too on how things were, now that she was back at home and what the dynamics between her and Michael had been like.

Olivia had always admired what Carol and Michael had, as a couple. Now that she and Steve were spending more time together as a couple, she realised that an individual didn't need to envy another person's lifestyle. Because in His own time, God could open doors for others too, giving them a similar experience, if not something more unique and special as a result. She was grateful that she had finally stopped fighting her feelings and succumbed to Steve's pursuit of her. Who knows, perhaps that might have been the final time he had decided to pursue her and where would she be now? She would have lost out on the love of her life. No, Olivia knew she had made the right decision and over the weeks that had ensued, God had been showing her, through various signs, that all His promises are yes and amen regarding their impending marriage.

Jen and Chris had also been making progress within their newish relationship, with Chris and Ben frequenting the house more often on the weekend. Olivia felt a sense of happiness for her housemate and was glad that it didn't feel awkward, especially if she still had any unresolved feelings towards Chris. Now that she had embarked on a relationship with Steve in her life, she had other things on her mind to keep her occupied. Not that Jen and Chris were aware of that fact, since Olivia and Steve were cautious to see each other outside the confines of her home, and usually frequented restaurants, the cinema and other communal areas to respect boundaries and to protect themselves from any forms of temptation.

Now that everyone appeared to be in a relationship of some kind, Olivia wanted to throw a dinner party to share her and Steve's news. She had run the idea by Steve, and he thought it was a good idea. He hadn't said anything to

Michael either, nor had Olivia spoken to Carol. However, they both wanted to share their good news with their close friends in person, prior to the dinner. Olivia was grateful when Carol had called her a few days prior to meet up for a catch up over coffee, as she would use that opportunity to share her news with Carol at that time. Steve too had arranged to touch base with Michael at some point just to see how he was doing, since Carol was now back home. He felt that would be a good opportunity also to share his good news with him then.

With surgery closing late on Wednesday evenings and Michael not being around, Carol had called Olivia the night before to change the venue and asked her to come around to the house instead. Home was cosier and with what she had to share with Olivia, she didn't want an outburst like their meet up in the coffee shop, where the conversation got a little bit heated to say the least. That was something Carol did not think she could handle again. Carol knew Olivia was going to be shocked by the revelations she had to share with her. Therefore, felt she could manage any fallout in a more intimate and neutral setting, as opposed to in front of strangers. Carol wasn't quite sure how she was going to broach the subject, but since she had been back from Manchester, the guilt had been eating her up, and keeping up the façade by living a lie on a day-to-day basis was something that Carol knew could not carry on for the foreseeable future.

Carol and Michael had been getting on well since she had returned home, but they were walking around each other on eggshells, so to speak. It felt like there was an elephant in the room, and Michael had no inclinations of what was looming or was about to shatter his world. At least if Carol offloaded her emotional baggage onto Olivia, she might feel better. Olivia would give her an honest opinion on what she needed to do, since she certainly wasn't listening to her own conscious on the matter. Carol did not always think things through and at times could be quite selfish with her relationships. Carol was used to getting her own way and individuals often gave way to her demands, if only to save the peace and not have to listen to Carol's whining tone.

The doorbell chimed. Since Carol had changed the venue, Olivia was glad she had been able to go home after work and freshen up first. She slipped into some comfortable clothes, a T-shirt and pair of jeans, before going around to see Carol.

As Carol opened the door, Olivia presented her with a bunch of tulips. "Here you go girl. Now don't say I don't bring you anything," Olivia exclaimed, whilst dusting her pumps on the mat at the entrance, pushing pass Carol through to the hallway.

"Why thank you hon, and why don't you come in, too?" Carol said sarcastically. Carol was glad that she and Olivia had ironed out whatever differences had tried to come between their friendship and that they could laugh once again with one another and at each other. They were always so good at that.

"It looks lovely, Caz," Olivia commented as she looked around the house, observing all that Carol and Michael had achieved since renovating the property. The neutral colours made the open plan lounge area look spacious, light and airy. And with Carol's keen eye for design, the furniture and unique pieces they chose blended and complimented each other well. Carol loved it when her work was admired and appreciated Olivia's sentiments. "Thanks very much. We love it. It feels like a home now, compared to the rundown shell that we bought when we first moved in. Take a seat, the coffee is brewing and if you're really nice you can have some shortbread too," Carol expressed with a wink in her eye.

Olivia took a seat, still looking around at the beauty of her surroundings. "Caz, please don't tell me that you were slaving over a hot oven to specially make me shortbread." Olivia pretended to faint, collapsing back into her seat.

"No, my dear, you know I'm no Mary Berry when it comes to the kitchen. Sainsbury's does it all the time for me, girl, and are just as good." They both fell about laughing. Carol came back from the kitchen with two mugs on a tray, which gave off a strong aromatic smell of Colombian coffee and enveloped the room, and a plate of, well presented, shop bought, shortbread biscuits, accompanied with a couple of napkins.

Olivia took one of the mugs and a couple of biscuits, which she rested on a coaster on a small side table next to her. "So, how have you been?" Olivia asked as her hands tightly clasped her coffee mug, keeping them warm, whilst taking a sip.

"Oh, you know," Carol sighed, as she sat on the sofa opposite Olivia. "We're getting there. Having been parted for a few months did put a strain on the relationship, and it feels a bit like we are courting again …." As the words 'courting again' innocently fell out of Carol's mouth, Olivia took a huge gulp which made her cough slightly. "Oh gosh are you alright hon?" Carol said as she looked at her anxiously.

"I'm alright." Olivia used a napkin to wipe off the coffee that spilled on her T-shirt. Thankfully, it was a dark colour so there wasn't much of a stain that could be seen.

Carol continued. She knew that there was no point drip feeding information to Olivia in bits and pieces. Olivia would not have appreciated that anyway. No, in her mind

Carol decided what was needed was straightforwardness and directness. Even though she wanted to run as far as to the ends of the earth, without ever having to deal with her past, in all honesty, Carol was tired of the deceit and lies and finally wanted it out in the open.

However, what Carol naively craved was that once her secret was out, that Michael would process it, forgive her and then they could move on with the rest of their lives. Michael was easy going and Carol was always able to wrap him around her little finger, and that was what she was relying on. Although this situation was a lot more serious than her trying to negotiate the colour scheme of the walls in the lounge or what style of kitchen/bathroom suites they would settle on.

Olivia noticed that, as the conversation between them was progressing, that Carol was getting a bit fidgety and agitated. Her jovial demeanour changed in an instant, and for no apparent reason that Olivia could not put her finger on. Olivia wondered if she had perhaps said something that she shouldn't have. But when she replayed the conversation over in her head, she felt at ease that she had not said anything to agitate Carol. She therefore reckoned that Carol was probably still trying to get back to her normal day-to-day reality.

"Are you okay Caz? You look a bit gaunt, hon."

Carol's shoulders dropped, and she put her hands to her face and started to sob uncontrollably.

"Caz, what is it?" Olivia rushed over to put her arm around Carol to console her.

"I've messed up Liv. I've made a big mistake in my life, and I don't think it can be rectified."

Olivia gave Carol a tissue, which she blew into, trying to control her sniffles. "Come on Caz, now what it is? Whatever it is, we know that our God can rectify anything, so I'm sure it's not that bad." Olivia rocked her as Carol rested her head on Olivia's shoulder.

Carol just blurted it out. "The reason why I took the job in Manchester was because Michael and I had been arguing a lot lately about starting a family and it had started to divide a wedge between us."

Before Carol could even finish her sentence, Olivia butted in, "Don't be too hard on yourself, Mother nature will happen in her own good time. Plus, Michael needs to be patient too."

Carol felt irritated since she wanted to give Olivia the full picture. But as usual, Olivia was trying to romanticise the situation and yet Carol knew the full weight of the truth hadn't yet been delivered and it was about to hit Olivia like a bullet right between the eyes.

Carol pulled away from sobbing on Olivia's top and sat up straight. She dabbed her eyes. "Mother nature won't be able to do her work because I messed up and now I can't have children."

Olivia's eyes widened. "What do you mean Carol?"

Carol continued with her delivery. "I got pregnant when I was 18. And was made to get rid of it by the father but I had complications with a botched-up abortion and now I can't have children. There, I've said it. Sod's law eh." Carol threw her hands in the air and stared blankly at Olivia, wondering how she was going to process the information.

Olivia tried to comprehend the enormity of what her best friend had just blurted out. As a teacher, Olivia was methodical in her thinking and so had to break things down so she could understand what had been relayed to her. "So, is that what you and Michael have been arguing about, the fact that you can't have children now?"

"If only it was that simple," Carol continued. "Michael doesn't know. I didn't tell him before we got married."

Olivia's eyes widened even further. "Ohh Caz, please don't tell me this. I can't believe it," uttered Olivia in a disappointing tone. Carol's secret was now paid forward, and Olivia didn't know what she was going to do with the revelation that Carol had just dumped into her lap. "So, what are you going to do now? The fact that you have told me, tells me that you want it out in the open now... And I know you. It's been eating you up, hasn't it, Caz? God knows it would have eaten me up. This is not just some little mistake, Caz. This is huge... especially to Michael. You know how much he wanted kids. Why did you keep something as serious as this from him......why, Caz?"

Olivia got up and walked back to her original seat. She tried to put herself in Michael's position. Now that she and Steve had been seeing each other, she tried to process in her mind how she would feel if Steve had some big secret that he was concealing that was detrimental to the success of their future marriage yet failed to disclose it. For whatever reasons he chose not to trust her enough to talk to her about it.

Michael did not deserve this. Carol knew right from the outset that children were important to Michael because of him being adopted. Olivia recalled all the times that Michael spoke about what life would look like when he and Carol had 2-3 kids running around the place, terrorising Carol's well-designed opulent environment. Michael's face always seemed to light up when he talked about being a father and had grand plans of the type of role model he would be and the love he would lavish on his children. Olivia wondered how he would get over what Carol had to tell him and if their relationship could sustain such deception.

Considering what Olivia now had to process, she chose not to share her own news with Carol after all. She reasoned that perhaps it was not the kind of news you should share when someone else is going through their own misery. It would be like a cold slap in the face and maybe slightly insensitive. There would be another occasion and for the most part Carol had more important matters to deal with and this mess needed to be sorted out sooner rather than later.

"It all makes sense now why you never wanted to talk about children when I used to bring up the subject." Olivia shook her head, still in a state of shock and bewilderment. "Will you tell Michael soon?" Olivia enquired.

Carol nodded. "I have to, He has a right to know. I don't know what this is going to do to our marriage, but I now have to deal with whatever fallout will transpire."

"But Caz, what I can't understand is why you felt you couldn't have told him right at the beginning of your relationship."

Tears were still streaming from Carol's eyes, and she continued to dab under her eyelids with a tissue. "Livy, he wouldn't have married me. I know that. No... I knew what I was doing. What I did was deliberate. I've gone over this a thousand times in my head. I can't make anymore excuses for what I have done."

"But Caz, you don't know that. He worships the ground you walk on. If you had shared your heart with him, I bet he would have understood. After all, this all happened prior to you being a Christian, and no decent individual would hold something like that against someone else. Especially when God forgives us when we mess up on so many occasions. We are all sinners saved by grace."

"Well, we will never know now, will we? Liv, do you mind if we call it a night? I don't feel too great and I'm sure Michael will be home soon, and there's no time like the present to deal with this now I have managed to actually voice it to another individual. Well apart from Jenny."

"Jenny knew?" Olivia did not realise that her voice shrieked louder than normal.

"Of course, she did. She helped me through it all. But to her credit, Jenny wasn't aware that Michael didn't know, so she's just as disappointed with me as you are. You both are disappointed with me, so how do I really expect Michael to react, and he's my husband." Carol got up and walked over to the door, as if to usher Olivia hastily out the door.

Olivia understood and took that as her cue to gather her things together. Olivia walked towards Carol and gave her a big hug and whispered in her ear, "Hon, God has got your back. He didn't bring you this far to leave you. Yes, the next few days are going to be challenging, but I believe you are going to get through this. Michael has a strong faith and, yes, this news is going to rock his world, but he's going to talk to God about it. You'll see. You're going to get through this and you're both going to come out stronger too."

Olivia slid her hands down the side of Carol's hair, straightening it in place. "If you need me, don't hesitate to call me. I'm here for you. You take care, hon." Carol struggled to smile assuredly and told Olivia that she would contact her if she felt she needed to and hugged Olivia again, waved her off and closed the door.

Chapter Eighteen

*T*he surgery's late midweek service had just ended, with the last appointment having left 10 mins prior. Janet was busily tidying up as best she could, so that the cleaners did not have too much of a mess to clear up. The doctors would often tease Janet in their attempt to get her to go home straight after the late nights, assuring her that tidying up the surgery was what the cleaners were paid to do, but Janet was old school and couldn't help herself. She would often laugh along with them, telling them to leave her alone. Janet switched the lights off to the main reception and waiting room area and said goodbye to Michael and Chris, the two doctors, who were on duty that evening.

Chris was always keen to get home straightaway after a late-night surgery as he wanted to relieve Mrs Jenkins, who would stay with Ben until he got back home. It was a relief to him that there was a rota for the midweek late-night shifts, so he only had to cover twice a month, which wasn't ideal. However, the surgery appreciated that some individuals who had city jobs, or worked unsociable hours, were not always able to get to the surgery within its normal surgery hours. The extension of their hours to accommodate such patients was received well when it was first introduced as a trial. And a unanimous decision, for the good of the practice, was reached to continue with it a while longer with a review in six months to see how things were progressing.

Chris organised the patients' files on his desk in an orderly fashion and placed them in his out-tray, ready for Janet to file away for the next morning. He grabbed his bag and jacket and rushed with speed out of his office, dangling his car keys in his hand and slamming the door. As he passed Michael's office, the door was ajar. He quickly tapped it, popped his head in, and said goodbye to him and left the surgery.

Michael was aware that Carol and Olivia were meeting up that night and he suspected that they would have a lot to catch up on. Probably nattering about various things, and putting the world to right, and he wanted to give them the space to do so uninterrupted. Michael had called Steve the night before to see if he wanted to catch up for a bite to eat and Steve agreed. Steve also wanted to tell him how things had developed between him and Olivia since they had last spoken or met up. So, the timing was perfect.

Steve arrived at the 'All-you-can-eat' Chinese buffet restaurant first. He secured a table and ordered a soft drink, whilst he waited for Michael to arrive. He took out his mobile phone and started to check his messages, to see if there was anything important, that he had missed, since he had back-to-back meetings throughout the day. Steve managed a Pupil Referral Unit (PRU) and, like Olivia, was in the education sector. As a qualified counsellor, he often met with pupils, and their parents, acting as an advocate whilst liaising with mainstream teachers, social workers and court officials.

Whilst Steve and Olivia could communicate passionately on their shared love, he would often remind her, in a playful manner, that his job was a lot more challenging than hers. He would tease her that she had it far easier, playing teddy bear tea parties with her pupils. Meanwhile, he had to negotiate his students staying out of trouble and not potentially ending up in prison. It was a job he loved, because he got the opportunity to speak into the lives of the young people who attended the PRU and could help change the trajectory of their lives by his mentoring, if they heeded the advice they were given. He won some battles but lost many. Sometimes it took quite a toll on his self-esteem, but his faith played a big part in that area of his life. When Steve got home after a demanding day, he enjoyed the fact that he had the tranquillity of his own space. Where he could relax, unwind and enjoy listening to worship music, watch sports, read his bible or a good book.

He started to imagine how different his life would look with a wife in the mix. It was something Steve had wanted for a long time. But the right person had never come along, until the day he met Olivia and then his world changed. From the get-go, Steve enjoyed the friendship that ensued between them. But he was instantly attracted to her, and took the opportunities, whenever they were in the same company, to watch and observe how Olivia conducted herself. Her likes and dislikes. How she interacted with individuals, regardless of their age, ethnicity or social standing. But more importantly Olivia's relationship with God.

Steve had grown up in a Christian home and one of the things that was drummed into him as a young man was not to be unequally yoked, in marriage, with someone who was an unbeliever. The mentors in Steve's youth club would communicate to the youth that marriage was a blessing, and yet challenging. And to be a Christian and marry someone who did not agree with your Christian values or persuasion would be very hard to negotiate.

Steve had, etched in his mind, a word picture that was given to them as an example. Of two oxen, with different heights, yoked together, with one pulling one way and the other pulling in a totally different direction.

Steve had made up his mind from all those years ago, that he would wait for the right person to marry. That she would be a Christian with the same values that complemented his, because Steve was aware that two Christians could still be unequally yoked if they were not in agreement and on the same page spiritually. And that was why Steve valued his job, because of the way his mentors inspired and challenged him all those years ago. Steve now wanted to do that for others to afford them the same privileges he had growing up.

"Hey, there mate, sorry to keep you waiting," Michael interrupted Steve's deep thoughts and he looked up from his mobile phone to see a friendly face peering at him. Michael placed his jacket on the back of his chair and sat down opposite Steve.

"Hi. Sorry, I was just checking my messages." Steve put his phone away as a sign of courtesy now that Michael had arrived. There was nothing more irritating than someone constantly checking their phone when they were out in company and not giving the other person their undivided attention. Steve knew how he would have felt if someone had done that to him, so he was going to ensure that he was not guilty of doing the exact same thing.

"Hope I didn't keep you too long."

"No, I got here early, so just thought I'd catch up on my email traffic. I've already ordered a drink, so if you want to order yours, I think we just go up to the buffet area and help ourselves to some food. As many times as we like, I might add." Steve smiled.

"Sounds good to me, because I'm famished." Michael ordered a soft drink also and then they both went to the buffet section and piled their plates high with a variety of Chinese cuisine.

"This food is tasty here," Steve verbalized as he picked up a sesame prawn toast with his fingers and took a bite.

"Yeah, this is one of mine and Caz's favourite restaurants," Michael agreed, and Steve was glad that Michael had introduced Carol into the conversation early on, which he took as his cue to enquire how things were between the two of them now that Carol had come back home.

"So, how are things between the two of you Michael since Carol has been back? I think the last time we spoke was just before she was due to come back, and you had shared that you were making progress via Skype?" Steve tried to tread carefully and didn't want to seem as if he was prying if Michael did not want to go there. Michael took a sip of his drink before answering.

"Thanks mate, it's good to have someone to talk to and you've been a good friend over these past few months. On the surface it seems things are going well, but I can't seem to put my finger on it, but something isn't right. I just feel Caz is holding back on something. I don't know if there is something weighing heavy on her mind, but I don't seem to be able to get her to open up about whatever it is." Michael put his cutlery down and gave Steve his full attention as he continued.

"I'm trying my best to remember the counsel I received from PT and not pressure her into talking about subjects she isn't comfortable with. And rather just try to keep the peace, but I don't even know if that really is the right way forward. Caz and I used to be able to talk about absolutely anything, whether we agreed or not. That's what I liked about how we communicated. We seemed to understand each other, but now…." Michael paused. "This is a whole new ball game, and I don't even think I know what the rules are." Michael shrugged his shoulders in despair. "You're a trained counsellor; what would you suggest?"

Steve shook his head. "Mate, that's a difficult one, because if there is something that needs bringing up and out in the open, it's something that should be addressed and tackled honestly. Is Carol open to counselling?"

Michael sharply cut into the conversation. "Carol isn't even aware that I have been meeting up with PT for counselling. She would be horrified to find out that I had gone to him, behind her back, about aspects concerning our marriage. You may not believe it, but as busy as Caz likes to get into the affairs of others, when it comes to her own issues, she's quite a private person, our Caz is, and likes to keep matters close to her chest. She's with Olivia tonight. I only hope Caz is able to open up to Olivia and get off her chest whatever has been keeping her from being my old Caz and that we can get back to the way things used to be."

Steve tried to play it cool when Michael mentioned Olivia's name, not wanting to disclose anything about his relationship with her until the time was right throughout the course of the evening. "Oh yes, I think Olivia may have mentioned something vaguely that she was meeting up with Carol. Was that tonight?"

Michael wasn't to know that the two of them were

constantly on the phone, exchanging conversations and other aspects of their lives that they shared with each other. So of course, Steve knew exactly where Olivia was tonight. In fact, Steve really wished, at that moment, that he was with her in person. Steve had been enjoying the various occasions they were spending with each other, because it was now on a totally different level to when they met up as friends in the past. Now they were in a committed relationship and Steve wanted to jump from the rooftop and tell the whole world, but they agreed to tell their close friends first, before going public with their relationship. Steve knew that he would be sharing his news with Michael that evening; he just did not know precisely when.

Michael and Carol's current relationship wasn't the only subject the men talked about that evening. They talked about their respective jobs, church life and reminisced over the past. Steve got him laughing as he regurgitated hilarious stories they were both involved in. They had been friends for over 20 years. Having first met at the local gym, they were drawn to each other simply by exchanging the odd glare and greeting now and then with their facial expressions. Until that is, they sat down in the canteen to get a drink and struck up a conversation. That was when they found out that they were both Christians and shared similar interests, which over the years developed into a strong friendship and has stood the test of times.

Both men went back to the buffet area and refilled their plates. When they got back to their table, Michael decided to flip the script, which took Steve off guard. "Anyway, enough about my love life. What's been happening in your life?"

Oh, so this is how we're doing it, God? Steve deliberated. *No worries, I can work with this; thanks for the intro.*

Michael continued whilst cramming more food in his mouth. "I know you briefly had a moment with Jen, but I didn't think that was serious. Plus, Jen and Chris seem to be enjoying each other's company somewhat of late."

Steve shifted in his seat and put down his cutlery. "Yeah, I only went out with Jen a few times and, as you say, it wasn't anything serious on my part. It was just two friends meeting up, as Jen was new to the church, and I wanted her to feel welcome at New Dawn."

Michael smiled. "Is any female ever going to have a fair shot, if you continue to compare every woman up against Olivia, your ideal woman? I don't know why the two of you just don't put everyone out of their misery and get your act together?"

"Okay, okay." Steve playfully put his hands in the air as an act of surrender and decided to have some fun with Michael's line of questioning. "Actually, it's funny that you should ask as I am seeing someone at the moment." Steve knew he had Michael's curiosity juices flowing with that comment and now just wanted to watch Michael try to unravel the gossip out of him. Just like Carol would do when she was trying to find out something new about another person. Michael put his cutlery down and his eyes widened.

"No way; you dark horse. Who is she? Is she someone we know?" Michael resembled an excited kid who had been handed a Christmas present early and wanted to know what was in it.

Steve pondered to himself, *now I wonder how long I can keep this up or should I just put him out of his misery?* "Oh, you know her," Steve said with a smile on his face.

Michael looked puzzled as he could not come up with a name. "Okay, I give up. There are a few ladies in your singles group, and I don't know all of their names so we could be here all night." He gasped.

"Well, you did say that I keep measuring up every woman against my ideal woman, and if that is the case, then why settle for less? I might as well go directly and get that ideal woman herself eh…"

Michael grabbed hold of Steve's arm. "Wowwww. I'm shocked, but at the same time very pleased for you," he reassured him. "How did you pull that off then? Olivia has been rejecting your advances for ages, man. And don't get me wrong, as my comment isn't meant in a bad way. I just mean, you've been knocking on that door for a while now and clearly it seems to have finally opened. Persistence certainly pays off eh?" Michael gave Steve a high five as a sign of approval. "So how did you do it?"

Steve laughed. "Yes, you're right, it has taken a while, but I just felt that, if I kept on pursuing Olivia it might one day happen. And to make a long story short; that one day happened a few weeks ago. But there's more, much more to the story." He smiled. "We aren't just dating each other and seeing how it goes, we have made a commitment to enter into a courtship, leading to marriage."

"Wowww, Stevie boy. When you make your mark, you go big, don't you? But I like your style and it makes perfect sense. You make such a great couple and I know Caz is going to go absolutely nuts when she hears the news."

"Well, we didn't really want to go public until we had both spoken to you and Carol. Olivia is most probably letting Carol know tonight what I have shared with you. And yes I did know that Olivia was going to be at yours tonight. I was just playing Mr Cool Dude, leading up to the big reveal." Steve smiled. "Thanks a lot for your approval, as it means a great deal to us."

"To us, listen to you. You're really getting the hang of this couple lark, aren't you?" Michael laughed as he tapped Steve on his shoulder. "I can't wait to get home and talk with Caz about this. But I bet she'll want to be the one to get in there first. You know what she's like." They both smiled and nodded.

The evening had come to an end and both men felt they were given the opportunity to share their heart. They gathered up their things as the waiter brought the bill to their table. Before Steve could go into his pocket to get out his wallet, Michael grabbed the receipt off the plate. "I got this one, mate. This is my treat to congratulate you on your good news, because to be honest that's the best news I've heard in a long time." Michael tapped his card on the contactless machine that the waiter had in his hand and left some cash on the table for a tip. They both left the restaurant and headed to their respective cars.

——◦——

Chapter Nineteen

*A*s Michael drove home, he reflected over the evening that he and Steve had spent together. His heart was full of joy because of the news that Steve had shared with him about his relationship with Olivia. Michael was excited to get home and discuss the news with Carol because he knew that she too would have heard the same news that night. He decided to let Carol break the news first as that was her thing. Carol always had to be the first to share whatever bit of gossip she heard, as if to win Brownie points that she had first dibs on the latest news as it got released.

As Michael drove into the drive, he noticed that there weren't any lights on in the front of the house. Which he thought was a bit odd, because when Carol had news she was bursting to share, she would wait up for him in the front room. *Perhaps, Carol was tired from all her nattering with Olivia, and she went upstairs to sit up in bed until I got home,* Michael deduced.

When Michael entered the house, it was eerily dark

and quiet. He flipped on the light switch, which flooded the hall with bright light, revealing that Carol was nowhere to be seen downstairs. Michael put his jacket on the coat rack, as was his norm. He didn't feel like making himself a hot drink, having had one before he left the restaurant, and instead went straight upstairs.

Michael entered the bedroom to find it in total darkness. He didn't want to wake Carol up and, therefore, tiptoed his way to his side of the bed and switched on his side lamp. Michael noticed that Carol was neatly tucked up in bed with the covers over her head. Which was her way of letting Michael know that she did not want conversation or to be disturbed.

Michael quietly made his way to the en-suite, since it emitted more light for him to see what he was doing and changed into pyjama bottoms. Shirtless was his norm, and he only wore a top in the winter months of the year. Michael once again quietly tiptoed back to his side of the bed, trying to be respectful as Carol did not like a lot of noise once she had hit the sack.

As Michael laid in bed beside his unresponsive wife, he gazed towards the ceiling. He pondered over how the meeting between Olivia and Carol might have gone that evening and whether something had transpired between the two of them that would cause Carol to go straight to bed and not wait up for him. He hoped that Carol wasn't upset by Olivia and Steve's good news. But then quickly dismissed that notion as ludicrous and instead put it down to perhaps him trying to put two and two together and coming up with five. Michael reasoned that tomorrow was another day and he would deal with the matter then after a good night's sleep and with fresh eyes.

After Steve got home and settled down for the evening, he changed into something casual and couldn't wait to give Olivia a call to see how she was. He sat in his favourite armchair, that enveloped him as he sunk into it, to get comfy. He picked up his mobile and rang Olivia's number. Olivia thought she would have got home much later that evening, as was always the case when she and Carol had met up. But what with Carol's abrupt end to the evening, almost kicking her out, she had time to spare and pottered around the house. Jen had already retreated to her room by the time Olivia had gotten home. She quickly rustled up herself something to eat, since she only had a couple of biscuits and a cup of coffee at Carol's, which after a hard day's work, was not very filling.

Olivia was in the lounge area, sitting down reading a magazine, when her phone rang. Steve's number illuminated on her screen. "Hey there, how are you?" The thought of his call excited her, and Olivia felt her heart flutter.

"Hi there. Thought I'd catch up with you, to see how you are doing and how your evening went?"

Olivia put the magazine down, so as not to be distracted by the various articles of the trappings of the celebrity world that would normally hold her attention. Olivia sighed. "Truthfully, I really don't know how to answer that. It's been quite an eventful evening." Olivia knew Steve would press her further as to what that comment meant.

"Oh, I'm sorry; didn't everything go well with your meet-up with Carol tonight then? Did you tell her about us?"

Olivia shook her head, not that Steve could see her reaction. "No, I didn't tell her about us as it just wasn't the right moment. Carol had news of her own to share with me and it was a bit difficult to take in. So to share our news would have seemed cruel to say the least. How about you, did you manage to tell Michael?" Olivia enquired, rather inquisitively.

"Yes, I did, and he was over the moon and extremely pleased for us. We had a great evening of male-bonding." Steve chuckled.

"Male-bonding eh! Well, I'm glad that you guys had a good evening."

Steve detected all was not well from the tone of Olivia's voice. He was curious and could not help himself from getting to the bottom of it. "So, the news Carol discussed with you, is it something that can be shared or is that something she swore you to secrecy and is staying with you ladies?"

"Actually, it's something that will come out in the end. I will eventually tell you about it, but right now, I'm still trying to get my head around processing it myself, that in all honestly I can't really talk about it until I first talk to God about it."

Steve could hear the emotion in Olivia's voice. He respected her judgement and yet he knew it must have been something serious, because Olivia was quite a strong individual and could usually handle difficult things that came her way. "Do you want me to just quickly pray with you that whatever it is, God will help you to deal with the enormity of it?"

"Yes, that would be great." Olivia valued that the man who would become her future husband was a man of prayer. Whilst she wanted to blurt everything out and tell him all of Carol's gory past there and then, Olivia knew that would not have been fair to dump such an emotional load onto Steve's shoulders. She needed to talk to God and allow the Holy Spirit to minister to her first. Steve prayed a heartfelt prayer and covered Olivia with God's comfort. Olivia felt a sense of peace after Steve's prayer. She knew she would sleep well and would not have a heavy heart. Which might have kept her up all night as she tossed and turned with the enormity of Carol's secret.

Mrs Jenkins had recovered from her accident and was back to her normal day-to-day duties working for the Harris household. Chris was still a little concerned that Mrs Jenkins had returned to work much too early, as he noticed that she still walked with a slight hobble. But Chris knew he was fighting a losing battle when it came to arguing with Mrs Jenkins. From the time Mrs Jenkins had taken up her position as Chris' housekeeper, it was evident from the way Chris interviewed her painstakingly, that the role and her commitment to it would be quite demanding. Chris had made it quite clear from the outset what he required, due to the nature of his busy schedule as a doctor. And the successful candidate would be expected to work up until he came home on an evening, Monday to Friday. Mrs Jenkins had become an invaluable asset to both Chris and Ben's life, and she didn't want to let them down, convincing herself that her ankle would heal fully in time. But in the meantime, that was the least of her worries as she had lots of housework and ironing to catch up on and wanted to get back to her normal routine as quickly as possible.

Chris was not the greatest of keeping on top of things around the house, and he had let things lapse into an untidy state whilst Mrs Jenkins was convalescing. There were piles of laundry on the floor in the utility room. Not to mention the clothes that were flung over a chair in the corner of Chris' room. Ben took his lead from his dad and followed suit, leaving clothes and toys lying around his room, without putting things back in their rightful places. Therefore, the entire house looked like a bomb had hit it.

As Mrs Jenkins looked around to observe the damage, she was relieved that Chris had managed to keep at least one room, the kitchen, in a half decent state. And was surprised to see that the sink was not full of dirty dishes, as she thought it might have been, especially in comparison to the rest of the house. That was until Mrs Jenkins opened the dishwasher and found it full of dishes, releasing a strong odour of stale food emanating from it. Mrs Jenkins went to the sink under the cupboard and retrieved the dishwasher powder and got the dishwasher cycle started. The next job Mrs Jenkins tackled on her list was picking up all the laundry from Chris and Ben's rooms, sorting them into three piles. Whites, colours, and darks, and loading the washing machine for the first wash.

Mrs Jenkins continued dusting and polishing furniture throughout the house. Hoovering, straightening out furniture and putting everything back in its rightful place. Mrs Jenkins pondered to herself. *How could two individuals make such a mess? I wasn't away for that long.* However, in another breath she could sympathise and forgive the two of them. She had grown quite fond of them and knew Chris' demanding job did not leave much room for him to keep on top of the domestic chores at home. And with having to pick up Ben after school also, whilst she was convalescing, that was sure to take out its toll on Chris. On top of that, then having to come home and prepare dinner; these were all duties Chris was not used to. He was used to Mrs Jenkins' meticulous schedule. Everything was always neat and tidy around the house. Ben was picked up from school, taken home and given something to eat. When Chris usually came home, Ben was almost ready for bed and there was a homecooked meal waiting for him. So, he rarely had anything to do before Mrs Jenkins left for the day.

It was Friday and Chris had a half day, which afforded him the rare occasion to pick up Ben from school. It also gave him the opportunity to exchange pleasantries with Olivia as Ben gathered his things. Whilst Chris wasn't aware of the relationship that had recently transpired between Olivia and Steve, he was glad that there was no awkwardness between him and Olivia now that he had been spending a lot more of his time with Jen. Chris was a frequent visitor to Olivia's house, whenever he came to pick Jen up for their various dates.

Chris wondered why it didn't work out with him and Olivia, but he felt it was a non-starter anyway. She was beautiful and intelligent, yet Chris couldn't put his finger on what it was. But in his mind, one thing he would have had an issue with was Olivia's close relationship with Steve. Chris felt their friendship would have been questionable if he and Olivia were to have made a go of things. Anyway, there wasn't any point in Chris torturing himself with those thoughts as that was now in the past. He was with Jen now, and he was comfortable with that. Chris was ten years older than Jen and at times, Chris felt his comparison of life's perspective was lost on Jen. But in his opinion, Jen was easy on the eye and, he reasoned, had a good job, and so wasn't unintelligent.

Chris convinced himself that sometimes opposites attract. He based his rationale on the fact that his late wife was the total opposite to him in character and social standing, and yet they still had a happy and fulfilling marriage. Also, the fact that Jen's features resembled his late wife might have had something to do with his initial attraction towards her.

By the time Chris and Ben had got home on entering the house, they were met with a burst of freshness. They could feel the cleanliness emanating from the house. Mrs Jenkins had fixed them something light to eat. Ben had a sleepover at the home of one of his classmates and Chris had arranged to go out for the evening with Jen. "Mrs Jenkins, wow, you have worked your magic again. The place looks and smells great." Chris put his hands on Ben's shoulders and guided him towards the living room where Mrs Jenkins had just sat down with a cup of tea.

"Yes, I thought I deserved to have a nice cup of tea and a 5-minute break. I don't know what you guys had been up to in my absence, but the place looked like World War 3 had come early." Mrs Jenkins rolled her eyes and smiled cheekily as she sipped her tea.

Ben ran over to give her a hug. "Mrs Jenkins, I'm so glad you're back."

"Ben, mind Mrs Jenkins. She's got a hot drink in her hand. We don't want an accident now, do we? Because Mrs Jenkins would have to go away again," Chris lamented. Chris knew Ben could get quite excited when he went charging over there and he was concerned for both of their safety.

"I don't want that," Ben said, and he stopped short of crashing into Mrs Jenkins on the sofa.

Mrs Jenkins pointed towards the kitchen. "I've left you something to eat, lasagne and a salad. You don't have to eat it all. Just eat what you can as I know you're both going out!"

"I'm staying at Jack's house tonight, Mrs Jenkins, and I'm really excited." Ben smiled.

"I know you are pet and you're going to have a wonderful time too."

"That's great, Mrs Jenkins." Chris opened the oven and to his delight the aroma of one of Mrs Jenkins hearty lasagne's waffled pass his nostrils. "It smells delicious, but I'm taking Jen out tonight and Ben is going to have his dinner at Jack's house. So, I think we will let this keep until tomorrow evening. That's the cooking sorted for tomorrow then." Chris smiled as he closed the oven door. "You like Mrs Jenkins' lasagnes don't you Ben?" Ben had a big grin on his face and nodded quickly as he ran to go upstairs and pack his favourite toys that he was taking for his sleepover.

Chris was glad that Ben had got over his shyness

and had come out of his shell to the point that he felt comfortable having sleepovers at his friend's house. He knew that was largely down to the excellent work that Olivia had done, working with Ben. Sometimes on a one-to-one to get the very best that she could get out of him, and her patience and perseverance paid off. Even though Ben was still a little bit on the clumsy side, he had a heart of gold. Olivia found him a delight to teach, which was often reflected in his weekly class report that he brought home for Chris to observe and sign.

Chris reflected on the evening he was going to spend with Jen. Sometimes he found it difficult to choose activities that he thought Jen would enjoy, because their tastes were on the opposite ends of the spectrum. Being more mature, Chris preferred evenings that were more cultured and relaxing, which helped take the load off his mind from the busyness of his week. But Jen was quite bubbly and outgoing and loved doing things that involved lots of noise, fun and crowds.

Chris wondered if God had been drawing them towards each other so that they could take a leaf out of each other's book that would make them appreciate sides of their characters that perhaps they both needed to work on. He felt he certainly needed to loosen up a bit. Something his late wife would often relay to him to try and get him to chill out a bit more. Perhaps, now being involved with a younger woman, that was what he needed. Chris hadn't thought about remarrying again, but he did know that at times he felt lonely and devoid of adult interaction with just him and Ben in the house. But didn't want to pursue a relationship with Jen if there was no long-term stability.

Chris was a bit of a commitment phobic when it came to relationships, which could have been the reason he didn't allow his feelings to develop any further with Olivia. Chris felt guilty that he got Olivia's hopes up, in a false sense of security, only to dash them away quite abruptly. It played on his mind if perhaps he owed Olivia an apology of some kind. However, when he saw her at school that afternoon, Chris had felt comfortable with the way they both were professional in their interaction with each other. And he reasoned within himself that if he were to say anything now that he could just be stirring up a hornet's nest that didn't need disturbing. No, Chris decided to let things be as they were. And going forward, to only interact with Olivia purely in a professional capacity.

—◦—

Chapter Twenty

*M*ichael had been tired of the mood in the house for the past few days. He wondered why Carol had not brought up the subject between Steve and Olivia. Instead, Carol just moped around the house, exchanging the odd grunt whenever Michael asked a question in an attempt to break the monotony and inject some life into the atmosphere. Michael determined that he was going to tackle the situation when he got home that evening, regardless of whether Carol wanted to talk or not.

Michael had called PT the evening before to air his frustration and PT advised him that as the head of his home, he was responsible to address anything that was affecting the harmonious atmosphere of his home and Michael knew that PT was right. Michael had several appointments before the close of business and was glad that his mind was kept busy, which meant he could push to the back of his mind how exactly he was going to approach the situation when he got home.

Chris was on call at the hospital and Joan was in

her room assessing the flow of appointments for the day. Olivia had a check-up appointment with Dr Webb that morning and had arranged for one of her teaching assistants to take her class as she would be running late. Dr Webb was pleased with Olivia's post-op progress following her procedure a few months prior and addressed some minor concerns Olivia raised regarding her being able to conceive naturally when the time came for her to start a family.

Olivia had started to think about her future a lot more seriously in the area of her health and, in the light of Carol's web of deceit, she wanted to be sure that if there were any issues, then that would be something she'd definitely discuss with Steve prior to their marriage. Olivia was relieved when Dr Webb confirmed that everything was looking well, post-surgery, and in fact there was nothing to hinder her conceiving naturally when the time was right.

Olivia felt slightly nervous with her line of enquiries, as she did not want Dr Webb to suspect anything and start asking questions. Not that it would have been out of the ordinary, as Olivia spoke with Dr Webb in detail on the matter extensively prior to her surgery. Especially when she was faced with the option as to whether she wanted to consider having a hysterectomy, which was something that Olivia categorically rejected. Olivia did her homework and looked at all the other alternatives to having an outright hysterectomy, thus denying her the opportunity to be a mother. That just didn't seem a natural option to her, given her love of children. Olivia was happy with the decision she had made, and her future looked bright knowing that children would feature in the life that she planned to have with her future husband.

Olivia thanked Dr Webb and left her office on a high. As she walked down the corridor towards Michael's office, he was saying goodbye to a patient when he glanced at Olivia walking in his direction. "Olivia, hey, how are you? I didn't know you had an appointment this morning." He lowered his voice in a whisper. "And may I say a big congratulations to you and Steve. I'm so happy for you both."

Olivia was hoping not to run into Michael that morning. She was banking on a quick dash in and out of Joan's office, undetected. She smiled and caught his gaze. "Hi Michael." Olivia extended her arms to give him an affectionate hug. "Thank you very much, but I thought you might be at the hospital this morning." Olivia tried to hide her disappointment of running into him, when clearly, she was trying to avoid them bumping into each other.

"No, not me today. Chris got the short straw, but since it's Friday, he shouldn't have that many clinics to run as they run fewer on Fridays. Have you got a quick minute, Olivia?" Michael opened his door, inviting Olivia into his office.

The very thing that Olivia was trying to avoid was taking place. From his mannerism, Olivia could tell that Michael was none the wiser of the nuclear bomb that was about to shatter his world. And she didn't know if she could keep up the pretence of wondering what he wanted to discuss. Olivia did not have a very good poker face. When she played board games, she always got rumbled because of that very fact. Olivia tried to get out of it by saying she had to get back to work, but Michael managed to convince her that it was only a quick question he wanted to run by her, and Olivia felt obliged to lend her ear.

"Sorry, I know you have to go back to school, but I just wanted to quickly ask you a question about your meet up with Caz the other day." Michael went over to his side of the desk and sat in his chair, whilst Olivia assumed the role as the patient on the opposite side of his desk. *I don't believe this. Why on earth did I agree to come into his office? I should have insisted I really needed to get back to school. Now what am I going to say?* Olivia's thoughts had gone into overdrive, and she wondered if she was going to come out of Michael's office in one piece.

Michael painstakingly attempted to offload his concerns onto Olivia. "I just wanted to know if everything went well the other night when you came over?" Michael's voice sounded troubled, and Olivia knew she was being pulled into a situation that really had nothing to do with her. This was Carol's mess and Carol should be the one to clean it up.

Olivia wriggled nervously on the edge of her seat. "You know me and Carol; we always put the world to right when we meet up." Olivia hoped she had done enough, but Michael pressed her further.

"Did she seem herself? How were matters left?"

Olivia had to do some quick thinking on her feet. *Come on Olivia, you're a teacher for goodness sake, this should come naturally to you to make up something plausible.* "Well, I do remember she didn't feel too well towards the end and asked if we could call it a night?" Olivia knew she should have just left it there but wanted to appear as if she was showing concern.

"Is there a reason why?" Michael scratched his head and continued, "Well, she hasn't been herself these last couple of days. I mean, she hasn't even talked about your good news and that's not like Caz; we both know that...."

Right!" That comment provoked a light-hearted reaction from them both.

"Oh, I haven't told her yet Michael. Carol didn't seem her jovial self, and I didn't want to add to whatever was on her mind."

"Ohh, well that makes sense then."

Olivia got up from her seat. "Michael, I don't mean to be rude. You know I'd love to chat, but I've got a class of six-year-olds to go and sort out."

"No of course, sorry Olivia, you've been more than helpful. Anyway, I have decided to discuss the matter with Caz tonight just to see if I can get to the bottom of whatever is bothering her. She didn't tell you if she was upset about anything, did she?"

Olivia made a bolt for the door. "Michael, I'm out of here." Olivia hugged Michael, and in an attempt to get out of the door as quick as possible, knocked over a vase which was on the table, which shattered, and the water went everywhere. "Oh, sorry Michael." Olivia was apologetic but couldn't get out of Michael's office any faster in case he fired more questions at her.

"Don't worry Olivia, I'll get Janet to help me tidy it up. You have a great day and I hope your kids don't drive you too crazy, leaving you some brain intact to enjoy your weekend with Steve." He smiled and perked up slightly following his chat with Olivia. Michael felt a bit guilty that he had used Olivia as a sounding board and felt that if anything were serious, surely Olivia would have said something. He felt relieved and confident that when he got home later, he could confront whatever he needed to.

Chapter Twenty-One

*F*riday night was usually take-out night in the Mills' household. Michael had not made his usual call to Carol to see what she wanted him to pick up. He was unsure what kind of mood he would be confronted with, therefore on his way home from the surgery he decided to be spontaneous and stop off at their local fish and chip shop, The Plaice To Be. Carol loved their cod and chips. Sometimes they would frequent the establishment for their date night and at other times they would just order a takeaway. It was a popular place amongst the locals, so Michael had to take his place in the queue of individuals who all clearly had the same idea of not cooking that night.

When it was Michael's turn to place his order at the counter, he ordered two portions of fish and chips and two pieces of their southern fried chicken, just in case Carol wasn't in the mood for fish. At least with an alternative, there would be something that she could still enjoy and not go hungry, he reasoned. The owners were a friendly

Greek family and knew Michael and Carol well from their numerous visits. Michael exchanged friendly banter with them and paid for his food and left, making his way to his car that was parked outside the restaurant.

Carol was finishing up on a design that she had been working on for her next project that she had recently bid for and had won the contract. This time, she would be working more closer to home, as in reality, Carol knew that she couldn't keep running from the inevitable. The sooner she spoke to Michael, the better she would feel and the weight of guilt she had been carrying around for years, would finally be lifted from off her shoulders. Carol looked at the clock and realised that Michael would be home soon and wondered why Michael hadn't called her like he usually did and contemplated if he was thinking about them going out instead, but going out and exhibiting public displays of affection was the last thing on Carol's mind.

She reasoned within herself that the time was right for her to talk to Michael and get everything out in the open, once and for all. Carol continued clearing her workspace in her design room which was one of the spare rooms she had designed for that very purpose. Michael thought the room would work better as a nursery, but Carol convinced him that as it was the smallest of the three bedrooms, that it was too small for a nursery and, again, won that argument, like she usually did. Carol heard the roar of an engine in the driveway and suspected that Michael had arrived home.

Carol came out of her office and made her way down the stairs, as Michael was coming in the front door. "Hi there," Carol warmly greeted Michael as she reached the bottom of the stairs.

Michael was surprised to see Carol right in front of him but was pleasantly surprised that she had a smile on her face, something that he hadn't seen brighten her countenance for a few days. Michael put his bag on the floor and held up the distinctive plastic bag in his hand. "I stopped off and got us fish and chips. Sorry I didn't call, so I hope it's alright."

"Yeah, that's great. I could do with some fish and chips right about now, plus it smells moreish. Let me take that from you whilst you go upstairs and freshen up." Carol stretched out her hands, taking the bag from Michael.

"Okay, great; thanks." Michael gave Carol the bag and ran up the stairs to get out of his work clothes and change into something more comfortable.

Carol dished up the fish and chips, arranging them on plates so that they could casually eat off trays on their laps in the lounge area in front of the TV. Michael was down shortly, having changed into black slacks and his favourite Arsenal T-shirt, and followed the aroma of the food and joined Carol in the lounge. "Umm I can't wait to tuck into this. I'm so hungry," Michael said as he sat down, having taken the tray that Carol handed him.

"I noticed that you bought chicken as well and I didn't know if you wanted that on the plate too, but I left it in the kitchen as the cod is huge. That fish and chip shop does the best value cod don't they?"

Michael smiled. "They sure do. No, that's alright. We can probably have the chicken tomorrow with something else." They both tucked into their food, exchanging pleasantries by asking each other how their day was. "Dimitris was in good spirits as usual, even though the shop was busy. And he told me that their son had got into Cambridge," Michael said, referring to his earlier interactions.

"Oh, that's great," Carol said with a genuine tone in her voice. "He has worked hard, so I'm sure they are very proud of him getting into University."

Michael sensed Olivia was feeling more relaxed in herself and he wanted to capitalise further on their shared conversation, since it was a while that they had sat down together to enjoy quality time. "I also bumped into Olivia at the surgery earlier in the day," Michael continued, but didn't divulge the nature of his conversation, although felt that was probably a good way to broach the topic he wanted to talk about that night.

Carol coughed on a chip that got caught in her throat when Michael mentioned that he had spoken to Olivia earlier and her mind raced ahead, wondering what the nature of that conversation resembled and whether Olivia had outed her. But then quickly pulled her thoughts together, knowing that Olivia would not be so insensitive. Olivia had already made it clear to Carol that it was something she needed to do and to do it sooner rather than later. Carol chose instead to deflect from talking about Olivia and in turn shared with Michael details of the new contract that she had just won.

Michael was genuinely pleased for her as he knew how passionate Carol was about her work and the satisfaction it gave her when a project was completed. Michael was even more thrilled when he learnt that it meant Carol wouldn't be going away for a lengthy amount of time. It still puzzled him, the fact that Carol had chosen that last project because she was a home girl by nature, and usually preferred jobs where she wasn't away for extended periods of time. But this was Carol he was dealing with, and it was just another one of those things he had to let slide, just to keep the peace.

As the evening progressed, it was obvious that they were both dancing around the elephant in the room and that someone had to be brave and make the first move. Michael got up after finishing his food. "Here, let me get that for you, since you kindly prepared and got the food ready."

"Why, thank you." Carol smiled and gladly handed her tray to Michael and sunk further into the corner of the settee, getting comfortable by placing her feet on the settee by her side. *I'm going to have to do it when he comes back into the room. LORD I need your help because I don't know what kind of reaction I am going to get and how I am going to handle his response.*

Michael scraped the unwanted food and put it in the green recycle bucket that was just under the kitchen window and placed the plates in the dishwasher. He shouted to Carol, "Hey Caz, do you want a cup of tea?"

Carol thought for a moment and responded favourably, "Yeah, that would be nice… thanks."

Michael put the kettle on and pondered within himself. PT's words kept reverberating over and over in his thoughts. *As the head of your home, you are responsible*

251

for the spiritual atmosphere in the house. Michael made two cups of tea and as he walked back to the lounge area, he started to give himself a pep-talk. *Come on Michael, man up and get a grip on the situation. Go in there and just have a decent conversation. You just want to know if anything has upset your wife and if something has, then you'll just have to comfort her as best you can and deal with it.*

"Here you go." Michael gave Carol her tea in her "C" cup and sat on the armchair opposite her, clutching his tea in his "M" cup. The set was one of their wedding gifts. Two white bore china cups with a gold rim and gold initials, which they both loved using because of the sentimental value attached to them.

They looked at each other in deadly silence. Both having something to get off their chest, but equally not aware that the other person also had something to share. Michael decided to be the man that PT referred to and take charge of the atmosphere.

"It's nice to see the old Caz back tonight. You don't seem to have been yourself these last few days." Michael hesitated, but continued… "Well, if I'm really being honest, I'd say it started before you left for Manchester." He looked directly into her eyes. "Is everything okay Caz? I hope I haven't done anything to upset you or that someone else has upset you for that matter of fact?"

Carol was stunned. She couldn't believe it. She felt like Michael had stolen her thunder as she was the one who was supposed to get in there first. Now he had flipped the tables and she had to respond and had no choice but to respond with the truth. Her voice softened as she struggled to get the words out, almost like a force was stopping her from saying what she knew she could no longer camouflage. "Yes, I know things have been a bit strained between us of late and I'm sorry for that because it has all been my fault. I've been struggling with something that I have wanted to tell you but haven't known how to go about it."

Michael sunk back comfortably into his armchair, intently giving Carol his full attention and intrigued to hear what Carol had to say. "What I would ask is that you let me completely finish before speaking, as I need to get this all out in one go." Carol exhaled intensely.

Just like Carol had done when she was sharing her quandary with Olivia, she started to well up and tears filled her eyes. "I need to let you know that I haven't been completely honest with you in an area of my life, which I have kept back from sharing with you. Actually, it's as far back as before we were married."

Michael felt an ache forming in the pit of his stomach. The anticipation was killing him, and he wished that Carol would just hurry up and spit out whatever it was that she wanted to share with him. But he promised not to interrupt her and continued to let her have the floor.

Carol started to shake her head from side to side. The time for sugar coating the truth was over and she couldn't beat about the bush any longer. It had to come out straight and as blunt as it was. She continued fumbling on her words. "Michael, I am sorry, but you can't be the father that you want to be because I am unable to have children."

There was an awkward deadly silence for about a few seconds and Michael broke the silence with a loud shriek, "What!"

"Michael, please, you said you would let me finish," Carol continued in a subdued manner. "When I was 18, I got pregnant and the person I was involved with was a married man. He did not want the baby and so he paid for and arranged that I have an abortion, but there were complications at the abortion clinic where I had the procedure, and as a result, I suffered irreversible damage to my reproduction organs, meaning that I can't ever have children." Carol was horrified that she just had to convey her terrible secret to Michael, which she knew was like an arrow shot right in the heart of his core being and limply bowed her head in utter shame.

Michael ran his fingers over his head in utter disbelief and just sat there in silence for about five minutes, but to Carol the time seemed like an eternity. *I wish he would say or do something. Scream or throw something at me, but this silence is killing me.* Michael wiped his brow and looked sternly at Carol with piercing eyes.

After Michael's five-minute silence of pondering and trying to comprehend what he had just heard, he managed to utter a response. "So, everything has been a lie then. Right from the get-go. Meaning that this marriage has been built on a pack of lies. All the conversations we had whilst we were courting, when we talked about having a family was all built on a deep-rooted lie." Michael was on an emotional roll and deduced he had nothing to lose. So, in his mind, there was no holding back or the protecting of Carol's honour like he normally would. "You not only deceived me, but you deceived yourself into thinking that you could continue this façade, without being found out. It was eating you up Caz, wasn't it? No wonder you have been falling apart these last few months, especially when I have tried to talk to you about trying for a family. It's all starting to make sense now. I just can't believe this, I really can't." Michael got up abruptly and went to the kitchen to get himself a glass of water.

Carol wasn't sure if she was over the worse or if there was more to come but suspected that Michael was not finished yet and mentally prepared herself to try and offer some kind of explanation for her dismal behaviour. Michael walked back into the lounge and sat back in the same place. "So why didn't you tell me any of this when we were courting and planning the rest of our lives together Caz, you tell me that?" Michael's tone was getting louder and more agitated.

"There were so many times when I wanted to tell you Michael, but you were so passionate about having a family and I was so in love with you that I knew if I had told you, you wouldn't have married me."

Michael's eyes widened in disbelief. "You're crazy, Caz. You have no idea what I would have done or how I would have reacted. But I guess we'll never know that now, will we? Because 'little Miss know-it-all' took matters into her own hands and decided that she knew best. In fact, you were so worried about me being disappointed of us not being able to have a family, when, in reality, it's the deception, at this moment in time, that I can't get my head around. The fact that you would stoop so low, for so long is beyond me. So, does anyone else know about this little charade of yours?" Michael threw his hands up in the air in anticipation of what was coming next.

"I only shared it with Olivia a couple of days ago when I just didn't know what to do about the situation. Also, my sister knows too, as she helped me through it at the time, but she wasn't aware that I did not tell you. She was horrified when I told her that I hadn't yet told you."

"Oh, this just gets better. So, everyone else knows and your husband is the last one to know. That's rich coming from you, Caz. The woman that doesn't like anyone knowing about her personal business. Now I can understand why Olivia didn't tell you her news that night you met up."

Carol dabbed her eyes as she questioned Michael's last remark. "What do you mean? Tell me what?"

Michael finally had one up on Carol in terms of news and smirked. "Well Caz, for a change, you're getting second-hand information. When I met up with Steve the other night, he told me that he and Olivia had been seeing each other and had made a commitment to each other, with a view to getting married. He confided in me, as his best friend, and likewise Olivia was also supposed to confide and share her good news with her best friend. But I guess you really spoilt what was supposed to be a happy moment for her, with your problem that you dumped in her lap. No wonder she wouldn't share it with you. And now I know why she was so keen to get out of the surgery

257

this morning too. I thought it was just me, but now I know, she couldn't look me in the eye, knowing what she knew."

"I'm genuinely pleased for Olivia. They make a lovely couple. I always told her she might end up with him."

"Caz, I am not in the mood for one of your matchmaker speeches on who you think make a lovely couple. You certainly didn't think much of us as a suitable couple when you were hatching your masterplan. You must have been pitying me, whenever we talked about starting a family. I feel such a fool now. How on earth did I get blindsided like this?"

"Michael, it got out of hand. When we first met and started talking about our goals, it was always my intention to tell you the truth. But the deeper we shared and the closer we got, it became harder. Especially the more you expressed your desire for a family."

"So, this is all my fault now?" Michael sarcastically bellowed.

"No that's not what I meant. I know this is all my fault and I'll have to live with whatever you decide to do."

"Yes, you're right, Carol, you will." Carol knew that Michael was extremely upset and frustrated, because he only called her Carol when he was annoyed with her, and she could only recall that being on two occasions in the past.

Michael stood up rather suddenly as if he had come to a snap decision. "You know what, I can't get my head around this and need to clear my thoughts, and I can't do this under the same roof as you. I'm going to call Steve and ask him if I can crash at his place for the night."

Carol looked up from having her face buried in her hands, absolutely shocked by what Michael had said. Carol felt for sure that, whilst, understandably, Michael would be angry, she thought he would probably just sleep in one of the spare rooms to cool off. But Carol did not envisage that Michael would walk out in disgust. Her secret was out, but the enormity of it was now taking shape and she only had herself to blame and had to wait on Michael, who now held all the cards and, more importantly, their future in his hands.

Michael had called Steve and asked if he could crash at his house for the night. He explained that he and Carol had an argument and that he needed space to clear his head. Steve told Michael that it wasn't a problem as he was at home and assured him that he could come over whenever he was ready. Michael ran up the stairs and got one of his sports bags from the wardrobe and threw a few items of clothing in it and put some toiletries together in a holdall and put that in the bag also. With the bag in his hand, he switched off the bedroom light and ran down the stairs.

He grabbed his jacket and keys that were in the hallway, where he had left them earlier, and exited the house without acknowledging or saying goodbye to Carol, who was left sitting on the settee, in what now seemed a hollow space. The slamming of the front door reverberated, and Carol was left with the deafening roar of Michael's engine as it left the drive in a hurry. As Carol reflected on the evening and the reaction of Michael, she burst into a flood of tears again. Her marriage was in tatters, and she wasn't sure if they would ever come back from the lies and betrayal that she was responsible for. In the natural, the situation was a disaster and yet Carol's only hope was to cling to divine inspiration that the Holy Spirit would intervene, and that God would make a way of reconciliation for her and Michael that only He could do.

—◦—

Chapter Twenty-Two

Steve lived about three miles from Michael and Carol's house, yet the drive to his house seemed like an eternity to Michael. The journey was filled with emotions as Michael contemplated the mammoth information Carol had just shared with him. The traffic was light, so Michael didn't need to concentrate too deeply on his driving. The route was a familiar one to him, having driven to Steve's house numerous times within the lifespan of their friendship, which afforded him the opportunity to widen his mind and ponder extensively as to what other things Carol might have lied about from the get-go. Was there anything in their relationship that was sacred or authentic? Michael questioned every detail as he reminisced over the time he had first met Carol and all that transpired in the lead up to their marriage.

One of the things he particularly admired about Carol was her ability to be genuine and honest in her dealings with him, her family, and her friends. So, in his mind, there was no excuse on Carol's part not to have come clean to him beforehand with her truth. She had had numerous opportunities from the time they first met throughout the duration of their courtship and even up to the time of their wedding day to come clean, and yet she chose to conceal the very thing that was most important to Michael and may or may not have been a dealbreaker to their relationship progressing beyond a friendship.

Michael continued to muse. *That means she also told a pack of lies at our pre-marital counselling sessions that we had undergone prior to our wedding.* PT was a stickler for engaged couples going through the course, which was designed primarily to highlight any issues that needed to be addressed and dealt with prior to marriage. At these meetings, this was where the 'rubber met the road', so to speak, as the couples sought to be raw and vulnerable with each other. It was also the perfect opportunity for either party to discuss anything that could potentially harm their future marriage or any issue that needed ironing out. Michael had felt their sessions went well as he was confident that his bride-to-be was honest and genuine. He had no reason to question her integrity.

In fact, Carol was the exact type of woman he had prayed for and imagined he would be with and, almost in a prideful way, felt that they had breezed through the sessions with flying colours. Likening the course to one of the medical examinations he took when he was studying to be a doctor, he was confident that he would get a distinction. In comparison, in the past Michael had relationships where there was deception at some level and this did not sit well with him, and he was adamant that he wasn't going to repeat the mistakes of his past. He was determined to marry someone who shared the same level of integrity as he did, which meant that telling the truth was high on his list of 'must haves'.

Michael drove into Steve's drive. Under the circumstances, he didn't feel he could have stayed at his home that night, with all the pretence that everything was fine with him and Carol. If Steve wasn't able to put him up, he was adamant that he would have gone to a local hotel instead for a couple of nights, whilst he processed the bomb that had shattered his world into pieces and had hit him like a ton of bricks.

Michael took his bag out of the car and rang the bell. Steve answered the door. "Hey mate, you okay?" He looked at Michael sympathetically, suspecting that it wasn't anything too serious, other than just a silly tiff between his two old friends. Their relationship was such that they could wind each other up at times, but he knew they loved each other and always found a way to turn things around. He tapped Michael on the back as he welcomed him in.

"Thanks Steve, I didn't really know what to do and would have gone to a hotel if it wasn't convenient. Sorry, I don't mean to put you out like this."

"Don't be silly, mate. You know you are always welcome. But I don't really understand, what has happened? You didn't seem to be making much sense on the phone." Michael and Steve strolled into the living room. "Can I get you something to drink?"

Michael sat down on the recliner chair, positioned in the corner of the room. "I'd say give me something strong, but I don't think that would do anyone any good. It might numb the pain, but it certainly won't sort out my problems, so just give me a strong black coffee."

"You got it mate. I'll be back shortly." Steve's place was simply decorated and quite sparce. It was a typical bachelor's pad, with only the essential things required, like a sofa, a 50-inch widescreen TV and a bookshelf filled with an eclectic range of books. But nonetheless, the room was quite tidy, and as Michael's gaze scanned around the room it reminded him of his own bachelor days, prior to him meeting Carol, when he did not have a care in the world and could live how he liked. He didn't have to answer to anyone in terms of how he spent his money, where he went and with whom he was out with.

He smiled inwardly to himself. *If Steve is expecting to share this house with Olivia, she'll definitely put her stamp on it, because it's crying out for a woman's touch.* Michael recalled that when he first met Carol, she had certainly put him straight and introduced him to colour, cushions, rugs, and the finer detail of design, that men are usually clueless on.

Steve interrupted Michael's thoughts as he came back into the room with two mugs of hot coffee. "Here you go mate."

"Oh thanks."

Steve took a seat on the settee and attempted to make sense of why Michael was at his house instead of being at his own house with his wife. "Well, I'm just going to be blunt and direct, because we've known each other far too long to beat around the bush. So why exactly are you spending the night here at my place and not at your own home, with that lovely wife of yours?"

Michael looked up after taking a sip of his coffee. He could either play this down, and not draw Steve into his world of chaos and not say anything, thereby protecting Carol's honour. Or as Steve had alluded to the fact, he could just be direct and put it out there. "I'm surprised you don't know already. Hasn't Olivia told you then?"

"Told me what?" Steve was puzzled and scratched his head wondering what he was missing.

Michael relayed the whole version of events verbatim to Steve, choosing to spare no details. Who in turn was stunned, shocked and yet in a strange sort of way, not surprised. He empathised and understood Michael's reaction in wanting space to gather his thoughts. And wasn't going to add fuel to the fire by saying something insensitive like Michael should have stayed and tried to work things out with Carol instead of walking out. Perhaps it was a good thing that they both had some space to clear their heads. And after a good night's sleep, he felt sure Michael would be able to decide how he wanted to deal with really thrashing things out, hopefully resulting in a reconciliation with Carol.

Steve tapped his head as if a lightbulb came on inside his head. "The night Olivia met up with Carol when I spoke to her after she got home, I sensed she was carrying something heavy within her spirit and I asked her if it was anything I could help her with. She insisted that it was something she had to pray about first and that she didn't want to burden me with it, and now I realise that this is what she didn't feel comfortable sharing with me."

Steve jumped to his feet in response to a thought he sensed in his spirit. "Michael, I'm going to quickly call Liv, because after what has happened, I don't think Carol should be on her own tonight either. Regardless of what she has done, she needs her best friend with her also. You don't mind me doing that do you?"

Michael shook his head by way of agreeing with Steve. "No, you do what you feel is right. I'm not at my best right now, so I don't feel qualified to give any kind of sound advice."

Steve went in the hallway to call Olivia, as he sat on the bottom stair, which creaked as it held his weight. It reminded him that the staircase needed to be ripped out and replaced with a sturdier one. He kept putting off calling Carol to come over and give him her professional opinion, but work commitments had distracted him, and he never got around to it. Olivia saw Steve's name illuminate on her phone.

She answered the call with a smile in her voice. "Hey there, how are you?"

With an urgency in his voice, Steve replied, "Not too bad. Look Liv, I can't talk for long as I need you to do me an urgent favour."

Olivia could hear an earnestness in Steve's voice

and wondered what was wrong and yet she trusted him that if he wanted a favour, then it was something he was confident she could handle. "Yeah, what is it Steve?"

Steve spoke softly, almost in a whisper, "Michael is here."

Almost teasing him in a whispered tone, Olivia mused, "Oh, that's nice; but why are we whispering? What, are you guys have a bonding session or something?"

Steve tried his best to be more direct with Olivia, which was something he found difficult because of his love for her. "No Liv. He's just told me some devastating news that Carol disclosed with him tonight." The phone went deadly silent. "Are you still there Liv?"

Olivia's silence was a giveaway. Eventually breaking the silence, she uttered "Ohh, I guess she told him then? I'm guessing he did not take it well. Then again, why would he take it well?" Olivia caught herself. *What a silly thing to think eh, of course Michael would not be happy to learn that his dreams of becoming a father and having a family of his own have now been shattered. All because of a lie that was left to fester.*

Olivia pulled herself back to focusing on the conversation. "Sorry I didn't tell you. It just wasn't my problem to share. Plus, I did not want you knowing before

Michael was told as that would have placed you in a really awkward position."

"You're such a wise woman and that's why I'm marrying you, because I wouldn't have wanted to know before Michael either."

"So, what's the favour then?" Olivia asked rather inquisitively.

"Liv, I believe Carol could do with your company about now. Would you go over and stay the night with her? I think she'll be going through a lot of emotions and with no one else in the home, who's to tell what she might get up to."

Olivia agreed wholeheartedly with Steve and did not hesitate to act. Not that she felt Carol was suicidal or anything of that nature. But the situation did call for Carol having a friend to be there for her. "Yeah sure. I'll call her and insist that I'm coming over and I won't take no for an answer."

Steve's voice got a bit louder. "You're the best. Anyway, I better get back to Michael. Thanks, Liv. Let's speak tomorrow."

Steve re-joined Michael in the front room where he had allowed him the space to be quiet and to process whatever was on his heart. "That's all sorted then. Liv has agreed to go around and spend the night with Carol." Steve could feel the trepidation in the atmosphere and knew that Michael was hurting deeply. Michael was quiet with his head bowed and Steve sat on the settee and prayed in the spirit under his breath. It felt like the scene when Job's friends found him in deep despair, after he had lost his family, livelihood and suffered harshly in his body. They chose to sit in silence with him because his suffering was so severe. Eventually Michael broke his silence and agreed to Steve's offer of prayer, which he gladly received. Steve prayed with authority and spoke to the situation, commanding God to turn the situation around and Michael felt the anxiety lift for that moment and went to bed a little lighter.

Olivia got through to Carol and was able to reach out to her, who appreciated the sentiment of her best friend coming to her aid. They talked, cried and prayed with each other into the early hours of the morning. Olivia was there to offer moral support and be that shoulder to cry on that Carol so desperately needed. It was not her place to question Carol's integrity or why she did what she did, for so long. Olivia could sense Carol's genuine repentance and she muttered under her breath. *LORD, please help my friends and help them to get through this.*

Carol was so exhausted that she had sobbed herself to sleep on the settee. Olivia glanced over at her friend who looked so snug that she didn't want to disturb her. She went and got a duvet from her bedroom and gently positioned Carol's feet on the settee and covered her body. Olivia threw her dressing gown over herself and snuggled in the recliner chair until she fell asleep.

Chapter Twenty-Three

*T*he Harris household was up early, which was unusual for a weekend, as Chris enjoyed a lie in to compensate for the heavy week he normally endured. In addition, that gave Ben the opportunity to benefit from not having to get up early, like he did on a weekday to go to the breakfast club that Chris dropped him off at on his way to the surgery.

They were spending the day with Jen as Chris had organised a few activities for them all to enjoy as a bonding exercise. Whilst Chris and Jen had been spending a lot more time together, Ben was not always included in the mix. Chris was trying to establish in his mind first, if he saw a potential future with Jen and whether he felt there was a place for her in Ben's life. Chris had not really dated anyone after his wife's death and felt protective over Ben and, therefore, didn't want to expose him emotionally to individuals who wouldn't be in his life for the long-haul.

For the sake of Ben, Chris wanted it to be a fun day, but realised that he would have to try and find the balance so that everyone concerned would be equally happy. Chris planned for them all to go to a trampoline park in Cheshunt called Jump City. He had researched the company on the internet and had read the reviews, which were favourable, confirming it to be a place to take the family for a fun day out. Ben's energy levels were already supercharged. Chris had previously told him ahead of time about the day so as to prepare him mentally of what to expect and how he was to behave, given the fact that it would be a crowded place.

The fact that Ben woke up first and ran into Chris' bedroom to ask him if it was time for them to leave yet was an indication of his excitement levels and anticipation for the day. Chris was also looking forward to the day, although his enthusiasm wasn't quite as apparent as Ben's was. Chris really didn't do much fun things like the day he had pre-planned, so a trampolining park was way out of his comfort zone. However, he had a relationship to work on, with someone a lot younger than himself, and was the parent to a son of an energetic disposition, which forced him to start making some changes to his life.

After their appointment at the trampoline centre, Chris planned for them to stay in the vicinity and googled a nearby park to picnic in. He had already asked Mrs Jenkins to help him prepare a picnic basket the night before and followed the meticulous note that she had left for him to add a few things to the basket in the morning to finish off the prep. Chris had checked the weather beforehand, and it was forecasted that it would be a bright and sunny day. He went to the shed and got out the foldaway chairs and rugs and put them in the boot of his car. The plan was to pick up Jen from her house en-route.

Jen woke up with an air of excitement. She hadn't spent a whole day with Chris and Ben before and wondered how the dynamics would work. She spent most of her time with Chris, trying to get to know him better since they had first met. Jen did think it odd at first that Chris didn't want her to get to know Ben better, because she felt a connection with Ben on the odd occasions when they did meet, which was generally at church on a Sunday and felt comfortable interacting with him.

Jen didn't know exactly where she was going, only that Chris had told her to wear comfortable clothes and to bring her trainers. As she got herself ready, it was evident that the house was eerily quiet. Olivia had knocked on her door the previous night explaining that she had to go and stay with a friend for moral support but did not say who the friend was. Olivia wanted to protect her friends for now, as the issue was still raw and the less people that knew about the breakdown of their relationship for the moment, the better.

Jen got her things together and rushed downstairs, as she heard Chris blow his horn signalling that he and Ben were outside. Jen paused at the front door and left a handwritten note on the side table for Olivia, explaining that she was out for the day. Olivia's departure was so quick the previous night that Jen forgot to mention that she was going out the next day.

Jen and Olivia had been getting on well since Jen had moved in and both ladies made great effort to be respectable of each other's space. Jen knew that she had big shoes to follow, as the relationship between Olivia and Carol was a strong bond, the two having shared a home together for several years. But from the get-go Jen wanted to be herself and forge her own unique style and footprint. Olivia was drawn immediately to Jen's personality more than the other individuals she had interviewed, which she deduced was a good recipe for a pleasing future.

Jen hopped into the passenger seat of the car and Chris took her bag and put it in the boot. Ben was quiet and comfortable in the back seat, donned in bulky blue headphones covering his ears, as he was watching a cartoon on his iPad. He looked up when Jen got into the car, cracked half a smile and then went back to what he was doing.

"Right, now that we are all set; are you ready for your

daytrip with the Harrises?" Chris said as he smiled and glanced over at Jen.

"Yes, I am a little bit intrigued to say the least, but excited nonetheless." She chuckled.

"Well, I hope you enjoy your day with us. It may not look like it now, but Ben has been looking forward to the day since yesterday." Chris sniggered.

The journey took 25 minutes via the M25, and the traffic was a steady flow due to their early start. Chris put on one of his worship CDs which served as background noise and the conversation flowed steadily between him and Jen on a range of topics. Chris found that the more time he and Jen spent together, the clearer the age gap between them was becoming more apparent. But he chose to ignore that noticeable detail, convincing himself that it was not a big deal at the present time.

The only trouble with that notion, was that Jen had started to become more emotionally invested in the relationship and was fantasizing over it as more long term. The fact that he was a lot older than she was and not really her type didn't ring any major alarm bells in her mind either. She had this unrealistic emotional attachment to meeting her prince charming and being swept off her feet. That was how her dad won over her mother, who was also 10 years older than she was. The age gap didn't seem to pose an issue and they somehow made it work and now had a strong marriage. One that Jen wanted to emulate.

As a kid, she enjoyed hearing the story repeatedly told of how they met. And whilst it wasn't love at first sight for Jen's mother, she pushed passed whatever reservations she had and in time learnt to love Jen's father. Chris met some of Jen's expectations in terms of his status, but the physical side was lacking somewhat. But she also chose to ignore that factor having the preconceived notion in her head that if it worked for her mother, it could also work for her.

As they reached their destination, Jen saw the flashing neon sign giving a clue as to what Chris had arranged and shouted, "Trampolining! That's great." Ben looked up to see what Jen's sudden outburst was all about and was also delighted that they had reached their destination and started to pack his iPad away, unplugging his earphones and putting everything back neatly in its case.

"Yes, I thought it might make you all excited. I also researched the company on the internet beforehand and the reviews were all good. So hopefully, we should have some fun today." Chris drove around the car park until he found an available bay and parked the car. Once the car was stationary, everyone unbuckled themselves to exit the car. Chris attempted to run around the other side to open the door for Jen, but she had already got out and was fixated on trying to see which way was the entrance. Chris then went to the other door to help Ben out of the car, to hold onto his hand so that he would not run after Jen in all the excitement to get inside. Chris sniggered to himself of how his chivalrous attempt, when he tried to open the car door for Jen, was totally lost on her and just put it down to an age thing.

Once they were inside of the centre, Chris was overwhelmed at how noisy and crowded the atmosphere was and wondered if he would last the two-hour slot that their booking was reserved for. Ben was dazzled and intrigued by the various trampolines, observing individuals of all ages jumping up and down, tumbling over and getting back up, whilst others steadily bounced alongside of each other in unison.

Jen started to laugh, directing her conversation towards Ben's earshot. "I'm really going to enjoy seeing you try to stay up, because I can bounce high, and I am sparing no prisoners." Jen put her hands around Ben's shoulder. "Are you ready Benny to have some fun?" Ben looked up in her face with the biggest grin on his face, reassuring her that he also was ready to enjoy himself.

Chris quickly got in between the two of them. "Okay,

well let's grab this corner and use it as our area, because I don't think I'll be on the trampoline as much as the two of you." Chris had planned to maximise his time to do some work on his laptop, which is why he brought it inside with him. He was swamped with a backlog of work and had a few patients' notes to update on the system.

With Jen and Ben occupied on the trampoline, Chris felt it was a good opportunity for him to catch up. Jen and Ben started to take their trainers off to get ready to take their place in the queue to get on one of the many huge trampolines that were positioned in square formats alongside each other all around the venue. Chris sat down, nestling himself into the V-shaped table, and got his laptop out.

"Oh, noooo Chris, you're not going to be working, are you?" Jen seemed annoyed as she thought that Chris had genuinely planned a day for them all to enjoy together, which wasn't work related.

Chris started to shake his head to reassure Jen that wasn't the case. "No, I'm not going to be long. You and Ben go on first, as we can't all go on together. Someone has to look after the bags. I'll go next when you have had a few jumps with him."

Jen wasn't convinced or impressed with Chris and

reluctantly took Ben by the hand to get on one of the trampolines as the queues were getting longer. Jen wasn't about to spoil Ben's day by making a scene, so she started joking around with him telling him that they were in a competition to see who fell over the most times. This excited Ben and he couldn't wait even more to get on the trampoline and win the competition.

Jen and Ben eventually got onto one of the trampolines and had fun jumping around, falling over and interacting with some of the other families. Jen sensed this was the norm and perhaps something that Chris did a lot by leaving Ben to fend for himself. Or not even doing fun, childlike things with him and she felt sorry for Ben. Jen understood the dynamics of being an only child, but at least she was blessed with two loving parents who doted on her, which more than made up for the absence of any sibling. Jen also grew up with a close-knit group of cousins, which compensated for the lack of siblings in her life, but it seemed that Ben did not even have that. Jen glanced over to see what Chris was doing, whose gaze was completely fixated on his laptop, looking up occasionally when he could hear Ben call his name.

"Dadddd; look how high I am jumping!" Ben shouted. Chris smiled, waved and went back to what he was doing.

This is supposed to be a bonding experience for all

of us, yet he is treating me like a glorified babysitter or better still, his housekeeper. Jen started to feel resentment over the way the morning was panning out, as it wasn't what she imagined it would be like.

After she and Ben had tried a few more different types of trampolines, Jen called time and went back to where she had left Chris, in the same position, who was still preoccupied with his work. Ben ran over and crashed pass Chris, nearly knocking over his drink, but clearly excited that he won the competition between him and Jen. Being a lot smaller, he had the upper hand and Jen fell over a lot more times than he did, which he thought was hilarious every time she fell over, as he was keeping a running total, which he told her was over 20.

"Hey, watch my drink, buddy," Chris said as he put his cup on a higher shelf out of Ben's reach.

"I thought you were supposed to relieve me so that you and Ben could enjoy some quality time together," Jen said slightly annoyed with Chris that he did not keep up with his end of the agreement.

"Oh, I was watching you both and you looked like you were having so much fun. I didn't want to spoil things." Chris smiled and went back to looking at his screen. "I got myself a drink. Do you guys want something? We still have another hour to go under our booking."

"I am sure Ben is thirsty, as that was quite exhausting," Jen said as she affectionately smoothed Ben's hair down. She loved children and it was her desire to have her own brood one day when she found her Boaz. She just had to figure out if that person was going to be Chris or whether she was to look for someone else. "I'll have a drink too and then it's your turn to take Ben on the assault course, because I don't think I have the energy for that one. Plus, I believe Ben would appreciate you doing it with him."

Chris looked at Jen and got the message from the tone of her voice and the piercing look in her eyes. "Okay buddy, after a drink break, it's me and you on the assault course. Are you up for that?"

"Yesssss Daddy, yippee. I can't wait." Chris went to the food kiosk and purchased a couple of soft drinks. After which he happily went on the assault course with Ben as well as a few other trampolines, which he had to admit to himself that he enjoyed seeing Ben just having a really good time. He would be the first to confess that he didn't do many things like that with Ben as he occupied himself with his work and his patients. And it made him think how perhaps he needed to make some sort of changes to ensure that Ben was his priority. He felt this sudden epiphany was down to Jen calling him out and highlighting this and bringing it to the forefront of his mind. Perhaps things could work with them after all he mused.

Their two-hour slot had expired. Chris, Jen and Ben started to pack up for the next half of their day. "Right; it's still early so, what's next?" Jen was zipping up her turquoise sweatshirt and ready for the next part of the adventure.

"Well, I researched that there is a park not far from here and I, with the help of Mrs Jenkins, I might add, have made up a picnic which I thought we could sit on the grass and enjoy."

They all started walking to the exit and Jen weighed in. "Sounds great, but on one condition". Her voice taking on that Head Mistress tone she used earlier.

"What's that then?"

"The laptop stays in the boot."

Chris smiled. "Deal." He realised for the first time how assertive Jen could be and that she was a young lady that wasn't to be trifled with and he liked that feistiness about her.

Their time in the park was a productive one. They enjoyed the contents of the picnic basket, Ben met some children on the climbing frames which kept him occupied, and Chris and Jen took the opportunity to further explore their relationship to see whether there was a future to pursue with each other. Jen shared the fact that she too was an only child, but that she did not feel she missed out because of the way her parents included her in everything they did and the fact that she had cousins of a similar age, who she always saw as the brothers and sisters she never had. Chris too had a vulnerable moment and shared how he threw himself into his work after the death of his wife and admitted that he felt guilty that his behaviour may have attributed to Ben's erratic behaviour of one minute being withdrawn and introverted to the next minute being very clumsy and over excited.

As the day ended, Chris and Jen, inwardly, both felt they had made a breakthrough in learning a bit more about each other and Chris was glad that Jen got to spend the day with him and Ben. He dropped her back home and Jen got out the car, whilst Chris got her bag out of the boot.

"Bye Ben." Jen tilted her head in the window towards the back of the car. "Thanks for letting me spend the day with you." Ben smiled, waved and then went back to watching his cartoon.

Chris walked Jen to her door and handed her bag to her. "Well, I hope you enjoyed your road trip with the Harrises?" He smiled, hoping that Jen would give a positive affirmation.

Jen took her bag. "Yes, I did, eventually," Emphasising the word 'eventually' sarcastically. "But you pulled it back with the picnic so, I'll give you that I guess." She chuckled. "Yes, I had fun. Hope we can do it again some time."

"Yes, I hope so too." Chris awkwardly gave Jen a kiss on her cheek. Even though they had kissed intimately in the past, Chris was mindful of Ben in the car and didn't want to confuse him as he hadn't really explained his relationship with Jen to him yet, continuing to stall until he himself knew where their relationship was going. Jen waved the car off as it left the drive and went inside the house.

———◄O►———

Chapter Twenty-Four

*O*ver the next couple of months that passed since Carol told Michael about the secret she had been keeping from him, they had been having weekly marriage counselling sessions with PT, to try and salvage what seemed to be the embers of their marriage. Yet, Michael continued to struggle. He could not get past the lying, betrayal and deceit that Carol so comfortably exhibited on a day-to-day basis, and felt he had no other option, but to temporarily leave the marital home for the time being.

This drastic decision was a route that PT had tried counselling against, preferring rather to see the couple make a more concerted effort to work out their differences in the marital home together, rather than separate. Whilst Carol was willing to do so and was very much repentant in all their counselling sessions, for Michael, all avenues had been exhausted and he was ready to have a temporary reprieve. He had reassured PT that it hadn't come to him thinking about a divorce, which stemmed from an idyllic perspective on his part that marriage was for life and that divorce was not an option. Yet here he was on the verge of such a contemplation, which was why he thought that a trial separation might help him to gather his thoughts and compartmentalise his life in the interim period.

News of the breakdown of the Mills' marriage was now common knowledge within their church community, friends and work colleagues, which came as a genuine shock to many, since Michael and Carol were seen somewhat as the dream couple who had it all. Michael threw himself into his work, taking on extra callouts as a locum for after-hours requests, which was a pattern Chris recognised and tried to offer moral support in. But he himself was not, perhaps, the best example, seeing that was the way he too dealt with his grief after his wife died.

Equally, Carol added more work to her portfolio, but was now left home alone to fend for herself in a bespoke house, which she had designed to match her and Michael's unique taste and requirements. Which was now empty of that warmth and affection that usually is felt in a home where love is at the very heart. A home that she and Michael had created together, which was intended for their long-term future.

It certainly wasn't the way she thought their first year of marriage would have panned out. Especially as they had so many plans that they talked about achieving together. And even though children were discussed, Carol naively believed that she could keep changing the goalposts to buy her some time. Failing to realise that for Michael, as soon as they tied the knot, trying for a family was something he was eager to pursue, sooner rather than later, given their age and especially if they wanted to have at least two to three children.

It broke Carol's heart on that final day when Michael cleared his side of the wardrobe and bedside cabinet and packed two suitcases with his things. Especially knowing that it was her fault why he was leaving, which could have been avoided had she the guts and gumption to trust Michael with her truth. With hindsight, Carol pondered what would have been the worst-case scenario that could have happened back then. Sure, Michael might have been sympathetic, but she had no guarantees that he would have stuck around and that is what she was reluctant to risk. Especially as she knew how important children were to him.

How on earth did I think I was going to get away with this. Surely, I knew Michael would have reacted like this. I have deeply hurt him. Carol, what on earth were you thinking. What a mess. You crazy woman. As Carol continued to ponder within herself, she wondered if Michael's departure would be a temporary measure or a final goodbye, with Michael never stepping foot back into the house again.

Carol convinced herself, however, that it was indeed only temporary, which she could just about live with. She recalled at their last session with PT Michael confessed he was not contemplating a divorce at this stage, but just needed some space. As Carol made herself scarce by pottering around in the kitchen, the noise upstairs of Michael gathering his things was thunderous. He wasn't the quietest person to live with, but Carol would have given anything, ruckus and all, for Michael not to leave. Preferring him to stay so that they could work things out together, under the same roof. But Carol recognised at this late stage in the game that she had to respect Michael's decision, as it was the least that she could do.

And yet had to come to terms with the fact that this time apart could go one of two ways. Either it would create a hunger between the two of them for each other's company again, as they reminisce over the history, they have with each other and how that love was forged. Or sadly, if forgiveness could not be reached, it could drive a wedge further between them. Carol inwardly dug deep and clung tightly to the clutches of optimism and hoped it wasn't going to be the latter.

Michael and Carol had left their final marriage

counselling session on speaking terms, so at least they were cordial to each other. Michael was mature enough to inform Carol that he had rented a small studio flat nearby the surgery and gave her the address for his mail to be forwarded on. Carol was disappointed that Michael was not planning to return home to collect his mail. However, Michael had agreed at their last session with PT that he wanted to treat their break from each other as an opportunity to see if he could indeed learn to respect Carol's trust again.

Carol resolved and gave herself hope that at least she would see Michael at church on Sundays and in the week when their small group met. Also at the surgery, whenever she needed to pop in. As she wanted the opportunity to talk with Janet personally to set the record straight and didn't want it left to the version of events by some nosey gossipers who wanted to make her and Michael the latest headline news in the community. Carol soon learnt that it wasn't pleasant being on the other side of the gossip and felt a deep sense of regret and remorse, remembering the times when she perhaps distorted the truth and the events of someone else's unfortunate downfall.

Life was moving on for others too. Steve and Olivia had started meeting up with PT. Whereas their close friends had been having counselling to save their marriage, they were getting pre-marital counselling to embark on a life together, which was challenging in the light of what Michael and Carol were going through. It seemed to weigh heavily on Steve and Olivia to avoid some of the pitfalls that their close friends fell into, which just added to the pressure of adapting to the idea of marriage.

Olivia had been enjoying the excitement of planning her wedding, which was something she had dreamt about for a long time. The type of dress she would choose, lace being her preferred choice, finished off with a long train. The décor of the venue would be a secluded country manor in beautiful spacious grounds, surrounded by green foliage, and beautiful wild flowers. But most importantly than being swept up by this fantasy world Olivia had imagined, was the man who would sweep her off her feet. Although if someone had told her, that man would be Steve Adams, she would not have believed it. But she was getting used to potentially becoming Mrs Adams and liked the ring to the way that sounded...*Olivia Adams, nice....*

Given Michael and Carol's present circumstances, Olivia kept her thoughts and the finer details of the planning to herself and didn't want to include Carol too much into the discussions, as she felt that might be a bit insensitive and raw for her at the current time. But Carol was her best friend, after all, and had a great eye for detail, and knowing Carol, she wouldn't have wanted to miss out on being there for her best friend. Olivia contemplated that when things had settled down a bit, she would pick Carol's brain and involve her in the process.

She smiled as she imagined the mischief they would get up to. Carol would be trying to force her ideas onto her, and Olivia would have to stay strong and true to what she and Steve wanted for their wedding. They had discussed it in great detail, and agreed, that they wanted it to be an intimate affair. Not a lot of all the fuss and fanfare that usually goes with planning weddings. They were clear and on the same page, that their priority was the marriage that was going to follow, and they weren't going to put all their efforts into the actual day which comes and goes by like a flash in the night.

Chris and Jen were also continuing to pursue their relationship, whilst still ignoring all the red flags and obvious negative signals they were encountering. Chris could be quite controlling in his temperament. He often made subtle suggestions as to how Jen should dress or style her hair, especially as her features resembled that of his late wife's, which perhaps was the reason he had felt drawn to her initially, given there wasn't that depth and richness of relationship there that he had had with Jill.

Equally, Jen too continued with her romantic notion that love and attraction would follow, even if it wasn't immediately evident. After that initial day out, introducing Ben into the mix, Chris continued to keep Ben protected by not including him in any of the other occasions he met up with Jen.

Ben didn't seem phased by that day out and did not ask his dad any further questions about the time they spent with Jen. Rather his recollections were more of a childlike manner, often smiling recalling how he won the competition between him and Jen in their trampoline battle off, and Chris had no intentions at this stage in building Ben's hopes up that Jen could potentially be his new mum. Ben was quite young when his mother had died, so remembering what it was like having a mother figure in his life in those formative years was vague and the introduction of Mrs Jenkins into his life had been a positive experience for him, one which he relished.

Since moving to Bricket Wood, Chris had been pleased with the way Ben's development had come along and attributed his rapid progress to Olivia's patience and care in the way she had taken Ben under her wings. A lot of his erratic behaviour seemed to calm down somewhat and Chris looked forward more to returning home after work to find a pleasant and pliable child, who showed eagerness and expectation when Chris tucked him into bed and read a story to him. The relationship between them was developing into a strong bond, despite the amount of time Chris spent away from the home. Employing Mrs Jenkins to handle all those areas he could not fill was a Godsend and brought a sense of balance to their lives, which had been missing since the death of his wife.

Jill was very much a hands-on individual that looked after her family well. She was like the model Proverbs 31 woman and there wasn't much that she could not do well. Jill was a stay-at-home mother and wife and up until those final months when her cancer progressed further and more aggressive, she was busy looking after her family, and seeing to their every need. Providing that support that Chris appreciated, which allowed him to do the thing that he loved most, caring for individuals. Jill's death had rocked Chris' world and for a long time, he could not come to terms with why God would allow a woman who was always a picture of health and who had everything going for her, to be snatched away from him, leaving behind a young son of three years old.

Chris' faith took a knock in those formative years as he questioned the goodness and fairness of God and drifted away from the God that he and Jill served faithfully as a couple and family. Even though it was an abrupt departure from all that he knew, moving to Bricket Wood seemed to be the clean break Chris needed from work, his surroundings and Jill's family, who were extremely close-knit.

Yet he struggled in his relationship with them, especially with Jill's twin sister, Tilly. Even though he couldn't always understand it, he had to appreciate the unique bond that they had as identical twins. He felt Tilly was too invested in their relationship after they had got married and was either always calling Jill on the telephone or turning up unannounced and intruding on what little time they had as a couple when he wasn't at the surgery. And that bond even intensified when Jill was first diagnosed with her cancer. When she eventually died, Tilly dealt with the news quite badly and pointed the finger of her sister's quick and sudden demise at Chris. Tilly's irrational behaviour rocked Chris' world and acted as an incentive for him to move away from what he felt was a toxic environment for his son to grow up in and was glad to get away from all the blame and accusations.

He and Ben had settled well in Bricket Wood, and they were rebuilding their lives. After years of not having a relationship in his life, Chris struggled to allow another woman into his heart that had hardened over the years as a result of Jill's death. It was why he wasn't as invested initially with pursuing a relationship with Olivia as perhaps he should have been, choosing rather to be drawn more to Jen only because of the similarities in her features to his late wife. Yet he was struggling with his emotions. He was having a change of heart, and feelings towards Olivia were starting to resurface, even though she was now with Steve, and they were embarking on getting married.

However, Chris did not let an important obstacle like that phase him and wondered if he had given up too easily and if indeed there was still a chance to explore the feelings he was now experiencing and could not shake.

Chapter Twenty-Five

*J*anet was busy tidying up the reception area at the surgery, making good use of the late start that was the usual norm on a Wednesday morning. The coffee was percolating, and a strong aroma of Colombian coffee filtered down the corridors pass the offices of the individual doctors' rooms. Joan was in her office, fixated to her computer screen, frantically searching for information that appeared to be missing. Rather than let it affect the rest of her day, she logged out and strolled down the corridor towards the kitchen.

"I'm getting myself a coffee, does anyone want one?" Joan bellowed as she passed Michael and Chris' offices.

Michael was quick to respond. "Yes please, I'm on my way."

"I don't think Dr Harris has come in yet," Janet added and hurriedly ran towards the kitchen to get there before Joan. Janet was very protective over the things she felt were specifically her role and even though the culture in the surgery was very relaxed, and the doctors were quite capable of getting a cup of coffee for themselves, Janet still preferred to spoil them as she knew that they had quite busy schedules and it was her pleasure to relieve them of at least one thing that they didn't have to worry over.

Michael fixed his tie as he reached the kitchen. "Ahh the aroma of that coffee is tantalizing, and a cup of coffee right now is just what I needed. Thanks Janet. Just the way I like it too." Michael took the cup of coffee that Janet had handed him and sat on the bar stool at the counter, savouring the flavour. Joan also took her cup and sat down next to him.

The microwave pinged, signalling that the croissants Janet had put in there to warm for their meeting were ready. "I'm going to take these to the conference room." Janet said, as she arranged the croissants on a plate, grabbing a few napkins from out of the cupboard, and exited the kitchen, heading to the conference room first on her way back to the reception area. Janet arranged the pastries in the middle of the conference table and covered them with one of the napkins. Janet proceeded to the reception area to feed the fish and then straightened up the chairs in the waiting room, whilst sorting the magazines on the table, throwing away the ones that were out of date.

Janet liked the patients to have up-to-date magazines to read which kept the conversations current and relevant. She was responsible for most of the magazines on the table, positioned in the middle of the room, being an avid reader herself of numerous magazines such as OK and Hello. She loved reading stories about the lives of the celebrities, especially the Royal Family, and relished being nosey seeing pictures of their exquisite houses and the extravagant lives they lived. Other magazines were also left by patients, and it was a bit like a take one, bring one, type of culture, which seemed to work well.

"You look like you needed that cup of coffee. Don't you have coffee where you are living?" Joan teased.

Michael smiled. "Actually, I do, but I'm out of it at the moment. I meant to go to the supermarket last night but had a late night here sorting out some things and then was too tired after to go." Michael shrugged his shoulders and raised his hands.

"How are things going living on your own then? What, it's been about a month now, hasn't it?" Joan didn't think that an intrusive question since her and Michael had a good working relationship and she also considered him a close friend and was concerned about his well-being.

"Well, it's not been as easy as I thought it would, as

I've been used to having Caz around for nearly coming up to a year now and miss her annoying ways and her meticulousness that she shows in everything. She certainly wouldn't have let the coffee be depleted, now would she?" Michael smiled, remembering Carol's unique way of doing things, yet getting things done well. "Anyway, that's how it is for me at the present time and I'm just trying to adjust to my new normal, whatever the heck that is. And tell me, Mrs Webb, why is it that I could hear a lot of huffing and puffing coming from your office this morning?" Michael teased as he addressed Joan by her full title and tried to use humour to divert from the subject of him and his faltering relationship with Carol, choosing rather for it not to be the topic of conversation.

"Ohh that," Joan exhaled. "I have been updating our records, making sure we are compliant with our CQC that is due, and for the life of me, I can't seem to find the references for Chris anywhere. By the way, where is he?"

"He called me this morning saying that he was running late and to go ahead and start the meeting without him. He didn't think he would make it. There seemed to be an issue with him waiting around for Mrs Jenkins, or something like that." The call from Chris seemed vague and Michael did not press for further information at the time. "I recall at the time that George had to take up his new position abroad fairly swiftly and being inundated with work, we were desperate for his replacement. When we interviewed Chris and were satisfied that he would be a good fit for the practice, we agreed a quick turnaround to him taking up the position, with his references to follow shortly thereafter, but I thought that was all done and dusted at the time."

"Well, if it was, there is nothing to show on our records that we have received those references and we really need to be compliant and have everything up-to-date." Joan was studious and a stickler for being on top of things, especially when it came to practice matters, and was the voice of reason at the surgery, being the go-to-person to bounce off any ideas and treatment plans when there was a challenging situation.

"Let's finish this conversation in the conference room," Michael said as he got up from resting on the countertop and made his way towards the door. "I'm sure there is a perfectly reasonable explanation, which can be sorted out with a quick chat with Chris or even a phone call to his previous practice. Don't worry, everything will be compliant. I'm sure it's nothing major and can easily be resolved."

In the conference room, Michael and Joan took advantage of consuming the croissants that Janet had so kindly prepared for them. They sat opposite each other in the spacious conference room, which they were fortunate to have as an extra area where they could gather, away from their individual offices, and bounce ideas around with each other. Joan took a bite of her croissant and sipped her coffee in between bites.

Joan continued the flow of their conversation they had started in the kitchen. "Also, there is a medical conference coming up in the next couple of weeks at the BMA and they have sent us two invitations. I think you and Chris should attend as I don't mind holding the fort here and we can get a locum in to assist if need be."

Michael contemplated as he finished off his croissant and leaned over to take another one. "Yeah, I think that would be a good idea, especially as Chris is the newbie and hasn't been to one of these events as a representative from this practice. I'm sure he'll relish the opportunity."

Going back to the topic of Chris' missing references, Joan was keen to get the matter sorted out sooner, rather than later. "So shall I approach Chris about the whereabouts of his references, or will you? As we don't want the practice to get a substandard report just because we failed to cross our 'T's' and dot our 'I's'."

"No, you are quite right," Michael agreed. "Let me

have a word with him when he gets in. I imagine he is going to be rather surprised that after such a long time, we are still asking about this and perhaps it has just been misplaced. Probably filed away in the wrong place I suspect. Is there anything else on the agenda for this morning's meeting?" Michael enquired.

"No, that question was the main thing to discuss, but Chris wasn't here to update us, and I wanted to talk about the conference at the BMA, also involving Chris and again, he isn't around to talk about this either, so I guess it's a short meeting this morning and its back to the daily grind." Joan smiled and got up from the table, gathering her cup and plate. "Do you have a busy schedule this morning?" she asked Michael as they both were preparing to leave the conference room.

"Thankfully, a quiet morning and later this afternoon I am heading to the hospital for a short stint and then I have some home visits to wrap up the day. What about you?"

Joan sighed. "Not so lucky, I'm afraid. It's the flu jab season and I have a number of elderly patients who need to be vaccinated, so that will take me right up until the end of the morning. And then this afternoon, I want to continue updating our records so that we don't have a last-minute dash around when we have our CQC, and

I hope that earlier comment wasn't directed towards me that I have somehow mislaid Chris' references."

Michael patted Joan on her shoulder as they left the conference room to go to their individual offices. "Of course, not. You're our very own 'Joan of Arc' at this surgery and if anyone can keep things up to date, you can."

"Yeah right." Joan chuckled. "Someone's got to keep this place in ship shape, so it might as well be me. Plus, we all know I can't help myself." They both laughed as they went into their respective offices to prepare for the day ahead.

It was 9.30 am and Janet prepared to open the surgery for the sudden rush of patients who were scheduled to see Joan and was surprised to see Chris as the first person in her gaze as she unlocked the door.

"Morning Dr Harris, how are you this morning?" Chris appeared dishevelled in his appearance, with his usual slickly styled hair ruffled and not in place, as if he had just grabbed his things and made a mad dash to get to the surgery.

"Good morning Janet." Chris greeted Janet in a hurried manner, as he proceeded to take the scarf from around his neck. "It's been a hectic morning, but I'll fill you on that later as I can see you have your hands full." He grimaced as he rolled his eyes referring to the queue of patients behind him, which he recognised as a few that were his for that morning.

Chris knocked Michael's door and peered his head into his office. "Sorry I wasn't around this morning for our staff meeting. What did I miss?"

Michael was sat at his desk waiting for Janet to buzz him with the name of his first patient and looked up from sorting the notes that were on his desk that looked like it had been hit by a storm. That was the way he worked, but there was a method to his madness, and he could account for every piece of item on his desk. Janet often attempted to bring order to his desk, but Michael politely told her not to disturb things as he liked it exactly the way it was. "Hey Chris, yes a few issues came up which I'll need to fill you in on. Are you available for a quick catch-up in the conference room about 1PM for about 15 mins, which I could squeeze in, prior to going to the hospital? By the way, is everything okay at home?"

"Yeah, it was just Mrs Jenkins. She was delayed picking up Ben for school, something about her husband not feeling well, so I'll have to leave a bit early today to pick Ben up from school as she doesn't want to leave him. I think he had been vomiting all night and could not keep anything down. She didn't want to let me down this morning and briefly left him so that she could take Ben to school. I reassured her that she did not have to worry about collecting Ben from school this afternoon, that I would. 1PM is fine. I have a busy morning myself. It's mayhem out there, but I'm sure that Janet will handle the patients as she usually does so professionally. The receptionist at my last place was not as competent. Often sending the wrong patient to the wrong doctor's room, it was quite something as we tried to correct her mistakes." Chris smiled as he reminisced over his past.

The morning rush was over, and calm resumed. The bulk of patients having been seen by Joan and vaccinated with the flu jab, with there being only a handful of patients to be seen up to lunch time. Janet had prepared a fresh brew of coffee and taken it into the conference room as Michael had informed her beforehand that he and Chris were going to have a brief catch up, prior to him leaving for the day to attend the hospital. When Michael and Chris strolled in, the tantalising aroma of coffee welcomed them in, and they both helped themselves to a cup.

Michael made himself comfortable as he eased into one of the conference room chairs and Chris positioned himself directly opposite him. "Well, I'll get down to matters since we don't have very long. It was a brief meeting this morning with Joan as a few of the issues on the agenda related to you personally and you were not there, which I already know, could not have been avoided. The long and short of it is that we have a CQC review coming up and Joan has been meticulously trying to make sure all our records are up-to-date and that we are compliant on all levels. Joan highlighted this morning that as she was going through our records, she could not find your references from your former practice. I told her it was probably mislaid or filed elsewhere, but you know what Joan is like, she panics and won't be satisfied until we have those references and that they are filed in the right place."

Chris shifted nervously in his seat and his eyes widened as he took a sip of his coffee. "Oh, I thought that was already done and dusted, since it has been quite a while ago."

"That's what I would have thought too, but there's a simple enough solution. We can just get Janet to give your former practice a quick call and ask them to email over a copy as we have mislaid ours."

Chris was quick to butt into Michael's flow of conversation. "No, that's fine. I'm still friendly with the doctors there and I'll....err, let me sort it out. There's no need to trouble Janet, she's got enough on her hands trying to keep the patients in line." Chris sounded as if his thoughts had drifted away, and mentally he was in a different headspace. "No, no, let me deal with this."

"I'm totally fine with that, mate, and you probably know exactly who to speak with directly. Janet may get passed around from pillar to post and it may take longer so thanks for dealing with this. See, I told Joan that it would be easily resolved. Sometimes I think that she just overthinks things, but don't tell her I said that." Michael smirked and Chris tried to reciprocate Michael's humour, but clearly, he had other things on his mind that seemed to be weighing him down, following the revelation that his references were not on the practice's system. "Finally, the last thing we discussed was going to a medical conference at the BMA in a couple of weeks' time. We have been afforded two invitations from the BMA and Joan and I made an executive decision that you and I should attend this year."

Again, Chris's demeanour changed, and he shifted agitatedly in his seat. "Surely, you and Joan should go since you both have been in the practice much longer than myself?"

"Yes, I can see your logic, but we felt, as the newbie, it would be good for you to go and represent the practice. I could introduce you to some colleagues of mine and, who knows, you might even bump into a few old colleagues from your former practice."

Chris could see that both Michael and Joan had already decided on this, and it wasn't something he was going to wriggle out of. "It would mean me having to ask Mrs Jenkins to stay on a bit longer as she picks up Ben after school. Don't these things go on for quite some time?"

"Yes, these events can drag on, but that's only due to the networking at the end of the conference. If you needed to leave at that time, then I guess that would be fine." Chris felt slightly more satisfied within himself that he wouldn't have to spend more time than was needed and convinced himself that he would make a clean break directly after the main session.

He had previously been to conferences at the BMA and just about mustered up enough mental energy to sit through the long presentations of the latest medical procedures that specific specialists shared. Having to sit through one after the other, each specialist shared their findings, was taxing on the brain, with the art of trying to position ones posture to look like if an individual was remotely interested. But the highlight of the day was definitely the break away from the monotonous of the medical talks, when the delegates stopped momentarily to have coffee/lunchbreaks and eventually got to network at the end of the event in a relaxed atmosphere.

"Okay, that's fine. You have given me enough notice, so I guess I can check with Mrs Jenkins that this will be fine. She already does above and beyond her allotted hours for us, and I don't like to take advantage of her good nature."

"I thought you said Mrs Jenkins was a God-send and loved to help out."

"Yes, I know that, but I like to prioritise and only choose the specific things I need her assistance in, as she has her own family to support as well."

"I see." Michael raised his eyebrows as if to suggest that Chris used that excuse about not wanting to take advantage of Mrs Jenkins when he wanted to avoid complying with other things and it suited him. "Let's hope she is agreeable then," Michael said as he got up, taking his cup with him. "Anyway, I have got to go now, if I'm going to get through that traffic across town. We can discuss this further, if need be, nearer to the date."

Chris agreed and they both left the conference room.

Chapter Twenty-Six

Olivia was glad the day was ending, as all she could envisage was going home to have a long soak in the bath. It had been a busy week, but she had had other things on her mind, such as hashing out the finer details of the wedding. Even though that wasn't going to be for another year, it was something that she enjoyed doing, letting her mind run away with how she and Steve wanted the day to transpire. Olivia had finally engaged Carol in the planning, and, like she knew would happen, Carol had been hands on with her suggestions regarding the design of the reception area, injecting life into the basic template that Olivia started off with.

Olivia and Steve had decided not to use a wedding planner, as they felt they had enough resources and individuals at their church who agreed that they were happy to assist them on their special day. Olivia reminisced over the many weddings she had helped at, and the numerous times she acted as a bridesmaid and now it was finally her turn, where everyone would now be running around her.

Olivia's parents were also delighted when she told them the news of her and Steve getting married as they had always liked Steve and felt that they made a nice couple, even if Olivia could not see it at first. And as Olivia was an only child and took her time in walking down the aisle, her parents relished the idea of being grandparents, and were equally excited about the possibility of that happening soon.

Olivia's thoughts were brought to an abrupt halt when the final bell rang indicating it was home time. Earlier in the day, one of the teaching assistants had alerted Olivia that Mrs Jenkins was not picking up Ben after school, and instead his father was coming to get him, which Olivia was not looking forward to. Even though things didn't work out between the two of them, Olivia had tried to avoid any unnecessary conversations with Chris, if she did not have to. Choosing to let matters stay on a professional level in her capacity as Ben's teacher. There were only a couple of times when she had to speak with him on the telephone if there was a need to exchange information regarding Ben's continued progress, which was growing in leaps and bounds. Anything other than talking about Ben, Olivia evaded.

The final bell always brought a lot of noise and activity as the children packed their books away in their desks and gathered their things, whilst they got ready for their parents to pick them up. "Ben, your dad will be collecting you today," Olivia alerted Ben, as she weaved herself into the middle of the children's joviality and chatter.

Ben looked up and smiled with Olivia. "Okay Miss Dupont, thank you."

Once all the children were ready, Olivia escorted them to the playground as the parents came one by one and collected their children. As the numbers dwindled, the noise of children coming and going decreased. Olivia had already predicted that Ben would be the last child to be collected, as Chris wasn't as prompt as Mrs Jenkins, and he usually came rushing in with an apology and some excuse or the other. Olivia wondered what lame excuse he was going to use today. After all the children had been collected, Olivia was left sitting with Ben on one of the benches, which was a bit uncomfortable for her given how low the bench was, but she wanted to be on Ben's level so that she could converse with him.

"Don't worry Ben, your dad will soon be here, he probably got stuck in traffic," Olivia tried to reassure Ben as she could see that he was getting fidgety and restless.

"He's always late," sighed Ben, clasping his hands around his cheeks, "and I'm always the last one here with no one to play with."

Olivia felt Ben's frustrations. "I know Benny, I'm sorry, but I bet it won't be long now. I tell you what, should we play a game of 'I spy with my little eye' whilst we wait for your dad?"

Ben smiled and perked up and appeared happy that his time waiting would not prove fruitless. "Yeahhh, I would love that," he chirped.

"Okay, I'll go first." Olivia smiled. "I spy with my little eye, something beginning with 'S'."

Ben giggled, "That's easy Miss Dupont...sky."

"Well done Benny, you are clever, aren't you? Right, now it's your turn."

Ben erred and ummed, finally seeping out a huge laugh. "I spy with my little eye, something beginning with 'C', and I bet you'll never get it." He smiled.

"Ummm, now let me see," Olivia said inquisitively. "I don't see any cats around, so it can't be that."

Ben chuckled. "There aren't any cats at school, Miss Dupont."

"Okay, then well let me try again. How about coat?"

Ben shook his head. "Nope."

"Okay, how about child?"

"Nope."

"Ooooh, I can see you might have tricked me, Ben, as I can't see that many things beginning with the letter 'C'. I think I am going to have to give up and you will have to let me have the answer."

Ben chuckled and jumped up from off the seat with his hands raised and shouted "Concrete!"

Olivia smiled. "Oh Ben, you are clever, aren't you? I never would have guessed that, and it is all around us, isn't it? Well done Ben you are a smart little boy." As they were about to play another round, they heard footsteps approaching.

"Hey, what's all this laughter I could hear from the school gates?"

Ben looked up and ran straight over to Chris and embraced him. "Daddy...me and Miss Dupont were playing a game of 'I spy' and I think I won."

"Oh, you did, did you? Well, that's great son and well done. I guess you get your brains from your old dad eh?" Ben laughed. Chris directed his gaze towards Olivia, who by that time was rubbing the arch of her back as she rose to her feet. "Olivia, I am really sorry that I am late. There was an accident en-route and I got stuck."

'*Yeah, yeah,*' Olivia reasoned, but tried not to let the expressions of her frustration show on her face. "Not to worry, Ben and I entertained ourselves whilst you were delayed." Olivia tried not to sound too annoyed and walked with Chris and Ben towards the school gate. Ben had excitedly run ahead.

"I hear congratulations are in order. I haven't seen you for a while, so have not been able to congratulate you."

Olivia was thrown back by the sudden accolade. "Oh, thank you, I appreciate your sentiments."

"I must admit, I didn't realise that yours and Steve's relationship was that close. I mean, I knew you were good friends, but I didn't realise it was on a romantic level." Chris was trying to tease out of Olivia the extent and depth of her relationship with Steve. How long it had been going on and when things started to develop deeper between the two of them. It was only a while back when individuals thought that they we were an item. Chris wondered whether his lack of commitment and drive to pursue a relationship with Olivia pushed her away and eventually into the arms of another man.

"Well, you know what they say, sometimes the thing that you are looking for is right under your nose. Steve and I have had a close friendship over the years, but sometimes something happens which causes you to take a second glance at the situation and that is when you see something with fresh eyes that you never saw before, and that's what happened with us. We weren't looking for it, well at least I wasn't." Olivia smiled but wanted to change the subject as she didn't really want to be taking to Chris about her love life, especially since he was like the one that got away.

"Well, here we are," Olivia said as they arrived at the school gate where the caretaker had opened the gate to let Chris and Ben out from off the premises as the last two. "Bye Ben, see you on Monday."

"Bye Miss Dupont." Ben waved and continued to walk ahead.

"Bye Olivia, and again sorry for keeping you back." Chris felt as if a wound had pierced his soul as he listened to Olivia's account of her new relationship, especially as he could hear in her voice how happy she appeared. Chris escorted Ben to the car, which was parked in the school car park and drove home. Olivia walked back to her classroom, collected her things, turned the lights off and left to enjoy the weekend.

317

Jen was exhausted when she arrived home that she went straight to the lounge, dropped her bag on the floor and just slumped on the couch and exhaled. Life as a paramedic had its challenges and today was quite a hard one on her on all levels, physically, mentally and emotionally. Her last pick up pulled every emotion from the depths of her soul. When Jen and her colleague arrived at the house in their ambulance, they were met with a hysterical mother who directed them upstairs towards the bathroom where her daughter was, who had cut her wrists in a suicide attempt. Jen and her partner immediately checked to see if the young lady was conscious, followed by the necessary procedures they needed to carry out to save her life, eventually taking her to the hospital.

As Jen sat on the couch, allowing the TV to play anything mindless that would take her attention off the scene, she recalled the mother's conversation in the back of the ambulance when they were on their way to the hospital. Her daughter had been upset about the fact that her boyfriend had dumped her for someone else and what was even more heart wrenching for the young woman, is that the person her boyfriend had dumped her for, was her best friend.

Jen was emotionally drawn in as the young girl could only have been a few years younger than herself and yet she had not felt driven to do anything that drastic. Jen would be the first to admit that her relationship with Chris over the last few months had no real depth to it and was barely hanging on, but she wouldn't have gone to such lengths of trying to kill herself over a relationship. And sympathised with how that young lady must have been feeling and how low she had got. Jen knew that when all hope was lost in any given situation that her relationship with God was the most important thing in her life, and there were times in her life that had been challenging, but her faith in God always got her through.

After some time of mediating on the couch, with her thoughts and emotions wandering, Jen dragged herself up the stairs to change and refresh and then came back downstairs into the kitchen to prepare something to eat, desperately looking in the fridge and cupboards to see what was there. She and Olivia had a system in the kitchen, that worked perfectly for them, where they had dedicated cupboard areas and shelves in the fridge for themselves. Jen saw on her shelf that there was some salmon and decided to have that with a stir-fry of mixed vegetables and quinoa. Jen had a petite figure which she maintained by regularly going to the gym and eating healthily and often made more food for one person, which she would save the next day for her lunch or offer it to Olivia.

Olivia was glad to get home, especially because her lower back was aching from sitting so long in a crouched position, whilst waiting for Chris to pick Ben up, and as she drove her car into the drive, she noticed the lights on in the front of the house. *Jen must have finished work early*, Olivia deduced, and made her way into the house. She headed straight towards the lounge, following the noise of the television she could hear blaringly loud, and stuck her head around the door.

"Hey girl, you're home early." Jen was slumped on the couch with the remote in her hand and a tray next to her which had on it her empty plate and cutlery.

Jen pulled herself up straight and responded to Olivia warmly. "Hi Olivia. Yeah, I swapped shifts with a colleague. He took my late one and I took his early one. Glad to be getting home at a decent hour for a change." Jen smiled.

"Well good for you. I'm off to have a nice long soak in the bath, as every bone in me is crying out for some love."

"A nice hot soak in the bath sounds like the solution and when you are finished, I've left some food in the kitchen, you are quite welcome to have it if you like."

"Girl, you are a God-send. That would be lovely as it

means I don't have to think about cooking and can spend longer soaking. I'm going to light a few aromatic candles and really make the most of it, making sure that I also de-stress my mind and meditate. Think I have one of those soaking tracks on my phone that I can play that will just do the trick and get me into the right headspace. I'll see you in an hour or so."

Olivia found a few candles that she positioned near the bath and laid there soaking, savouring the moment, de-stressing any thoughts that did not need to be in her headspace. *I'm not sure why Chris thought it was okay to quiz me on my love life, but it really isn't his business. I don't want to talk with him about things pertaining to my personal life and would prefer to keep things on a professional level.* Olivia pondered on the earlier conversation she had with Chris and treated the memory as one of those conversations that she needed to file towards the back of her mind, never to be looked at again.

The soaking music played, and Olivia could feel herself softening and loosening as she sunk deeper in the bubbles that surrounded her. After staying in the bath for well over an hour, Olivia got out, went to her room and changed into a flowy, auburn paisley kaftan and slipped on her flip flops and headed back downstairs.

Jen was still slouched on the couch when Olivia

brought the food that Jen had left for her on a tray into the lounge and sat down in front of the TV to engage with her.

"I can see you're still just about alive," Olivia teased as she comfortably positioned herself on a smaller armchair opposite Jen. "You look like you had a hard day. By the way, thanks for the food, it smells divine. I love the way you do your quinoa, mixing the vegetables into it. I'll have to try it some time. I'm looking forward to enjoying this food."

Jen glared towards Olivia's direction. "It was a full-on day in the life of a paramedic, but it was the last call that really shook me up." Jen proceeded to tell Olivia all about the young girl who had slit her wrists in an attempt to take her own life.

"Oh gosh that's awful Jen." Olivia showed empathy towards Jen's account of things in between bites of her food, as she relayed the full gruesome story verbatim. "Are you okay hon? How are you really feeling?"

"I feel a bit numb. I'm a paramedic, so I'm used to seeing blood, but there was so much blood everywhere and just seeing her body slumped over the sink like that was something I never want to see again. And, yet in reality, I know it is something that I will be faced with again in the future."

"Hon I am so sorry that you are exposed to such tragedies, but we are going to pray later, as you shouldn't have to bring your work home with you, which on a mental level is easier said than done, I know."

Jen continued trying to get a grasp of the situation. "I mean, what drives someone so low to want to take their own life over another individual's actions?" Jen shared with Olivia the conversation she had with the mother of the young lady in the back of the ambulance. "It's such a shame when you get dumped like that. I should know because it has happened to me once or twice, but I have never thought of taking my own life as a result." Jen sighed, as she tried to make sense of the young lady's actions.

"Jen, some individuals have a lot going on in their mental state and I can guarantee you that this young lady did not want to die, but merely her actions were a desperate cry for help. Thankfully, she did not die, and you and your colleague got there just in time to give her the medical help and assistance that she needed. Well done hon, you should be proud of the work you do, even if at times it is hard-going."

Jen felt comforted by Olivia's words but had other things that she wanted to get off her chest and felt the time was right to pick Olivia's brain on them.

"Olivia there is something I have been meaning to ask you since you and Steve connected with each other." Jen had Olivia's full attention, so she felt comfortable to proceed in what she felt was an intimate, yet private matter.

"Yes, what is it?" Olivia said curiously.

"I just wondered how you handled the physical intimacy of your relationship with Steve. Just tell me to mind my own business if you would rather not divulge any personal details, but I am going somewhere with my line of questioning, so there is a method to what may seem like my madness."

Olivia smiled. "No, that's okay, hon. I don't mind being upfront about mine and Steve's relationship. Well, as you know, we are human beings after all, so feelings will be evoked from time to time, but we manage in the best way we can to keep it respectful, remembering first and foremost that our duty is to God in the way we carry ourselves. Plus, we try to ensure that I don't stay too late at his house, and you'll know that he isn't here late either. It's easy to fall into bad habits, which is why it's important to have boundaries in a relationship right at the outset, so you have something to respect if those lines get blurred from time to time."

Jen listened intently to Olivia and nervously shifted in her seat. "Ohh okay. Well, I think my lines are getting blurred then as Chris has been pressuring me to take things to the next level, but I don't feel comfortable or think it is right. He said that there was nothing wrong with it, if the two individuals were consenting adults and were comfortable with what they are doing." Jen's voice loudened as she continued. "But it's something I don't want to do. I know I could lose him over this, if I don't conform to his request, which is why I thought I would ask you in case this is what others are doing and I am just old-fashioned."

"You are not old-fashioned, missy." Olivia was infuriated by what Jen had told her. "You do not have to satisfy the wishes of someone else, who clearly is trying to take advantage of your innocent nature, as he should know better that sex before marriage is not acceptable within the Christian faith. I am sorry that he has made you feel uncomfortable like this, Jen. It's really not okay and I am disappointed with him. So, what are you going to do? Are you going to take some time out to create some space so that you can gather your thoughts?"

"I don't know what I am going to do at the moment. We seem to get on, but then there are times when I feel that he is not really interested in pursuing a relationship with me and I feel that he is passing the time until something better comes along."

"You know you deserve better right, Jen? It seems to me like Chris has other deeper issues that he has not really got to the bottom of, and I just want you to be careful that you don't get hurt. Just make sure that you don't decide with your head instead of your heart that's all I would add."

"I know, I have a lot to think about, but thanks so much for your honesty and transparency as it has really helped to put things into perspective." The two embraced each other with a hug and as promised, Olivia prayed for Jen regarding the earlier matter she talked about, but Olivia extended her prayer to ask God to give Jen the wisdom and confidence to protect her heart that she would be faithful to Him and the purpose that God had for her life.

It was obvious that the weight of such a revelation had been plaguing Jen for some time that she felt she needed to offload the enormity of it onto Olivia's shoulders, but she was glad that she finally released it and got freedom. As Olivia got ready for bed and leant over the sink brushing her teeth, she gazed into the mirror at her reflection and uncomfortable thoughts towards Chris overcrowded her mind. *Girl, that could have been your reality were you to have gone down that route with a man who clearly has no respect for women. Thank you, Lord, for protecting me from that, but help Jen to make the right decision.*

Olivia wondered how she would be able to relate to Chris following the revelation of what she had learned that night, which was going to be particularly difficult seeing that she would need to deal with him on a professional level for the sake of Ben. Olivia knew what she had to do going forward, which was to put her personal feelings aside and do the job she was paid to do, which would prove a challenging feat.

Chapter Twenty-Seven

*T*he day of the medical conference had arrived, and Chris was getting himself ready as Michael was driving and picking him up. Mrs Jenkins had happily agreed to help out for the day as it gave her the opportunity to take Ben to her house after school and treat and spoil him like the grandchild she never had, as a result of her and her husband not having any children. Chris frantically ran around the house trying to get Ben ready and packed a small bag for him, which contained a change of clothes, his iPad and a few personal things to keep him entertained after school, since Chris was not sure what length of time he was going to be gone for or if indeed there was any way he could get away early.

Mrs Jenkins arrived promptly and picked Ben up, gathered his things and took him to school. Chris hurried to finish getting ready, as Michael had already warned him that he did not want them turning up to the conference late and be the attention of everyone for the wrong reasons. Chris wasn't looking forward to the conference. Leading up to the conference he had tried on several occasions to persuade his colleagues that he felt Joan shouldn't have to miss out on the experience and that he was happy to hold the fort. But instead of getting a locum to cover, they decided to close the practice for half a day, giving Joan the afternoon to finish off the audit preparation that she was still very much on course to finish before the CQC review.

Chris heard Michael's horn and dashed out the door with his coat and bag in his hand. Michael had wanted to get an early start so as not to get stuck in traffic for considerable lengths of time and to get one of the few parking spaces that were afforded to delegates. Chris made himself comfortable in the passenger seat, whilst Michael concentrated on the drive. Chris attempted to keep the conversation light and at a steady pace as Michael seemed tense and anxious to get to the conference on time.

"Have you stopped going to church then, as I haven't seen you for a month or so now" Chris enquired.

"No, I haven't abandoned my faith, if that's what you are referring to. I felt it was going to be awkward with Caz and I attending the same church with onlookers watching our every move. You know that New Dawn is quite a tight community. I just didn't want Caz or me either, for that matter, feeling uncomfortable so I found another church where I have been going."

"Oh, I see. I totally understand and I guess it makes sense too. So, are you guys any closer to getting things resolved or do you plan to live out the rest of your marriage in that small bedsit you are calling home these days?"

"I am trying my best to control my thoughts about where our marriage is going and what the future looks like for us. I have been having personal counselling sessions with PT also, but I'm not going to lie, it's really been hard. When someone you have known for so long throws a curve ball at you like that, the impact is shattering. With hindsight, you take a second glance at someone, and you see something totally different and lying has always been a big thing for me. I hate liars. Well, perhaps hate is too strong a word, but you know what I mean. Why can't people just be honest at the outset and allow whatever it is they are hiding to rise to the surface, out in the open, and eventually things will take their natural course?"

Chris didn't say much and made grunts in the right pauses of Michael's conversation to indicate that he was sympathetic and understood where Michael was coming from. "I hear what you are saying, man, but sometimes if you know a person's backstory, perhaps you can understand what made them go to such lengths to hide their truth. I think what I am saying is that rather than be judgemental we should seek to try and be more empathetic and understanding."

"Well, that's where I am at the moment and PT is helping me to break things down and evaluate it from a different point of view and I am working on that." Michael wanted to shift the talk from his personal situation to something else and threw the ball right back into Chris's court. "Anyway, enough about me, how have things been going with you and Jen? It's been a few months now hasn't it that you have been seeing each other? It must feel good to be moving forward with your life in terms of a fresh start relationship wise?"

"I guess I'm still treating things in the friend zone. Don't get me wrong, Jen is a very nice person, but you do know that there is a 10-year age gap between us right? And at times that gap is very evident in the type of things we want to do or the maturity in how we interact with one another. I'm an older man who has been married before, with a young son to look after and perhaps that is too much experience to put on her young shoulders. I am pacing myself for now and therefore not pushing forward on a serious level. Also, I am not sure if I'm ready emotionally to invest in another serious relationship."

Michael quickly glanced at Chris and then went back to concentrating on his driving. "Wow, I didn't realise that you were toying with your feelings in such a way. But whatever you decide Chris, please be honest with her as no one deserves to be left hanging in a relationship if the other person does not feel there is any potential in it."

"I know, it's something that I have to think long and hard about before we both get emotionally drawn into something that might be potentially going nowhere."

Just as Michael had meticulously planned, they arrived at the BMA's offices in good time, got one of the designated parking bays for the delegates, and were able to enjoy a cup of coffee before going into the main auditorium, which was heaving with medical practitioners from all parts of the country. Michael and Chris took their seats towards the middle of the auditorium and positioned themselves comfortably for what was going to be a long day of listening to presentations, taking notes, and gathering ideas that could best help them improve the way their practice functioned.

Throughout the day there were opportunities to go into different seminars in other breakout rooms and Michael and Chris decided between them which ones they would go to separately to be able to maximise as much as they could out of the day, meeting back together in the reception area at the relevant coffee breaks that were interspersed throughout the day.

The BMA provided an impressive lunch buffet style where Michael and Chris took the opportunity to catch up and compare notes on how their various sessions went. The lunchbreak only allowed for 45 minutes to eat, take a toilet break and then it was back into breakout rooms for smaller sessions. With the final presentation in the main auditorium, followed by the networking opportunity at the end of the conference, which for some was the highlight, bringing the formality right down to a more relaxed level.

"That was hard-going," Michael said as he stretched his hands in the air to release the tension that had built up from sitting most of the day and concentrating on a mindful of information that was thrown at them. Chris agreed as they made their way out of the main auditorium to the reception area, where teas, coffees and light refreshments were provided. "I got some good ideas though and I can see how implementing them in the practice will improve things greatly. Joan will be pleased," Michael teased.

"Yes, she will," Chris responded. "Has she always been so thorough with her work?"

"Yes, I guess she has, but we are very fortunate to have her as she has been the driving force behind the smooth run of the practice. I'd be lost without her."

"It's good to have a respectable working relationship

with your colleagues, it makes for an easier life and a happy practice," Chris commented as he sipped his coffee.

As the day was ending, Chris contemplated how he was going to get Michael to leave early and not extend their stay since Michael drove, and technically was his ride home. Whilst Chris was pondering a good excuse for getting back home, he thought he could hear his name being called and as he paid attention to that, he could see a man waving his hand and making his way directly towards him. Chris recognised the man as one of the doctors in his previous practice. Chris became nervous and his demeanour changed from relaxed to agitated and he abruptly excused himself to Michael, making an excuse that he needed to go to the bathroom and then make a quick call to Mrs Jenkins to see if everything was okay.

Michael was left standing alone sipping on his coffee, scanning the room to see if there was anyone he could network with, when he heard a voice calling Chris' name and saw a man desperately waving at him heading in his direction.

"Hi, I'm Nathan Kelly." The man who had been waving and walking towards Michael extended his hand as he introduced himself.

"Hi, I'm Michael Mills." Michael and Nathan

continued with small talk as they both talked about the nature of the conference and what parts of the country, they were both from and then Nathan dropped an inquisitive question.

"Sorry, I don't mean to be direct, but I could have sworn the man you were talking to before I came over was Chris Harris."

Michael responded with a glee in his voice. "Yes, you are right that was Chris. He had to make an important phone call, but he's my colleague and we work together at the same practice."

Nathan sounded relieved in his response. "Well thank goodness for that, as I thought my eyes were deceiving me. Now I know I don't need to make that appointment with Specsavers after all." They both smiled. Nathan continued, "I haven't seen Chris for a year or so. We used to work together at the same practice, but I must admit, I thought he had left the game and wasn't practicing anymore."

Michael was intrigued to know more and lent in trying to ascertain what exactly Nathan had meant by that comment. "What do you mean?"

Nathan discerned the confusion on Michael's face and didn't want to say anything out of turn and just stuck to the facts and what he knew. "Perhaps I've got my wires crossed, as I thought Chris was suspended, following an investigation that the practice was carrying out regarding a serious allegation that was aimed at him. I did leave the practice shortly after that, so perhaps everything got sorted and the suspension was lifted. Anyway, he is practising at your surgery now which goes to show that I don't know what I am talking about. So just ignore what I have said as I don't want to resurrect history that Chris would rather not have dragged up again, especially since he was an emotional wreck when his wife, Jill, died. To be accused of having something to do with her death, when he was supposed to be grieving, really couldn't have been easy. Well, Michael it was nice chatting with you. I've just seen someone who I haven't seen for a while, and I'm going to run over there and catch up with him. Tell Chris I said Hi."

Nathan was in and out like a tornado, creating a storm but not sticking around to deal with the aftermath. Michael stood there, with his cup in his hand, stunned about the revelation about Chris that he had just heard. *Was this the reason why we have not yet been able to get Chris' references through from his old practice? And how were things left there? Can he legally practice or not? With the CQC imminent, has he put our practice in jeopardy?* Michael's thoughts were racing ahead of him, and he had to quickly decide if he was going to confront Chris now to try and get some sort of explanation, or if he would leave matters as they were to get his head around it a bit more, and perhaps do his own probing.

However, before he could finish his thoughts, Chris came back into the auditorium to find him, oblivious of what had transpired earlier. "Sorry I was so long. Firstly, I was on the phone to Mrs Jenkins and then I got chatting to a few people on the way back to you."

Michael seemed intrigued to know exactly who Chris was talking to. "That's great that you met up with some old colleagues."

Chris quickly jumped in to correct him. "Oh, no I didn't know them. As you rightly said, this part of the day is about networking, and they approached me to make contact."

"Very true, I too met a few individuals myself. It's always interesting to hear from other practitioners and get their perspective on things. By the way, was everything okay with Mrs Jenkins?"

"Ahh yes, about that. Sounds like Ben is acting up and has been crying for me to come and pick him up. I told Mrs Jenkins that the main part of the day had finished, and we were just winding up and I would ask and see if you wouldn't mind us leaving now, so that I can get back in good time to pick Ben up." Chris was using his son as a pawn to free himself from an environment where he would have to continue interacting with individuals who might be familiar with his past and felt the net closing in on him.

Michael was not surprised that Chris wanted to leave early and decided to tease out Chris' lame excuse to see how far it would go. "I always thought Ben enjoyed his time with Mrs Jenkins. Bit like having one's own personal grandma to spoil and pamper him," Michael said in a 'matter of fact' manner.

"He does usually, but I think he is just having an off day and I don't want him to get agitated for the rest of the evening, as you know what he is like and how hard it is to settle him down once he is in that kind of state."

Michael started to feel exasperated within himself. And from the information he had just learned, he now understood why Chris would not have wanted to stick around to be further exposed to anyone else that might remotely know him. However, he decided to humour Chris and agreed to his request, letting him think that he had got the upper hand over the situation. When indeed it was him who had the upper hand over something Chris did not know that he was now aware of. He had also made the decision not to quiz Chris on his past, but rather would do his own investigation to get to the bottom of things. Once again, someone had lied to him, and he was left having to unravel their mess and envisaged that the ride back home would not be a comfortable one.

Michael placed his empty cup on the table with the other used cups and beckoned to Chris. "Yes, we can leave now. We wouldn't want you to have to deal with an agitated child for the rest of the evening, now would we?"

Chris smiled mistaking Michael's sarcasm as a joke and was relieved that they were finally going to be leaving. "That's great, let's hit the road then, hopefully the traffic will be kind to us too."

"Let's hope."

The ride home was quiet with Michael not really engaging in the conversation that Chris was trying to keep going, only giving the occasional grunt in the appropriate places. Chris put it down to the fact that Michael might have been tired after such a long day of listening to one presentation after the other and needed to concentrate as they drove home.

Chris played the scene over again in his mind, seeing Nathan waving to him and wondered how that might have transpired. He hadn't seen Nathan since he left his former practice and didn't want to make small talk with him, especially not in front of Michael. Nathan might have started discussing matters he had laid to rest when he left Chichester and Chris was not in the frame of mind to start going down memory lane. With any luck, he had dodged the bullet on that one and when Nathan made his way through the crowd and did not see him. Hopefully he would have thought he had made a mistake and gone back to what he was originally doing.

There was a build-up of traffic on the way home, but Michael's skillful manoeuvring got them home in good time. When they got to Chris' house, he thanked Michael for the lift and waved him off.

<hr/>

Chapter Twenty-Eight

*M*ichael had a restless night, tossing and turning, as he processed everything that had transpired the day before. He felt that he was in a tug of war all over again, wrestling to decipher the facts and what was truth from what wasn't. He still had his relationship with Carol to get around in his thoughts, so did not appreciate the added pressure that had arrived at his door, once again, for him to sort out.

When it came to issues concerning the practice, Michael always relied on Joan's acumen to sort matters out, which is why he had called her the night before as soon as he had got home and arranged to meet her the next morning for an urgent meeting before opening hours. Michael did not explain to Joan what the matter was about, only that it was urgent and needed immediate attention. With the CQC due in a matter of weeks, this was not something that could be swept under the carpet and forgotten about as if it had never happened. This was now a matter of importance, and Michael and Joan would have to determine how they were going to deal with the issue.

Michael arrived at the surgery first and opened the door, disengaging the alarm in the process and then headed straight to his office. Once he had taken off his coat and turned on his laptop, Michael headed straight into the kitchen to put the coffee on so that it would be fresh and ready for when Joan got there, who he was expecting imminently. He heard a sound of keys and the front door being opened and popped his head out of the kitchen to check that it was indeed Joan who had arrived. Michael would not have made a good detective, as he was too jittery when being involved in secret encounters. Of course, it would be Joan arriving as none of the other staff members needed to be in the office as early as their planned 8 am meet-up time. "Hey, it's you Joan, good morning."

"Yes, it is me Michael, who else are you expecting?" Joan said intrigued. Michael's conversation the night before was very cryptic, and he did not divulge much, only that it was imperative that they met up early the next morning. "Where's Chris then?"

Michael walked back to the kitchen. "Just sort yourself out and I'll meet you in the conference room. I've put the coffee on, so I'll explain everything when we are sat down."

Joan dutifully did as she was told and went to her office to put her things down. Not stopping to do anything else and strolled down the corridor into the conference room where the smell of coffee enveloped the room. "Ooooh, that coffee smells good, thanks Michael." Joan took the cup of coffee Michael had poured out for her and sat at the conference table, whilst he poured one for himself. "Now what's this all about Dr Mills?" Joan used Michael's title as she teased about why they were meeting so early in the office.

Michael tutted and looked directly towards Joan's gaze. "Houston, we have a problem on our hands." Michael then explained to Joan verbatim everything that had transpired at the conference, the previous day, culminating with the revelatory conversation he had had with Dr Nathan Kelly.

Joan gasped and had a shocked look on her face as she put her hand across her mouth. "Michael, this is not good. We have the CQC coming up in a matter of weeks and this is one of the first things they are going to check, our credentials as doctors. What does Chris think he is playing at, jeopardising our practice like this?"

"I know, Joan. I was just as shocked as you when

I first heard and even though Nathan was trying not to divulge the entire facts, he dropped enough breadcrumbs for there to be a trail. Come to think of it, Chris seemed very jittery all morning and we both know that he did not really want to go to the conference in the first place and tried on numerous occasions for you to go instead. Now we know why. So, what are we going to do about this?" Michael threw his hands up in the air.

"This one really got away from us didn't it and it's my fault. I'm usually so on board with matters of such importance, But I recall now, at that time when George was leaving, we were desperate to find his replacement and we dropped the ball by taking on Chris rather quickly, with the proviso that his references would follow shortly after him and then we just got on with practice life and sadly the matter got buried."

"No, Joan, I won't have you blaming yourself. We both got played in a sense if that's even a word that can be used in this situation. Chris Harris knew exactly what he was doing, and we were just the unfortunate suckers who got hoodwinked on this occasion."

"Well, I'm going to follow through on this straightaway and get to the bottom of what happened and why we did not get the references we asked for. So, in the meantime how do we play this with Chris? Do we just act like nothing has happened?" Joan asked.

"Yes, we do exactly that. At this moment in time, we do not have any hard evidence, so anything we say would be circumstantial and then he could turn things around and try to back pedal his way out of the situation. No, let you and I play this one as smooth as he has for all these months. Let's get our facts first and then we can confront him with whatever we find." Michael was determined to get to the bottom of whatever was going on and wanted to do it following the right protocol.

"So, what I need to do is call Chris' previous practice and establish if I can arrange a video conference via our Cisco WebEx system where we both can speak with the appropriate individual to ascertain the exact circumstances as to why Chris left their employ. I think that is the best way forward, don't you?" Joan was just as keen as Michael to get matters sorted out sooner, rather than later, considering the upcoming CQC review.

"I think that's a great plan, Joan, as we need this dealt with as soon as possible." The meeting between Michael and Joan lasted approximately 20 minutes and they still had plenty of time before Janet was due in. Chris was at the hospital that morning, so was not due into the surgery until late in the afternoon. "Well, I guess we better get back to our desks and do what we know to do best."

Michael smiled as he got up and took the empty cups with him.

He was determined not to let Chris' indiscretions ruin the good reputation of the practice that he and Joan had worked hard to build and would put on his professional hat to make sure that was not done. Joan agreed and followed behind Michael.

When Janet arrived, it was evident that the doctors were in the surgery before her. But she was none the wiser by the secret meeting that Michael and Joan had earlier, as the doctors would often arrive early to get ahead if they wanted to prepare for a busy day and from the look of the appointment book, Michael and Joan had appointments back-to-back for the entire morning. Janet cleared the cups in the kitchen and put a fresh pot of coffee on, to be on tap, as and when the doctors needed a refreshment break, and then prepared the reception area for their first influx of patients.

The first thing Joan did as she went back to her office was pull up Chris' profile on her laptop, which gave her the details of his previous practice. She noted that there was a note stating that they would take Chris on with his references to follow. However, felt personally responsible as there was no diary note made for a future date to follow this through. Joan used and relied on her Outlook tasks reminder to help keep herself in check, which clearly failed on this particular occasion. *I can't believe that I forgot to put a reminder regarding this issue and the matter has now got to where it is. Where was my head back then?*

Joan was in the middle of a divorce at the time when Chris had started, which may have contributed to her ambiguity and not being as perceptive as she usually was. It was a divorce she did not see coming, with her ex-husband being unfaithful, blaming her that she cared more about her work than their marriage. However, Joan was thankful that they did not have any children and therefore it was a clean break. When she first heard about Michael's issues, she could empathise somewhat with the emotions he was going through, knowing what it felt like to be betrayed in a relationship.

Joan only had half an hour before her first patient and called the number on file and spoke to a lady who dealt with the administrative matters at Chris' former practice. Joan explained that she needed to set up a video conference meeting with the appropriate individual as they needed to discuss an important matter concerning one of their ex-colleagues.

The person on the other end, seemed taken aback at first, when she mentioned Chris Harris' name and put her on hold for about five minutes. The individual came back saying that was something she could sort out and offered Joan a time when the meeting could be set up. Joan was ecstatic that they were on the right track to sorting out the mess she felt responsible for causing and thanked the individual as she put the phone down. Joan then dialled Michael's number. "Hey Michael, just quickly. I wanted to say that I just rang Chris' former practice."

"My goodness Joan, you really weren't joking when you said you would get on to the matter were you?" Michael was impressed with the speed and thoroughness that Joan showed in wanting to resolve the matter.

"Well, you know what I'm like. Strike whilst the iron is hot is my motto." She chuckled. "Anyway, I've arranged an early video conference meeting tomorrow at the same time of 8 am, if you're up for that."

"Sounds good to me, Joan. The sooner we can find out what we are dealing with, the better. Thanks a lot for getting this sorted before we started work, as looking at the diary, it looks like we have a busy morning, so I'll talk to you later."

"Yes, we do Michael. Okay until tomorrow's meeting then. Have a great day."

Michael and Joan were up at the crack of dawn and

in the surgery poised for their meeting with Chris' former practice. They followed the same routine as the morning before, but this time, they turned the widescreen monitor on in the conference room, which was adjacent to the wall and was used for video conferencing calls or training, whenever it was needed for that purpose.

"We really must stop meeting like this," Michael joked as he sipped his coffee and relaxed himself into his chair.

"Yes, I know what you mean. These early meetings are seriously damaging my beauty sleep," Joan responded. "Right, are you ready?"

"As ready as I'll ever be," Michael responded with a sense of urgency and yet he was intrigued as to what can of worms they were going to unearth.

"Okay, then let's do this." Joan dialled the number and after a few minutes, a distinguished looking gentleman, with silvery hair and who appeared to be peering over his glasses fumbling around with the technology, answered the call. Joan took the opportunity to introduce herself and Michael and in turn, the gentleman on the other side of the screen, introduced himself as Dr Kelly, the Senior Partner at the practice. Michael enquired if he was related in any way to a Dr Nathan Kelly he had met a couple of days prior at the medical conference he attended. Dr Kelly senior confirmed that Nathan was indeed his son, who used to work with him at the practice.

Following the introductions, Joan was keen to get started to state the nature of their call. "Well, firstly may we say, thank you Dr Kelly for agreeing to meet with us at such short notice, as I know your time must be very valuable, as is ours, but we have an urgent matter that has arisen, which we wanted to address as soon as possible."

Dr Kelly was an elderly gentleman and not at all familiar with the technology he was using and seemed distracted with his headphones, that kept falling out of his ears and he was muttering under his breath. "Rebecca, please can you help me with this?" Dr Kelly beckoned to someone who also was in the room, presumably to aid him if he got stuck on the call. "Sorry about this." He apologised profusely to Michael and Joan. "I'm not really familiar with all this fancy technology. Just give me a simple telephone or an actual face to face meeting and I'm fine with that."

"That's quite alright Dr Kelly, you take your time."

Rebecca, presumably his PA, lent over to him and adjusted his headphones and appeared to quickly coach him through what he had to do.

"Ahh that's better." Dr Kelly straightened up himself, ready to start again. "Sorry, please continue." Rebecca was visible in the monitor, deciding to stay by his side in case anything else went wrong whilst he was in the meeting.

Joan continued, "Again, Dr Kelly, our thanks for meeting with us. We wanted to talk with you about Chris Harris, who we believe used to work at your practice about a year ago."

Dr Kelly responded, "Ahh yes, Dr Harris. Is he still around?"

"Well, yes he is." Joan tapped her fingers on the desk in anticipation of what was coming next and continued. "He joined our practice, following the departure of one of our colleagues who urgently took up a post abroad. We were inundated with a lot of work at the time. However, we were happy with Chris' interview and agreed to take him on with the understanding that his references were to follow thereafter. But having recently checked our records, we have noticed that those references never did materialise, which was the fault on our part for not requesting them from your practice."

Michael lent his voice to the conversation. "It was only after briefly meeting your son, Nathan, at the conference that threw disparity as to whether he thought Chris was still practicing medicine, which was something that caught my attention. When I got back, we checked our files and found that we did not really have anything substantial on Chris by way of recommendation from your practice and we have a CQC due anytime soon.

Dr Kelly nodded and rubbed his chin with his hand. "Yes, I can see how that would look with the CQC if your credentials were not up to scratch. Well, you're probably not going to like what I have to say. Dr Harris was with us for about five years, and by all accounts, he was a brilliant doctor. But lived somewhat on the edge in terms of administering new drugs, especially the types of medicine we should be prescribing to our patients, which got him into hot water a couple of times, I can tell you." Dr Kelly seemed concerned over that point. "Well, I am sure you are aware that his wife died."

"Yes, we were aware of that," Michael confirmed.

"Well, here is the strange thing. His family was not convinced that his wife died of the cancer she was severely suffering with, and they accused Dr Harris of perhaps helping his wife to ease the extreme pain she was in by giving her a concoction of drugs to ease her suffering. Now, I know, that's one serious accusation, but we were duty bound to take their complaint on board and launch an investigation. His wife, Jill was a twin, and her sister Tilly, took her death the hardest and she was convinced that Chris had something to do with her quick demise and, therefore, was the driving force behind pushing for this investigation and getting to the bottom of the matter. We spoke to Dr Harris to let him know that we had no other choice but to start the proceedings and then just like that, Dr Harris disappeared, and we have not seen or heard from him since. It was only when my son mentioned to me that he thought he saw him at the conference, that we assumed that he had relocated somewhere else and must have still been practising medicine."

Michael and Joan both sat glued to their seats stunned at the revelation that was just dropped into their laps. Michael was the first to speak, clearing his throat. "So, what you are saying is that Chris was not struck off the register and technically he is still within the law to practice medicine?"

"Well, yes, I guess if you put it like that, he is free to still practice, but his family won't be dropping this matter any time soon, and whenever they find him, they will continue to pursue proceedings. Whilst I had no way of knowing whether they were right or wrong in their assumptions, the fact that Dr Harris just up and left would suggest some sort of guilt on his part, don't you think?"

Dr Kelly peered over his glasses, wide-eyed, with that schoolmaster look on his face as if someone were about to be scolded. "I understand how that must have looked at the time and certainly Chris did not do himself any favours by not sticking around and facing the music, but could that have been attributed to his state of mind at the time, having just lost his wife and then being accused that perhaps he helped her to end her suffering?"

Having now heard the full side of the story, Joan was showing empathy as to Chris' state of mind and what would have made him just up and leave, his work, loved ones and his surroundings.

Michael was inquisitive as to where Dr Kelly's practice stood in terms of still releasing a reference, as the upcoming CQC was dominant in his thoughts. "So, Dr Kelly, can I ask you where you are in terms of agreeing to give Chris a reference now?"

Dr Kelly paused, took his glasses off and put one of the handles in the tip of his mouth. He had to think long and hard as to what he felt was the right course of action. "Technically, we would have given you a reference based on the work Dr Harris did at the practice, which as I said, would have been glowing at the time. But we can't dismiss the investigation element that we were faced with." Dr Kelly continued to ponder as he lent back in his chair.

Michael and Joan glanced at each other, using facial expressions to communicate with each other, wondering which way the decision was going to be swayed. After about five minutes of Dr Kelly contemplating, he was ready to give his conclusion of the matter. "Given the circumstances, we would still be prepared to give a reference based on his professional acumen at the time, but we would have to add in a clause explaining that we were about to start an investigation on him regarding a complaint of malpractice. It would then be for you to decide whether you would have been happy at the time to get such a reference and whether you would still have employed Dr Harris under those terms. One further thing that we would request is the whereabouts of where Dr Harris is residing, so that the family can continue to pursue their investigation. I am not sure what can or cannot be proved now, after such a length of time has passed, but we owe it to them to help them be able to put the matter to rest, seeing that the grandparents haven't seen their grandson for over a year. Nor do they know where he is."

Joan responded first. "Can you just give us a couple of minutes Dr Kelly to discuss the matter?"

"Yes, sure, that is fine."

Joan muted the volume on the remote and her and Michael started to have a serious conversation as to what they felt was the best course of action. "I think we're just going to have to go with what Dr Kelly is offering. At least we will have a reference for our records, albeit somewhat ambiguous." Joan shuddered and continued. "We can't ask him to backdate the reference, as the CQC will want to know why we did not do anything about the matter at the time that it was made known to us. So, I think we will have to face the music with them when we cross that bridge."

Michael voiced annoyingly, "I can't believe Chris put us in a position like this and blatantly tried to deceive us. Thinking that we would never find out about this. But you are right, we have no other choice than to take the deal that is being offered on the table and, as you say, face whatever consequences is coming our way."

"Okay, so we are in agreement then." Joan unmuted their volume and they both faced the monitor to speak directly with Dr Kelly. "Thanks, Dr Kelly, for your understanding in the matter," Joan said. "We would be prepared to accept the terms and conditions that you have proposed."

"Good, I will get my secretary to prepare the reference and then we will forward it on to you. Can I suggest that when you sit down and talk with Dr Harris that you impress on him that it is within his best interest to get the matter resolved sooner rather than later? If he has nothing to hide, then the investigation will reveal that. Anyway, good luck with things. I have a meeting to prepare for so I must go now."

Michael and Joan both thanked Dr Kelly for his assistance and understanding in the matter and ended the conference call. "Well that certainly was a lot of information to take in, wasn't it? And now comes the fun part, in confronting our Dr Harris. Although, I wonder what that will conjure up, now we know his backstory and that his cover is blown." Joan winced.

"Indeed," Michael added. "This should be interesting. So be ready for anything."

———◆◇◆———

Chapter Twenty-Nine

*C*arol was in the kitchen finishing off the dishes she had started preparing earlier. Even though she was not the world's best cook, Carol was determined that her guests would enjoy what little culinary skills she felt she was blessed with. Olivia and Steve were due to arrive shortly, and Carol still had not laid the table or got herself ready. Carol was looking forward to entertaining her friends. It was something she hadn't done in a while and had kept promising Olivia that she would have her and Steve over for a meal, although it saddened her that the picture would be incomplete.

She had always imagined her and Olivia in a foursome, meeting up with their respective husbands or partners and just enjoying each other's company, around a meal or some other fun activity. And yet here she was all alone, not knowing where things were really going with her and Michael. Carol's hopes of getting a glimpse of Michael on Sundays were also dashed, since she noticed that he had not been coming to church and wondered what that was all about. It was something she was hoping to prize out of Steve when he came over to ascertain what the reason was and to learn anything else that Michael had got up to, as the interaction with him since he had left the marital home was next to none.

Carol wondered with them not seeing or interacting with each other, how that was supposed to solve the problem or bring them back closer together. Yet she had to accept that this was the plan for now and she just had to sit tight and hope that things would change soon for the better.

Like clockwork, Steve was at Olivia's house for 7 pm and tooted his horn to indicate that he was outside. Olivia quickly gathered her things and made a dash for the door. She was looking forward to seeing Carol and spending an evening with her. Although she had hoped that the circumstances could have been different and that Steve could have at least had some male company to even things out, she prayed that he would feel comfortable and not out of place, which is something she was keen to talk with him about in the car before they got there. Steve watched as Olivia locked her door and he got out to open the passenger side of his Porsche.

"Why thank you, Mr Adams." Olivia smiled as she graciously responded to Steve's act of chivalry. He was old school when it came to little touches like that and how he felt a woman should be treated. And it was something that Olivia was growing accustomed to, as she relished the attention to detail that Steve had exhibited in their relationship that had turned from friendship into a courtship.

Once Olivia was settled comfortably in the car, she was keen for her and Steve to know the nature of conversation they planned to have when they saw Carol and the sensitivity that would no doubt be needed. "You are welcome, Miss Dupont. How has your day been?"

"It was good, thanks. You know how much I love those kids, so going into school every day is always such a blessing rather than a chore, as some may feel."

"Yes, I do know how much you love that job, and also how much your students love you. They are blessed to have someone as caring and loving as you, teaching them."

"Ahh thanks Steve, I appreciate that. So, how did your day go?"

"Well, not as good as I would have hoped." Steve appeared exhausted as if he would just have sooner stayed at home to chill and relax and did not feel that he would be the best company, but he wanted to support

Olivia. He also did not want to offend Carol by cancelling at the last minute, especially as he imagined that she would have gone to great efforts to prepare for their visit. Steve continued, "As you know, some days are quite challenging, and today was one of those days. There is this particular kid who is hell bent on destroying his life. He is always getting into trouble with the authorities, and he just doesn't seem to care about the trajectory of where his life is going, as it continues to spiral out of control. But that's what I am there for and with God's help, I am determined that he will make something out of his life."

Olivia rested her hand on Steve's shoulder by way of comfort. "You're a good man, Steve Adams, and I know that the students you manage are sometimes a bit of a handful to say the least, but if anyone can straighten them out and set them on the right course, it's you. So be encouraged that God will give you the wisdom and direction to handle each student and change the course of their lives."

"Thanks Liv, you always know the right things to say, at just the right time and that's what I've always admired about you."

Olivia smiled and appreciated Steve's compliment. "Now, just a quick battle plan for when we get to Carol's house, as I want us to be on the same page in what we talk about. Obviously, the conversation will veer towards her and Michael at some point, but if we can keep it light rather than prying, I think that might be respective of her. What do you think?" Olivia was keen to get Steve's perspective on things and didn't want it to seem as though she was dominating the way how things should play out that evening.

Steve nodded in agreement with Olivia. "Oh, I totally agree. However, I can only be honest in how things have been because as you know, Michael and I have been meeting up regularly to play badminton and go to the gym and I have seen the vulnerable side of him in all of this, but I won't divulge the nature of our conversations since he has told me about those things in private."

"Yeah, I appreciate that, and neither should you have to. Just be prepared for Carol quizzing you in a roundabout way just to find out where Michael is at these days. As she's good at that." Steve agreed and appreciated that the evening wasn't going to be an easy one for Carol and he valued the sentiments too in the invite they had been afforded.

Steve and Olivia arrived at the house and were unanimous as to where they both stood as they walked up the drive. Olivia was armed with a pot plant of Carol's favourite flower, an orchid. And Steve was empty handed, not realising what the protocol was when being invited to dinner.

"Sorry, Liv, I didn't bring anything," he winced.

"Don't worry, Carol won't be offended. She'll just be glad we both turned up." Olivia smiled as she rang the doorbell.

Carol had managed to get herself ready in the nick of time, having laid the table to her specification. Attention to detail was her middle name and if she was going to do something, she was going to do it right.

"Hey, you two," Carol said with a glee as she opened the door. "Nice to see you both, come on in." Carol showed her guests in and took their coats.

"This is for you, hon," Olivia said extending her hands with the pot plant towards Carol.

"Ohh wowww, you shouldn't have. And it's my favourite plant too, as you well know. But thank you both, it's lovely and I know just the place for it." Carol placed the plant on a shelf by the window to allow it to get sufficient light, whilst Olivia and Steve made themselves comfortable in the lounge area.

Steve was mesmerised, as he looked around, by the décor and the way the room felt warm and inviting and was keen to let Carol know, being careful with his wording and remembering the conversation between him and Olivia in the car. "Carol, the place looks amazing. You've done such a great job, although I would not have expected anything less considering the line of work you are in." Steve sipped on a drink that Carol had brought in for them to enjoy and had appropriately placed some nibbles on a coffee table in front of them both.

"Thanks Steve, we have worked hard to get this place to the way we wanted it. You were there on demolition day. I recall you helping us getting all the rubbish out of the place, so you know what it looked like before. It was a labour of love, but we got there in the end."

Carol was reflective as she pondered over the history of her and Michael's journey together and the days of laughter they had working on the house. The furniture hunting they did to ensure they got the right pieces to match the décor that Carol had designed. Michael knew he wasn't going to win any arguments in that department and was happy to leave that part to Carol. But he was adamant that he was going to have some sort of say in the matter and put his foot down when it came to some of the pieces of furniture they bought for the house. Carol was happy to give them both a tour around the house which only added to the depth of her talent and yet she was enjoying this all without the one person who it was meant for, her beloved husband.

After the tour, Carol invited her guests to come to the table as she brought the food in from the kitchen. "Wowww, it smells lovely, Carol, and I'm intrigued to see what you've made for us." Olivia smiled, knowing that it was a big deal for Carol to even attempt to put this dinner party on singlehanded.

"Well, I kept it simple and did something I knew I could do well, so I hope you both don't mind having Spaghetti Bolognese."

Steve was the first to jump in. "Works for me and actually, I'm quite famished, as it goes."

"Good Steve, as I've made enough to go around, as I know how much you guys love your food. This is one of Michael's favourites too." Steve and Olivia glanced at each other intensively at the mention of his name as they knew it was only a matter of time when he would be introduced to their conversation. "Have you seen much of him?" Carol asked in an inquisitive way as she passed the large serving bowl of pasta to Steve for him to help himself with what he wanted.

"Err, yeah, we are still doing our regular meet ups."

"Oh, that's good" Carol commented.

"I need that six pack intact for when he comes home. I've not really seen much of him myself as I send his mail on to his temporary address. I had hoped that at least I might get a glance of him on Sundays, and get the opportunity to have a catch up, but again haven't seen him. Unless he has been going to the early service that is."

Steve braced himself mentally as to how much he was prepared to divulge to Carol that evening. However, he could hear the concern in her voice and appreciated how hard this must be for her in all that she was going through.

Carol passed the other bowl with the mince towards Olivia's direction. "Here you go Olivia, made just the way you like it and I incorporated some of your secrets you entrusted to me."

Olivia smiled as she took the bowl. "Well, I'm glad to see my hard work paid off and you were actually paying attention all those times when I was trying to make a master chef out of you."

The conversation throughout the evening remained light and jovial, with Carol asking Steve and Olivia about how things were progressing with their plans. The couple shared that they planned to get married within the next 6-9 months since they really didn't need a long courtship, having known each other for a number of years.

"Carol, that was a lovely meal. I really enjoyed it." Olivia was keen to let her friend know that she really had done a great job, especially as she knew words of affirmation was Carol's love language and to put her mind at rest, as such words would be relished and appreciated by Carol.

Steve was quick to second that. "Yes, thanks Carol. That was hearty and delicious and filled the empty hole I had, even if I had a few helpings." They all laughed.

Changing the subject, Carol wanted to enquire about Chris and Jen's relationship, since now that Michael wasn't around, she wasn't getting her regular fill of the latest gossip and that was killing her. "Olivia, how's your housemate's relationship with Chris going these days?" Carol cleverly slipped the question into the conversation as she attempted to clear away the dishes from the table.

"Oh, you mean Jen?" Olivia said surprisingly, as the question had caught her off guard. "To be honest, I really don't know how it is going. There is a 10-year age gap between them and I'm not sure that they have a lot in common, but that's just my opinion and observation of the matter." Olivia didn't want it to appear evident that she did not really approve of the relationship between the two of them, especially in light of some of the issues Jen had shared with her, such as Chris' controlling nature and his erratic behaviour at times.

Carol seemed intrigued, but still pushed for more information, in her usual inquisitive way. "Ahh, that's a shame, as I was hopeful that Chris had finally found someone he could move on with, He seems a nice chap."

Olivia tried hard to hide any emotions that her face might have revealed. "Carol, you act as if he's one of your best buddies. How well do you know him?"

"Well, I guess, I don't know him that well. But ever since he came to the practice, Michael was keen to make him feel welcome, and I occasionally talked to him whenever I was at the surgery, and he was always pleasant to me; that's all I am referring to." Olivia was quick to respond.

"Well sometimes, looks aren't always what they appear to be," Olivia said and hoped that might bring to the conclusion that you cannot always judge a book by its cover.

"Yes, I hear you," Carol said as she got up from the table to take the plates into the kitchen.

"Here, let me help you with those, Carol," Steve said

as he hurried to assist her with the awkward way she had piled the plates on top of each other, also trying to juggle the bigger serving bowls.

"Oh, thanks Steve, that would be great as I don't seem to be doing a very good job on my own am I. Anyone for dessert? I made a banoffee pie."

"You really are spoiling us tonight, aren't you?" Olivia responded with a hint of excitement in her voice.

"Well, I'll not say no to banoffee pie if it's on offer," Steve said gladly as he followed behind Carol towards the kitchen. The banoffee pie went down well, which they finished off with coffees in the lounge area. All in all, it was a good night considering that it was Carol's first dinner party having guests around without Michael by her side, hovering over her to see what she was doing. Olivia and Steve left having thanked their host for an enjoyable evening.

Chapter Thirty

*O*livia was looking forward to a relaxing evening and having some well-deserved 'me' time. She had not made any plans to see Steve as she needed to start on the prep work as she was teaching a Sunday School class the next day. She had over ambitiously told the children that she was going to prepare them a model ark with various animals depicting the story in the Bible of Noah and the ark. For anyone else, that would not be classed as a relaxing evening, but Olivia loved the buzz of being creative and could not wait to see the excitement of the children as she used the props to teach them truths from the Bible. She couldn't help from thinking that one day, someone could be doing the same thing for her and teaching any children that she and Steve might be blessed with.

Olivia had the larger of the three rooms in the house, which could comfortably fit a table in the corner of the room, which was covered with an array of arts and crafts needed to create her masterpiece. She was careful to stay in her room as she had a frank conversation with Jen a few days prior, who informed her that she was ending her relationship with Chris and wondered if she could invite him around to have a chat with him. Olivia had confirmed that it would be okay and wanted to give them the space and privacy to be able to meet in the lounge area.

Olivia popped downstairs to check on Jen, as she imagined how she might be feeling. Even though Jen was young in age, there was a tender and vulnerable side to her nature that Olivia felt inclined to protect as a protective big sister and it was Olivia who pressed Jen to examine her relationship with Chris to see if indeed it was the best for her and whether she was getting everything out of it that she deserved.

"Hey, how are you doing? Are you okay?" Olivia appeared concerned as she walked into the lounge and saw Jen nervously shuffle the cushions from one settee to the next, pumping them up and repositioning them to appear staged, like a showroom.

"I'm doing okay. No, that's not totally true," Jen said nervously. "To be honest, I am absolutely terrified as to how he is going to react. Following the many chats, we have had, you are right. You have helped me to see that if this relationship, or whatever it is we have, is not working, then I shouldn't keep trying to force something that isn't taking its natural course. I know I often refer to my parents and the fact that when they first got together it was not necessarily love at first sight, but in time, they learnt to love each other. But I've come to realise that that is their story, not mine, and I think I allowed that to cloud by judgment when it came to Chris."

It was almost as if Jen had an epiphany of what life could be like with Chris if she continued in the relationship. If she was being honest with herself, she could see there was still unresolved emotional issues with Chris over the loss of his wife, who Jen came to realise that he idolised somewhat, and she wondered if Chris was using her as a way to unconsciously feel connected to Jill.

On a rare occasion that Jen visited Chris at his house, she spotted on the mantelpiece a picture of Jill who bore an uncanny similarity to her appearance, in terms of hair colour and physical features. Jen wondered if perhaps that was the reason Chris suggested she wore her hair in a particular way or advised on colours or styles he thought looked best on her and accentuated her physique. Jen was young and had a lot going for her and didn't want to be restricted by a man telling her what she could or could not do. Or how to wear her hair or style of clothing.

Olivia walked over and gave Jen a hug. "You've got this girl. All you have to do is be honest and God will help you with the rest." As they were both in an embrace, the doorbell rang. "That's probably him now, so let me quickly get out of the way.... and, Jen, you're going to be just fine." Olivia gave her a thumbs up, tiptoed out of the room and ran back upstairs so that she would be inconspicuous for the evening and out of the way.

Jen showed Chris into the lounge and they both sat opposite each other engaging in small talk. "So, does Ben have one of his sleepovers tonight then?" Talking about Ben, Jen hoped would help ease the flow of the conversation into what might be a bit heavier towards the end of the evening.

"Yeah, he's at his best friend Simon's house for the night. Actually, he was so looking forward to it this evening that he couldn't wait for me to drop him off. Kids, eh?" Chris smiled as he recalled the way Ben jumped out of the car as they pulled in the drive to Simon's house and nearly forgot to take with him his overnight case.

"That's good," Jen commented. "Oh, I forgot to ask you how the conference went, since we haven't spoken for a while regarding that? I bet you were surrounded by too many likeminded professionals, eh?"

"Yes, you know what it can be like. But I must admit, Michael and I picked up some good ideas to be implemented in the future and I especially enjoyed the seminar talking about the latest news drugs and medicine that are being trialled." Chris' tone heightened in excitement talking about a subject he was passionate about.

Jen continued in her line of questioning appearing to be interested in Chris' life. "And how is life at the surgery?"

Chris stumbled with his answer and Jen detected a note of concern that perhaps not all was well. "Work has been busy. I've had quite a few periods where I have been at the hospital a lot."

Jen jumped in. "Yes, I briefly glanced you there on Friday, but we had an emergency, so I didn't have time to stop and say hello."

Chris continued, "Oh, okay. No, surgery life is fine, although I always get the sense that I am being left out of things, as Michael and Joan seem to whisper a lot, have meetings in each other's rooms and Michael seems a bit off with me at the moment and I can't really put my finger on what the problem seems to be."

Chris knew that technically he was still considered as the newbie, having gone into an already established practice where relationships were strongly forged. But he thought that he had seemingly passed that probation period and was being accepted as one of the elite and, yet at times, it felt like he was still an outsider, looking in.

"That must be hard trying to find your place." Jen empathised with what Chris was going through, herself being new to the area, having taken up a new assignment, being thrown into the mix, also going to a new church. It wasn't always easy trying to know where you fitted in. "I hope you don't mind, but I didn't want to cook and have ordered an Indian takeaway for us." Jen got up and went in the corner to retrieve her bag.

"Sounds great," Chris said.

"The only snag is that I have to quickly pop out to get it. It's only a 10 min walk."

"Do you want some company then?" Chris said chivalrously.

"No, you stay and relax. I'll put on some music, and I will literally be there and back in a jiffy."

"Okay, well if you insist, I'll just let the music do its magic."

Jen smiled as she handed Chris the remote. "Here, you can change the tracks and control the volume yourself until I get back." And on that note, Jen was out of the door. The Indian takeaway was a favourite of hers and Olivia's when they wanted to be lazy and not slave over a hot stove. They especially liked their lamb biryani and poppadom and Jen enjoyed spending nights in with Olivia who took great care to pour into her life and be like the big sister she never had.

Olivia heard the door close and wondered what made Chris leave so early. *Oh my gosh, he must not have taken the breakup well, slammed the door and walked out. I hope Jen is alright. Perhaps I'll quickly go downstairs to check.*

Meanwhile, Chris had got up to stretch his legs. Jen had left him with a drink, which he had in his hand, as he manoeuvred around the room, looking with interest at the art on the wall and appreciating that it was similar in taste to what he would have bought. He assumed Olivia had gone out and that he and Jen had the place to themselves for the evening. Olivia strolled down the stairs and heard loud music coming from the lounge and wondered why Jen had the volume up so loud.

Olivia burst into the room "Hey Jen, the music is a bit loud, isn't it?" She was startled and surprised to see that instead it was Chris in the room. "Oh…, hi Chris…err, I didn't realise…. You were here." Her gaze spun around the room as she wondered where Jen was.

"Oh, hi too. Sorry, I was just enjoying this particular track by Marvin Sapp and didn't realise that you were at home." Chris also seemed stunned by Olivia's appearance and yet pleasantly surprised by the way she looked in her casual attire, a flowy kaftan and her hair tied loosely in a bun on the top of her head.

Chris turned the volume down which was evidently loud as they seemed to be shouting above the music. "Jen popped out to get us a takeaway. I didn't realise that you were here and had assumed that perhaps you were out with Steve." Chris sat back down on the settee and Olivia made a concerted effort to exit the room as quickly as she barged in, since she did not feel that she was appropriately addressed for company.

Slipping into a kaftan was her safe mode, and her way of saying, I'm at home, I'm chilling, and I don't really have to dress up as no one is going to see the way I look, which made her comfortable and relaxed. It was not an attire she would have greeted Steve in either, choosing rather to keep things respectable, free from anything that could be construed as temptation, since it was sheer, and the shape of her body was visible through the material.

"No, I was upstairs, prepping work for a Sunday school class that I am teaching tomorrow and I only popped downstairs to get a drink." Olivia bended her truth slightly as it was obvious that Jen had not spoken to Chris yet about the real reason he was there, and she didn't want him to know that she was aware of what was about to transpire when Jen got back. Olivia slipped out of the room and headed for the kitchen to get a drink, with the intention of going back to her room as quickly as possible.

Chris appeared relaxed and comfortable in his skin Olivia thought, *It's a pity he doesn't know what is about to hit him.* Olivia was deep in thought and didn't hear the door behind her open as she stood in front of the fridge looking to see which juice she was going to choose.

Chris had entered the kitchen and came up very close behind her and almost startled her. "So, how are things between you and Steve going these days?" Chris thought this was as good a time as any, to quiz Olivia as to where her relationship with Steve really stood.

Olivia felt uncomfortable with how close Chris had come up behind her and slammed the fridge door quite sharply as she attempted to move away from him before she answered. "Emmm, we are doing fine. Thanks for asking." Olivia managed to step aside with the box of juice in her hand and reached into the cupboard to get an empty glass.

Chris sensed Olivia's discomfort, but still pushed ahead with his line of questioning. "Don't you think it all happened a bit fast between you and Steve? I mean, we were only talking with each other prior to you getting together. Don't you wonder how things would have panned out if we were still together?"

Olivia's expression dropped as she struggled to understand where on earth the conversation was going and why Chris felt he had the need to bring up something that was really a non-starter in terms of them being together. "I would hardly call what we had a relationship, Chris. You made it quite clear that I was not worth pursuing and I was okay with that, since that was your choice. And I certainly wouldn't want to force any man to be with me if he was having second thoughts. What happened with me and Steve was actually a God-thing. Neither of us saw it coming. Well, let me rephrase that. I didn't see it coming, because if you ask Steve for his version of events, he will tell you that he always knew that we would end up together, and that it was only a matter of time and him waiting on God for it to happen. Now that's the type of faith that I like. A man who knows what he wants and goes after it."

Chris listened intently, whilst positioning himself at the door, blocking Olivia from leaving until he was done with the conversation. "And how do you know that I don't know what I want? What if it's you I want?"

Olivia felt intimidated by Chris and wondered if he

was teasing her or if he was serious. But whichever one it was, she knew that she didn't want to be in the position she felt herself in, trapped in a room with Chris literally breathing down her neck. "Chris, this is not the time or the place to be discussing something like this. Don't be silly. Besides, you are with Jen."

Chris interjected quickly, "But what if I have realised that she is much too young for me, as we have nothing in common, and the feelings I was developing for you before have recently started to resurface?"

Olivia attempted to try and get out of the room, but Chris continued to stand in the doorway making it impossible for her to do so without Olivia physically having to push him out of the way. "Chris, get out of my way. You're being delusional now and you are making me feel uncomfortable."

All sorts of scenarios flashed across Olivia's mind as to how out of hand the matter could get, and she wasn't about to be a victim to any of those thoughts. As she managed to prise her way through the door, Chris grabbed Olivia's waist as she tried to get pass him.

"Get off me, Chris." Olivia pushed him off her and ran. She was in such a hurry, that she spilt some of her juice on the floor but had no time to stick around and clean it up. As she got to the top of the stairs, she heard the front door open, which signalled that Jen had got back home.

Once Olivia got to her room, she put the drink on the table and sat on the edge of her bed, hyperventilating and trying to catch her breath. *What on earth did Chris think he was playing at and how dare he corner and touch me like that, putting me in such a vulnerable position?* Olivia was taken aback by Chris' behaviour as she had never saw him in that light before and wondered if indeed that was the real Chris Harris she had experienced moments earlier and not the persona of dutiful father and downcast widower that he wanted everyone to perceive. Olivia was grateful that Jen had come to her senses in deciding Chris was not her knight in shining armour, which given what had just transpired between them, only reinforced why it was the right decision.

She only hoped it was sooner rather than later and then that man would be out of her house. She also made the decision that it wasn't going to be something she would divulge to Jen, nor Steve for that matter. Olivia deduced that the incident was probably a one-off opportunity that Chris thought he would take, which failed, and she didn't feel that it was worth blowing out of proportion by telling others, even though he crossed the line, big time.

Chris was left standing by the kitchen door when he

heard Jen come back in. He himself didn't even know what just transpired between him and Olivia or why he went for her like that. It was just an opportunity that arose which he wanted to explore in case there was anything left between him and Olivia to pursue. Now that he got Olivia's perspective on the matter, Chris felt he was left with no other choice, but to continue seeing how things developed between him and Jen. He reasoned that perhaps he just needed to try harder and get out of his comfort zone a bit and try activities that were new to him.

"Hey, let me help you with those." Chris walked towards Jen to relieve her from the two bags she had in her hand.

"Thanks Chris. What are you doing out here?" Jen was surprised to see Chris just lurking in the hallway. "Oh, I just briefly popped to the loo and don't worry, I did wash my hands." Jen smiled as Chris followed her to the kitchen. She tumbled slightly, almost losing her balance, when she got to the entrance of the kitchen. "Ohh dear; looks like something has been spilt. I must have done that when I brought your drink out to you earlier. I'll get the mop and clean that up."

"Yeah, you must have. Are you okay?" Chris' performance was stellar considering what had just transpired between him and Olivia and would have won the BAFTA hands down for best villain in a soap opera, the way he did not flinch or react to the situation. Jen mopped up the area in question and Chris helped her to arrange the food on plates for them to eat in the lounge.

They both ate and enjoyed the takeaway and true to form, Jen chose the lamb biriyani and poppadoms, since that was considerably mild compared to other Indian dishes where they might have needed gallons of water to cool down their tongues. Jen was mindful of why she invited Chris around and was gauging the mood of the evening as to when she would drop her bombshell. Now seemed as good a time as any. Jen cleared away their plates and came back into the lounge with two cups of coffee.

"Chris, there's something that I have been meaning to discuss with you, and we haven't had much time to meet in person, which is why I specifically invited you around tonight." Jen cleared her throat and shifted nervously in her seat.

"Oh, yeah?" Chris responded as he sipped his drink, glaring directly into her face, analysing her expressions.

"I don't think this is working Chris." Chris looked puzzled.

"What isn't working?"

383

Jen continued timidly. "I mean us. I don't see the relationship really going anywhere and if you were honest with yourself, you'd agree too that we have some major differences."

"Where is this coming from, Jen? I wasn't aware that you weren't happy." Chris' eyes widened as he put his cup on the side table in a state of confusion. That was the last thing he thought he was going to hear after the pleasant evening he thought they were having. Chris attempted to justify himself, "I mean, I know that I'm not always accessible and that my priority is Ben, but I thought we were doing all right and getting there slowly."

"You see Chris, that's the problem, I want and deserve more than alright. I deserve the best. I don't mean that to sound condescending in any way, but I have seen time and time again, girlfriends of mine who just settle. They aren't always happy in their relationships and instead of doing something about it, they just continually try to fix and patch up a relationship that has run its course. I think what we had was what it was. Just two lonely people looking for love, but in all the wrong places."

"Have you been talking to anyone? Did someone put you up to this?" Chris' mind spiralled trying to understand how Jen had arrived at the conclusion she was making, especially when he did not pick up on any signals that she wasn't happy with what they had.

"No, no-one has put me up to this. I may have spoken to a girlfriend and ran my thoughts by her, but at the end of the day, the decision was mine."

The penny started to drop in Chris' mind. "And I bet that girlfriend is Olivia, isn't it?" Chris suddenly felt threatened that Jen would talk to someone else about their relationship, without discussing things with him first and there was a hint of sarcasm in this voice when he mentioned Olivia's name.

"I'm not going to divulge a confidant. Chris, I am sorry, and I wish you all the best for the future, but I think you need to take some time out to realign your emotions because I don't think you are totally over losing your wife, which is something you must deal with before entering into another relationship."

Chris became defensive at Jen's remarks. "What is that supposed to mean? I admit, I have the odd moment, when I have a trigger of a memory and Jill comes to my thoughts, but I have dealt with my feelings and believe that I am ready to move on."

Jen did not want to labour the point but wanted to let Chris know some of the things he did which brought her to that conclusion. "Chris, you tried to control the way I did my hair or made suggestions about the style of clothes I should wear."

"Well, that was me trying to show interest in you as an individual."

"I don't think it was, Chris. You don't know this, but I saw that creased up photo you carry around in your wallet. It dropped out when we were at the trampoline park. It was a picture of you and a woman, which I presumed was your wife and I had to admit, I had to do a double-take as I thought it was a picture of you and me."

Chris fumbled over his words. "Yes, you are right. You and Jill have uncanny similarities in the way you look, but that has nothing to do with why I wanted to be with you."

"Well, anyway, whether that has anything to do with it or not, my mind is still made up and we have to go our separate ways. Let's not make this complicated. We are both adults and have the same circle of friends and go to the same church so we can at least be civil with each other and just put it down to the fact that we tried, and it did not work. There's no harm or shame in trying."

Chris could see that Jen's mind was made up. Even though he felt in his heart that somehow the girlfriend that Jen confided in was Olivia, he had no proof and had to concede to his fate. "Well, I too am sorry it has come to this Jen, but I will respect your wishes and apologise for anything that I have done to make you feel uncomfortable. Perhaps in a few months you might feel different."

Before Chris could finish his sentence, Jen interrupted him, "No, Chris this is not a temporary separation of some kind, this is a permanent goodbye." Jen did not want to leave Chris under any false impressions that she would be a gullible young lady waiting to reconnect with him after a period had passed and had to be firm and direct with him so that he knew where they stood. Chris rose to his feet realising that there was nothing more to be said. Jen showed him to the door and as she watched him walk away, she closed the door and breathed a sigh of relief that she was finally out of what was potentially turning into a toxic relationship and thanked God that she had the bravery and wisdom to listen to that still small voice in her spirit warning her that all was not what it purported to be.

Chapter Thirty-One

*O*livia was delighted all her hard work had paid off by the reaction she got from her class. The kids were captivated by the hand painted individual animal pieces that Olivia had meticulously taken the time to craft. The colours were vibrant and dazzling giving the kids a visual picture of what Noah's ark would probably have looked like. Olivia was busy tidying up the remnant of what was left after the children asked to take home their favourite animal. Olivia was disappointed not to see Ben in class as she imagined how excited he would have been to see her presentation but understood why he wasn't there. *I see Chris is probably licking his wounds*, Olivia thought, *and if I were him, I wouldn't show up either after what he has done.*

Olivia hurried out the room as she wanted to catch Steve before he left. She had noticed that morning that Carol was not in church either. It was unusual for Carol not to call or text Olivia if she wasn't going to be at church that morning, which worried Olivia as to whether anything was up.

Olivia and Jen travelled to church together and she wanted to find Jen to let her know that she wasn't going to go straight home, but rather would make a detour to check in on Carol. Olivia made her way through the auditorium, greeting individuals as she headed towards the hospitality area, where Jen's bright red jacket gave her away.

"Caught you." Olivia crept up behind Jen just as she was about to put another biscuit in her mouth.

"Guilty as charged," Jen said with a mouth full of biscuit and a cup of coffee in her hand.

"I just wanted to let you know that I am going to pop over to see Carol on my way home, as I haven't seen her this morning, which isn't like her not to let me know. Can I give you a lift halfway? Sorry for the short notice."

"No, don't worry about that. It's a lovely day and the walk home will be good for me to clear my head and breathe in God's beautiful fresh air." Jen was referring to the fact that Chris was finally out of her life, and it felt refreshing to have her life back again, where she could just be herself and not a replica of what others wanted her to be.

"Thanks for being so understanding Jen. I've just

seen Steve over there and I want to catch him too. Enjoy your stroll, girl, and I'll see you at home later. I think I defrosted some lamb chops from the freezer. Well, I hope they were, as I couldn't make out if the bag contained lamb chops, beef or chicken." Olivia smiled. "Anyway, whatever they are, please could you put them in the oven for me and by the time I get home, I'll rustle up something to go with it. I hope I won't be too long with Carol. She was probably having a lazy day or something like that, but either way, it's good to know."

"Yeah, no probs, I'll go ahead and make the dinner, so don't worry. You stay as long as it takes with Carol and your dinner will be waiting for you when you get home."

"You're a doll, Jen; see you later, hon." Olivia made her way to the other side of the room where Steve was just finishing talking to PT.

"Hey there." Steve leant forward to embrace Olivia, giving her a peck on the cheek.

PT started to walk off. "I look forward to seeing you both at your next session."

Olivia greeted PT by shaking his hand. "Yes, will do. Sorry I missed your sermon this morning, but I'll get the CD or listen to it online."

"That's alright, Olivia, you can't be in two places at once you know. Plus, we here at New Dawn value the time and effort you put into our children's programme, given your capacity as a teacher in your chosen profession."

Steve seconded that. "Yes, they are lucky to have her aren't they. And, yes, we will be there, PT, and are looking forward to it. The sessions are helping us tremendously and we feel that they are really preparing us for the road ahead." Olivia agreed and PT left them, continuing on with his rounds of greeting the congregation. It was something he saw as his personal duty to make sure everyone felt included. After all that was the motto and culture of New Dawn.

"I'm glad you found me as I was going to come looking for you to see if you wanted to come to lunch with Michael and I."

"Ohh, I would have loved to, but Carol didn't come to church today, and you know that's not like her to not let me know if she wasn't going to be around, since she seems to think that I need to know her every move these days."

"Very true. That does sound out of character for Carol doesn't it. You go ahead and be with your friend, and I'll be with her other half. Perhaps it's for the best if you don't come after all as I just remembered that Michael said he had something important that he wanted to pick my brains on. I'm hoping that he has finally come to his senses and is planning on going back home. Well, I'm certainly going to have that conversation with him, if it isn't. It's been two months now and he should have sorted his thoughts out by now as to which way things are going to go." Olivia nodded her head in agreement. "But please don't mention any of this to Carol as I wouldn't want her to get her hopes up, if Michael is still on a downward spiral with his life."

"If she asks for you, I might mention that you're having lunch with Michael today, but my lips are sealed on anything else." Olivia motioned and zipped her mouth with her hand to labour the point. "Anyway, I must dash, so you have a nice lunch with Michael and tell him I said hi."

"I will and likewise, I hope you and Carol have some good bonding time, or whatever it is you ladies do when you get together," he teased and they embraced again and went their separate ways.

Olivia arrived at Carol's house and as she pulled into the drive, she noticed Carol's car there, but saw that the drapes were still closed. *At least she's in thank goodness.* Olivia got out of the car and rang the doorbell. After about five minutes with there being no answer, Olivia rang again and went to the window to try and peer in, but she could see no sign of visibility. She walked backwards and looked upstairs to see if she could see the curtains twitching, but again there was no sign of movement. *Where is that girl? I hope she is okay.*

Olivia took out her mobile phone and rang Carol's number. After a few minutes, a groggily sounding voice answered the phone. "Hellooooo?"

"Caz, it's me, Olivia. I've been ringing the doorbell. Can't you hear it? You weren't in church this morning and I just wanted to check in on you."

"No, sorry, I didn't. I'm still in bed."

"Well, you need to let me in. Can you throw the keys out of the window, and I'll let myself in?"

After a few minutes, Olivia noticed movement and Carol opened the window and threw her keys out. Olivia was pleased that her efforts playing netball as a youngster was not wasted and caught the keys that were aimed at her. Olivia let herself in and was met with complete darkness. She first went into the lounge area and opened the blinds to let some light flood into the house. It was such an attractive room, Olivia thought and really was the soul to the entire house.

Olivia ran upstairs and when she reached the top, she turned left and headed towards the master bedroom. Olivia knocked the door and waited for Carol to answer, indicating that it was all right to enter. As she entered, again the darkness of the room met her, and Olivia headed straight towards the window and opened the blinds. Immediately a burst of light hit the room that she had to adjust the blinds slightly to filter some of the natural sunlight. Carol was sat up in bed.

"Caz, what's the matter? Why are you still in bed? Aren't you well?" Olivia was concerned with the way her friend looked and the fact that she was still in bed after 2PM. Carol's face looked drained, which ordinarily isn't an unusual feature for someone who had just woken up suddenly. Yet to Olivia there seemed to be more to the story, since it wasn't like Carol to let anything defeat her. She was such a go-getter and always had a positive outlook on life.

Carol straightened up herself and tried to pat her hair down, thinking it must be sprouting in all directions. "I just felt out of sort, Liv. I had every intention of coming to church this morning, but when I tried to get out of bed, I just felt really awful and the next thing I knew, I just turned on my side and went back to sleep."

"Oh dear, that's not good, is it? So how are you

feeling now?"

"I still have a sickly feeling; perhaps it was something I ate, I don't know."

"Caz, let me go downstairs and make you a mint tea and do you think you could manage some toast if I did that for you too?"

"Let's start with the mint tea and see how I go. In the meantime, I'll just go in the bathroom and have a quick shower, if you don't mind."

"Not at all hon, you take your time. I'm not going anywhere until I know you are fine." Carol slowly dragged herself out of bed and walked towards the en-suite, which was a lifesaver, in such incidences, having a bathroom adjacent to the bedroom.

Olivia ran downstairs towards the kitchen to make the mint tea. She had to open a few cupboards to find where Carol kept the boxes of herbal teas and noticed that there wasn't much food in the cupboards. Olivia became suspicious of the fact that perhaps Carol wasn't looking after herself as well as she ought to and took a sneak peek in the fridge which, again, barely had anything in it which confirmed her suspicions.

With her mobile phone in her pocket, Olivia took it

out and started to make a list of some of the basic things that were needed. She anticipated that it would take Carol about 20 minutes to get herself decent. As she still had Carol's keys with her, she ran upstairs to get her bag. Olivia could hear the water running from the shower and did not want to alert Carol as to what she intended to do and instead allowed her to happily indulge in getting herself aroused and refreshed.

Olivia was familiar with the area and was aware that there was a local food shop very close to Carol's house and drove there to get a few supplies to stock up Carol's empty shelves and fridge. *Goodness knows how long that girl hasn't been to the shops,* Olivia thought and wondered if Carol could be suffering from some sort of depression or breakdown regarding the way her life was panning out, especially since Michael wasn't around and there were no signs of when he would return.

Olivia timed it nicely and got back before Carol had come down the stairs. She stocked up the cupboards and fridge with the items she knew Carol liked, which was not hard to guess, especially as they were roommates for several years and most of the time back then, Olivia did the shopping anyway. Carol always appreciated Olivia's taste and went along with whatever Olivia bought. As Olivia put the last few items in the fridge, she could hear steps coming down the stairs, which was her cue to put the kettle on and get the mint tea ready, as was her original assignment. The door to the kitchen creaked.

"Ohh sorry I was a bit long in the shower, I think I was just enjoying myself too much. It felt so good to feel the warmth of that water just wash over me, almost as if it were washing my troubles away."

"Ahh bless, hon. Come and sit down. I've put the kettle on, and it won't be long now. Are you sure you couldn't manage a bit of toast now that you feel a bit more alive?"

"I suppose I could do, but I don't think I have any bread. I was meant to go shopping yesterday, but I wasn't up to it and just pottered around the house, doing practically nothing I guess." Carol slouched herself on a seat at the kitchen table.

"Don't you worry about that. When I was looking for the herbal tea, I noticed that there wasn't much in the cupboards, so I took the liberty of popping out and getting you a few bits and pieces and bread was on my list." Olivia smiled as she went to the fridge to get the bread and butter.

"You're amazing Liv, what would I do without a friend like you? And thanks for stopping by to check in on me."

"Of course, I would. What are best friends for, eh? Even if not to check up to see if everything is all right. So how have things been going these past few months, Caz?" Olivia knew it was only right to allow Carol to air whatever concerns she had been having, since apart from her, there probably wasn't anyone Carol would divulge her personal details with, seeing she was a private person. Jenny, her sister, was based in the North, so she wasn't too readily accessible in terms of having a chat in person.

Carol took the cup of herbal tea and toast Olivia had made for her and attempted to respond to the question posed to her. "The truth of the matter, Liv, is that it hasn't been easy. I've hardly had much contact with Michael. He doesn't pop back home for anything. He's not taking my calls when I contact the surgery, and as you know I don't get to see him on Sundays either, since he has been going somewhere else."

Carol's tone was subdued as she continued, "How are we ever going to solve matters, if he is too deep rooted in his man cave and won't surface to engage in conversation? That has surprised me about Michael as I always thought him to be a strong character with the ability to deal with anything. That's what I loved about him. And yes, I know that what I landed in his lap wasn't the best of bombshells to drop on anyone, but I really didn't think he would react by literally walking out on me."

Olivia listened and tried to see the situation from all sides. "Caz, I think you're just going to have to be patient and let him process how he wants to deal with things. You are right, that was a whopper of bombshells to drop on anyone and in hindsight I'm sure you wish you had done it much sooner rather than later. But you know what, it's done now, and you both just have to concentrate on how to get past this."

Carol nodded her head in agreement with all that Olivia had said. "Well let me tell you, Liv, please don't keep anything back from Steve before you both get married. Take it from someone who has been there and has got the T-shirt."

Olivia processed what Carol was saying, and her mind went back to the previous evening and her encounter with Chris. Surely that was something she didn't have to mention to Steve since it was a one-off and yet Olivia knew that having secrets between them, regardless of what the issue was, wouldn't bode well. Olivia's thoughts returned to the matter in hand. "There was one piece of good news that they announced in church today and that's the Annual Summer Fete next week. Now I know that Steve is meeting Michael for lunch today and I'm sure

399

he will push him to attend, since PT encouraged us all to invite our friends and family and anyone else we knew who might like to come along."

The Annual Summer Fete was New Dawn's effort at incorporating the entire church socially for a day of activities, such as sport related events, food booths, a children's play area and a host of other related events, which started at midday and went on into the evening. Olivia and the gang had all attended in previous years, and the event was the highlight of the church's calendar.

"Oh, I forgot that was coming up," Carol said with a hint of optimism in her voice, especially as she hoped it would be an opportunity for her to touch base with Michael and possibly exchange a word or two. That would be her only way of cornering him, since all the other attempts she tried were failing.

"Yep, that has been a great event over the years for bringing the whole church together and if Steve manages to convince Michael to attend…well you never know what can happen." Olivia wanted to give her friend something hopeful to hold onto in the coming week.

"Yes, perhaps."

"I just had an idea. Would you like to come over for dinner? I left Jen to start it for me, whilst I came to look for you." Olivia sounded hopeful as she thought it would give Carol a change of scenery and an opportunity to have some fun with a few girlfriends.

"No, I'm fine Liv. Just getting out of bed and talking with you has made me feel slightly more with it, although I still have an ache in my stomach. But I'm sure with a few paracetamols, the pain will subside. Thanks for the offer anyway."

"Well alright then if you're sure. And if the pain doesn't go, make sure you book yourself in to see the doctor. If not your hubby, then Joan," Olivia gave Carol strict orders as she grabbed her bag and started getting ready to leave.

"I'm fine Liv. I don't think I will need to take such drastic measures. I probably just haven't been taking care of myself, that's all. I'll be good, you'll see, and again, thanks for popping in, hon. I really appreciate that." Carol stood up to embrace Olivia and showed her to the door and waved her off when she got into her car.

———◦○◦———

Chapter Thirty-Two

*M*ichael arrived at the restaurant first and waited outside for Steve to join him. The church he had started attending finished their service 30 minutes earlier than New Dawn's, so he had plenty of time on his hands to browse in the shops on his way there. Michael wasn't really a big shopper, that was Carol's department. He usually went along to keep her company and hold the bags and could never understand why it took her ages to find what she wanted, especially when she'd eventually purchase an item she saw in the first shop anyway. Carol loved a bargain, which Michael didn't think was a bad thing as at least Carol did not waste money and appreciated the value of a pound.

Michael leaned up against the window of the restaurant and peered in. It was fairly empty, which he was glad to see since they failed to make a booking, having made the decision to meet up after church at the last minute. The last time he saw Steve was a couple of weeks ago when they played badminton, so he was looking forward to catching up with him. Michael didn't have to wait that long as Steve turned up 10 minutes later.

"Hello, my man." Steve walked up to Michael and slapped him on the back.

Michael turned around, smiling from his friend's gesture. "Mind the back. Are you trying to break it?"

"Thought you were stronger than that, mate. You need to man up." They playfully went backward and forwards with their innuendos and entered the restaurant.

A waitress showed them to a corner area where a table set for two was neatly nestled into the space. "Would this table be okay for you gentlemen?" They both nodded in agreement and made themselves comfortable, taking off their jackets and putting them on the back of the chairs. Once they were settled, the waitress came back to get their drinks order and gave them a few more minutes to decide on what they wanted for their entrees and main course.

"Shall we get a platter?" Steve suggested. "I know how much we guys love our food and the platter will give us a choice of chicken, lamb and pork, alongside rice, salad, naan bread etc."

"Sounds good to me," Michael agreed as he put the menu down that he was scrutinising and sipped on his apple juice that the waitress had brought to the table.

Steve was first to break the ice. "So, how have things been with you since we last caught up?" Steve was genuinely interested in hearing how far Michael had gotten in his decision as to whether he was going to forgive Carol and go back home. And if not, then he wanted to get to the bottom of what he intended doing for the long-term.

"Getting through the best I can. Have had a few issues at work, which I can't really talk about, but it has been doing my head in, because it has put the practice in jeopardy somewhat, but by the grace of God, we will get there."

"Sorry to hear that, mate."

"And also, I need to decide what I am going to do about the studio flat where I am staying, as I only took it on a short-term basis, as a temporary measure to clear my head, and it's due to expire very soon."

"I'm glad you brought that up as I really wanted to know where you are at in that regard."

Their conversation was interrupted by the waitress who brought a large platter and put it in the centre of the table. She returned with plates and cutlery for them.

"Gentlemen, please enjoy your meal and if there is anything else you need, please do not hesitate to let me know." They thanked her in unison and started helping themselves to the array of scrumptious looking food that was in front of them, with tantalising smells encouraging them to dive in quickly.

Michael returned to the question posed to him before they were disturbed in their flow of conversation. "Steve, I know I have to make a decision, but this is one of the hardest things I have ever had to do. Inwardly, I'm so angry with Caz. I don't think she'll ever know how much this has rocked me and my confidence in us as a couple. Of course, I still love her, there is no question of that, but every time I look at her or have a conversation with her, you can bet what is going on in my head and what is number one in my thoughts."

"Michael, I am not going to pretend I know remotely what you are going through, or what it even feels like to be betrayed like that, but at the end of the day man, she is your wife. I was stood right next to you as your best man, when you echoed those words 'for richer, for poorer; in sickness and in health; till death do us part'. That's got to mean something to you." Steve tried to imagine how he would react if anything as drastic as that came between him and Olivia and what he would do differently to

Michael.

"It does mean something to me, Steve, which has been the difficult part. I know me and Caz are going to have to sit down again and try and get pass the lies, deceit and betrayal and I pray we can do that. I've always wanted to be a father and knowing that I may not be able to have biological children of my own has been hard to process."

Steve put his cutlery down and looked intently into Michael's face, as if he were about to give him the third degree. "Michael, I'm going to ask you a bold question now, so don't shoot the messenger and hear me out. If Carol had told you at the time you guys were courting that she was unable to have children, do you think you would still have wanted to marry her?"

Michael paused and leant back into the seat, clenching his chin. "I've thought long and hard about that question Steve, since I found out, and to be brutally honest, I think I still would have. I fell in love with Caz the individual, and not what I could get from her."

"Then mate, I think you've got your answer and the battle to moving forward has already been halved. You know we have the Annual Summer Fete event next Saturday right? And PT said he wanted everyone to be there, so maybe this would be a great opportunity for you to try and patch things up with Carol by at least having some sort of conversation with her. You of all people should know that we can't bury our problems in a ditch and hope they will go away. Michael, it's time to get this sorted."

"Yeah, I know you're right. I didn't realise it was that time already for the Annual Summer Fete. The time goes by so quickly, it seemed like only yesterday that Caz and I were there as an engaged couple, and we all had a good day. Perhaps that would be a good place for us to talk. I just need to ask the Holy Spirit to heal my heart so that I can get pass the anger I have been feeling. I keep recalling something PT said in one of his sermons about unforgiveness. He said unforgiveness is like drinking poison and hoping the other person would die. His point being that unforgiveness eats you up far worse than the individual you are reluctant to forgive. I guess that poison has done a number on me, hasn't it?"

"Look, Michael, as I said, I am not going to pretend I can understand how hard this has been for you, as I can imagine that it has been extremely painful. But I do know that you cannot continue the way you have been going and now is the right time to get this sorted."

As they continued to talk and hash out Michael's waning relationship, the waitress came over and cleared away their plates and the empty platter and asked them if they wanted any desserts, which they declined and instead opted for two cups of filtered coffee. Michael felt a sigh of relief, since he hadn't really spoken to anyone in depth about his feelings and the situation, and decided he was going to go back to his pad and spend some time in prayer, as admittedly, he also tried to avoid discussing the matter with God, which he was aware was a big mistake.

"And how are things going with you and Olivia? Have you guys set a date yet?"

"Yeah, things are going well, and we are looking at sometime early next year. We are currently attending our pre-marital classes and only have a few more sessions to go."

"Ahh pre-marital classes. How well I remember those. Pity none of the stuff that me and Caz are going through was brought up at that time and goodness knows there were numerous opportunities." Michael's voice sounded agitated again. "You see Steve, it's little things like that which trips me up and forces me into my cave of damaging emotions. How could she really conceal all of that, even in our pre-marital sessions?"

Steve could hear how frustrated his friend was and didn't know what more to say. This was something that

Michael had to work out for himself, with God and with Carol, and Steve hoped that he would find the peace he so yearned for, to be able to get pass the hurt that was crippling his heart. "Mate, I'm really sorry, but I know by God's grace, you're going to get through this as prayer really changes things. There is a song by Don Moen that says, 'God will make a way, where there seems to be no way'. Remember that song? I think we have sung it in church before. Well, God has to step in and do for you supernaturally what you can't do for yourself, and that is repair your hurting heart. Once He does that, I believe you'll be able to move forward. So just take some time out and really seek His face on this matter. Look, sorry to cut our time abruptly, but I need to go now as I have a few files to review for a meeting I have tomorrow, so do you mind if we wrap this up?"

Michael looked up at Steve, having felt he just endured a masterclass in the art of relationships. "No, that's fine, Steve, I also need to go. As you say, I have a lot of soul-searching to do, and I guess there is no time like the present to start. Let me get this and pay for the bill, as you've helped me more than you'll know."

"Thanks, mate. Just being a good friend. I know if the boot was on the other foot, that you'd be there for me too, so I haven't done anything out of the ordinary."

The waitress arrived with their bill, which Michael paid for, and he and Steve gathered their things and left the restaurant promising to touch base with one another on Saturday at the Summer Fete.

Michael and Joan continued to wrestle with the information they had learnt about Chris' past and were looking for an appropriate opportunity to confront Chris. However work restraints had prevented them from doing so. The impending CQC inspection that was expected within the next week had to be put back a month or so due to another inspection running over unexpectedly, which was a blessing in disguise for Michael and Joan. However, the short reprieve they had been afforded, did not deter from the fact that the matter still had to be addressed, sooner rather than later.

They had continued to have discussions as to what would be an amicable conclusion, but that was dependent upon on how co-operative Chris was going to be. Having checked with Janet as to a time when they all were going to be free, she gave them a specific time and date, which Janet electronically entered in all their diaries.

And as Chris did not seem to object, they took that to mean that he had no issues with having a 4PM meeting on a Tuesday.

Chris had had a lot on his mind over the last few days. From his relationship with Jen ending and the mishap with Olivia, he had allowed the stuff going around in his head to cloud his judgement. As a result, the fogginess affected his work with him not checking his diary as to where he should be, whether that was staying in the surgery, or having to be at the hospital. And a few times it was left to Janet to gently remind him of his various commitments, so he hadn't noticed the staff meeting that was scheduled in his diary for that day. Chris' last patient left his office and he pulled up the patient's records on his computer to update what was discussed. He found that if he did not update the records as soon as a patient had left, he would accumulate a pile of work and would then be trying to play catch up to get everything in an orderly fashion.

Chris pulled up his diary to see what were the next few appointments that were scheduled for him, when he noticed an entry that said, 'staff meeting @ 4PM in the boardroom.' Chris was puzzled by the entry and slightly taken back, since there was usually a staff meeting the following morning as the surgery opened late on a Wednesday morning to accommodate such meetings. Chris dialled through to reception.

"Hi Janet. I've just noticed that there is a staff meeting in the diary at 4PM. I must admit that I really didn't notice

411

it this morning. Do you know what it's about?" Chris appeared irritated, since he did not like to constantly be running late and of late, was taking advantage of Mrs Jenkins' good nature. Not that she would ever complain as she loved Ben's company.

"Hi Dr Harris, Dr Mills just asked me to find an available time when you were all free, but he didn't say what the meeting was about. Nor did he ask me to provide any supporting documentation. I just assumed it might have something to do with our CQC inspection that is due. It most probably won't last more than half an hour as I know you'll be keen to get away as soon as you can."

"You're absolutely right, Janet. We've only got half an hour before it starts, but I just may quickly call Mrs Jenkins just to pre-warn her, in case, for reasons unbeknownst, it decides to run on.

At 4PM, Michael, Joan and Chris stopped what they were doing and headed to the boardroom for their planned meeting. Janet had prepared the boardroom prior to their arrival, where a fresh brew of coffee was awaiting their arrival. They each helped themselves to a drink and sat around the table.

Chris was the first to break the ice. "So, what's going on then? Why the sudden reason for meeting up now and not tomorrow morning as per our usual custom?"

Michael cleared his throat. "This is true, but the matter in hand needed to be discussed as soon as possible."

"Sounds ominous," Chris joked. However, the others did not share in his joviality.

Michael continued, maintaining a more professional stance as he did not want the meeting to appear as if it was of a social nature, given the seriousness of what was going to be discussed. "Chris, the last time we met up, we discussed the matter of the references from your previous practice that we have yet to receive, which is something that you said you would sort out. Where are we on that?"

Chris' eyes widened which spoke volumes than the words he was yet to voice. Stumbling on his words, Chris tried to offer a lame excuse as to why it was not done yet. Citing it on the fact that he called the surgery, but no one had gotten back to him yet.

However, Joan wasn't going to let him off the hook so quickly. "Chris, quit trying to fob us off, as this isn't the time to be flippant. Thankfully, our CQC inspection has been postponed for another month, but were we to have had them inspect our credentials, we could have found ourselves in some serious hot water."

Joan leant forward and looked intently into Chris' eyes. "Anyway, let's cut to the chase, Chris. We took the liberty of having a conference call with Dr Nathan Kelly Snr and he filled in the blanks for us and told us about the investigation that they were about to start, prior to you absconding."

Before Joan could finish her sentence, Chris interrupted her in mid-flow. "Why did you guys feel the need to go behind my back, when I told you I was going to sort things out?"

"And when exactly was that going to ever happen Chris?" Michael interjected furiously. "I don't believe you did anything about it, as you already knew what the response was going to be. You won't be aware of this, but at the medical conference, when you so conveniently tried to avoid Nathan Kelly, he spoke with me instead and it was something he said, which alerted me to the fact that you had not been straight with us from the outset."

Chris was loss for words as he recalled the moment when he saw Nathan making his way over to him but was unaware that Michael had had a conversation with him. Chris was rumbled and he did not have a leg to stand on and tried changing tactics in an attempt to appeal to his colleagues' emotional side. Chris explained that at the time, he was going through enormous stress, having just lost his wife and on top of that, he felt hurt by Jill's family with the accusations they were directing at him. He was not thinking straight, and him leaving abruptly was out of character for him, but under the circumstances he felt there was nothing else he could have done.

Michael and Joan took into consideration all that Chris had told them but encouraged him that the best thing for him to do, was to go back and face the music in person. Clear his name and allow Ben to be reunited with his family. They told Chris that they would have to suspend him until he had gotten things sorted to protect their practice. Chris was reluctant to go back and deal with his past and address whatever needed to be addressed, but he was left with no option as to where Michael and Joan stood unanimously.

Chris agreed that he would go back to sort things out but said he would need at least a week to try and sort something out with Ben's school and that he couldn't just up and leave immediately. Also, he would need to let Mrs Jenkins know that he had to go away for a few weeks on personal business. They all agreed that this course of action was the best way forward and Michael made it clear to Chris that he was not dismissed as such, but that the lifting of his suspension was down to him clearing his name and having a record that was free from accusations that would not impact upon their practice. Everyone left on an amicable note, believing they were all on the same page and the meeting ended.

Chapter Thirty-Three

*T*he day of the Summer Fete had arrived and there were mixed emotions as to what the day might bring. For some, it was an opportunity to catch up with old friends and enjoy some much-needed fellowship, whilst for others it was something they would have liked to avoid, if they were able to, as was the case for Chris.

There were varying reasons why Chris did not want to be at the Summer Fete, in light of his relationship break up with Jen, the mishap with Olivia and now the fall out with his work colleagues, so that was the last place he would have wanted to find himself. But for the sake of Ben who had been excited about the Fete for the longest time and kept reminding and asking Chris when Saturday had arrived, Chris knew that it was something he had no choice in attending and had to put on a brave face for the sake of his son, in spite of his reservations.

Carol woke up feeling a little under the weather, but she wasn't going to let a little dizziness stop her from getting herself ready to attend the Fete, especially when she heard on the grapevine that Michael would be attending. Olivia had let the cat out of the bag previously, as Carol was thinking of giving it a miss this year, feeling embarrassed that last year she and Michael had arrived hand in hand and yet, what a difference a year made. Carol coaxed herself into thinking that perhaps this was finally going to be the break she needed in getting Michael to acknowledge her and at least have a decent conversation and hoped that in his time out, he had some time to really think about where their future was going.

Olivia had agreed to pick her up, so Carol was grateful that she did not have to think about driving and could just concentrate on making sure she felt physically up to the task of being out for most of the day.

Olivia grabbed her keys and coat and headed for the door. Steve had offered to pick her up so that they could go together. But Olivia had told him that she had already arranged to pick up Carol and again didn't want to rub in Carol's face the sight of a happy couple interacting when she herself was going through what she was undergoing. Whilst Steve appreciated Olivia's concerns, he reminded her that she could not keep mollycoddling Carol, as that wasn't real life and even though she was unfortunately suffering in the way she was, couples would always be around her, no matter where she went. Olivia knew that

Steve was right, but just couldn't help herself as it pained her to see Carol in such a way.

As Olivia made herself comfortable in the car, her thoughts recalled the last time she had seen Chris and she wasn't even remotely looking forward to setting eyes on him. But she knew that Ben would be with him and would most probably make a dart straight towards her, so avoiding Chris wasn't going to prove as easy as she would have liked. Olivia convinced herself that at the end of the day she had nothing to be ashamed of, since she didn't do anything to provoke the type of reaction she got from Chris. Neither did she know what had come over him to make him think that there could ever be anything more between them other than the relationship they already had as parent and teacher, since she wouldn't even consider him as a friend, but more of an acquaintance.

Again, her conscious told her that she didn't need to bring the matter to Steve's attention as she was confident that it was an unfortunate incident, which would not be repeated given the way she had reacted. Jen had arranged to go to the Fete with a friend from church, who had already picked her up and they had left 10 minutes prior.

Michael was in the middle of packing his things when the phone rang. "Hi Michael, it's Steve. I just wanted to check if you were still planning on going to the Fete and if so, would you like a lift as Olivia is going with Carol."

Michael had his phone under his chin as he piled clothes into his suitcase whilst trying to talk with Steve at the same time. "Hey there…right…. oh yeah. I still plan on going. Just have clothes everywhere as I am getting my things together. Actually, come to think of it, a lift wouldn't go amiss. Is 10 minutes okay?"

"Sure, I'll pass around and pick you up. Anyway, I wouldn't have thought you had that many things to pack, considering us men don't own that many clothes," Steve teased.

"Well, you may only have one pair of trousers and two tops, but some of us like to have a bit of variety and style," Michael laughed back. "Olivia really is going to put you through your paces when you're married. You mark my words. Okay, so in 10 it is, see you then."

The weather was perfect, as the sun shone brightly, with there not being a cloud in sight. The car park was heaving with cars as individuals arrived for the Annual Fete. Parking attendants were helping to manage the flow, ensuring that the spaces were being utilised adequately, since the car park to the church was not as big as the grounds adjacent to the church where the Fete was being held. Olivia planned to get there early for that very reason and was pleased that she managed to get one of the spaces. Her and Carol made their way to the grounds, where in the distance they saw Jen waving at them, alongside her friend.

"I see you got here then. When we arrived, there weren't that many spaces left, so I'm glad you guys got a space also and didn't have to park down the road and then have to walk back up." Jen acknowledged Carol with a smile. They didn't know each other that well, but Olivia was the connection between them both and they knew of each other because of that fact.

"Yeah, we're glad too and just about squeezed into a small space in a corner. I just hope no one blocks me in, in case I need to leave early for some reason," Olivia reasoned. "Have you looked around much then and seen where everything is?"

"We had a quick look, but I must say, everything looks really good. I've not been to one of these before, so I didn't know what to expect." Being new to the church, Jen wouldn't have been at the previous Fetes so would not have been familiar with how things went.

In the past, Carol was always keen to lend her creative eye to make sure things ran and looked a picture but didn't offer her services this year and neither did PT push her or ask her to assist, considering the load she already had on her plate was a full one.

"Well, I'm heading straight to the cake stand to sample their delights. Anyone joining me?" Olivia smiled, darting towards the furthest part of the vicinity.

"No, you go on. We're going to stay here by the music stand and listen to the various groups perform."

Olivia laughed. "You see Carol, they think we are old."

"Well perhaps we are Liv, as at one point, that's exactly where we would have been found." Carol winked at Jen and gave her a thumbs up, giving her a sign of approval and Jen gave her a thumbs up back.

Chris arrived with Ben and straightaway signed him into the kid's programme, where he would be occupied for the next two hours, whilst Chris got to stroll around the grounds and see what took his fancy. Ben was excited to see the large, red and yellow stripey bouncy castle and indicated to Chris that was the first thing he was going to go on. And knowing his son that meant Ben would spend the entire two-hour slot bouncing around on it and having fun. Chris was relieved to know that Ben would be taken good care of whilst having fun, even if he didn't particularly think he was going to have a good time.

He made his way over to the hotdog stand to get himself a cool beverage, where he saw Michael and Steve in the line a few spaces in front of him. They were the last two people he wanted to see at this point, but it was inevitable that he would bump into individuals he knew throughout the course of the day.

Steve turned around and noticed Chris in the line. "Hey, isn't that Chris back there?"

Michael turned around and saw Chris standing in the line with his head towards the floor. "Oh yeah, so it is." He turned back around in the line whilst waiting to be served. Steve thought it odd that Michael would be so dismissive of Chris and seemed slightly puzzled.

"So, should we invite him to join us? He looks like he is on his own."

"He's a grown man, I'm sure he's fine. If he wants company, I'm sure he'll come over and say hello." Given the conversation they had with Chris earlier in the week, Michael didn't know where Chris' head was at the moment or whether he had started making any plans to return to his former town and could not predict what type of temperament he was going to be in.

"Michael, we aren't like that. I'm going to call him over and see if he'll join us." Before Michael could say another word, Steve was beckoning Chris and calling him over. He didn't know Chris that well, but they had had a few interactions over time, and Steve did not want it to seem as if they saw Chris and were deliberately ignoring him.

Chris walked over to them both. "Oh, hi guys. How are you doing?"

"I'm well, thanks," Steve replied.

"Yeah good, mate," Michael responded. "No Ben then?" Michael noticed that Ben wasn't with him and tried to use that factor to engage in small talk with Chris.

"Ohh, I've signed up the little man for the kids programme. I'll pick him up in a couple of hours."

"Oh right."

"So, what's the main attraction around here?" Chris too was trying his hand at small talk, not really wanting to be in their company.

"Well, we can have a game of pool inside if you're up for it, but I think we have to put our names down to play, so it could be in another hour or so." Steve noticed that something wasn't right between Michael and Chris' body language. He could cut the tension with a knife and thought he would be the go-between, since the pair were not communicating much or looking towards the direction of each other.

Chris got his drink and started to walk off. "Okay, I'll meet you in an hour's time inside. I'll just stroll around and see what else is going on." Michael and Steve were left standing with their drinks as Chris walked off into the crowds.

"So, what on earth was that all about?" Steve threw his hands in the air, waiting for an explanation from Michael.

"It's just stuff, which is work related and it's best you don't know the details either." Michael shrugged off explaining any further why he wasn't really interested in hanging around with Chris for the day.

"Well, whatever it is, that sure was uncomfortable. I hope you guys can get things sorted out soon, as that can't be good for morale at work."

Michael nodded his head in agreement. "Yeah, I know. I believe we are on the road to things sorting themselves out though. Perhaps I've got a lot on my mind and Chris really isn't on my list of priorities."

"Talking of priorities, look who's walking over this way," Steve said as he elbowed Michael.

Olivia and Carol had spent a considerable time at the

cake stand, mostly sampled by Olivia, as Carol wasn't hungry, and they were just on their way to the hotdog stand to get themselves a drink. As Carol walked towards the two men, she wondered what type of greeting she would get from Michael.

"Well, if it isn't my two favourite men." Olivia smiled as she embraced Steve first with a hug, followed by Michael. Steve in turn hugged Carol and Michael likewise went in for an embrace with her, which felt slightly awkward to them both. Almost as if rehearsed, Olivia told Steve that she wanted him to accompany them to a stand where she saw some arts and crafts that might suit the décor of their wedding theme and arm in arm she whisked Steve off, leaving Michael and Carol to make up their own small talk.

Michael seemed fidgety, and Carol nervously looked at the buzz around her, but as the man, he was keen to make the first move. "So how are you, Caz? Sorry, it's been a while."

"Yeah, it has. Just been keeping myself busy with work."

"Oh okay, any new projects then?"

"There's been quite a few tenders I have been awarded, which have got me feeling a bit tired and by the time I get home, I'm just exhausted and ready for bed."

Michael appeared concerned as he knew what Carol was like when she pushed herself too hard. "Are you still taking your vitamins? You don't want to overdo things and it affect your health."

For the first time in a long while, Carol had a glimmer of hope that Michael still cared for her and inwardly her stomach was doing somersaults. "Thanks Michael. I think I just need a little pick me up. Or some kind of tonic and then I'll be right as rain."

"Well pass by the surgery on Monday and we'll get you sorted out."

Carol smiled. "Okay, I might just do that." Carol didn't know what the protocol was regarding them moving forward. Was she supposed to ask Michael when he was moving back home or was he supposed to ask her when he could come back home. Thus, they both continued to dance around the subject.

"So, how are your digs then?" Carol's bold question meant that she was going to address the matter.

"It's very small. Only a studio flat, but my two months rental is coming to an end, and I've got to decide what I am going to do." Michael knew that he should be

427

suggesting that he come back home, because that's what PT counselled him to do, but his hurt feelings and pride had prevented him from uttering the words.

"Well, you can always come back home you know, and we can take things slow. If you wanted to occupy one of the rooms in the meantime, then that would be fine by me. At least we'd be under the same roof and in a better position to move forward in repairing our marriage." Carol sounded desperate, but she did not care. She was going to fight for what was rightly hers.

"Ohh I don't know, Caz." Michael sounded reluctant; however, he did not have a better alternative solution in place.

"Michael, what do we have to lose by trying, eh?"

Michael realised that there was no other plan, especially as he was still paying for a mortgage on their home. It just didn't make any sense forking out extra money all because he couldn't get his act together. "Can you give me a few days to think about it, Caz?" Michael wanted it to seem as though he would think things over, when in reality, it was the only sensible way forward.

"Yeah, sure, take all the time you need. This sun is a bit too hot for me. I'm just going to get some shade inside. If Liv comes back, can you tell her that's where I have gone."

"Yeah sure, Caz. Well, take care of yourself." *Well, take care of yourself. Who actually says that to their wife in passing?* Michael watched as Carol walked away from him and in that second, a floodgate of emotions enveloped his heart and for the first time he felt convicted in his spirit for the way he had acted. He hadn't acted honourably as a husband, regardless of what Carol had done. He still had a duty of care and commitment to her as he recited to her on their wedding day.

As he was wallowing in self-pity, Steve and Olivia came back. "Where's Carol?" Olivia was quick to ask.

"She went inside to get some shade as the sun was too much for her."

"Let me see if I can find her. See you later, boys." Olivia rushed inside the main church building to see if she could find Carol.

In the meantime, Steve and Michael headed towards the area where the pool was taking place, since Steve was keen to honour his commitment to Chris. Michael was reluctant but tagged along anyway. When they got there, Chris was already there and had a cue in his hand, as the individuals playing previously had just finished their game. Steve chose a cue that he felt comfortable with, and he and Chris proceeded to play.

Michael still couldn't shake the image of Carol walking off and him not following her, so he just sat on the side and watched them play. Steve and Chris were bantering and exchanging light conversation as they played. Steve was very competitive, and Chris was good, so he had his work cut out to stay on top and pulled out his A-game and won the first game. They asked Michael if he wanted to play either of them, but Michael waved his hand indicating that he was fine and happy to sit on the side.

Chris placed the balls in the triangular track, made the break and potted the first ball; since Steve potted the first ball in the last game, which was a solid ball, leaving the striped balls for Steve to play with. After a few shots, Steve felt more comfortable with Chris and dropped his guard by asking him a personal question regarding his relationship with Jen. "Didn't Jen come with you today then?"

Chris was surprised by Steve's line of questioning since they weren't exactly that close with each other and took it upon himself to cease the opportunity to get even and turn the tables around. "No, she didn't. We aren't seeing each other anymore."

"Oh, I'm sorry mate, I didn't know that." Steve felt embarrassed that he brought up something that Chris was still clearly trying to process.

"I thought Olivia would have clued you up on that. Don't you guys talk?" Chris said in a sarcastic tone.

"We do talk; she just didn't mention that for whatever reason."

"I think I might know the reason why she didn't tell you. Perhaps the reason was that she may have had something to do with our break up."

Steve looked at Chris inquisitively wondering what he meant by his comment. "Excuse me?"

Chris continued with his tirade of comments, "Jen and I were doing fine, until she started allowing Olivia to fill her head with all sorts of things about me and I believe that's what contributed to Jen ending the relationship."

Steve became defensive and wasn't about to tolerate Chris accusing Olivia over his failed relationship. "That's a bit strong don't you think? Olivia isn't like that and whatever discussions they might have had; at the end of the day, Jen is a grown woman and can make her own decisions."

"You say, you and Olivia talk, but I doubt she told you

how she came onto me, dressed in an inappropriate attire, the evening Jen ended our relationship?"

"Chris, I'm not sure why you are making these things up, but let's stop here before things get out of hand."

"No, worries mate. I can stop there, but you need to know the type of person who you are thinking of walking down the aisle with. Perhaps you don't know her as well as you thought if she is keeping things from you already. Take a leaf out of Michael's book and see that lies in a relationship don't bode too well in the long run."

Chris' work was done. He had dropped enough seeds to put doubt in Steve's mind to potentially sabotage his relationship with Olivia.

Michael saw a bit of commotion that was building up between Steve and Chris and before he could come over to see what was happening, his mobile phone rang, and it was Olivia on the other end. "Michael, can you come to the main sanctuary? It's Carol, she's just fainted," Olivia said frantically.

"Ohh no, I'm coming right now." Michael jumped up.

"What is it, Michael?" Steve said as he noticed Michael was extremely agitated.

"It's Caz, she's fainted. I've got to go to her."

"I'll come with you." Steve left the cue stick on the table in mid-flow of his game with Chris to support Michael. When they arrived in the main sanctuary, there was a crowd of people who had surrounded Carol.

Michael ran over and tried to disperse the crowd. "Please, everyone, step back and let her have some air."

Olivia was anxiously fanning Carol trying to get her to come around. "I've called for an ambulance as well as I did not know what to do. Is she going to be all right, Michael?"

"She should be fine Olivia, but you did the right thing, it's better to be safe. I'll go with her in the ambulance when it comes so don't worry about that and thanks for being such a good friend to her."

After much fanning and tapping of her face by Olivia, Carol started to come around just as the ambulance arrived with the paramedic, one of who turned out to be Jen as she had left the Fete earlier, because she was on duty that afternoon. "Okay, let us get to the patient," Jen said as she and her colleague made their way to where Carol lay, and they helped her onto a stretcher and took her into the ambulance.

Michael went along and assisted the paramedics by sharing with them what he found when he first arrived on the scene. Jen thanked him and they closed the ambulance doors and sped off with urgency.

———◆◇◆———

Chapter Thirty-Four

The crowds disbursed as the ambulance fled away and Olivia was still sitting down distraught and worried over what might be wrong with Carol, since this was not the first time she encountered Carol not feeling well. A mirage of possibilities flooded her mind and she prayed that it was not anything as serious as cancer, as she couldn't afford to lose her friend to that dreaded disease. Steve was also left behind and tried to be of support to her as he could see that she was clearly in distress, but at the back of his mind were the accusations that Chris had wielded around that he couldn't quite shift and wondered if he should bring it up or wait for a more convenient time when Olivia was in a better headspace.

As Steve wanted to show consideration, he decided to wait and discuss the matter later with Olivia. "Come on, let me walk you to your car as you are clearly shaken up over what has happened. Will you be okay to drive yourself home?" Steve said as he helped Olivia to her feet.

"Thanks. I think I should be fine. Just seeing Carol in

such a vulnerable way is so heart wrenching. You know, she wasn't well last Sunday either when I went around to see why she hadn't come to church."

"Why didn't you mention this to anyone then?"

"Well, I just thought it was one of those overnight bugs and that she would get over it in a day or two. I really hope it isn't anything serious. I couldn't take losing my best friend."

"Liv, you really are getting ahead of yourself. Carol will be fine, plus she has Michael with her now. Perhaps it has just been the emotional stress that has finally caught up with her body, over what they have been going through. We can call Michael a bit later to check in on them and see what's happening." Steve's reasoning reassured Olivia that perhaps she was jumping the gun with her concerns and that Carol was a strong enough individual to handle whatever she was experiencing. Steve walked Olivia to her car and watched her get in.

"So, what will you do Steve? are you going to stick around here?"

"No, I don't fancy it now. Think I'll go home myself, unless you'd like some company? I could come around later as there was something I needed to run by you." Steve's voice sounded serious, and Olivia detected that he seemed concerned.

"Yeah, that would be lovely but give me a couple of hours as I just need to clear my head and spend some time in prayer for Carol."

"Works for me," Steve said as he closed the car door. "See you later." He watched Olivia drive off and reasoned that it was best to deal with Chris' silly accusations sooner, whilst they were fresh in his mind, rather than let them fester and potentially turn into something more sinister.

Chris stayed at the Fete. The time to pick up Ben had expired, and he was on his way to collect him. He knew that what he had done earlier wasn't really called for, as he did not consider Steve an enemy, but his annoyance over being dumped by Jen and rejected by Olivia still very much dominated his thoughts. It was almost like if he couldn't be happy, he didn't see why anyone else should be either. Also, there was the issue of him having to go back to Chichester and sort out the mess he left behind and tried so hard to forget. Everything was spiralling out of control in Chris' life, and he was losing the ability to handle all the balls that he was juggling.

Chris got to the children's area and picked up Ben who was excited to see him and it was evident that he enjoyed his two hours playing with his friends from

Sunday School. "You look exhausted buddy; you want something to eat?"

Ben's clothes were all ruffled and out of place and his laces were undone from where he took his shoes off to play on the bouncy castle. Ben nodded and smiled as he looked up into Chris' face. "Yes Daddy, I'm really hungry now."

"I bet you are, buddy. And just look at you, I can't take you anywhere, can I?" Chris smiled as he ruffled Ben's hair and knelt down to tie up his laces. "Let me tie these before you trip over them. Would you like a hot dog?"

An enthusiastic Ben confirmed that he would, and they made their way over to the hotdog stand and joined the queue to get their refreshments. "Buddy, after this, we'll stay just a little bit longer as Daddy needs to sort some things out at home. Is that all right?" Ben nodded and didn't seem phased by the fact that he had to leave the Fete early. He had his two hours enjoying himself and that was good enough for him.

Michael sat with Carol in A&E holding her hand, whilst they waited to be called in so that she could be assessed by one of the doctors. He had indicated to them that he was a doctor and regularly practiced at the hospital, but the individuals behind the counter weren't giving him any preferential treatment and Carol was made to wait in line with all the other patients who were in the waiting area.

"Hopefully, it won't be too long, Caz. How are you feeling now?"

Carol's voice sounded laboured. "I feel a lot better than I did before. Everything was just a blur and then the next minute, I was gone."

Michael seemed concerned. "Caz, has anything like this happened before?"

"No, I've never fainted. Lately I have felt a little run down, but I put that down to me working too hard and not eating well. I've not really been cooking for myself and have only had snacks here and there."

"Caz, you shouldn't be skipping meals and I bet you didn't have any breakfast this morning, did you?"

"No, I didn't. Before I knew it, Olivia was outside blowing her horn to pick me up and I just managed to have a cup of coffee."

"Well, it will be that then." Michael sighed a breath of relief that Carol's condition was not life threatening and was probably down to her not taking care of herself as well as she should have, which he realised that him not being there played a major part in. After waiting several hours in the waiting area, Carol was called and Michael accompanied her. The female doctor overseeing Carol's case took her vitals and examined her to rule out anything that was of concern.

Michael was familiar with the doctor, and she allowed Michael to accompany Carol in an area that was normally reserved for patients only, whilst their loved ones waited on the other side. After much poking and prodding, the doctor wanted to check one more thing just to rule it out. "Do you think you might be pregnant?" the doctor asked as she felt Carol's stomach?

Carol's eyes widened. "Pregnant?" she shrieked, and Michael looked intently at Carol in utter confusion.

The doctor continued, "I mean, have you taken a pregnancy test recently? Your abdomen feels quite swollen and all the symptoms you are experiencing are in conjunction with early signs of pregnancy."

Michael interjected, "We can't have children. There must be some mistake."

"Well let's get your wife to take a pregnancy test and we'll know for sure. Give me a few minutes and I'll come back with a few tests."

As the doctor left the room, Michael was keen to start the dialogue first. "Caz, I thought you told me that you couldn't have any children."

"Well, I can't. At least that's what I was told," Carol fumbled over her words and her mind drifted back to the time when she was given the prognosis that children would not factor in her life.

"But didn't you have it checked out in the years following that prognosis?"

"Well, no I didn't. If a doctor tells you that you can't have children, then that's gospel.....right?"

"No, it isn't Caz; there are always second opinions that you can get as not all doctors get things right, I'm afraid to say."

"Well, I don't know about that and there wouldn't have been any reason for me to have things checked out as I wasn't going to have a baby outside of marriage once I became a Christian. Anyway, once I told you that I couldn't have children, why didn't you push me to have some tests to see if that was indeed the case? No, you just ran off didn't you and made me feel like I had taken the one thing away from you that you longed for: the ability of you being a father."

Michael felt a sense of guilt as Carol was right. He allowed his anger of the situation to cloud his judgement, instead of putting on his medical hat and pressing for more information as to the extent of her condition. "Caz, let's not argue about this now, since we both have clearly been in the wrong in some aspects of this matter."

Carol turned her head away from Michael. She didn't want to get into a slanging match either over who was right or who was wrong. After their little spat, the doctor came back into the room with two pregnancy tests and asked Carol to go into the toilet and when she had finished taking both tests, to bring them back to her. Having two tests done would most definitely reveal an accurate reading.

Michael waited in anticipation, confused, but hopeful at the prospects of their being a slight glimmer of hope of him finally being the father he had always longed to be. The doctor came back in with the results. It was hard for them to read the expression on her face, as she gave nothing away. Michael clasped onto Carol's hand as they waited nervously to hear what the results revealed. The pause seemed like an eternity. Had the doctors gotten things wrong all those years ago and were they indeed now going to be parents or not? The answers to the questions that were swimming around in both their minds, but they were not verbalising to each other, now laid in the hands of the doctor.

Olivia had exchanged a few text messages with Michael, when she got home who could only confirm what he knew at the time: that Carol was okay, and they were waiting for the results of some tests she had taken. Michael did not divulge what type of tests they were as he didn't want to confuse Olivia, when they themselves did not know exactly what was going on. Olivia's concerns were immediately put at ease.

If something major was happening to Carol, she didn't know how she would have coped, but would have been strong for her to support her in whatever she was going through. Olivia wanted to take her mind off things and with Steve arriving later, she went into the kitchen to prepare dinner for them to share a meal together. Now that her head was a bit clearer, she recalled that Steve didn't seem himself when he had walked her to the car. Steve was a caring individual and Olivia loved that about him. The way he could be so masculine yet have such a sensitive nature. She wondered if everything was okay and put it down to perhaps him having a hard day at work the day before, as some of his cases did take their toll out of him at times.

Olivia looked in the fridge to see what she could

rustle up. There was half a chorizo ring left and a packet of frozen stir-fry vegetables in the freezer, so she decided to put some noodles on and make a stir-fry to serve with naan bread. Olivia cooked the food and got it ready awaiting Steve's arrival and on cue, the doorbell rang.

Olivia went to the door and Steve was outside poised on the doorstep. "Hey, how are you? Come on in." Steve greeted Olivia and walked inside with his hands in his pocket.

"I've made us some dinner; are you hungry?" Steve followed Olivia into the lounge and found himself a seat.

"Okay, I wasn't really thinking of dinner, but that would be nice. Have you found out anything more about Carol? I have been texting Michael, but he hasn't really responded."

"Yeah, I have, I believe all is well and they are just waiting for the results of some tests, but she'll be okay. I've been praying and I have left her into God's hands. Excuse me for a minute whilst I go and get the food. Would you like something to drink?"

"If you have something soft, that would be great."

Olivia left the room and Steve's gaze scanned the room, admiring Olivia's taste in décor. He wondered how he was going to approach the topic he had really come around to discuss and didn't want it to get out of hand, but rather for it to be a rounded conversation that would give clarity to the disparaging comments Chris had made earlier. They enjoyed a meal together and talked about what type of week they had and after dinner they sat side by side on the sofa with a cup of coffee.

Steve took the opportunity whilst the atmosphere was mellow to bring up the comments that had overtook his thoughts and that he could not put to bed until he had heard Olivia's side of things. "Olivia, did you see Chris and Ben today?"

The thought of Chris' name made Olivia shudder in her thoughts. "Nope, I didn't. Were they there then?" Olivia was grateful for the fact that it was a large enough event, and she did not bump into Chris, since she didn't know how she would have reacted if she saw him.

"Michael and I spent some time with him earlier and played a few games of pool with him. Well actually that's incorrect. In fact, it was I that played pool with him since Michael wasn't really giving him the time of day and I didn't really press as to what was going on there."

"Oh right." Olivia didn't want to really have a conversation about Chris, but felt she had to keep her composure and hear Steve out. "I don't really know Chris that way and half-way through I was trying to be cordial with him to get to know him better and asked him if Jen was at the Fete with him and apparently, I did not realise that it was a sore topic of conversation for him right now."

Olivia's demeanour changed and she started to feel uncomfortable wondering if Chris would have said anything about what happened to them or not. Surely Chris wouldn't have been that insensitive to jeopardise her relationship with Steve out of spite for her rejecting his advances towards her Olivia pondered. "Yes, Jen ended the relationship about a week ago. She was uncomfortable with the way it was going and the age-gap between them played a large factor."

"Well, I don't think he has taken it very well and seems to think that you had something to do with the split in that you perhaps coerced Jen into making the decision to end things with him."

Olivia's voiced heightened. "Me! Why would I coerce Jen into ending her relationship with Chris?" Olivia was astounded by the fact that Chris would cite her as the instigator.

"Actually, he didn't stop there. He went on to accusing you of coming onto him and that you were dressed inappropriately in see-through attire when you did so." Steve didn't feel comfortable relaying back Chris' words, but he had to say verbatim the disparaging comments that Chris was spouting.

Olivia lent back into the seat and put her hands in the air. "Oh, my goodness, that guy is a piece of work. In fact, it was the other way around, he was the one who tried to come onto me, and I pushed him away as he cornered me whilst I was in the kitchen and would not let me get out." Olivia was understandably upset that Chris had turned the truth of the situation around and now she stood to get the blame for his actions.

"Liv, why didn't you tell me any of this before? I feel such an idiot now as I tried to be friendly to that dude not knowing all the while what he had been up to." Steve was agitated over the fact that Olivia chose to hide something as important as that from him, especially as they were on a journey to trust each other with everything that was going on in their lives.

"Steve, you're right and I am sorry, but I was embarrassed by the whole thing and thought I could handle it and that it was just a one-off."

"Things are never a one-off with characters like that. There seems to be something very sinister about that guy and I know Michael isn't happy with him either. Liv, if we are to go forward together on this journey, there needs to be complete transparency and we need to talk about everything, no matter how hard."

"Yes, I agree, and again I'm sorry that I thought I couldn't trust you with all that happened between me and Chris."

"Has he ever tried anything like that before?" Steve had to be sure in his mind that this incident was indeed a one-off and Olivia was not hiding other things from him.

"No, he hasn't, and the strange thing is that I don't even know where that behaviour came from."

"I ought to go around to his house and knock his lights out, but I'm not going to give a character like that the satisfaction. You know what Liv, it's getting late and I'm tired and I have some stuff to do at home, so I'm going to call it a night." Steve tried to conceal his annoyance over the situation and thought it best to leave to process his thoughts in the confines of his own home.

Olivia continued to apologise profusely, but she could see the pain and disappointment in Steve's face that she had caused and reassured him that she would never keep anything from him that was of importance and detrimental to their relationship.

Steve left the house abruptly, and with mixed emotions, Olivia watched as his car sped away. Olivia immediately found her mobile phone and called Chris to ask him what he was playing at in telling a bunch of lies about her, but Chris showed no signs of remorse, standing by his story and that she brought it on herself, parading around the house in a see-through, flimsy outfit when she knew he was in the house. Olivia's eyes widened, and she could see that she was dealing with a narcissist, with Chris thinking he was untouchable and could get away with almost anything.

"I ought to come around to your house and slap your face for the lies you have told on me," Olivia shouted as she became more and more troubled at Chris' apparent 'I'm not bothered' attitude. Olivia slammed the phone down as Chris wasn't worth anymore of her effort. Her main priority now was getting her relationship with Steve back on track.

Chris sat there on the sofa, with his remote in his hand, contemplating the day he had had. He had just put Ben to bed early as he was exhausted from the day's activities, and they stopped off at McDonalds on their way home from the Fete and spent some time there for a while. It didn't seem to bother Chris that he was upsetting his whole community of friends. That was three individuals that he had now had an altercation with, and he failed to recognise that the common denominator at the heart of it all was himself. He reasoned inwardly that he was under a great deal of stress and that everything had come on top of him all at once, with the main bone of contention being him having to return to Chichester to clear his name.

Chris turned the volume up on the remote to drown the thoughts that were vehemently swimming around in his head, eventually nodding off with the television glaring at him. Chris had nodded off for a good hour or so and woke up to a consistent loud banging on his front door. He wasn't expecting anyone and wondered who could be knocking the door with such force after 10PM at night.

As Chris rubbed his eyes and tried to compose himself, Olivia's words ran through his mind, '*I ought to come around to your house and slap your face,*' and Chris wondered if after a few hours to process her thoughts, whether Olivia had indeed come around to do just that, which he wouldn't have put it pass her, since Olivia had a mind of her own and did not suffer fools gladly. Chris made his way to the door, stopping to glance in the mirror at his melancholy face and fixing his hair, which had become ruffled from him falling asleep on the sofa. A long sound of the doorbell vibrated as it was left prolonged.

"All right, all right, I'm coming," Chris angrily

shouted as he opened the door. Chris was shocked and stunned as if he had seen a ghost and his eyes widened until they could expand no more. "Tilly!"

"Hello Chris, you have been a hard man to track down, but I did tell you that I would eventually find you, and now I have."

Olivia was about to get herself ready for bed, knowing that she would have to get up early the next morning for church. Thankfully, she wasn't teaching Sunday School, and considering the traumatic day she had endured, Olivia did not think God would mind if she took a Sunday off and decided to see how she felt when she woke up. Olivia's mobile rang and she scuffled quickly to find it, hoping it was Steve wanting to apologise for his quick departure and to wish her goodnight before she went to bed, as that was a call she wouldn't have wanted to miss. Instead, it was Jen's name that flashed up on her phone.

Jen was still at work doing the nightshift and Olivia wasn't due to see her until the next morning. Jen did not normally call her when she was on duty, so Olivia was a little apprehensive even before Jen had said a word. "Hey Jen, is everything okay?"

There was a long pause before Jen composed herself. "Olivia, I don't want you to panic, but Steve's been in a motor accident. I was one of the paramedics at the scene, when I noticed he was the patient we were dealing with."

Olivia screamed and dropped the phone in hysterics, but quickly picked it up again when she realised what she had done. "Is he alive, Jen?" Olivia said frantically. Again, the phone went silent. "It's touch and go at the moment. Just make your way to the hospital and I'll bring you up to speed when you get here."

Olivia put the phone down and knew she had to be strong and composed before leaving the house and muttered a pray in her heart, *'LORD, if ever I need you, it's now. This is one of the hardest prayers I have ever had to pray, but I am pleading with you, please don't let my fiancé die. Please preserve his life so that we can have our happy ever after life together'.*

The End – Sequel To Follow

About The Author

Andrea Best is currently the author of two books. 'Insightful Tips for The Unique Mature Single in Her 'Wait' For Mr Right' and 'Second Glances'. A romance novel.

When Andrea isn't plotting out the 'in's' and 'outs' of her next book, she is busy travelling the Globe, actively speaking and sharing her experiences as a mature single at women's conferences in countries like Sudan, Uganda and South Africa, as well as in the UK.

Andrea is passionate about seeing young women empowered and walking in their full potential in God and also facilitates a small singles group for mature singles.

During the 2020 pandemic, Andrea got to tick off one of her long-time goals, to learn to play the saxophone, which she currently continues to enjoy.

Printed in Great Britain
by Amazon